OF LIGHT AND SHADOW

PRAISE FOR
TANAZ BHATHENA

PRAISE FOR THE WRATH OF AMBAR DUOLOGY

★ "A breath of fresh air in the fantasy adventure genre . . .
Readers will be mesmerized by Bhathena's vivid storytelling and
the deeply felt connection between the two main characters. This
fantasy adventure featuring protagonists of color will be enjoyed
by fans of the Legacy of Orïsha and Ember in the Ashes series."

—*School Library Journal*, **starred review, on** *Hunted by the Sky*

★ "A novel of palace intrigue, supplication and resistance, romance,
and betrayal. Bhathena takes her time unfolding the story, allowing
the reader full immersion not only in the richly drawn characters but
the world itself—a world inspired by medieval India. The result is an
intoxicating novel that is at once leisurely and keenly enthralling."

—*Quill & Quire*, **starred review, on** *Hunted by the Sky*

"A compelling mythology-based fantasy."

—*Kirkus Reviews* **on** *Rising Like a Storm*

"A thrilling start to an exciting new series set in a fresh, magical
new world . . . I couldn't put it down!"

—**S. A. Chakraborty, author of** *The City of Brass* **and**
The Kingdom of Copper, **on** *Hunted by the Sky*

"Perfect for fans of thoughtful world-building and fantastical mirrors to
our own reality. A whirlwind of heartfelt storytelling."

—**Jodi Meadows,** *New York Times*—**bestselling coauthor of** *My Plain
Jane* **and author of the Fallen Isles trilogy, on** *Hunted by the Sky*

"Lush and well-researched, Bhathena brings her series to a satisfying close as Gul and Cavas resist tyranny as they work to build a more just world."

—*Teen Vogue* on *Rising Like a Storm*

"With stellar characters, epic battles, and exploration of power, this spectacular duology comes to a roaring end."

—**BuzzFeed** on *Rising Like a Storm*

PRAISE FOR *THE BEAUTY OF THE MOMENT*

"Fans of Nicola Yoon's *The Sun Is Also a Star* will enjoy this bicultural romance. A strong purchase for most YA collections, especially where contemporary romance is in demand."

—*School Library Journal*

"This dramatic romance, told from Susan and Malcolm's alternating viewpoints, authentically traces the teens' gradual changes as they come to terms with mistakes they've made and who they want to be."

—*Publishers Weekly*

PRAISE FOR *A GIRL LIKE THAT*

★ "Bhathena makes an impressive debut with this eye-opening novel . . . Should spur heated discussions about sexist double standards and the ways societies restrict, control, and punish women and girls."

—*Publishers Weekly*, **starred review**

★ "Bhathena's lithe prose effortlessly wends between past and present . . . A powerful debut."

—*School Library Journal*, **starred review**

ALSO BY TANAZ BHATHENA

Hunted by the Sky

Rising Like a Storm

The Beauty of the Moment

A Girl Like That

OF LIGHT AND SHADOW

TANAZ BHATHENA

FARRAR STRAUS GIROUX

NEW YORK

Farrar Straus Giroux Books for Young Readers
An imprint of Macmillan Publishing Group, LLC
120 Broadway, New York, NY 10271 • fiercereads.com

Our books may be purchased in bulk for promotional, educational, or business use.
Please contact your local bookseller or the Macmillan Corporate and Premium Sales Department
at (800) 221-7945 ext. 5442 or by email at MacmillanSpecialMarkets@macmillan.com.

Library of Congress Cataloging-in-Publication Data is available.

First edition, 2023
Book design by Samira Iravani and Maria Williams
Printed in the United States of America

ISBN 978-0-374-38911-6
1 3 5 7 9 10 8 6 4 2

We acknowledge the support of the Canada Council for the Arts.

ONTARIO ARTS COUNCIL
CONSEIL DES ARTS DE L'ONTARIO
an Ontario government agency
un organisme du gouvernement de l'Ontario

In loving memory of Homai D. Bhathena

Koh

Atash

Subedar's
Warehou

The
Maw

Bagbol

Iro

The Western Pass

Mohr

Raigarh

Asi

Samudra

Dakkin

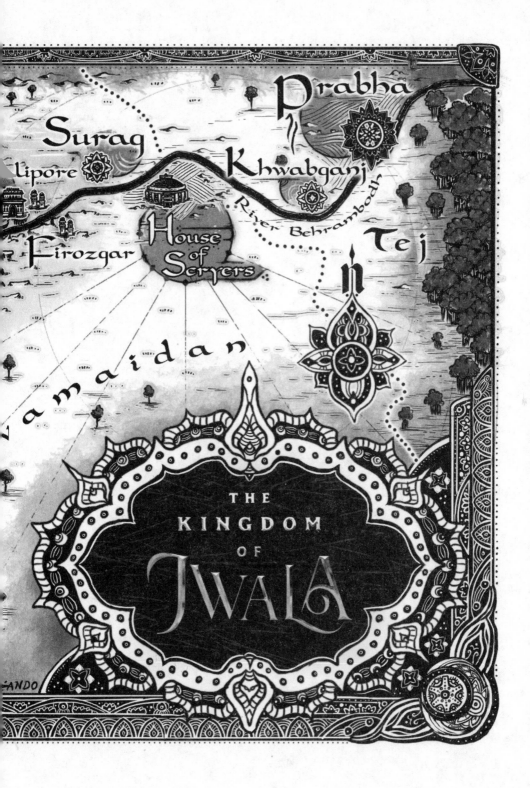

OF LIGHT AND SHADOW

With the blessings of our Goddess of Fire and Light, we bring you

THE
JWALA KHABRI

THE ORIGINAL
Voice of the Kingdom

Day 16 Drought, 39 Bhairavi Kāl

MINISTER OF TREASURE BEMOANS DAUGHTER'S BROKEN ENGAGEMENT

In an extraordinary turn of events, the much-celebrated binding proposal of Kumari Damini of Clan Tej (also daughter of Minister Manoharlal of the kingdom treasury) to Jwala's royal heartthrob and resident heartbreaker, Rajkumar Navin, now appears to be off.

While Kiran Mahal has remained mum about the cause of the broken engagement (as the palace normally does during scandals about either of the two princes), reliable sources say that a sobbing Damini was spotted last night without her maids and retinue along the capital's pleasure strip, where her betrothed was found in a passionate embrace with a tavern boy.

Unlike his daughter, who refused to answer our hawks, the Minister of Treasure was much more forthcoming about the scandal.

"If I see that aiyaash lout anywhere near my daughter again, I will make a murga of him!" Manoharlal threatened.

The minister did not clarify if he *did*, indeed, intend to turn

Jwala's Peri Prince into a cockerel or if the murga in question simply referred to the punishment ladled out by irate schoolmasters to young children.

FRESH HORROR IN
ASHVAMAIDAN VALLEY

Barely a month after the death of Bhim Chaya, leader of the infamous Shadow Clan, the western province of Ashvamaidan faces fresh resurgence of banditry. A new, terrorizing Shadow Bandit—rumored to be Bhim's daughter—broke into the Ministry of Treasure in the city of Surag, looting as much as fifteen hundred gold mohurs, eight hundred silver sikkas, and a hundred copper dām.

An anonymous masked figure, the Shadow Clan's new leader is rumored to use healing magic in abominable ways, her favored technique of murder being strangulation.

FATE AND FOLLY

Along the River Behrambodh
in the kingdom of Jwala

DAY 5 of the Month of Drought
YEAR 40 of Queen Bhairavi's reign

1

THE MORNING OF THE RAID SUNHERI HUNG FULL AND BRASSY in the sky, dappling the black water with a trail of gold. The blue moon, Neel, was invisible and would remain so until the night of the moon festival next year—a small blessing as far as Roshan Chaya was concerned. The light of one moon was bad enough; two moons together would have likely given away her position by the riverbank, along with every other member of the Shadow Clan.

Her breath fogged the air before her; nights were chilly here in Jwala's westernmost province, no matter the time of year. But tonight, Roshan barely felt the cold. She watched the vessel emerge from the darkness, a large cargo dhow slowly making its way across the gleaming river, its sails rolled up. The carved figurehead of the fire goddess gleamed eerily on the bow, protective enchantments lending it a dull blue sheen.

Roshan whistled: a passable imitation of a bulbul in a tree. An owl hooted back perfectly: confirmation that Governor Yazad Aspa's weekly shipment of grain was on its way to the capital city of Prabha. Smack-dab in the middle of the river.

Completely out of reach.

Another hoot followed and Chotu rose into the air, small and wingless, his slender form slowly blending in with the sky. He would soon be invisible to everyone, except for Roshan, who knew exactly where to look. If she didn't love the little boy with her whole heart, Roshan would have been envious of Chotu's gifts. Levitation was hard enough magic without adding a reflector spell to the mix. Now she watched him float toward the dhow, his body but a blur against a scene that would have appeared tranquil—if not for the bloated corpse of a ruddy shelduck floating in the water nearby, its sour, peaty odor lingering in the air.

Without thinking, Roshan reached up to touch the amulet between her collarbones. Made of firebloom wood, it was a perfect, flat square embossed with a tree, the remnant of parents she had never known. That is . . . if it *had* been her parents who'd gifted her the one object that best amplified her magic—before abandoning her as a newborn eighteen years ago.

Do not dwell on the past, bitiya, Baba had told her whenever she'd asked him questions about them. *It is best left behind.*

It had been difficult for Roshan to drink in her bitterness. To leave thoughts of her parents behind. But for Baba, she'd done her best. Baba, who'd called her his bitiya, even though he wasn't her father. Baba, who took her in, taught her to pick locks without magic, to fight. To kill, if necessary—and only if necessary.

After Baba's death a year ago, Roshan had had no choice but to kill. As Bandit Bhim Chaya's adoptee and favored successor, she had known that someday she would have to prove herself, even fight for the clan's leadership. She had not expected a battle to the death mere hours after Baba was killed. Roshan still remembered the way her hands had locked around her rival's throat. How she'd blocked his arteries with a magic normally used to fix broken bones, smooth bruised skin, and knit torn flesh. The world classified life magic and death magic as two separate things—the first wielded by healers and the second by warriors. But healers like Roshan knew that those who breathed life into a body or extended it with magic could also take it away.

Last year was the only time Roshan had used her life magic against a member of the Shadow Clan—an act that had earned her its leadership and also cleaved it in two.

She could hear some of the bandits behind her now: viperous susurrations followed by loud giggles, an intentional violation of her order for silence on this raid. Roshan hadn't taken the bait before. And she wouldn't tonight.

"When they don't give us our birthright, we steal it," she whispered the Shadow Clan's motto to steady herself.

Baba had bellowed the same words when he was last alive, his coat as bright as flame, his atashban glowing with death magic. He'd been shot in the back by four Brights—gold-armored brutes from Governor Yazad's private army. Ultimately, though, it had been the leader of the Brights—the governor's son, Shera Aspa—who had killed Baba, severing his head from his body and then levitating it onto a pike for all throughout Ashvamaidan valley to see.

"Bhim Chaya is dead!" Shera had cried out. "And we'll kill his witch of a daughter next!"

A jagged streak of light interrupted her reverie: Chotu had shot the first atashgola at the blue shield. A gong sounded all the way to the coast, the small grenade ricocheting off the enchantments, shooting fragments of clay and fireworks into the sky. But that was not the end of it.

Not even close.

Chotu launched more atashgolas at the dhow's barrier, gongs erupting like a frenzied devotee ringing the bell at a temple, invoking the fire goddess herself.

"Wake uuuuuup, you gold-plated bastards!" a voice sang out next to Roshan. Lalit winked from over the top of the black cloth masking his face, strands of coppery hair sticking to his pale forehead from under a tightly wrapped black turban. He was Roshan's right hand and one of the few people in the world she would trust with her life.

Roshan smiled under her own mask. "If they aren't awake already, they certainly will be now," she said.

She hoped they would try to shoot Chotu—a feat that could be accomplished only if the dhow's protective barrier was raised. It was risky, certainly. Chotu could die. Or the Brights could ignore them entirely, causing their mission to fail. Yet Roshan and the clan were used to risks like these. Used to teetering on the edge between life and death, their laughs masking their fear.

Also, the Brights had been turning complacent recently. Falling asleep on watches at the governor's warehouses. Using shortcuts like simple blue deflector shields that, when hit correctly, completely disappeared on impact. Chotu shot yet another atashgola, and this time, instead of a gong, Roshan heard a resounding *boom* and watched an enormous blue star explode in the dark sky. She waited until the shield surrounding the dhow vanished, allowing the enemy to shoot a couple of red spells into the air.

"*Now,*" she commanded.

Lalit's hands glowed red on the grip of his Lohar-era atashban, an old but powerful magical crossbow, and he shot a spell that split into a dozen flaming arrows from its tip, piercing holes in the ship's hull, right at the waterline.

That would get them moving in a hurry.

"Arms at the ready," she called out.

"Haan, Sardar!" a few voices chorused in acknowledgment.

It felt odd at times to wear Baba's former title the way she did his old red jama, the silk coat magically shrunk and cleverly altered to fit her smaller form. But not now. Right now, Roshan's skin thrummed with excitement, and her face warmed the way it did whenever a raid went exactly how she planned.

To avoid sinking, the dhow rapidly changed course, curving toward the beach, its trajectory leading right to where Roshan stood, in a space between two large rocks. A web of yellow light cast out like a fishing net; a few yards away, the clan's best conjurer, Vijali Fui, was drawing the dhow to shore with wrinkled hands, faster than the lightning she was named for, her braid like old gold in the dim light.

There would likely be enough grain inside that dhow to feed the clan and at least four of the five villages in the valley they'd allied with. Most of the villages had barely survived the governor's blood tithes last year. The tithes—tax collection sprees—usually ended in farmers' deaths or left families on the brink of starvation. No amount of earth magic could regrow three months' worth of bajra and sorghum in a week's time. And magically conjured food, Roshan knew from experience, had little nutrition, often tasting like dirt in the mouth.

The sky lightened from midnight to slate blue. Sunheri was now the color of a fading orange ember and would soon disappear completely.

They had little time to spare. In an hour or so, constables from a neighboring village would likely begin patrolling the coast and raise an alarm.

But, again, Vijali Fui was quicker. Within moments she'd raised the rocks by the coast, summoning a pathway that led right to the dhow's deck, anchoring it to the shore.

"Let's go!" Roshan said.

As one, the forty-four clan members stormed the dhow, their spells and ancient sabers clashing with gleaming new-era atashbans and the Brights' gold armor. Roshan got nicked in the arm by a stray dagger, rolled out of the way of another fiery red spell. A hard arm began curling around her throat, seconds before it trembled and let go. She ignored the squelch that always came when she withdrew her katar from human flesh, the grunt of the Bright who fell dead, his blood now trailing down its short, triangular blade.

Her father had gifted Roshan the punch-dagger once he'd learned death magic wasn't her strong suit, and she'd spent years drilling hard in the intricacies of nonmagical combat. Getting caught in a simple choke hold would have only made Baba say: "Fight like that and you deserve to die."

As she plunged the katar into another unprotected Bright nape, the cut on Roshan's arm burned. She ignored it. It would soon heal. Already the magic in her blood was cooling the injured skin, knitting it back in place.

The battle, too, turned in their favor, Lalit and two others making quick work of the remaining Brights with their atashbans. Corpses lay strewn across the blood-soaked upper deck. Roshan averted her eyes, ignoring the twist in her belly that always accompanied these killings, and headed down a set of wooden stairs to the storage area below, a glowing lightorb illuminating her way.

She found the bounty they'd anticipated—to be divided among their allied villages, the smallest portion going to the clan—gunnysacks of bajra, sorghum, and various lentils, stamped in ink with the symbol of Ashvamaidan's flying mare. This dhow carried spices as well, probably meant for a wealthy city merchant, grown magically in glass domes surrounding the governor's haveli in Surag. There was cumin, pepper, and—Roshan grinned under her mask—cloves that would last her a year. Maybe more. She reached for a sack, about to toss it over her shoulder, when she heard the sound.

An unmistakably human snore.

A boy of around eighteen or nineteen blue moons lay partially hidden behind the sacks of sorghum, fast asleep, a thin trail of drool seeping from his mouth. A length of cloth curled nearby like snakeskin, the sort of finely woven, block-printed, green-and-gold turban wrap available only in big towns or in cities like Surag.

A rich Jwaliyan brat, Roshan assessed. A boy who stank of alcohol, sweat, and—her nose wrinkled—vomit. She frowned at the familiarity of his features: high cheekbones, a beaked nose, hair a mess of red-brown curls.

Why did it feel like she'd seen him before?

The boy's deep emerald jama fell to his ankles in city fashion and was untied at the front, exposing a slender torso and deep brown skin like Roshan's own. She froze in place when she saw the tattoo on his chest: a small golden bird with uncanny black eyes, its feathered white crown in full bloom, wings and tail feathers spreading out like flames.

Oh. That was why.

"Wait!" She caught hold of Lalit before he shot the boy dead. "Don't. See that?" She pointed at the tattoo.

"It can't be," he murmured, staring at it.

"Fire and ashes! It has to be," someone else said. "Who else outside the royal family would get a *homāi* inked on their chest?"

In Ashvamaidan, some saw the homāi as a cursed bird, saying she brought more bad luck than good. But Baba had called the homāi a harbinger of fate, saying that she was the fire goddess's own companion.

When you see the homāi, know that the fire goddess has played a part in it, bitiya. Know that your future is going to change.

Queen Bhairavi had claimed to have seen the homāi before her three siblings were killed in a carriage accident, bringing her to the throne far sooner than she'd anticipated. There had been rumors, of course, the way there always are. But Bhairavi had been cleared by every investigation and had later adopted the bird as the royal family's official symbol.

Roshan wondered if the queen had seen the bird again when her only daughter had indulged in a love affair so scandalous that it had reached every corner of the kingdom. Crown Princess Athiya, from what Roshan remembered, had been bound to a prince from the northern kingdom of Prithvi, then had taken various lovers, including a handsome peri.

The lovers in themselves had not caused the scandal. Affairs were common among royals, even more so when two people were bound for political reasons. But no royal in Jwaliyan history had insisted on bearing a lover's child and—worse—endangering an existing political alliance by naming the child second in line to the throne. Neither her consort's fury nor his subsequent return to Prithvi changed Crown Princess Athiya's mind. Five years after birthing her heir, she delivered an inconvenient spare, and then died shortly afterward in the arms of her peri lover. Or so the story went. Eventually, the peri had abandoned his son, leaving him and the heir to be raised alone by their grandmother, the queen.

Roshan examined the homāi inked on the boy's chest. She had seen the heir a few years ago—the then twenty-year-old Crown Prince Farhad—leaving the palace in a horseless carriage. It had been on a rare trip with Baba and a few others to the capital to buy saltpeter for firebombs from the black market. They'd stared at the crown prince's serious, handsome face, watched as he'd politely smiled and waved at the crowds flanking the carriage's sides, desperate for a glimpse of Jwala's future king. "Corrupt to the core," Baba had whispered to Roshan. "All of them."

The spare—Roshan could tell by now that the boy on the dhow *wasn't* the crown prince—was taller and broader than his brother. Was he also as powerful or influential? Roshan couldn't be sure. Inconvenient though he may have been called, Queen Bhairavi *had* raised the spare as her grandson. He could be of *some* use. And right now, he was the only link the clan had to the queen and the throne.

When they don't give us our birthright, we steal it.

She sheathed her katar and slowly walked over to him, lightly touching his collarbones, shoulders, and arms with glowing fingers. She followed the movement downward—over torso, hips, knees, and finally, feet encased in dusty jootis lined with shadowlynx fur.

There. Immobilized from the neck down for a few hours.

When he woke, she would have to confirm his identity, of course. No villager in Ashvamaidan would flirt with fate in this manner, but you never knew with these arrogant city boys. The tattoo could very well be a fake.

She reached up to touch his face. Roshan's whole body glowed, her every nerve attuned to his, the sound of his blood pulsing in her ears. Sweat beaded her forehead the way it always did when performing life magic, especially when she needed to transfer some of her own energy to someone else.

The boy's breathing quickened and he coughed sharply, black lashes flickering open to reveal eyes the color of molten gold, their pupils not round but elliptical like a cat's.

Peri eyes, Roshan realized as they slowly focused on her, taking in the turban that covered her hair and the mask that shielded her face.

She had not seen a peri before except maybe in old scrolls or paintings. Peri were supposed to have wings; they were among a race of part-human and part-animal beings called the Pashu, who lived in the kingdom of Aman, northwest of Jwala.

The spare prince had no wings. Nothing to indicate his heritage except for those eerie gold eyes that made her want to pull away from him and simultaneously draw closer.

"Speak," she commanded.

"Are you sure about that, Roshni?"

Roshan started. Surely . . . surely, he couldn't know her name.

But he was still watching her, examining her from covered face to glowing arms . . . and that's when she understood. He had called her

Light in the Common Tongue, referring to her illuminated form, completely unaware that he'd referred to her by a variant of her real name.

"Or would you prefer I do something else for you with this very gifted mouth of mine," he went on, his voice like honey, sinuous and smooth. "I hear the bandits of Ashvamaidan are rather ... lonely ... most of the time."

In the background, someone snorted. Roshan suppressed the urge to roll her eyes. Normally she would have told the boy to bite his tongue—or better yet, magically forced him to bite it himself. Yet, if this boy was who she thought he was ...

"Your name," she ordered.

He raised a thin, perfectly arched eyebrow. "You don't know who I am?"

"I can guess. But I'd rather you tell me yourself," she replied, perfectly mimicking his arrogant tone.

"Well, then," he murmured. "Let it be known that I am Rajkumar Navin of Clan Behram, the first of his name and second in line to Jwala's throne." As the prince spoke, his voice seemed to magnify in volume, sending shivers up her skin. "I command you to unhand me now and take me back to Prabha." The words vibrated in her ears, hammered painfully under her skull. *A soul magus*, she realized, as tendrils of his magic began curling around her brain like a vise.

"I then command you to surrender to the authori—" The prince's voice cut off abruptly as Roshan's hands locked around his throat.

Her grip wasn't *too* tight—she did not want to choke him by any means—but it was firm enough to silence. Sweat slid between her breasts and heated her back, magic and anger burning her body with a red light, until she turned it chilly and blue, her fingers numbing painfully at the prince's throat, freezing his voice until nothing emerged from his mouth except for gasps.

"Sometimes, the best thing for a mouth to do is to remain shut, Rajkumar."

2

As a prince of Jwala, Navin was used to being greeted with flower garlands. With servile bows, honorifics, and false compliments about his "blindingly gold" eyes, wherever he went.

The Shadow Bandit of Ashvamaidan didn't care for such formalities. She had wielded her magic with cold brutality, her spell painfully icing his vocal cords in a way that reminded him of the palace hakim, who'd been asked to examine Navin's throat when he'd abruptly stopped singing as a child.

Navin knew who the Shadow Bandit was, of course. Everyone in Jwala did. When she'd first appeared on the scene last year, looting a branch of the Ministry of Treasure in Surag and then disappearing without a trace, every news scroll in the kingdom, including the widely circulated *Jwala Khabri*, had tried to uncover her identity. This mysterious, masked daughter of the bandit Bhim Chaya—a young woman notoriously good at killing people, usually with magic meant for healing. Hakims in Jwala called the Shadow Bandit an abomination—someone who clearly did not care about the sanctity of life magic, someone whose soul had rotted through and through.

She watched him now with dark brown eyes that could skewer, a look that burned like a hand stuck in a tandoor. Even the colors of her aura, which should have been distinctly visible to him, had faded, but that was probably the effect of binge drinking with Shera earlier that night. Alcohol always dimmed Navin's soul magic to a degree—not that he'd ever listened to anyone who'd warned him against consuming it. The roof of his mouth was blistered over with tiny bumps—a side effect of using soul magic—blood now added to the rotting mix of flavors in his mouth.

Yet, as painful as the blisters could be when he overexerted his powers, Navin preferred them to the dizzy spells or incapacitating stomachaches his brother, Farhad, got. While all kinds of magic drained energy, the magic that drew the most power from a person—soul magic, in Navin and Farhad's case—always had the worst effect. His blisters were a reminder of this, one of the rare times he envied Jwala's small non-magus population.

Tonight, Navin hadn't even expected to use magic. His morning had been spent racing horses with Shera across the Aspa haveli grounds in Ashvamaidan and the evening at a tavern in the nearby port city of Surag, where they both downed glass after glass of strong tharra.

Later, while Shera had slipped off somewhere with a giggling maid, Navin had spent an hour conversing with a beautiful young Suragi man and woman. Their hands had brushed Navin's fingers, his arm, and his cheeks in an unmistakable suggestion. Unfortunately, by then, all the alcohol he'd drunk began churning in Navin's belly, threatening to expel itself from his mouth.

He'd declined the couple's invitation to get a room and, for reasons he could no longer recall, bypassed the Aspa haveli altogether to head for the docks. There he clambered onto the first dhow headed to the capital. It didn't matter that it was a cargo boat, or that Governor Yazad Aspa's guards had fretted over Navin's presence and security. Once Navin had turned on the magic in his voice, their eyes had glazed over like puppets, and all he'd had to do was pull the strings.

Should've just had the threesome, Navin thought now as he examined his captors.

Dressed in shades of brown and black, the bandits wore turbans wrapped on a hard angle in the manner of provincial farmers, the coiled fabric nearly covering their left ears. Unlike the farmers, though, who tucked in every stray bit of fabric, the bandits had purposefully left one end of their turbans longer than the other, using the spare cloth to mask their features.

Navin held still, though every inch of his body ached to move. Hungover as he was, he knew what folly it would be to try to push past a healer's magic, to strain his powers when he was this weak. Navin hadn't spoken to nor seen his father in a decade, but in this moment, he couldn't help but wish he'd taken more after the peri: especially when it came to the power of song and making human ears bleed.

A boatful of ear bleeds would be so damned convenient right now.

"What happened, Roshan Didi?" someone murmured. A small boy of ten or eleven looked up at Navin, his brown eyes wide.

Curiosity stirred. Navin watched as the Shadow Bandit stiffened.

So her name was Roshan, then.

In Paras, the word could mean both light and fame, and strangely enough, it suited her. She was both bright and famous—in all the wrong ways.

"He's a soul magus, Chotu." Roshan's voice was like sandpaper, raspy and oddly pleasing to the ear. Navin had to give her credit for not snapping at the boy or scolding him for giving her away.

"What does that mean?" the boy asked, more curious than afraid.

"It means he can use his voice to magically manipulate your emotions and make you do exactly what he wants. It is why we're going to gag him now."

A rag that smelled like stale grass-oil and piss was promptly stuffed into his mouth. Roshan touched Navin's numbed throat again.

Heat rushed back in pinpricks of pain. His voice—thank goddess, his *voice*—emerged in muffled sounds and grunts of retribution.

"Don't worry, Rajkumar," the Shadow Bandit said, her brown eyes glinting. "You'll end up home with the parasmani. Eventually."

"Are you sure?" another man asked. He carried an old-fashioned atashban on one shoulder and assessed Navin the way one did a target, deciding which part to shoot first. "Maybe we should get rid of him."

"Not yet. He's more valuable alive at the moment. Parcel him up."

It was the last Navin would see and hear of the Shadow Bandit before someone bludgeoned him over the head and darkness fell all over again.

3

"LALIT! DID YOU HAVE TO HIT HIM SO HARD?"

Roshan knelt on the floor, examining the prince's head for bumps or cuts.

"*You* told me to parcel him up. Parcels should be silent and immobile." Lalit patted the wooden stock of his atashban, which had been used to do the bludgeoning, and then bent over to heft a sack of rice into his arms. "He's all yours, *Roshni*."

She ignored the light mockery of her name. "I don't want you damaging his brain," she said. Healing a concussion—even magically—wasn't the easiest thing to do. Pain curled up the back of her left ear and needled the bridge of her nose, a remnant of the headache that had pounded her skull when she'd frozen the prince's vocal cords earlier. She was lucky it hadn't progressed to a full migraine, though the latter usually happened after more strenuous healing sessions. As the old Jwaliyan saying went: *The power that burns brightest within will ultimately kill you.*

"Vijali Fui! Navaz Didi!" Roshan called over a pair of their strongest members: two women who'd fulfilled the roles of adoptive aunt and elder sister respectively over the years, Vijali feeding her spiced poha and rocking her to sleep as a child, Navaz sparring with her like a brute during training.

The three of them now tied several empty gunnysacks securely to a pair of spears, forming a makeshift palanquin onto which, with many grunts and huffs, they managed to move the prince's tall frame. It wasn't perfect, but it would have to do for their hour-long journey on foot through the ravines. The women took the brunt of the prince's weight up front, while Roshan took up the rear, where his feet were. After the excitement of the raid, the journey back to the ravines was blessedly uneventful, except for one small thing.

Hemant. Brother to Deepak, the man Roshan had killed in a duel for the Shadow Clan's leadership.

"Not that big a haul, is it?" Hemant said now in a voice both clear and carrying. There were murmurs of agreement from his small posse of loyal friends. "Sardar Bhim would've targeted a better dhow. There were so many to choose from. And now with this prince—"

"Want me to shut him up?" Vijali asked Roshan.

"No need. Baba always said that a barrel sounds the loudest when it's empty."

"Maybe. But you need to put him in his place, bitiya. He undermines your authority."

Roshan knew. Yet she also knew that rising to Hemant's taunts would give him exactly what he wanted: proof that she had no control over her temper. That she hid her weaknesses as a leader by curbing any dissenting voices. A knot formed in her throat. *Could* she have talked to Deepak on that terrible day? Forgiven him for selling Baba out to Governor Yazad and his Brights? She wasn't sure. What she did know was that if she hadn't killed Deepak back then, he would've most certainly killed her.

In either case, she had other things to worry about. Like the spare prince of Jwala, whose legs felt heavier than four sacks of barley.

Using her strong hips for leverage, she followed the others up and then down a steep hill choked with dying elephant grass, under a jagged rock arch, and then over a tangle of thorny shrubs. The air here tasted of salt, carried the lingering scents of dust and old metal. The river shrank the farther they moved westward, patches of dry earth interspersed with stagnant tea-colored pools surrounded by knolls of ribboning red and blue rock.

When Roshan was young, the river still flowed through the path they walked, rich with glassfish and waterfowl. She remembered being four or maybe five and being perched on Baba's shoulders as he carried her through the dense, rustling canopy of their earlier hideouts, the air fragrant with champa, sandalwood, and firebloom. But over the past decade or so, the forest had mostly died, leaving behind only inedible scrub and ber trees, their fruit as hard as stone, not softening even when pickled.

Badlands rose around them: terra-cotta ravines and V-shaped gullies on both sides of the river like tremendous, craggy fortresses. It was the sort of landscape easy to get lost in. Impossible to escape—unless you knew the way.

The path narrowed considerably as they climbed up to their newest hideout, forced into a single file. This also meant that Navaz Didi had taken the full load of Prince Navin's shoulders, and without Vijali Fui's added support, the weight in Roshan's hands instantly felt like it had doubled.

"Need help?" a voice asked from the back. It was Lalit, who was probably still secretly laughing at her about her parcel. But Roshan did need help, so she gratefully swapped Lalit for his gunnysack of rice, letting him take over the prince's load for those final few steps up into a wide, spacious cavern.

Magical shields, invisible to the eye, brushed Roshan's face and clothes like velvety curtains, the pleasant buzz of a sound barrier filling her ears. The cave's sole entrance and exit was fortified to withstand most attacks, including a barrage of atashgolas.

But not forever.

As Lalit and Vijali placed the prince and his makeshift stretcher on the floor, Roshan began softly chanting the shield spells Baba had taught her to confine someone to a place without shackling them. A web of blue and orange emerged from her hands across the floor where the prince lay, several feet in a circle around and above him. It was, in essence, an invisible cage—one no one except for Roshan and the prince's guards could breach.

Pain rolled in tiny increments up her neck and ears: a side effect of performing the magic. But, unlike healing, it was tolerable and faded within a few seconds.

Roshan eyed the chattering and laughing crowd of bandits, most of them happy from a fairly successful raid. Even Hemant and his posse seemed content for the time being, more interested in examining their loot.

Lalit stood next to her, eyeing the unconscious prince. "This is really risky," he said.

"I know. But Baba never shied away from taking risks." She lowered her voice. "This is my one chance to prove myself as the leader of this clan, Lalit."

"You *did* prove yourself. You challenged Deepak for the title of sardar and won."

"It's not enough."

Despite Roshan's best efforts, Bhim Chaya's death still hung heavy over the rest of the clan. A life of banditry held more danger than it did excitement, consisted of more days hiding than raiding, often without end. The Shadow Clan had been formed five years before Roshan was born, which meant that some bandits had been part of it for twenty-three years. It was a long time to fight for justice—and it felt worse when there seemed to be none whatsoever.

"I need to do more," she told Lalit. "Something Baba wasn't able to accomplish."

I need to get us back our lands.

"Goddess's flaming hair!" Lalit tugged down the cloth masking his face, which was red and blotchy from the heat. "I understand the pressure you're under, Roshan. But kidnapping a prince of Jwala? That's far more dangerous than anything we've done in the past."

"The most dangerous thing about the rajkumar is his mouth, which is now gagged," she retorted. "Soul magi can't influence us if they can't speak to us."

"Sardar!" someone called to her from the clan's makeshift kitchen at the front of the cave. "Breakfast!"

She nodded at Lalit. "Come. Let's eat and I'll explain."

After making sure that a decent-size portion was set aside for the prince, Roshan accepted her meal—steaming poha ladled into a dented steel bowl. She settled cross-legged next to Lalit, who was inhaling his meal, already halfway done.

Roshan was equally hungry, but she paced herself, chewing each morsel several times before swallowing it. Once they distributed the gunnysacks to the five villages, food would become scarce again. She'd learned, through experience, that the longer she took to eat her food now, the easier it would be to fool her mind into thinking she wasn't starving again an hour later.

Lalit gulped and swallowed audibly from a small steel tumbler, droplets of water dribbling down his chin and onto his dark brown jama. "So, tell me," he said, wiping his mouth. "What's your grand plan? Don't tell me you're planning to ransom the prince for coin or crown jewels."

"I'm not. But I am going to ask Parasmani Bhairavi to give us back our lands."

She hadn't seen Lalit look this stunned since he'd shot an atashban for the first time at age seven. "You're . . . are you all right?" he asked. "Don't tell me I need to fetch *you* a healer."

"Don't be so dramatic. Look, I'm not naive. I know the chances of us actually getting back our lands is slim. But at least, with the prince in our captivity, we can negotiate to have her remove Yazad Aspa as governor of this province."

"Maybe," Lalit allowed. "But who's to say that the parasmani's choice of replacement will be any better?"

"Because *we* will demand a say in that. There are several people I can think of in the villages—elders and panchayat leaders who have been loyal to the clan for years—whose names we can suggest. If she doesn't agree to our terms, then . . ." Roshan's voice trailed off, a finger delicately curving the underside of her chin. "Alvida, Rajkumar Navin."

Lalit snorted at her airy farewell to the prince. "You seem to have this figured out. But seriously? You're going to kill him if she doesn't agree to our demands?"

Killing a Bright in battle was one thing. Killing an unarmed captive was quite another. It wasn't something Bhim Chaya would have approved of—even if their captive was a corrupt royal.

"No," Roshan assured Lalit. "That'll be a threat. I don't want the queen and the rest of Jwala coming after me for killing their precious Peri Prince."

Roshan had read enough scrolls of the *Jwala Khabri* to know the spare prince's nickname, to gauge how popular he was with the rest of the kingdom. "Now that we have the prince here, we can send the queen a message: *Give us back our lands and we give you back your prince unharmed.* Until we negotiate a deal, he stays here as our prisoner," she explained.

"What if she sends sipahis again?" Lalit asked. The sipahis were Queen Bhairavi's elite force of soldiers, reputed to be the best trackers in the land.

"They weren't able to penetrate these ravines in the past," Roshan reminded him. "Besides, the queen can't have the sipahis conjure atash-golas and drop them on us from the sky without knowing where the prince is. She'd risk injuring or killing him."

Lalit frowned, saying nothing.

Swallowing the last bit of her water, Roshan reached into her kamarband, where she kept a small, embroidered pouch, the black silk gone gray with age. The pouch had once belonged to Baba, who'd used it to store fresh betel leaves for his paan. Roshan, who loved her father but hated paan, kept the pouch stuffed with cloves instead—one of which she popped into her mouth now.

"Look," Lalit said. "He's waking up."

Roshan turned to watch the prince again, noting the way his eyelids and fingers had begun to move. "Maybe you should go over and wish him a good morning," she said.

"That I will." Lalit wiped a hand across his mouth and rose to his feet. "But I hope for your sake that you're right about this, Roshan."

The spice from the clove stung her tongue, burning a trail down her throat.

I hope I am, too, she thought.

4

NAVIN SENSED THE SHIFT IN THE AIR AS HE CAME AWAKE, NO longer smelling the dhow's wet wood and the water lilies along the river, but smoke and sweat, the closeness created by stale bodies. Sounds filled his ears, the scrape of feet and sharpening knives, voices full of indistinct words. The smell of fried onions permeated the space, making his dry mouth water.

For years, Navin had gained a reputation for obliviousness, cultivating it as both weapon and shield, lying in bed for hours as servants chattered in his room, discussing him and everything else about the royal family. He did the same thing now with the bandits from Ashvamaidan, keeping his eyes shut and his breaths deep and even. His sensitive ears tuned outward, identifying a pair of voices.

Parting an eyelid, he spotted the Shadow Bandit and the man with the atashban—the one who'd wanted to shoot Navin on the dhow. The man, whose name was Lalit, still did not like the idea of holding a prince hostage. But Navin was more intrigued by the hitch in the Shadow Bandit's voice. Her admission that not everyone in the clan approved of her as their leader.

That could be useful.

With his magic not fully functional at the moment, Navin needed to exploit each of his enemy's weaknesses and insecurities. He tried to shift discreetly and listen to more of their conversation, but by then the Shadow Bandit and Lalit had walked out of hearing range and other voices began replacing them.

". . . getting worse every day," a man said. "Hemant Bhai said more ravines sprang up near Alipore last week. This is the fastest we've seen them spread."

"Perhaps the parasmani will listen to us now, with *him* here," a woman replied. "You must have faith."

"Faith in whom?" the man spat noisily. "In this slip of a girl who now calls herself our sardar? Or in a queen who has, for years, ignored our appeals and petitions?"

"There are rumors that the queen hasn't been herself since Yuvrani Athiya died." The woman's casual reference to his mother made Navin's heart seize. "She used to be much more active before, visiting different parts of the kingdom with her entourage. I still remember Parasmani Bhairavi as a young woman. She stopped at a village upriver, ate off banana leaves with the rest of us. She even laughed when a baby soiled her expensive sari."

Navin didn't recognize the person this woman described. The Queen Bhairavi he knew rarely encouraged talk that led to laughter— even with her favorite grandson, Farhad. The few times Navin had initiated conversation with her, it had tapered off like a flame sputtering at the end of a wick. Goddess's hair, he didn't remember the last time either he or his brother had called her Nani, the way other children did their maternal grandmothers, and not her official title, Parasmani ji.

Invisible fingers plucked at what felt like strings inside Navin's ribs, releasing a song full of discordant notes.

He pushed aside the feeling and forced himself to listen as a pair of footsteps approached, a strange creaking sound accompanying them. *What is that?* he wondered. And found out seconds later, jerking and sputtering from a bucketful of cold water that drenched his face. Air rushed through his mouth as the gag was removed from it.

"Suprabhat, Rajkumar . . . or wait. Maybe I ought to say *Shubh* pra-bhat," someone mocked in a stuffy city accent meant to mimic Navin's own. Navin would have wished a mocking good morning in return, if not for the atashban aimed right at his mouth.

Sunlight poured in from a crack overhead, revealing rock walls—*a cave?* he guessed—and a boy of around his own age. The boy was tall and pale-skinned, with hazel eyes and bright copper hair that fell straight across his forehead, his mouth reddened from chewing paan. The atashban identi-fied him as Lalit. Behind Lalit stood several others: from youths of Navin's age to older men and women, their brown skin deepened by the sun, gold streaking their auburn hair. The bandits were dressed similarly in trousers and loose jamas, a few still wearing hip-belts sheathed with knives. There appeared to be no children, except for the boy named Chotu, who was also staring at Navin while levitating a few inches off the floor.

A silhouette fell across his lap. He looked up, breath catching for a split second. It was her. The Shadow Bandit, Roshan, unmasked. He'd recognize those dark brown eyes—and the anger in them—anywhere. She had a round face with acne scars on the chin, an upturned nose, and full brown lips that bloomed pink at the center. There was no evidence of laugh lines anywhere. Yet, despite the obvious lack of humor on her face, the flirt in Navin had to admit the obvious: She was pretty. Dangerously so.

The worn red jama and black trousers she wore did little to hide her curves or the muscles on her arms and thighs. As if sensing the turn of his thoughts, one of her sturdy brown hands settled on the wide, crossbar grip of a punch-dagger strapped to her waist, sheathed in a scabbard under a wide black waistband. A warning. Navin's gaze moved back to her face, to wavy hair that ended in a crop below her ears, a red so dark it appeared nearly black. In Prabha, people called the shade a true Jwaliyan red. A color that was not quite fire, not quite coal. The palace courtiers spent hours in beauty houses across the capital, used countless concoctions of magic, henna, beetroot, and jatamansi to mimic what appeared to be the Shadow Bandit's natural hair color.

"Looks like the rajkumar has too much weight on him. We should relieve him of it." Lalit was eyeing Navin's pearl and ruby earrings and matching four-strand necklace, the white jade bracelets on his wrists.

"Good point," she said. "One of those trinkets could be amplifying his powers. Take it all off, Rajkumar."

That goddess-forsaken tharra. He should've never tried to outdrink Shera.

Though the bandits' auras were slowly emerging again, most were still invisible to Navin's eyes or indeterminate wisps of color around their heads. Every person's aura was made up of different colors, and each color identified a specific emotion. It would be folly to attempt a spell, even on a small scale, without seeing the exact colors within their auras or even ascertaining the group's general emotional state.

Naturally, the Shadow Bandit would be worried about Navin's amplifiers, though she really needed only his bracelets. Embedded with firestones and seaglass, their ends shaped to form two alligator heads joined in an open-mouthed kiss. They'd been gifted to Navin by his grandmother shortly after his father had abandoned him.

Navin didn't particularly enjoy wearing the bracelets; they felt like shackles on a good day. But the combination of white jade, firestones, and seaglass worked like a dream when it came to amplifying soul magic. The only other amplifier he had on his person was the signet ring he'd worn since he'd come of age—a plain but comfortable band made of polished Jwaliyan teak.

"Take it *all* off?" Navin drawled, hoping she didn't see the rapid pulse at his throat. "Is this your idea of foreplay? I'd prefer we get to know each other a little. Perhaps over a meal and a few cups of wine."

A few snickers followed his comment. The Shadow Bandit's eyes narrowed. "I have little inclination of bedding anyone who smells like a drunk water buffalo."

Laughter echoed in the cavern. Even Navin's mouth fought a smile. The girl was right. He *did* stink. Well, then. Perhaps it was time to change that.

As he slowly rose to his feet, he felt the buzz of magic—*a barrier*, he guessed, by the thornlike sensation against his skin. In the blink of an eye, the katar was pricking his throat.

Ah. So *she*, at least, could cross the barrier.

"What do you think you're doing?" she demanded. This close, he could see the fine lines of her deep brown irises, smell the cloves on her breath and the sweat beading her skin. His gaze trailed her throat, pausing at the wooden amulet between her collarbones. Something was carved there—a tree, maybe—but it was the grain of the wood that caught his attention. The fiery swirls of firebloom bark. *An amplifier, perhaps?*

The blade burned his skin this time; the Shadow Bandit had drawn blood. He wrenched his gaze up from her amulet back to those murderous brown eyes.

"Take it all off, *Navin*," he whispered. "Call me by my name and I'll do exactly what you say."

A tremor curved her mouth. The katar did not budge.

Dear goddess, let her take the bait.

It was a gamble, challenging the Shadow Bandit in this way. But names bred familiarity and familiarity was the first step to creating a bond in soul magic. If she chose to say his name of her own volition, their bond would grow stronger, making her more susceptible to his influence. Right now, despite the challenge he'd issued, she still had the upper hand. She could order her minions to strip Navin of his jewels. She could torture him until he chose to remove them himself.

An apology crawled up his throat, ready to emerge, when the Shadow Bandit spoke:

"Take it all off. *Navin*." She spat out the last word as if it was tainted. As if *he* was tainted in some way.

Yet the moment she spoke his name, the faded colors of her aura darkened to a single shade, surrounded her face like the sun. *Raging russet*, Navin named the color, relieved at being able to see her emotions, angry as they were. The more vibrant her aura became, the stronger their bond would grow, allowing him to manipulate her emotions without her noticing. As long as he could still speak, of course.

He curbed a grin. "As you wish. *Roshan.*"

Undoing the hoops in his ears, he dropped them to the floor. The necklace followed, and then, more reluctantly, his bracelets. There was no way he could hide them; their mere ostentatiousness made it impossible. His only hope now lay in the unassuming teak ring still on his finger. Still unnoticed—though that could change at any moment.

Unless . . .

Navin grinned wide and let his jama slip off his shoulders.

As expected, the move caused more than a few raised eyebrows. "What are you—" the Shadow Bandit began.

"You did say to take it *all* off, Roshni. And I don't want you to remember me smelling like water buffalo." Then, with a quickness he normally reserved for rapid, lust-filled interludes in quiet alleys or secluded public baths, he undid the drawstring of his trousers and let them fall to the floor.

"Goddess's flaming hair," he murmured, watching the Shadow Bandit's eyes grow wide. The red light of her aura now started mingling with another color: the delicate pink of embarrassment. "It seems I'm not wearing underclothes today."

A few snickers erupted around them.

Navin smiled, hoping the bandits didn't see his tightening jaw. If they had, they didn't say anything. No one seemed to have spotted the ring on his left pinkie, either. Curling the finger inward, he placed his hands on bare hips and pretended to be utterly at ease while their eyes roved over his form. He was already worse off without his bracelets than his clothes. But the teak ring could work as an amplifier. It was small and not enough for a truly powerful spell like the one he'd attempted on the dhow. But his mind and body were now throwing off the effects of the alcohol, and his soul magic was beginning to emerge, evidenced by the faded wisps of bandit auras around him. None, of course, were as clear as their leader's, with whom he'd daringly formed a name bond. This, of course, would not last forever.

Already the Shadow Bandit was looking at him like he was a pile of dung, her nose wrinkled, her mouth pinched at the corners. Whatever embarrassment he'd seen in her aura had faded, a streak of cobalt muddying the red. Was she worried? Or worse: Was she suspicious?

Quietly, she scooped up Navin's discarded jewels and clothes from within the barrier and handed them to Chotu, who stood beside her.

"Get the rajkumar some new clothes," she said, her low voice a cold wash of water over Navin's skin. "Since he has generously donated his overpriced garments, we might as well give him some suitable replacements."

"Haan, Sardar."

Moments passed during which Navin began to sorely regret his attempt at bravado, his skin prickling under multiple gazes. But Chotu reappeared soon enough, his small hands holding out what appeared to be bits of folded gunnysack. Roshan took the clothes from Chotu and dropped them at Navin's feet.

High hell. Was he really expected to wear *that?*

The curve of the Shadow Bandit's mouth was as sharp as a blade. "Am I sensing regret, Rajkumar?"

"*Navin,*" he corrected. "And my only regret is that I'm naked and you're not here touching me."

It was dangerous to play like this—to try to strengthen their bond with lust. His stomach churned as the Shadow Bandit stepped forward, crossing his barrier with the ease of a hot knife slicing through butter. Her cool fingers brushed the cut at his throat. Ice coated Navin's skin, making the fine hairs on his neck rise. He wondered if she'd frozen his voice again. He swallowed hard.

"Well, *Navin?*" she asked. "Are you happy now?"

Before he could reply, her hand dropped, leaving the skin at his throat tingling. Colors wafted around her: a blue cloud of worry, tinged with the slightest hint of yellow.

Fear? Was the Shadow Bandit afraid?

Not of him, certainly. She could kill him if she wanted to. No, something greater was at stake here. Something that had—he touched his throat with his fingers—made her heal his injury shortly after causing it.

Navin never had been and never would be good at physical combat. With a poor amplifier, he had no hope of taking on so many bandits. He would have to bide his time until he could escape. He would have to play the Shadow Bandit, play each of these bandits, the way he once did his tanpura, lightly plucking each of the instrument's four strings, tuning it until it made the perfect sound. For now, he waited a few moments, allowing the slightest bit of magic to seep toward his throat—a subtle tingling sensation that only he was aware of.

"Tell me more, Roshni," he said, ensuring that his voice was warm, but not too warm. Sweet, but not too sweet. "What do you want from me?"

For whatever she wanted, Navin would promise to give. Over and over, until she believed him, heart and soul.

Then, slowly, carefully, he would slide it out of reach.

5

ROSHAN STUDIED THE PRINCE'S FACE: THE RAISED LEFT EYE-
brow, the smirk on his sensual lips.

I want freedom, she could tell him. *Justice for Ashvamaidan's villagers
and our people.*

But what would the spoiled brat know about either? Would he
believe Roshan if she told him how corrupt Governor Yazad Aspa and
his son were or that the corruption climbed all the way to his grandmother, the queen? Roshan wasn't ignorant of the spare prince's close
friendship with Shera Aspa. Prince Navin wasn't their ally and he never
would be.

"Everything in good time, Rajkumar," she said.

A slight frown marred his smooth forehead. He didn't think it was
going to be *that* easy, did he?

"Get dressed," she said. "If you need to relieve yourself, raise a hand
and someone will come fetch me."

"And what if you're not around?"

"I'll make sure someone else is. Any other questions?"

Before the prince could answer, she snapped her fingers, a buzzing
filling the air. Cutting him off with a sound barrier was petty, perhaps.
But she couldn't let him get away with mocking her in front of the clan.

She turned around, knowing they were assessing her now, likely wondering if she was way in over her head.

Time to put those doubts to rest.

"If the rajkumar raises his hand, I must be informed right away." She spoke with what Baba called her belly voice, her words reaching the farthest parts of the cave, her gaze briefly connecting to every single bandit. "Do not attempt to otherwise befriend or communicate with him. Understand?"

"Haan, Sardar," they chorused.

"Any questions?"

"Naah, Sardar."

Roshan headed to the opposite end of the cave, through a short tunnel, and into a hollow that was her room—a sleeping pallet in one corner and a small trunk of her belongings in another: clothes, an extra punch-dagger with a broken handle, and a small pile of well-thumbed farmer's almanacs.

Moments later, Lalit's familiar head poked through, his shoulders hunching to fit the small space. "Have a moment?"

"Sure."

He plopped down on her pallet, the scents of poha and his sweat mingling in the air. "Maybe you *should* tell the rajkumar about what we want."

"What do you mean?" Roshan pulled out a spare bit of parchment, a pen made of bone, and a bottle of charcoal ink. "He's not going to care."

"Why not? He should know what's going on in his kingdom, too. He could inherit it if the crown prince snuffs out."

"*If,*" Roshan repeated with emphasis. She dipped the nib into the inkwell, waiting for it to soak up the black. "I wouldn't bet on the early death of a healthy young man who never travels without his own private force of sipahis. Besides, we don't have any idea what this spare prince thinks of his kingdom."

"Then why not find out? Maybe he doesn't even know about how bad it is here. How many rich city folk do you see this far out west? Most spend their time in Surag, locked up in those fancy bathhouses or throwing drinking parties at inns. The wealthy are often sheltered from the realities of the poor."

"Or they intentionally choose to shelter themselves." She started writing a letter, beginning with: *Exalted Parasmani of Jwala.* "Besides, since when do you empathize with silk-tongued pretty boys?"

"I don't. Not since the last one who broke my heart, at least." Lalit grinned, but not before Roshan glimpsed the flash of pain on his face.

"Lalit, I'm sorry—"

"No need to be. You distracted me well enough," he said lightly.

It was a testament to their friendship that Roshan didn't wince. She *had* distracted Lalit. They'd distracted each other last year, first with sparring practices and later with play fights that ended in bed—on this very pallet. Fiery as their time together was, the romance played itself out a couple of months later, with Roshan's grief over Baba's death easing to a dull ache and Lalit admitting he was still in love with an unnamed boy from a neighboring village. Seamlessly, they'd fallen back into a relationship that was as platonic as it was old—a blessing that Roshan would have thanked each of the four gods for if she believed in them.

"Back to my earlier point," Lalit went on when Roshan didn't acknowledge his comment. "I think you should try to talk to the rajkumar. Turn him if you must. Bring him over to *our* side."

Roshan suppressed a laugh. "Like that's going to happen."

"Why not? He's attracted to you. Use that to your advantage."

"Nonsense." She pushed away the memory of the way the prince's gaze had flickered over her form. "He's only a compulsive flirt. He likely uses seduction to get his way."

"So can you." Lalit grinned. "Don't make that face. *You're* the one who called him pretty."

"Doesn't mean I'm going to take advantage of him. That's the sort of thing the Brights do."

There was always, *always*, some desperate young man or woman in a dying Ashvamaidani village hoping that a few rolls in the hay with a Bright would get them their ancestral lands back. The thought sickened Roshan.

Lalit's smile slipped. "Roshan, I didn't mean—"

"I know you didn't," she assured him. "But we've always had one goal, remember? When they don't give us our birthright—"

"—we steal it." A thoughtful frown overtook Lalit's face. "I still think it's dangerous, what we're planning to do. But I don't see another way out, either. We'll have to keep an eye on the rajkumar. Make sure he doesn't try to escape."

"We'll have to watch Hemant and his cronies, too." The confinement barrier she'd placed around Prince Navin was strong but not foolproof. She had put Chotu on lookout and told him to let her know if any trouble was afoot.

"Chhe! Hemant." Lalit made a face. "Can't we expel him? He's such a nuisance."

"Salute the wicked first and then the good," she responded, quoting the old Jwaliyan proverb. "If we expel Hemant, the first thing he'll do is run to Subedar Yazad Aspa and tell him our whereabouts."

It was what Hemant's brother, Deepak, had done last year—leaking information about their raid to Governor Yazad, along with Baba's tactics. It had taken a while for Roshan to guess this, realization sinking in like a shard of broken glass, moments after Deepak had suggested disbanding the Shadow Clan.

"We're fighting a lost cause, Roshan bitiya," Deepak had declared, his hands reaching out to her in a poor attempt at mimicking Baba. "Why continue living like this? Why not stop banditry and cut a deal with the subedar instead? He's not so terrible a man. The Brights and those who are loyal to him are treated well. They have homes of their own instead of a cave, food instead of scraps, real clothes instead of rags."

Arguments had broken out, some, like Lalit and Vijali Fui, pushing back hard against these points. But several others had remained noticeably silent. As if they agreed with Deepak.

"You are not a Chaya," Roshan had addressed Deepak, her words silencing everyone. "You don't get to decide the future of this clan—not while I'm still here." She'd unsheathed her katar—an act that instantly resulted in a number of clan members drawing their weapons as well, cries ringing on both sides of the cave.

Ultimately, Roshan and Deepak had agreed to face off alone, one holding a katar, the other an atashban. Deepak had had the upper hand with experience and cunning, an expertise in combat magic, and the more powerful weapon. Roshan had only two things: the utter certainty that this man would destroy them for his own benefit and the knowledge that she had only one chance to kill him. She'd taken that chance, throwing the katar at Deepak's face and then, as he'd stepped out of its way, lunging forward, locking her hands around his throat, magic pulsing white hot under her skin. Deepak hadn't been an easy adversary. Apart from cuts and bruises, the kill had resulted in one of the worst migraines she'd had in years, one that had her blacking out and throwing up for two whole days, the left side of her head feeling as if it would shatter at the slightest touch.

She'd expected Hemant and his followers to retaliate after the duel and rat out the clan to the governor. But, for some reason, they hadn't. Perhaps Hemant didn't trust the governor as much as his brother had. Or perhaps he was simply waiting to see which way the dice would roll in this war over Ashvamaidan valley. Either way, there was no chance of Roshan entertaining any deal from Yazad Aspa. Baba hadn't lost his land and his family—he hadn't *died*—for things to come to that point.

And they wouldn't, Roshan promised. Not as long as she was alive.

With Prince Navin in her hands, she would bargain with the queen, stealing back everything that had been taken from the Shadow Clan and the villagers. Killing Deepak had earned Roshan the clan's fear. This wild plan, if successful, could earn her their respect—and their trust. Hemant or no Hemant.

"Come on," she told Lalit. "Help me write this letter to our queen."

6

His new clothes were no better than a gunnysack. Navin's captors had given him a mud-brown jama that ended at the knees and matching drawstring trousers that made his legs itch. At least they appeared sturdily made. And clean. He'd been fed breakfast as well, the Shadow Bandit bringing him a bowl of cold but edible poha, over-loaded with the blue river onions these westerners seemed to throw in every bit of their food. It had been too much to expect her to let him bathe in the river outside (and also scan the ravines for escape routes)—not that Navin hadn't tried.

Pain slid up the back of his neck, pulsing behind his ears. It was the cursed sound barrier, buzzing at that terrible low frequency. No matter how hard Navin tried, he couldn't lift it. Maybe he should have paid more attention to Dastur Jamshid during their lessons on everyday spells. But the very thought of blocking sound—the breath of every bit of music in this world—had made Navin resist performing such magic. And now, he was here. Stuck in this foul cave in the middle of nowhere, surrounded by murderous bandits.

Think.

He might not be able to lift the sound barrier or the confinement bar-rier restricting him to this small square of space, but he couldn't waste his time *waiting*. Surely not all the bandits were like their leader. In a group this big, there had to be at least one weak link.

He spotted Chotu in the distance, floating idly, peering through the crack in the ceiling. After the Shadow Bandit and Lalit had disappeared in the cavern's depths, most of the others had stepped out to eat, drink, or talk, leaving Navin alone with the little boy. Chotu somersaulted several times, as easily as an acrobat at a fair, but the boy used no trapezes, only his magic. Light wisps of color wafted around his small, bored face. Navin waited until Chotu's gaze fell on him, and then he clapped hard. It wasn't false applause. The boy was performing the sort of levitation that most magi in Prabha would cut off an arm or leg for. (Some actually had.)

The boy grinned and took a bow before spinning in the air like a wheel let loose, so fast that it made Navin dizzy to watch him.

Navin clapped again. *Wah!* he mouthed.

Chotu grinned. He was about to mouth a thanks for the praise—of that Navin was certain—when his smile froze and he shot back up to his old spot, floating several feet away. Navin cursed out loud. The others must have returned.

Sure enough, a group of bandits entered the cave a second later. At the center was a man over thirty-five blue moons in age, his body thin and muscular, his hair and beard nearly as red-black as the Shadow Bandit's, except his were already peppered gold. Spotting Navin, he paused mid-laugh, a sneer on his pale lips.

Then, without warning, he tossed something at Navin—or rather his barrier—a rock that made it crackle faintly before falling to the floor. Navin started, forgetting he was both caged and shielded, which the bandits found hilarious, their widely parted mouths revealing teeth in different states of disrepair.

Navin shot a glance at the ceiling, but Chotu was gone; he probably disliked this lot as much as Navin did. Someone handed the pale-lipped bandit an atashban.

Goddess of Fire and Light. Navin swallowed. *Please let not today be the day I see you.*

But before the bandit could do more than point his weapon, a pair of figures raced into sight: the Shadow Bandit and her second, Lalit. Chotu flying close behind them.

The boy flashed Navin a quick look, a gray wisp of relief sliding through his aura.

That's right, Chotu. I'm not dead yet, thank goddess.

Or maybe he ought to thank the Shadow Bandit.

She was talking to Navin's pale-lipped tormentor, her face carved into hard lines. The man sneered in response and then, without speaking, stalked out of the cave. A couple of others followed. But the rest of the bandits remained where they were, no longer laughing.

Eventually, the Shadow Bandit marched up to Navin and snapped her fingers twice. The sound barrier faded from his ears, but this time it did little to relieve him. Even without the bright red tingeing her aura, Roshan Chaya looked like she wanted to kill someone.

"Rajkumar," she began.

"Navin," he corrected. Angry as she was, it would do him no good if she reinforced that emotional wall he'd breached earlier today.

Her aura deepened to the shade of dried blood: annoyance. "Navin," she conceded. "I think it's time we told you why you're here."

Finally. Navin hoped his relief didn't show on his face. *But first—*

"Perhaps you ought to tell me why your friend was trying to use me as target practice," he retorted, using exactly the tone his grandmother would while dealing with him at his unruliest. "Or is that how you bandits treat your honored guests?"

"Don't worry about Hemant. He's like a wild dog. More bark than bite."

Navin stored away the name for future reference. "There've been plenty of reports in the news scrolls about wild dogs feasting on human flesh over the years."

Roshan ignored the comment. "We have some demands of your grandmother, Parasmani Bhairavi," she said. "Until those are met, you will stay with us. Do as we say and we'll make sure you're taken care of."

How touching. He bit back the acerbic response as her aura faded completely from his vision. *Curses.* His teak ring was clearly too weak an amplifier.

"What kind of demands?" he asked. "Alluring and mysterious as you are, Roshni, you *might* be better off sharing them with me first. I do happen to know the parasmani a little. I might be able to help."

A vein feathered up her jaw. "Have you wondered why Ashvamaidan is so poor, Rajkumar? Why a province that was lush with crops has now morphed into a wasteland within the last three decades?"

Navin had expected her to talk about the clan's poverty, their need for food and gold. *This* was the last answer he'd expected.

"Is this some sort of warped test on Jwaliyan geography?" he asked. "Will I be caned for not knowing the difference between a gully and a ravine?"

The Shadow Bandit's mouth twitched. With anger? Or amusement? Without her aura, Navin couldn't tell.

"Years before I was born, the badlands formed only a small part of this province," she went on as if Navin hadn't spoken. "Where we are now wasn't a cave but a village green with trees and fields. But then Subedar Yazad came along and introduced his blood tithes, doubling the amount of crops farmers had to send to Prabha. Farmers worked to the bone, growing crop after crop until the soil would no longer respond to their earth magic. Those who revolted were displaced. Or killed by Shera Aspa and his Brights."

Navin said nothing for a moment. He was sure he'd never heard of these blood tithes. In nearly two decades of expensive tutoring at the palace and university, no one had mentioned such a thing—not in a lecture, not even in casual conversation. Was the Shadow Bandit making things up? Or had she been brainwashed by her adoptive father—the infamous Bhim Chaya?

Suggesting the latter didn't seem wise—even in jest—so Navin said: "I don't understand. Earth magic lets farmers grow crops anywhere and in any soil. Even without rainfall. It does not drain a land of magic."

"It does if too much is used," someone else spoke, an older woman with midnight skin, her hair like hammered gold. "It changes the nature of the soil. Watch this, Rajkumar."

The woman knelt, pressing a gnarled, glowing hand to the soil. Green stalks slid between the cracks in the ground, growing upward, blooming into a bright blue flower that wilted before his eyes and thickened into a thorny shrub. "The magic I used should have sprouted starblooms," she said. "Now the only thing I can grow on this land are thorns, no matter what I do."

Navin hesitated. Though the woman had no aura, something in her voice tugged at his gut, urging him to believe her. "That still doesn't explain the badlands," he said. "Don't those take thousands of years to form? Even if the land is drained of magic?"

"That's something we don't understand, either," the woman admitted. "In this part of Ashvamaidan, ravines have erupted like the pox over the past three decades. Some appeared in a matter of *weeks*, forcing villagers to leave their homes and move elsewhere—even other provinces. There used to be over a hundred villages in our valley. Now there may be twenty, if that."

Was there magic at play here? Navin wondered. If so, what kind of magic could kill the land altogether?

"We also know that things weren't this bad until Yazad Aspa introduced the blood tithes," the Shadow Bandit spoke again, her tone low, urgent. "It's why we want our lands back. And we want him gone."

Again, those mythical blood tithes. "So those are your demands of the queen, then," Navin guessed, not knowing if he wanted to laugh or cringe. "Don't you think it's a stretch to think she'll accept them?"

"That's why you're here, isn't it?" The Shadow Bandit smiled coldly. "Or are you telling me you're as useless as the rumors say? That I'd be better off breaking into the palace and kidnapping Yuvraj Farhad instead?"

Acid burned his throat and sternum. But Navin had spent far too long at the palace to let his emotions color his face. He had no intention of letting this awful girl know how close she was to the truth.

"Why don't you kill me and find out, Roshni?" He raised a cool, indifferent eyebrow. "See if the queen is indifferent or if she decides to reduce your precious province to ash."

His words hung between them: a challenge and a rebuke.

The Shadow Bandit's eyes glinted, and for a split second, Navin wondered if he'd gone too far. But then, unexpectedly, she cackled, mirth bubbling out of her like a hot spring. The sound made Navin think of cool wind on a summer day, of a lover's slow, wicked caress.

"Well played, Rajkumar." A smirk that could rival his own crept up her face. "I'll make sure someone keeps an eye on you. We wouldn't want our honored guest leaving us so soon."

7

ROSHAN FELT THE LIVING SPECTER'S PRESENCE LIKE A ZEPHYR stirring the brush outside the cave, cold stanching the afternoon heat, her skin prickling as invisible fingers took the sealed square of parchment held flat on her palm. She watched her seer, seventeen-year-old half magus Khizer, talk to the air, his instructions to the specter utterly clear: *Deliver this to Parasmani Bhairavi of Jwala at once. The letter should fall in no other hands.*

Waiting until the boy had once again turned to her, she called out her thanks: "Meherbani, Khizer." And to the space around him, where she still felt the specter's presence: "Meherbani, Khush."

"It is our duty, Sardar," Khizer acknowledged.

"No thanks needed, my little hakim," a childlike, disembodied voice mocked before blowing Roshan a series of air kisses.

Roshan smiled. Khush had given her the nickname ten years ago, when he first learned of her healing powers. Khizer said that his brother appeared gray in his spectral form, immortalized in the eight-year-old body he'd died in, even though they were both only a year apart in age. Born of a magus mother and non-magus father, the brothers' time together in the living world had been cut short by a blood tithe that also had taken their parents. Yet, unlike their parents, whose spirits had faded into oblivion, Khush had morphed into a living specter, a spirit chained to the world by a single, desperate wish: keeping his brother safe. Dragging an unconscious Khizer away from their burning home in Jyoti, Khush had taken his brother into the ravines. Somehow, the young specter had known where to find the Shadow Clan and talked Bhim Chaya into keeping them both.

"Travel safe," Roshan told Khush now. "Beware of sipahis."

"Chhe! Those trussed up royal soldiers with their glowing tattoos don't stand a chance against me."

A few years ago, the sipahis had invaded the ravines, sending dozens of living specters to discover the Shadow Clan's whereabouts. Khush and Khizer, however, not only spotted the enemy spies from a mile away but also persuaded them to feed the sipahis false information. It hadn't been difficult. The specters sent by the sipahis were former prisoners who'd been tortured or killed by the queen's soldiers. Playing on the specters' resentment of the sipahis, the Shadow Clan had urged the spirits to lead the soldiers through the badlands and into the Maw, a tunnel no one used if they could help it. The unfortunate sipahis were neither seen nor heard from again.

Yet right now, Roshan found herself gritting her teeth as the air around her grew warm again, indicating Khush's absence.

"He'll be fine, Sardar," Khizer said softly. "He's carried messages for us before."

She exhaled. "I know." Yet back then, Baba was still alive. Why the brothers stayed loyal to her after Baba's death was a question she still didn't have the courage to ask.

Maybe Khizer had an inkling of what she was thinking, because he said, "We trust you, Sardar. We know that, given a choice, you'd never put anyone in this clan in danger."

Oh, Khizer. She didn't know if she wanted to kiss or shake him for being so naive. "I have put the clan in danger countless times," she pointed out. "I do so every time we go on a raid."

"Yes, but that is because we have no choice," Khizer replied matter-of-factly. "If we didn't raid the subedar's boats and warehouses, we would starve. So would many of the villagers."

True enough. Yet there were times when she wondered, rather guiltily, if they were fighting a losing battle. Was Deepak right? *Would* they be better off cutting their losses and leaving Ashvamaidan to find new homes, new lives elsewhere?

"Roshan Di?" Chotu's voice interrupted her thoughts. "The rajkumar wants to use the bathroom."

Again? She frowned. Prince Navin had been with them for only twelve hours so far, but he'd already used the bathroom more times than anyone else in the clan. Roshan hoped he hadn't fallen sick from the food or water. The clan needed to change hideouts tonight, and she didn't want to waste precious energy magically curing his royal bowels.

"I'll be right there, Chotu." She turned to Khizer. "Thank you again, Khizer. For your loyalty."

"Till death, Sardar." It was a phrase she'd heard clan members use often for her father. Until now, though, no one had ever used it for her.

Lighter than before, she entered the cave and found the prince on his feet, bouncing from one end of his barrier to another, clearly raring to go. She snapped her fingers, removing the sound barrier.

"Are you all right?" she asked.

"What do you mean?"

"I mean, are you sure you don't have diarrhea?"

"Does that worry you, Roshni?" He sneered. "Me stinking up your already smelly cave?"

His new clothes were wrinkled already and his hair mussed from sleeping on the ground. But his skin appeared normal to Roshan—brown and healthy, with no undertones of gray. To make sure, she caught hold of his wrist.

"No fever," she verified. "Heart rate appears normal, too."

"How," he said slowly, "do *you* not stink when nearly everyone else around you does?"

Roshan pressed her lips together, holding back a smile. He had a point. The cave *was* rather odorous, its air thick with the smell of grease and sweat from various bodies. "Stay still," she said.

"Stay still, *Navin*," he corrected. Then winced as a pair of stinging blue shackles appeared on his wrists.

"Is the blindfold necessary?" A trace of panic crept into his voice as she tied one around his eyes. "Last time, I pissed on myself. Don't force me to walk around naked again, Roshni."

The ends of her traitorous mouth curved up. Fire and ashes, but he *was* an amusing bastard.

"There's no need to exaggerate, Raj—*Navin*," she amended. His name seemed important to the prince, for some reason, and while Roshan didn't care for overfamiliarity with a hostage, it was really a small whim to cater to.

The prince stepped out of the barrier, his hand tightly clutched in hers, and then out of the cave to a nearby stone wall that was used by other clan members as well to do their business. While she refused to turn her back to him (shackles and a blindfold wouldn't prevent him from seeking out a rock or other weapon), Roshan did keep her gaze somewhere above his head for a modicum of privacy.

"Did you send my grandmother your ransom note?" he asked her.

"I did."

"Really?" A hiss, followed by a stream of urine hitting the wall. "I don't see any hawks around here."

Nice try, Rajkumar.

She lowered her gaze a notch, noting the stiff set of his shoulders, the way he strained his head sideways, as if itching to see her face. Clearly, the blindfold unnerved him.

"We have our ways," she said. "She'll know soon enough."

He turned back around, the front of his jama dropping to his knees.

"What will you do if you get your lands back?" he asked. "Or if the queen agrees to get rid of Subedar Yazad?"

Roshan wasn't as surprised by the question as she was by its lack of mockery. As if he was genuinely curious.

It was probably why she gave him the real answer: "We'll try to rebuild. Start afresh with what's left of the land." *If* there was anything left of it.

"What will you do, Rajkumar, when you are free?" she asked, changing the subject.

His throat bobbed. "*When* I'm free?"

"Of course," she said. "You don't think your own grandmother will leave you here with us, do you?"

"She might if she doesn't believe your claims about the subedar." There was a strange undercurrent of resignation in his voice. "I've been coming to Ashvamaidan since I was a child. From what I've seen, it's really well developed, with thriving villages and farmland. People love Subedar Yazad."

"It's *only* the port of Surag and its surrounding area that's thriving," Roshan corrected. "Those lands have always belonged to the subedar and his family. Tell me, Ra—Navin. Have you ever traveled ten miles west of Surag?"

"No."

"Then you haven't really seen Ashvamaidan. You don't even know what it's like here. You're like every other rich city brat who hasn't bothered to glance beyond his own nose."

"*You're* not letting me see it, either, blindfolding me like this! Do you expect me to believe you based on a single thornbush growing in your cave?"

People refuse to understand the scars they cannot see. It was something Baba had said once, the day he'd told Roshan the story of how the Shadow Clan was born.

She frowned now. Was Lalit right? Was the spare prince truly ignorant about the goings-on in his own kingdom?

A skylark perched overhead on a rocky ledge jutting from the entrance of the cave, where it trilled a song. To anyone else, the scene might have appeared idyllic.

Yet Roshan had grown up in these parts, had spent her whole life on the run. Her healing magic had taught her to not only distinguish between every ache and strain in her body but also trust its reactions during times of danger. And right now, from the way her jaw and left shoulder blade continued to tense, she sensed that danger wasn't far. Things were quiet. Too quiet. After that first altercation with the prince, Hemant was behaving himself. There had been no sign of any gold armor within a five-mile radius, either—even though by now she was sure the Aspas must have noticed their missing guest.

"Come," she told Navin. "Let's get you back inside."

At a living specter's speed, Queen Bhairavi would get the clan's ransom note in a few hours. By then, they would be on the move again—to a new hideout she and Lalit had found over a month earlier in case of raids or other contingencies.

Like kidnapping a prince.

"Rest," she said after escorting Navin back into his invisible prison and taking off his shackles and blindfold. "You'll need it tonight."

"Why? Are you planning an orgy, Roshni?" With the blindfold gone, his lazy, arrogant drawl had returned. His eyes glowed like newly minted mohurs—the way they did when he was amused, she realized. Or scornful. "If so, then you'll need rest, too. Or is there no rest for the wicked, as they say?"

More like no rest for the poor, she thought.

But what would the prince know about that? He had yet to learn what it meant to go to bed hungry, your bones as sharp as rocks even against the softest sleeping pallet.

Something about her face must have revealed her irritation, because he quickly added: "It was a joke. Haven't you heard any?"

Roshan said nothing. To think she'd considered giving him the benefit of the doubt only moments earlier. This boy deserved neither her empathy nor her anger. Ultimately, he was royal: a part of an institution that had forced her baba into a criminal life; an institution that continued to grow while the villages in her valley shriveled away.

Corrupt to the core. All of them.

"Rest, Rajkumar," she repeated, turning away. "Don't say I didn't warn you."

8

"Up!" Navin felt someone roughly shaking his shoulder. "Now!"

He bit back a groan, forcing himself to sit. It was pitch dark in the cave even when he opened his eyes. Nighttime. The Shadow Bandit hadn't been joking when she'd told him to rest up.

Soft murmurs reached his ears—the words *go* and *danger*—the last word being his only motivation to shake loose his aching limbs. The moment he stood, however, Navin felt the lash of magic against his wrists, the bright blue light of the shackles revealing Roshan's distinctive red hair.

"Were you a shadowlynx in a previous life?" he grumbled. "Or can you simply see in the dark?"

The left side of her mouth curled up in what might have been a half smile. Navin wasn't sure. In the dim light, the colors of her aura weren't as clear, though it was still—thank the gods—visible.

"I've been awake longer," she said. "My eyes are now accustomed to the darkness." Under her breath, she added: "Though I wouldn't mind a shadowlynx's speed right now."

Why did they need speed? His mind raced, latching onto something he heard before. *Danger.* Why? Were the governor's soldiers here?

"Put these on." She thrust a pair of boots at him. "You'll be doing a lot of walking tonight."

Navin obeyed in silence. Earlier that afternoon, when the Shadow Bandit had interrogated him about traveling into the deepest parts of the province, Navin had told her the truth. He *hadn't* been to these parts—and she and her bandits were the reason why.

"It's not safe west of the haveli," Shera had told him. "I mean, the villages are nice, but there are bandits in those parts. Dirty, greasy, illiterate creatures, always looting travelers for coin or trinkets embedded with magic. The Brights and I try to keep them in control, but there's still a risk of our being robbed if we go there."

Shera was partially right: Some of the bandits *were* dirty. The one named Hemant and his friends appeared constantly muddy and disheveled, their stench reminding Navin of a sewer. But the rest of the clan appeared to be reasonably clean, their faces free of dirt, hair glistening after dunks in the nearby river. The Shadow Bandit always smelled of the cloves she kept chewing. She'd even made Navin wash up with a bucket of river water and a clean rag a few hours ago.

Despite being relatively clean now, Navin's face still itched. He wished he had some soap as well. But, from what he'd seen, no one here had soap or any of the things he'd taken for granted at home. Not that this cave *could* be called a home. Clearly the bandits thought so, too, packed up as they were, heaving the sacks of grain they'd stolen from the governor's dhow back on their shoulders. Apart from the flying mare, the sacks were now also marked with black paint: JYOTI, MOHR, RAIGARH, ALIPORE . . .

Villages, Navin realized, trying to remember what little geography he knew of this area. Strange. He'd have expected the bandits to keep the loot for themselves. Then again, normal brigands might have demanded a thousand trunks of mohurs from the queen or elephant-loads of firestones—not that you could find much of the latter in Jwala anymore, even in the royal treasury. Navin hadn't expected the Shadow Clan to ask the queen for Ashvamaidan valley itself—a laughable request—and if not that, then a new governor of their own choosing—even more laughable.

"Take your blanket with you." The Shadow Bandit gestured to the itchy, woolly mess Navin had left on the floor. "It's cold out tonight."

A flame cut through the dark, dancing lightly on a fingertip before it turned into a small white lightorb, illuminating Roshan's face, her hair now hidden under a black turban. With the light, Navin could see her aura clearly again, though this time one emotion dominated: brown for calm.

"Moving houses, Roshni?" he asked, keeping his voice light. "What happened? Didn't like the view?"

Something flickered in her aura, a dash of scarlet that Navin hoped would push her into revealing her plans. But then she smiled—*a first*, Navin thought, if he discounted the time he'd unexpectedly made her laugh.

"Kitchen's too small," she replied, her tone equally airy. "And there's no gusalkhana."

Navin nearly laughed. Gusalkhana was probably the most pretentious Paras word used in reference to a bathroom—usually by courtiers trying to impress the queen or elderly servants at the palace.

Goddess help him. He didn't want to find the Shadow Bandit funny. He didn't want anything that could, in any way, soften his feelings toward her. Navin had learned long ago how detrimental his own emotions were to his magic, weakening it in situations where he needed it the most. Like that time in Aman, ten years ago. Right before his father had banished him for good.

So instead of joking back the way he would have, Navin remained silent.

Her smile flattened. "Right," she said. She reached into her pocket, pulling out that wretched blindfold again.

"Is this necessary?" he demanded. "I'm already shackled. And it's so dark out! How am I supposed to walk?"

"Your hands are shackled, Rajkumar, not your feet." She tucked a loose end of her turban over her mouth and nose. "Besides, you don't exactly have a choice."

Navin gritted his teeth, saying nothing. He'd rarely, if ever, come across someone this infuriating. But right now, there was no way to fight her and—belatedly—he realized that this was his own fault. Instead of hesitating, he should have continued bantering with her, spent a little more time developing a deeper bond—risky as it was.

As she blindfolded him, Navin's other senses grew heightened. Smell: cloves and lemongrass; touch: a fingernail accidentally scraping his ear; taste: the stale reminder of the evening's chai on his tongue; and sound: a whisper in the background, a man saying: ". . . no, no. That's too close to Surag."

Navin's heartbeat kicked up a notch. Surag was the province's capital, a port directly under Governor Yazad's control. Was it possible that the bandits were heading east? Closer to the Aspas—to a chance at freedom?

"Fire and ashes." The Shadow Bandit's whisper, so unexpectedly close to his ear, sent a shiver down his spine. "Look at you stiffening at the mention of your precious Surag."

When he stiffened even more, she laughed. "Funny, isn't it, Rajkumar, how much your body betrays you when you can't see? I'm not surprised. You've never had to try much with anyone, have you? Always using soul magic to manipulate them."

"Like you're any better," he retorted, his fear temporarily vanishing at her prickly words. "All you do is give orders and threaten people when you don't get your way."

Dead silence hung between them, and for a moment, he wondered if she'd raised a sound barrier around him again.

What followed, however, was worse: a strip of rough cloth that the Shadow Bandit tied tightly around his mouth.

"Enough with the talking, I think," she said coldly. "Let's move."

There was a sharp, magical tug on his shackles, urging him to walk. When he didn't move, the Shadow Bandit tugged again, harder this time, tiny shocks going through his wrists.

Fine. He'd move.

The ground was unpaved, rocks jagged and sharp under his boots. Night air enveloped his body, its grip like ice. Despite the heavy blanket, Navin shivered with each step. If not for the occasional tug on the shackles guiding him, he would not have known where to go.

The bandits were quiet, except for the sudden spate of loud coughing, which instantly made the Shadow Bandit turn around and silence the offender—"Shhhh, Hemant!"

Navin didn't register the exact moment they'd stopped in their tracks—until he walked right into someone else. He recognized the grip, the small, firm hand on his arm. Roshan.

"Wait," she whispered. "Don't move."

He jerked to a stop.

"Lalit." Her voice was now directed somewhere above his left ear. "Take the others through the western pass. I'll take the rajkumar through the Maw and meet you at the new hideout."

"The Maw?" Navin *really* didn't like the mix of shock and panic he heard in Lalit's voice. "But that's—"

Whatever Lalit was going to say was cut off abruptly when something thundered from overhead—*boulders*, Navin realized as he was pushed sideways, cheek-first against a rocky wall.

"Brights!" Roshan shouted, her voice ringing in his ears. "Brights up ahead!"

9

Brights? Navin's heart raced, his face stinging with scrapes. *They were here?*

Somewhere behind him, Lalit was shouting rapid instructions to the bandits, but the sound was drowned out by another voice, magically magnified, filling every pair of ears over the radius of a mile: "Don't bother running, witch!" Shera's rage urged Navin's frozen limbs back into action. "I know you have the prince with you!"

Navin tried to shout as loudly as he could from behind the gag. What came out was only a series of grunts.

A dagger pricked his throat. "Not a sound," Roshan snarled. "Move!"

The highest of hells I won't.

He focused on the warmth of the teak ring on his left pinkie, magic spiraling delicately up his arm and shoulder, to his tongue. Somehow, he managed to catch the cloth of the gag between his teeth and mumble two words: "Unhand me."

For a split second, he felt the Shadow Bandit tremble, her grip on him loosening. But then there was another thundering of rocks and she pitched sideways. The sudden movement made Navin accidentally bite the blister forming on the side of his tongue, pain exploding in his mouth like needles.

Fire and ashes.

Whatever magic he'd managed earlier faded to a dull hum, his amplifier growing cold again. Blood and saliva welled rapidly, dribbling from the corners of his lips. Coughs racked at his chest, his vision blurring, nearly forcing him to his knees.

When Navin came to again, he found himself miraculously freed of the gag. The Shadow Bandit's warm breath brushed his cheek, her cold fingers holding his mouth open wide.

"You bit the inside of your cheek pretty badly," she muttered, releasing him. "You could have choked on your own spit. Or blood."

Thank goddess she didn't suspect any attempts at soul magic.

Navin continued taking long, painful breaths. He waited for her to replace his gag, but she didn't. That was when he noticed the silence around them. A silence that, despite his best efforts at straining his ears, told him that the Brights and the rest of the clan were gone.

It made sense, he thought bitterly. Why shut him up when there was no one to hear his voice?

As the pain in his mouth began to fade, however, logic began to set in. At the moment, he was shackled and blindfolded, his soul magic reduced to a trickle by a pathetic amplifier. Loath as he was to admit it, now wasn't the time to escape the Shadow Bandit.

He breathed hard for several moments and then raised his fettered hands, palms facing the sky. It was a gesture used by priests in temples while praying to the fire goddess, by warriors offering a truce on the battlefield. Slowly, the Shadow Bandit helped him to his feet.

"Move," she ordered, her voice hoarse. Her dagger pointed at his back, right between the shoulder blades.

He stumbled ahead, one doddering step at a time. To his relief, the Shadow Bandit didn't shock him again through his shackles, merely nudging him with her katar when he didn't move fast enough for her liking. After what felt like an hour, maybe even a day, she ordered him to stop.

"Listen to me, Rajkumar, and listen hard. I am not going to gag you right now. And I am going to remove your blindfold. We will be entering the Maw, which is . . ."

Her words faded from his hearing as the first sentence registered. *His blindfold would be gone.* He'd be able to *see* again, maybe even manipulate her aura and—

"Understand?" Her voice held a bite, as if she'd already asked the question once. "We will not be able to hear each other in there. But *they* will. So remember to keep your mouth shut."

Who will? Navin bit back the question.

Did it matter? Clearly whoever it was frightened the Shadow Bandit. Any enemy of hers would only be an advantage in this moment.

"Yes," he whispered.

A sound that might have been an exhale. The Shadow Bandit ripped off his blindfold. But before his vision could adjust to the surroundings outside, Navin found himself being nudged forward, back into darkness—through the opening of what appeared to be a tunnel.

Seconds later, a lightorb floated over his head, revealing toothy rocks jutting from the walls and the ceiling, like the inside of some terrible creature's mouth. Even in the dim light, he could tell there was little room to move in this place; they'd be single file, the whole way through. A sour scent rose in the air, the copper of old blood and piss and puke. But it was the sound—or lack of it—that really got to Navin.

The ravines were quiet, no doubt, but there was the occasional screech of a field crow, the rustle of wind against the shrubs and the dead trees. Even the Shadow Bandit's sound barrier had made some noise by buzzing against his ears.

In the Maw, there was nothing. No wind. No feet shuffling the ground. Not even the sound of his own breath reached Navin's ears. His throat balled as if a stone had formed there, fixed and unmoving.

Sing for me, hatchling, his father used to say, pressing a long golden finger to Navin's throat. *Let me feel your voice.*

Navin would sing his father's favorite song—about the sun and other fiery stars—allowing the vibrations to fill his throat. His father would sing as well, gently coaxing Navin to modulate his tone, correcting him until both of their voices matched perfectly.

Now, in this tunnel without sound, Navin raised his shackled hands, carefully pressing his fingers to his throat. Another memory intruded— the one of his last day with his father.

Pitaji, I didn't do it! a nine-year-old Navin had begged. *Please! Believe me!*

The final two words had emerged as a command, the only time he'd attempted to use soul magic on his father. Navin had known it was a mistake the moment Peri Tir's aura had vanished from his sight. His enormous wings had unfurled, spanning six feet, every iridescent feather flaring outward.

Oh, hatchling. Your act, as terrible as it was, does not hurt me as much as your lies do in this moment. I can't see you right now. Not until you admit the truth.

No, Pitaji, I am telling the truth! I swear it!

Navin had not known then that *right now* would become *forever,* that his hawks to his father would never be answered again.

As he walked ahead, Roshan's lightorb and katar nudging him onward, Navin slowly began humming a song about a bird lost in the rain. His fingers picked out each shifting note from the vibrations, from the roll of hyoid and cartilage under his skin. The stone in his throat dissipated. Warmth filled the hollow it had left behind, like the sun emerging from the clouds. The song moved through his fingers, his limbs, eventually reaching his ears, freeing them of that awful, unending silence.

He barely realized he had stopped moving when Roshan clamped his shoulders, her crushing grip cutting off the song, her voice emerging as clear as a bell:

"Curse the gods, what did you do?"

There was no time to answer. Other sounds overlapped her voice— scrapes against rock, the patter of little feet, the high squeals of unknown animals raising the hairs on Navin's nape.

"Get behind me!" Roshan shoved him aside and stepped forward, her katar gleaming under the lightorb. Her aura was visible again: a bright cloud of anger and fear. "Quickly! They're up ahead!"

Who's up ahead? Navin wanted to ask.

But then he saw the creatures—possibly ten, possibly fifty—scrambling toward them on four legs, their sockets glowing green in the dark, large birdlike skulls open in screams, bits of rotting flesh and fur still clinging to their long, skeletal bodies. The stench, which had been bad enough when Navin had entered the tunnel, worsened, nearly making him throw up.

Bone demons.

Navin had never seen one before except in an old painting at the university. "Products of the darkest magic," his professors had called them, without elaborating any further.

Exterminated half a century ago, bone demons were now regarded as a myth in Jwala, used to trick small children into doing your bidding and then to laugh until your stomachs ached.

Navin wasn't laughing now. He raised his hands, weaponless save for his teak ring, which would be useless against what appeared to be not fifty, but a hundred bone demons, their screeches filling the tunnel, burrowing deep in his skull.

"Hide!" Roshan's voice came to him from what felt like a great distance. "Don't just stand there!"

As Navin slid into a crevasse between two jutting rocks, her blade flashed, piercing the center of a bone demon's long, triangular skull. Navin crept farther back, wishing he could turn into a rock himself, when his ears picked out another sound.

One right by his ear.

He had seconds, maybe less, to dodge the bone demon perched next to him, sending him back into the middle of the fighting.

"Roll!" Roshan shouted. "Roll!"

Navin crouched and rolled out of the way, just as a bone demon lunged—and then watched a dagger flash, sink through bone, severing its evil, skeletal head from its body.

"Come on," Roshan said, gasping under her mask. She caught hold of Navin's arm and pulled him to his feet. His hand burned where he'd scratched it against a rock, blood beading on the inside of his palm. Head spinning, he watched as she dug into the pocket of her trousers and pulled out a small, spherical object made of clay.

Cracking the seal with her teeth, she hurled it at the ceiling, where it exploded in a shower of sparks. Following Roshan's lead, Navin dived for cover as rocks came crashing down on the bone demons, leaving behind a silence that felt louder than their screams.

Roshan turned to face him, ripping off her mask.

"How," she snarled, "in the highest of hells did you *break* a sound barrier?"

I hummed, Navin thought. *For the first time in ten years, I attempted something close to singing.*

But something else had happened in this foul cave. Something that made his throat grow warm the way it did whenever he performed soul magic. That still allowed him to see the Shadow Bandit's aura vividly, every smaller emotion narrowing to one: suspicion.

Navin fisted the hand that wore the teak ring. "I don't know."

"Really." Roshan caught hold of his hands and held them up. Ice burned his palms, his fingers spreading wide of their own accord.

"Jwaliyan teak." She pulled the ring off. "Face the wall. Hands over your head."

She patted him down, firm but not rough in her movements, a degree of efficiency in her touch, even when it veered close to the space between his thighs.

"Turn around. Keep those hands up," she ordered.

Navin did, observing the cloud of blue around her head—no longer as vivid, but still, for some reason, visible even though she'd relieved him of his amplifier. He could take his chance now. Could, with a few words, melt the blue like sugar to a rich, complacent brown, ordering her to unshackle him and shackle herself instead.

But then what?

Though the ceiling was now pockmarked with holes from where the atashgola had hit it, the tunnel was still dark. What if more bone demons were ahead? Navin *could* double back to where they'd come from, but he wasn't sure what he'd find outside the Maw. The Brights and Shera? What if he found more Shadow Clan members, armed to the teeth and waiting for their leader? Worse: What if he found no one and died of starvation in the badlands?

Roshan was examining the ring with a frown. "Not much teak to be a great amplifier and yet . . ." She looked up at Navin, who did his best to keep his face still. For several moments, neither spoke. If not for her sharp exhale, Navin would have thought the sound barrier had fallen in place again.

"It doesn't matter." She rose to her feet and pocketed the ring. "Maybe next time you'll actually keep your mouth shut when I tell you to."

Right. Like I'd trust anything you say.

On another day, he might have spoken the words out loud. But for now, Navin chose silence, swallowing his anger like a mouthful of blood. He loosened his jaw and let calm bloom over his face.

"Where did the bone demons come from?" he asked. The abrupt change in subject and his demeanor made the Shadow Bandit pause.

"I'm not sure. They started appearing a few years ago," she said. Yellow ribboned the blue and red of her aura, which was slowly beginning to fragment again. His magic was fading. "Lalit and I discovered them by accident here in the Maw. We barely managed to escape. We later found that if anyone tried to talk here, the foul things would appear; somehow, they could hear our voices even if we couldn't hear ourselves."

"Bone demons don't appear out of nowhere, do they?" Navin asked. "I've heard that they have to be made."

"And who do you think is making them?" When he didn't answer, she went on. "They appear nearly every time the Brights raid a village or kill someone."

First blood tithes, now this?

"You're implying Subedar Yazad is somehow involved," Navin stated flatly. "The subedar is an earth magus, Roshni. I don't know how much history you've studied, but the last known maker of bone demons was a healer—like you."

Dead silence during which he heard nothing except the Shadow Bandit's labored breaths.

"She was also executed over fifty years ago," he added. As far as he knew, no bone demons had been seen in Jwala since, the knowledge of their making severed along with the old healer's head.

Roshan's aura began turning red again. "I am not the one making these abominations."

"But you have proof that Subedar Yazad is?"

Navin couldn't believe it. Not of the man who'd roused him and Shera at dawn whenever Navin visited them, dragging them both to the temple in his massive courtyard.

"Fear the fire goddess if you don't fear me," Yazad Aspa had always told the boys.

And, for all his vices, Navin always had. He'd prayed to the goddess for forgiveness after each drunken escapade, had even seen her once in a dream, his memory colored by the governor's grave words and the smoky scent of sandalwood. He prayed to her now.

Blessed Goddess, let me get out of this alive.

"Proof." Roshan's low voice crackled like the fiery lightorb overhead. "You want *proof*, haan? But that's what Parasmani Bhairavi always asks for, too, doesn't she? Even when the truth stares her in the face."

Navin didn't need to see her aura right now to note her anger. What was amazing was that he *could* still see her aura, fragmented as it was. He didn't understand how his magic hadn't faded yet. He hadn't done anything different today than what he had for the last few years—except hum that stupid song.

Wait . . .

"What's wrong?" Roshan demanded. Worry overtook her aura, dissipating the red. "You look like you're going to be sick."

"I'm fine," he mumbled.

He was barely aware of the Shadow Bandit, who now walked over to him and examined his face with a frown. Without another word, she pressed her fingers to his cheek, startling him into awareness. Light limned her shoulders, drove away the shadows under her eyes. For a blink, Navin forgot who she was—thief, captor, and murderer—and only saw what she'd become. A healer, her gaze luminous, the fire and ice of her magic transferring from her body to his—mending the scrape on his face, the dagger wound on his neck, the stinging cut on his hand, even the blisters inside his mouth from the last time he'd attempted soul magic. The skin on his palm grew taut, clean, and unbroken again, every trace of the wound gone.

"Good enough," she said. As the light pervading her faded, he saw that she was tired, a hint of ash tinting her smooth brown skin. Healing him had taken a toll on her. "Time to get moving."

Navin's heartbeat quickened when he saw her retrieve the blindfold from her pocket.

"Please. Not that again!"

He expected her to mock him, to laugh at his panic.

But she merely raised her eyebrows. "The sound barrier is gone, Rajkumar, and so are the bone demons. We both can hear now. It will not be difficult for me to guide you or for you to follow instructions."

She was back again to using his title instead of his name. Navin took a deep breath. It was apparent from the way she spoke that her emotions were influenced by logic. If he wanted this small bit of freedom, he had to appeal to her pragmatic side—while he could still see her aura. It could change later, of course, once his magic faded. But for now, Navin took the risk of allowing magic to trickle into his voice:

"Think, Roshni. It's already dark in this tunnel. I have no idea where we are. If I can see a couple of feet ahead of me, I am less likely to get injured. Don't you want a break from healing me? I promise I won't scream or try to run." Unless an opportunity presented itself, of course.

"Please," he asked, the word a perfect mix of persuasion and humility. "Let me see."

She frowned, and for a moment, he thought he saw her aura shift, a drop of brown seeping through the blue. But then she shook her head and it scattered. Almost as if she'd sensed his magic nudging at her emotions. Pain flooded Navin's mouth; he'd accidentally bitten his tongue again.

"Lower your head, Rajkumar." Whatever sympathy he'd thought he'd sensed before was gone. The Shadow Bandit of Ashvamaidan tied the blindfold tightly around his skull, close enough again so that he could feel her breath on his cheek, smell the cloves she always chewed.

"It's unfortunate that I don't believe you," she whispered. "But you aren't the only one who needs proof."

10

THEY TRUDGED THROUGH THE MAW WITHOUT FURTHER INCI-
dent, taking a single break to let the prince relieve himself. When they
finally emerged from the tunnel, dawn trickled across the scarred brown
landscape along with a familiar wetness between Roshan's thighs. She
sighed. Thanks to recent events, she'd forgotten to account for her
monthly cycle, further confirmed by the cramping in her lower back.
Luckily, her jama was red. And the clan wouldn't judge her for a few
bloodstains. Also, Roshan and the prince weren't very far from the new
hideout.

A twinge of sympathy rose inside her as the prince stumbled over a
jutting rock next to the ruin of an old Zaalian prayer house, his broad
shoulders hunched over, his jama patched with sweat. In the Maw, she'd
nearly been swayed by the plea to remove his blindfold. The prince
epitomized most things Roshan found annoying in a person: spoiled,
wealthy, offensively self-assured, yet . . .

He wasn't unintelligent. That much was clear from the questions
he'd asked. He could be funny, too—though that wasn't something she
would admit out loud. And that *voice*. It had sent chills up her spine,
reminding her of things she'd thought she'd forgotten: tracing shapes in
clouds as a child, the taste of spring rain, of a hope she was sometimes
too scared to feel.

Was his ignorance about Ashvamaidan as real as Lalit had suggested? Or was it a facade?

Ultimately, she hadn't taken any chances. She'd risked enough by moving forward with the prince alone while Lalit and the others distracted the Brights. It was luck that the Brights hadn't thought of the Maw—or perhaps they simply assumed Roshan wouldn't risk the creatures that roamed it.

Now she could only hope that her clan had escaped unscathed as well.

"We're heading downhill," she called out when they paused at the top of the incline. "I'm going to hold your arm and guide you." She slipped a hand between his forearm and bicep, both surprisingly strong for a man of leisure. "Two steps left. Four steps forward. A step slightly to the right. That's it. Twelve steps forward. Stop."

A trapdoor had appeared in the ground. It slid open to reveal an underground staircase when Roshan approached. The telltale magic of Lalit's familiar shield enchantment brushed her cheeks, easing the tension coiled in her ribs. The clan had arrived safely—further indicated by the small copper soldier left on the top step, its tiny face and atashban green with patina. Roshan pocketed the toy, which clicked gently against the prince's confiscated ring.

"I'm going to lead you down some stairs," she told Navin. "There are shields and other barriers in place." The trapdoor, in fact, had been visible only to Roshan because of the wooden horse-shaped charm she carried in her pocket, one that Baba had carved for each member of the clan.

"Stop," she said once they reached the bottom of the stairs, a torch flickering against the rock wall. She removed the prince's blindfold, watching as he blinked, his eyes adjusting to the dimly lit passage and the ancient rail track embedded in the ground.

"What is this place?" he whispered.

"Probably an abandoned mine." Or so it seemed from the broken barrows they'd found in one of the passages, along with the indents in the walls. "We turn here."

Making their way through a complex maze of passages, Navin still ahead of her, they emerged into a wide, cavernous space lit brightly with more torches.

"Didi!" Chotu flew across the cave, colliding with Roshan as she stepped in, his skinny arms winding around her neck. "You're here!"

She laughed, hugging him back hard. "Where else would I go, silly boy?"

As Chotu flew away, Roshan nodded at Lalit. "Anyone hurt?" she asked, trying to stay calm.

"No more than scrapes and bruises," Lalit assured her. "Your plan to disguise Vijali Fui and Khizer as decoys worked like a charm. The Brights followed them instead of you and the rajkumar and fell right into that nasty little pit by our old hideout. A good half of them got stuck there. The rest were scattered, waiting for instructions. We heard Shera braying at them to dig him out as our two escaped."

Roshan grinned, noting the spare prince's frown, the taut set of his jaw.

Annoyed, are you? Well, that's too bad.

It was also time to lay down the rules again. She gestured to a raised, flattened stone in the corner. "Have a seat, Rajkumar. Unless you'd like to strip naked again and show us more amplifiers."

"Amplifiers?" Lalit echoed. "Didn't we take his jewels from him?"

She pulled out the wooden ring and held it up for Lalit's inspection. "Jwaliyan teak," she said. "He's been using it to strengthen his soul magic this whole time. Not that it worked much, did it, Rajkumar?"

"Wouldn't you like to know," the prince drawled.

Something about his tone made Roshan frown. She thought back to her interactions with him a few hours ago. How he'd fought to get Shera's attention, grunting all the while through his gag. She remembered how, for the barest blink, she'd felt the urge to move aside. To drop her hands and let him go.

Soul magic. The realization tasted bitter. She'd nearly lost him then.

"Lalit," she said, her voice hardening. "Get me parchment, ink, and a pen, would you?"

Moments later, she ignored the prince's stare and scribbled out a single sentence on a sheet.

"Here," she said. "Sign this."

His gaze narrowed at the words, the ink gleaming in iridescent letters:

I, Rajkumar Navin of Clan Behram, will not escape nor try to escape the Shadow Clan in any way.

"What in goddess's flaming hair is this?" he demanded. "Are you making me sign a *contract?*"

"A magical one, of course. To cover our bases."

She *should* have made him sign a contract the night they first found him. Or, at least, yesterday, before changing hideouts. But she'd been foolish. She'd underestimated the spare prince. And nearly cost the clan.

"*Sign it,*" Roshan emphasized the words. "I won't repeat myself again."

That strong jaw tightened even more. Snatching the pen from her fingers, he scrawled his name across the parchment. Yet, it wouldn't have mattered if he'd drawn a line there. It was how magical contracts worked to bind the user. If the prince reneged on his, he would die. Or get a severe injury he wouldn't be able to recover from—even with healing magic.

He now sat stiffly on the rock while she magicked both confinement and sound barriers around him. Though she was pretty sure he had no other amplifiers on his person, the shackles on his wrists would also remain for now.

Good thing she'd already buried his other jewelry deep, about a mile away from their old hideout. It'd be difficult to sell or barter for new weapons momentarily, even in a black market, because by now everyone and their mother would be looking for clues about the missing prince. Roshan would have to wait until things calmed down—which they would at some point. Minds were fickle when people remained out of sight. Which reminded her—

"Any news about Khush?" she asked Lalit. By now the living specter should have hopefully delivered her missive to Prabha and returned.

"He caught up with us on our way here. Apparently, our letter to Parasmani Bhairavi spiced up a really boring state dinner. Want to hear him mimic the palace steward's squeals?"

Shaking her head, Roshan dug into her pocket and dropped the copper sipahi back in Lalit's palm. "Good thing you still keep this."

Lalit grinned. "And I see *you're* keeping the ring."

"Why not?" She slipped it over her calloused right thumb, where it fit rather well. "I could use some new jewelry."

"Also, a smart move with the contract," Lalit commented as she tucked the folded parchment into her jama. "It'll allow us to sleep easy at night."

I learn from my mistakes, she thought, grateful that Lalit couldn't read her thoughts. Or know how close she'd come to screwing everything up. She patted the parchment, reassuring herself of its presence. She'd hide it later in a safe place.

She scanned the cave for faces now, responded to various greetings and waves.

She paused at the sight of Hemant in the back, laughing and holding court before his cronies. They'd yet to acknowledge Roshan's presence.

"Darab!" she barked. "Fariyal, Saloni!"

A man and two women slowly rose to their feet, glancing nervously between Hemant and Roshan. "What?" Fariyal demanded, her voice sounding squeaky instead of belligerent.

"You three will be making deliveries tomorrow to Raigarh," Roshan said, then gestured to the others still sitting around Hemant. "The rest of you can clean this place and make it livable."

Hemant snorted. "What's with the *do this, do that*? Are we Sardar Roshan's servants now?"

She shrugged. "Your choice. Everyone who works will get two portions at dinner tomorrow. We have a little more food to spare this week."

They didn't. Not really. But the mention of extra food almost instantly resulted in several brightened faces.

"So?" Roshan raised an eyebrow after a pause. "Will you work?"

"Haan," some, including Fariyal, mumbled.

"Haan, *what*?" Roshan raised her voice ever so slightly.

"Haan, Sardar!"

"I can't hear you."

"Haan, Sardar!" they cried out, their voices echoing in the cavern.

She didn't have to look at Hemant to know he was fuming. Or turn around to sense the others watching them. She headed to the makeshift kitchen area, where Lalit handed her a steaming bowl of bajra and blue onion porridge, along with an approving wink.

Roshan allowed herself a tiny smile. Cutthroats as they all were in this cave, everyone needed an occasional reminder of who the biggest cutthroat was.

11

"Bajra and onions?" Navin grumbled as the Shadow Bandit's hand disappeared through the barriers, leaving behind a steaming bowl of food. "Again?"

Two days had passed since they'd arrived at the new hideout, indicated by the three meals Navin received each day. Seven everlasting torches lined the cavern wall, their flames magically turning blue at exactly dawn, morning, midday, sunset, dusk, evening, and midnight. Seven phases of the day for the fire goddess's seven prayers. At the palace, Navin would have prayed a couple of times, then skipped the remaining phases, claiming some prior engagement or another. Now he had nothing to do *except* kneel and pray—not that anyone seemed to be listening. Maybe even the goddess had trouble hearing him over this cursed sound barrier.

His contract with the Shadow Clan made things worse. Navin had felt its magic tug at his solar plexus the moment he'd signed the parchment—like an atashgola set to go off at any second. But all contracts had loopholes, including magical ones. Navin simply had to find out what they were—without dying first.

Slowly, he grew aware of someone watching. Chotu, who glanced away at once, his pale cheeks flushing.

An uncomfortable sensation curled in his belly as Navin examined Chotu's face, the sharp edges of his cheekbones and clavicles. There wasn't *that* much food in Navin's bowl. At the palace, this would be an average portion for a meal, excluding second servings.

But over here . . .

He glanced at the other bandits, who were eating from bowls half the size of his. How many would get another serving if they asked? Even the Shadow Bandit, from what Navin had seen, ate the same as the others. Sometimes, she ate less or skipped a meal altogether.

Waiting until Chotu's gaze turned to him again, Navin waved to the boy and pointed at the bowl. *Share with me?* he mouthed, rubbing his tummy. *It's too much.*

The boy at once glanced from side to side. He wanted the food. Badly. But neither of them could cross Navin's confinement barrier. There had been moments this week when Navin had been tempted to hum again. To see if his song could shatter the Shadow Bandit's sound barrier as it did the Maw's. But he'd held back. It might not even work, but what if his singing *did* shatter the barrier? The Shadow Bandit would grow even more suspicious of him than she was already and would likely cage him away somewhere in the tunnels, where he saw no one except rats.

Navin gave Chotu a smile, hoping it didn't look as strained as he felt it did. *You shouldn't rely so much on your magic, little brother,* Farhad had told him more than once. Fortunately—or unfortunately—until now, magic *had* solved a lot of Navin's problems. Curse Farhad and his foresight. Curse their grandmother, too, and her last words to Navin: *I will treat you with respect when you prove yourself worthy.*

Proof. He suddenly understood the Shadow Bandit's bitterness when she spoke the word. Farhad was likely the only family member who cared the most about Navin, but he wasn't here now. Right now, Navin had only himself. A body in borrowed clothes, a brain, his unreliable instincts, and no amplifiers whatsoever.

His smile remained in place as a pair of figures appeared from the back of the cave. The Shadow Bandit and Lalit were frowning at something Chotu was saying. Roshan walked up to Navin and snapped her fingers, sound rushing back into his ears.

"Is there something wrong with your food, Rajkumar?" she asked sharply.

"Nothing," he said. Well, it *was* bland. But it wasn't bad. Bajra porridge had tasted like the fire goddess's own food when they'd first arrived here, starving and exhausted. "It's . . . a lot. I wanted to share it with the boy. He's young. He needs strength. All I do is sit here."

Silence. Several heads turned to look. Roshan and Lalit watched him for so long that Navin wondered if he had, indeed, sprouted an extra head or limb.

"You *do* realize"—he switched to the lazy drawl he'd perfected, one that made the most malicious courtiers in Prabha cower—"that I'd like to fit in my clothes again when I return home, don't you? The newest fashions in the city are rather formfitting. And alterations are *such* a pain, Roshni."

Lalit smirked at the comment. Roshan didn't. She was still staring at Navin as if she couldn't quite believe his words.

"All right," she said after a moment. She stepped through the confinement barrier and picked up the bowl, handing it to the boy. "Chotu, what do we tell the rajkumar?"

"Meherbani!" Chotu's genuine delight at being given more food warmed Navin's insides and also made him feel oddly small. "Meherbani, Rajkumar Navin!"

"It's nothing," Navin replied truthfully. Growing up, he'd never had— nor been allowed—to share food. The one time he'd offered his brother a crispy eggplant bhajia, Navin had been reprimanded severely by the palace steward: "Rajkumar, those are *not* meant for the yuvraj! You must eat from your own plate and he from his. Please adhere to palace decorum and tradition."

Now, as he watched Chotu, Navin wondered why they'd even bothered with such a tradition. There was something rather satisfying about sharing one's meal, plain as it was—to feel the warm rush of having done something right for once. It was why, when the same large bowl came back to Navin for lunch, brimming over with steaming rice and a gravy of rich brown lentils, he shared it with Chotu again.

By dinnertime, however, moments into the fifth torch turning blue, the Shadow Bandit intervened.

"What's this nonsense?" she asked Navin. "If you don't want more food, say so."

He shrugged. "I like sharing with Chotu," he said truthfully. "His joy brings me pleasure in this dreary place."

"Did you expect us to put on a dance recital in your honor?"

"No. But I didn't expect to sit in one place. My hands will rot and fall off at this rate."

He raised the hands in question, the wrists bruised by now from perpetually being in shackles. The Shadow Bandit scowled, and for a second, he thought she would stalk off, the way she sometimes did when annoyed or at a loss for words.

But then she said, "Fine. You want work? You'll get it. The toilets need cleaning."

Goddess's flaming hair, he'd wanted to be unshackled—not put on cleaning duty! Still . . . this was freedom of a sort, wasn't it? It would allow him to stretch his legs, to see more of this underground mine. To learn if there was any way out. Magical contract or not, Navin didn't plan to give up without a fight. So he held on to his disgust, which wasn't entirely difficult, and began mumbling an excuse:

"I didn't mean—"

"No, no," Roshan cut in. There was an evil smile on her pretty face. "There's always work to be done with so many people and you are, as you said, an extra pair of hands. With a little supervision, I don't see why you can't be put to use. Starting tonight."

She snapped her fingers before he could respond, locking the sound barrier in place. Navin raised his fists, mouthing curses into the buzzing void until everyone, even Chotu, turned away.

And that was when he stopped. And smiled.

12

THE ONLY BENEFIT OF LIVING UNDERGROUND WAS NOT HAVING to wear a blindfold at all times. Navin used this advantage, mentally mapping the Shadow Clan's new lair as best as he could. He was confined to the central cavern, which made up the general living space and kitchen. As many as thirty bandits napped or slept here at night on blankets and pillows made of old gunnies. Then there were the inner tunnels, where Roshan, Lalit, and a few others seemed to sleep—though Navin hadn't seen their "rooms." The bathroom was the farthest from the main living area, accessible through a maze of tunnels, including a steep incline that made him breathless each time he climbed it.

At the top of the incline waited a wooden bucket filled with sand, a filthy shovel, and a wave of odors so strong they nearly made Navin throw up the rice he'd had for dinner.

"Are you going to faint?" The Shadow Bandit sounded disgusted. "You visit this bathroom, too, Rajkumar. You should be used to the smell by now."

"You didn't have to come—" Navin sucked in a breath through his mouth, leaning uncomfortably against the ridged wall "—supervise me." He'd thought the leader of the Shadow Clan would delegate less pleasant tasks to a subordinate. He was clearly wrong. "What happened?" he taunted. "Can't stay away, Rosh-niiiiiii?" He drew her name out, lifting it high in an unknown melody.

She rolled her eyes. Pale fragments of color floated around her deep red hair, dissipating nearly as soon as they'd emerged. So he was right. It *had* been the singing that had amplified his magic in the Maw. Yet, short of conducting an entire conversation in song, Navin doubted he'd be able to see or manipulate her aura right now. Let alone breathe. He gasped again, sucking in more air through his mouth.

"All right, Rajkumar. Get to work."

Scooping sand from the bucket and dumping it into deep, foul-smelling pits. Work, with shackled hands, trying desperately not to inhale the stench, every movement sending a sharp shock up his arms. Feces littered the empty drainage tunnels bordering the pits, an ancient bamboo pipe the only remnant of whatever plumbing had existed in the mine eons ago. By the time the bucket was half full, Navin was already retching, his ribs and forehead drenched with sweat.

"... all right," he heard someone say from a great distance. "It's all right, Rajkumar. Come out. Let's get you some air."

A cool hand lightly brushed his burning forehead. By the time his vision cleared, he was back out on the incline, seated on the upturned bucket, his head tilted upward, eyes focusing slowly on the Shadow Bandit.

"You able to sit?" she asked, her voice softer than he'd ever heard it before.

"I think so," he whispered back. A part of him wanted to laugh at the scene and also simultaneously bury his face in the ground.

"You actually shoveled," she said flatly. As if she was surprised.

"Isn't that what you ordered me to do?"

"You could have refused. Pretended to be sick. You didn't have to *really* get sick!"

"I could have refused?" he asked sarcastically. "You mean, I had a *choice* in the matter?"

Her lips flattened ever so slightly. Again, he wished he had his amplifiers—if only to know when exactly she would shut him up.

"Hold up your hands," she instructed, her voice abrupt.

Fire and ashes, was he going to be spanked?

But he did as he'd been told. Might as well face whatever lay ahead. There was a *crack*, followed by a flash of bright light and a sense of weightlessness on his wrists. And no wonder. His shackles were gone. Her calloused fingers slid up the backs of his hands. If it was someone else, he'd assume they were copping a feel. But not Roshan. Her gaze was on his wrists and the bruises purpling them. Magic outlined her form, left behind a sparkling residue on his newly healed skin. If that hadn't shocked him already, then the words she spoke now certainly did:

"I apologize." Sweat beaded her forehead—from the healing or nerves, he couldn't tell. "I thought it would be funny to see you gag and make faces. I didn't realize you would . . ." Her voice trailed off.

Panic so badly that I'd faint? he wanted to respond wryly. And he would have—if not for the tight set of her jaw, the tremor he now sensed in her hands.

"Does it happen often?" she asked. "The fainting."

"Not really. Well, it happened when I las—when I was nine." He'd nearly blurted out *when I last saw my father*. Another episode had recurred a month later when his grandmother had gifted him the jade bracelets—when Navin realized he'd never see his father again. But he didn't mention that to her. "Hasn't happened since . . . well. Until now."

She placed his hands back in his lap. "All right."

He sighed. "Don't worry, Roshni. Your bargaining chip for the queen still lives."

"That's not why I—you know what?" She shook her head. "Never mind."

"What? Are you going to tell me I'm wrong? That you and your so-called clan have my best interests at heart?"

A pause before she said: "No."

At least she was honest. Ignoring the pinch in his chest, Navin closed his eyes.

"There was a time," she said slowly, "when my baba, too, used to believe in Parasmani Bhairavi. That she had our—and Ashvamaidan's—best interests at heart."

Curse her for drawing his attention again. His eyes flickered open.

"Your baba," he said. "Are you referring to the criminal Bhim Chaya?"

"I don't have patience for mockery tonight, Rajkumar."

"Do I look like I have the energy to mock anyone?" he asked wearily. "I'm merely curious, Roshan." And he was. Curious about this man who had left behind a legacy of war and bloodshed. A man still beloved by this girl.

Navin's use of her proper name—or perhaps the rare, serious tone of his voice—seemed to startle the Shadow Bandit. For the first time, she simply looked at him without a smirk or a scowl. As if she was as curious about him as he was about her.

"Bhim Chaya wasn't always a criminal," she said. "He was a farmer with a few bigha of land in the village of Alipore, where he grew sorghum. His greatest joys were his mate and his little girl. Baba said they had a mare, too, back then—a sturdy Jwaliyan redmane."

There was another pause, which Navin did not fill with either an "and" or a "go on." He barely knew the Shadow Bandit, but he sensed that any comment from him right now would likely stop her from speaking altogether. And he didn't want her to.

"They sold the mare first to try to pay Subedar Yazad's blood tithes," Roshan said, her voice low, as if trying to rein in her emotions. "Then they began rationing grain from what they kept for themselves. But it wasn't enough. Eventually, the Brights came to their door and demanded the land for ten dām. Ten copper coins for land worth a thousand gold. When Baba refused, they broke his legs and killed his mate and daughter while he watched. Baba said many times he wished they'd killed him, too."

Navin had the strangest urge to reach out and touch her hand. To soothe her the way she had him only moments earlier.

"He decided to go and try to see Parasmani Bhairavi," Roshan continued. "A whole group of farmers from Ashvamaidan went. But the queen wouldn't even see them. Her steward declaring her booked for the next five years. When the farmers protested, he accused them of spoiling decorum."

Sounds familiar, Navin thought, frowning.

"That was the day Baba understood that the queen, too, was complicit with the subedar. There would be no justice that day and there would be no freedom. Not unless he snatched it with his bare hands. That night,

Baba and the farmers made a pact in the shadows of an old tavern in Prabha. They promised to fight for their lands as a unit. A family."

The Shadow Clan.

"Well," he said, "if it makes you feel any better, Parasmani Bhairavi pays little attention to anyone who isn't the steward or the crown prince." They were words he'd rarely spoken out loud. But something about the Shadow Bandit's story and her disappointment in his grandmother had spurred his own. "Most of my own conversations with her are dressing-downs I rightfully deserve. Now I've added to her troubles by getting kidnapped. I bet she'd have been happier if I'd never been born."

A long silence followed.

"I don't think you're right about that, Navin," Roshan said.

The shock of hearing his name from her lips—without any prodding—nearly made him fall off his seat. "What?"

"If your grandmother didn't want you, she'd have given you away to someone else—or gotten rid of you altogether. Baba said he found me by the river when I was a baby, lying on one of those garbage piles meant for burning. I guess I should be happy he got to me before the fire did." She tried for a wry smile, nearly succeeded at it, too. Again, Navin felt that pesky urge to touch her hand—partly to reassure and partly to build on whatever was happening here between them. A bond, however fragile, would only help him later when the time was right to use his soul magic again.

Think. After a few seconds, he decided to speak a truth. "It makes sense," he said. "Your loyalty to Bhim Chaya. To his clan."

"It's my clan, too."

Did he sense possessiveness there? "Your friend, the wild dog, would disagree."

She released a short breath that could have possibly been a laugh. "You mean Hemant. He isn't bothering you, is he?"

"No. But he watches you all the time." Fire and ashes, he sounded like a jealous lover. "Not in that way! I meant, he looks like—"

"—he wants to kill me." She sighed. "I know. It's been going on for a whole year now. I wouldn't worry if I were you, Rajkumar."

"Back to titles again?" He made a face even as he memorized that little bit of information about Hemant. "I'm hurt, Roshni. I liked it when you called me by my name."

A smile hovered on her lips. "Doesn't that break royal decorum or something of the sort?"

"Probably. Shove it and everything else up the palace steward's arse."

Another laugh, this one reminding him of warm, firebloom-scented nights in Prabha, and for a split second, he wondered what it would be like to hear it again. Softer. A little more breathless. Pinching his thigh through his clothes, Navin focused on the pain there, pretending his heart didn't thump twice as fast when Roshan said, "All right. *Navin.*"

She rose to her feet. "Do you want to head back now or give the shoveling another go?"

He stood up so quickly he nearly felt light-headed. "Spare me the shoveling, please."

"Even if decorum and your palace steward's arse are involved?"

Laughter burst out of him—loud and belly deep. He pinched his thigh again, certain he'd find bruises the next day. But the pain was also a warning. A reminder that he couldn't—by any means—*like* this girl. No matter how funny she was.

Yet maybe it wasn't so bad that he'd laughed at her joke, because from that night onward, she let him sleep without his shackles and the sound barrier. His confinement barrier, of course, still remained in place.

The next evening—perhaps not wanting a repeat of the bathroom incident—Roshan switched him over to dish duty.

It took a while to get the hang of scrubbing crusty pots and pans with the shell of an old coconut, a mix of ash and sawdust, and the river water Chotu brought him in a bucket. But Navin could feel the Shadow Clan watching, so he bit back his complaints, even refused the Shadow Bandit's offer to heal his bruised hands.

Patience, he told himself. Cleaning dishes wasn't as bad as shoveling sand in the bathroom. It let him move out of his confinement barrier for a good hour, walk a few feet to the kitchen on the opposite side of the cavern, where he could, without raising suspicion, hum a song or two.

Roshan came to check on him later as she put up his confinement barrier. This time, she lingered for a while as they talked, their conversation easier, more relaxed.

Patience, Navin reminded himself when he felt exhaustion creeping in. *Make her like you.* The more she did, the more influence he'd have over her when the time finally came to use his soul magic. While his contract prevented Navin from making direct attempts at escaping the clan on his own, it didn't preclude *tricking* the Shadow Bandit into helping him escape. All he needed to do was bide his time and keep up this pretext of docility.

It began to pay off the very next night. In the careful nod he received from Lalit as he worked. In shared smiles with Chotu when someone cracked a joke. In the shifting auras of color that began to emerge around various heads as he hummed. Once, when he glanced up from rinsing his hands, he caught Roshan looking at him and looking away almost instantly, a vivid pink flooding her aura. As if she had been caught doing something wrong.

He bit back a smile. *Patience.*

It wasn't a virtue as far as Navin was concerned, more like a curse. But after six long days of captivity, he was learning not to take things for granted.

Especially not his freedom.

13

"SHE NEEDS TIME TO CONSIDER OUR REQUEST?" LALIT'S VOICE rose in outrage. "By the goddess, we have a *prince* in our captivity, not a street urchin!"

Queen Bhairavi's response to Roshan's carefully worded, week-old ransom letter—a single perfunctory sentence on a scroll—had arrived seconds earlier via Khush, who'd found an exhausted palace hawk circling a mile away from their hideout during his morning patrols.

The queen's response, however, wasn't the only problem.

"Brights? Near here?" Roshan demanded of the living specter. "How many were there?"

"Two. They were trailing the hawk," Khush reported. "I pulled the note from its leg midflight. I don't think they noticed, though. Last I saw, they were still following it."

"Fine. No harm done," Roshan told the specter, dismissing him.

Inwardly, though, she was disturbed. She'd expected pushback from the queen on her demands; she hadn't expected the monarch to be soft. But for the queen to give no indication of what she was planning or how much time she needed even when her grandson was involved?

Roshan couldn't help but remember Navin's words: *I bet she'd have been happier if I'd never been born.*

"We need to send her another message," Lalit muttered. "One that makes her speed up. I don't like the sound of the Brights having been so close to our new hideout."

Neither did Roshan. "We can send her a lock of his hair and write: *Next time, it'll be his thumb.*"

"Right." Lalit snorted. "What if she calls your bluff? Or *are* you going to cut off his thumb?"

"I'll ask Vijali Fui to conjure a severed one from an animal bone and send it across," she replied quickly. And before Lalit could counter that suggestion, too, she added: "Let's just *see* what happens when we send her the lock of hair. We'll need to be patient, Lalit. Besides, the rajkumar hasn't been a very difficult prisoner so far."

"Don't you mean *Navin*? Isn't that what you're calling him lately?" Lalit pulled out two bits of parchment and expertly folded one into a flat pouch. "Don't bother rolling your eyes. I saw you talking to him last night."

"And what's wrong with that?" She hoped she didn't sound defensive. "It's not like I tell him anything important. Now let me focus. I need to write this letter to the queen."

As she wrote, though, her mind wandered back to Navin. She wasn't lying to Lalit. Navin hadn't asked her—even in jest—about the Shadow Clan's plans for him or their raids or anything of that sort. Instead, he'd ask her random questions, ranging from her favorite color, snack, and season to situational ones such as: *Would you pick perennial summer or perennial rain?* Or: *Given a choice between bloodworms and snake guts, what would you eat?*

Roshan, who'd faced the last situation during a raid gone wrong, had given the obvious answer: "Bloodworms. Less chance of being poisoned."

Navin, on the other hand, had refused to make a choice: "I'd rather starve!"

"Bloodworms are not bad fried. They turn nice and crispy—like a bhajia."

His expression of utter disgust—probably because Roshan had mentally ruined the image of his favorite snack—had made her collapse with laughter. Shortly afterward, he'd begun laughing as well. It was odd how he was the one person with whom Roshan felt herself grow lighter, easier, since he was also the biggest risk she'd taken so far. But somehow, after their conversation by the bathroom, Navin seemed to have settled down, mostly keeping to himself, occasionally humming quietly when he worked.

Right now, she found him washing the last of the breakfast dishes in the kitchen as he hummed, Chotu keeping watch from overhead. For some reason, she hesitated, unwilling to approach him right away.

Don't be a fool. You need his hair.

She stared at it now, hennaed at the ends, revealing a deep onyx shade extending from the roots. She wondered why he'd dyed it in the first place. Perhaps he thought the henna helped him fit in better with most other redheaded Jwaliyans. Or perhaps red hair was in fashion at the moment. Where the spare prince was concerned, it was likely a mix of both.

She gave herself a pinch—in time for Navin to turn and smile when he spotted her.

"Suprabhat!" he called out.

"Suprabhat." She walked over to him and blurted out: "I'll need a lock of your hair."

He raised one perfect, questioning eyebrow.

Baba would have spent time chatting a little more, easing into it. But Roshan despised dancing around uncomfortable subjects, preferring to get them out in the open as soon as possible.

"Parasmani Bhairavi wrote back," she explained, holding up the queen's note.

Navin didn't touch it, though he was frowning at the neatly lettered reply. "And?" he asked coolly.

"I believe she needs a little proof that it's really you. We thought it best to send her evidence. What better than a lock of hair?"

His earlier smile was gone. Without a word, he stood up and turned around, offering the back of his head to her. Roshan stepped forward and carefully cut off a small section from the side with a pair of scissors. The lock she'd picked was both red-brown and black in color—enough for the queen to identify it as his.

"That's it," she said, wondering why her stomach felt like it was in knots. She tucked the hair into the small paper pouch Lalit had prepared to go along with their reply for Queen Bhairavi. Using the heated tip of his atashban and a stick of wax, Lalit expertly sealed the pouch.

Lalit would deliver the pouch to Khizer, who would give it to his brother, Khush. This time, by Roshan's orders, the living specter wouldn't return without a reply from the queen—would badger her for one, if needed. Roshan would not run the risk of a palace hawk exposing their hideout again.

Slowly, Navin turned back around. "What if this doesn't work?" he asked, crossing his arms across his chest. "Will you cut off my nose and send the parasmani that instead?"

"It's not like that," she said.

"Then what's it like, Roshan?" The acid in his voice nearly made her wince. "What do I need to do to stay alive?"

"I am not going to kill you, Navin," she said, hoping she sounded patient and not angry. "Nor dismember you, if you're worried."

"How do I believe that?" he demanded, his voice rising. "I've had a hard time believing *anything* you've said so far—about your Shadow Clan, about Subedar Yazad, about the *real* Ashvamaidan, as you call it. And how can I—holed up as I am in this cage?"

Roshan bit the side of her cheek to rein in her temper. He was right, of course. This *was* a cage for him. She'd forgotten herself these last couple of days, allowed herself to be fooled by the prince's easy banter and friendliness. Both were likely a facade he'd adopted to protect himself from the clan. From *her*.

Several feet behind Navin, she caught Lalit watching them. Her friend raised his pale red brows and mouthed two words: *Show him.*

Roshan allowed her lungs to fill with air. It was a huge risk taking him outside. *No.* No, she couldn't. Even if she did show him everything, what guarantee would there be that he'd believe her?

But what if he does?

The thought lightly brushed the edges of her consciousness, tugged at something deep within. Roshan exhaled softly, turning again to face those angry gold eyes.

"All right," she told Navin. "You want to see the real Ashvamaidan? Put on your boots. We're making a delivery in the next hour."

14

It worked. Navin was sure he looked as stunned as he felt. Somehow his angry tirade, along with persistent nudges of soul magic in the Shadow Bandit's direction had shifted her emotions, adding a new trace of color: cobalt for doubt to the mix of red and yellow, neutralizing most of her aura to a calming brown. If he needed confirmation that his magic had worked, all he needed to do was feel the soft skin that had bubbled to the size of a pearl behind his left molar. The magic in the contract hadn't been triggered, either—which made sense as Navin had only wanted to go outside in that moment, not run away from the clan.

But would the Shadow Bandit's emotions hold?

"We'll have to disguise you first." She was still scowling at him. For now, she didn't appear to have changed her mind. "Lower your head."

"What? Why?"

"Those eyes of yours are a dead giveaway. I'm going to change the color to something more . . . ordinary. Might tweak your face a little, too."

"If you maim my eyes or disfigure my face in any way, Roshni—"

"Your eyes and vanity will remain intact," she cut in dryly. "Changes last only a few hours. Now look at me."

Her fingers felt rough against his cheeks, the touch oddly delicate.

Warmth curled around his neck, crept up his face. Roshan was glowing the way she had on the dhow and outside the bathroom, her fingers lightly tingling against his temples. Navin braced himself, expecting his eyes or face to burn, but a few seconds later, she dropped her hands.

"That will do," she said. "Chotu, a looking glass?"

Chotu brought out an oval of polished tin that fit the inside of Navin's palm. He looked into it and, instead of his usual gold, saw one deep brown iris reflecting back. Only his pupils were the same: elliptical instead of round—but no one would notice that unless they looked at him closely or in direct sunlight.

"It's just a color veil. Nothing permanent," Roshan said. "I've also added a few wrinkles to your skin and made your beard fuller."

He held the mirror farther away to see if it could capture his face. It could—and the changes weren't . . . bad. But they did make him look different. More ordinary, as Roshan had said.

"Not bad," Lalit spoke, examining him as well. "He'll also need a turban. That black in his hair might tip someone off."

Patience. He was lucky Lalit hadn't argued with Roshan—that no one else listening had seemed to challenge her about taking Navin outside. He was also fortunate that right now Hemant and his crew were either stuck doing another delivery or cleaning the hideout. So Navin bit back a retort and forced himself to stay still as Lalit wrapped the turban tightly around his head.

"Let's get going!" Roshan announced when they were done. "Think you can carry a gunny of rice, Rajkumar? You need to blend in with the rest of us."

"I'll manage." He wasn't sure if he could, really, not without collapsing.

But he hadn't missed how Roshan had reverted to using his title again instead of his name. She nodded at one of the other bandits, who helped Navin heave a sack onto his shoulders. It was heavy, but not terribly so.

Navin wasn't a fighter, nor had he done a day's hard work in his life. But he had spent long years at a viperous court. His task right now was to observe everything he could about Ashvamaidan. To seek out and exploit every potential crack he could within the Shadow Clan's so-called alliances with these villages.

He trudged up the staircase, Roshan's firm hand on his back—*likely another barrier here that I can cross only with her or a clan member*, he realized—and out of the hole, his shoulders straining against the weight of the gunny, his masked face hit with a blast of hot air. But for once, he wasn't complaining. He could finally *see*.

Vast swaths of undulating brown land, broken up by the barbed shrubs that the bandit called Vijali had grown in the old hideaway, and a maze of narrowly spaced, twisting ravines. Over two hundred feet high, the ravines were not only difficult to navigate, sometimes requiring the ten or so clan members to move in a single file, but they were also impossible to memorize.

Navin still tried. Some sort of ruined temple was near the hideout—the unornamented dome suggested Zaalian origins. He heard birdsong and the roar of the river, caught glimpses of the sun sparkling on water from time to time. As the land flattened, more of the Behrambodh rushed past, brown with sediment, its surface peppered with burned bits of wood and other unidentified debris. A dust-covered fire goddess temple rose in the distance, sculptures of Ashvamaidan's distinct flying mare flanking the entrance at both ends.

"Are we headed to that temple?" he huffed. For long moments, no one answered.

"That temple is abandoned." It was Roshan, who had paused to let him catch up with her. "Jyoti—the village it belonged to—has long since moved. That's where we're headed now."

A sour stench wafted through the air, and suddenly he was immensely grateful for the barrier of cloth covering his face. "What about the river water?" he asked her. "Is it safe to drink?"

"Not unless boiled. You might find dead fish floating in there. Or even a dead bird."

"Is that what haunts your nightmares, Roshni?" He didn't bother hiding his sarcasm. "Dead fish and dead birds?"

"My dead father, actually."

Irritable as he was, Navin couldn't come up with a suitable reply to that. It wouldn't have mattered. Roshan wasn't looking at him anymore, her eyes squinting over her mask against the road ahead. He itched to hum again, to see her aura. In the moment, though, he doubted that even that would be of much use. Already, he could feel her distancing herself, putting up a wall between them. The more time he let lapse, the stronger it would grow.

And it'll be your own fault.

"I'm sorry," he blurted out. "For blowing up at you in the cave."

A blatant lie, but Navin guessed that right now his usual humor and flirtation wouldn't work. "I see what you mean about the land. It's . . . bad." This, admittedly, was true. The land here was desolate, with no fields nor trees, not even a hamlet perched along the river. A pesky little thought crept up on him: *What if she's right about Subedar Yazad?* He swatted it away.

Roshan said nothing, but he sensed her watching, assessing his words.

"This way," she said after a moment, then slipped through a slender gap between two rocks.

"Where . . ." Navin stared at the small house before them, its outside wall plastered with dung cakes. A wild dog lay sleeping in the shade of a dead neem, flies perched on its long nose, its ribs barely moving under striped blue fur.

"Welcome to Jyoti," Roshan said quietly.

15

"DROP YOUR GUNNYSACK BY THE DOOR," ROSHAN TOLD THE prince, who was staring at the mud-brick hut as if he'd never seen one before. She frowned. Something nagged at her, a small voice that suggested it might be a mistake bringing him here. She shook it off. She was being paranoid. The prince had signed a magical contract. There was no way he could escape them right now.

"Go on," she prodded when he didn't move.

Trudging the last few steps, he dropped the sack by the side of the hut with a *thud* before rolling his shoulders slowly. Roshan followed suit.

The sounds drew old Dinamai to the door. She peered out cautiously, dark eyes widening on her wrinkled face. She was thinner than she had been last month, Roshan noted with a pang, the gray blouse of her sari hanging loose on her small frame, the tan skin of her skull visible through the parting in her gilded hair.

"Oh." The old lady's shoulders sagged with relief when she saw Roshan. "It's only you, bitiya. I thought it was one of those Brights again—asking for more coin."

Roshan shot a sideways glance at Navin, who was frowning. "Suprabhat, Dinamai," she greeted.

Dinamai nodded curtly at Navin, who did the same, and then watched as more bandits slipped through the opening between the rocks. Seven approached the hut, piling more sacks of grain atop the ones Roshan and Navin had already deposited.

Three bandits held back gunnies. These, reserved for the village of Firozgar, were temporarily placed near the rock wall, where someone from the clan would stand guard until it was time to head to the next delivery stop.

"Come in, come in. No need to remove your shoes," Dinamai added hastily when she saw Lalit bending. "You'll soon see why."

Almost instantly upon entering, they spotted the cracked mud floor, its strange, undulating shape.

"I didn't realize the ravines had reached this far," Roshan said, feeling her throat tighten.

"A new development. It doesn't matter. The village will move again. It's not like we haven't before," Dinamai said, forcing cheer into her voice. "Oh, don't be sad, Roshan bitiya. Everyone knew it would happen the way the badlands keep growing. I *told* the village heads not to infuse the land with magic again this year and leave it fallow. But no one pays attention to us old women anymore. Isn't that so?" She directed the final question to Navin, who started.

"Uh—"

"Dinamai, is the sarpanch around?" Roshan cut in. She glared at Navin, who'd begun to fidget with his mask. He dropped his hand. "I'd like to speak to him before we leave."

"He usually visits the temple in the morning," Dinamai said. "Why don't you have some chai and wait for him here?"

"Oh, no, we couldn't! We've had breakfast already!" Roshan declared.

"Also, we have another delivery to make today," Lalit added. "We don't have much time."

Meherbani, Lalit, Roshan thought gratefully.

It was bad enough that Dinamai had been forced to sell most of what she'd owned, her belongings reduced to a single netted cot and a few rusting pots and pans that hung on a wall. They didn't need to impose on her hospitality and eat her food—not when she barely had enough to feed herself.

"Oh, all right," Dinamai said, sounding only a tiny bit disappointed. "Sarpanch Vilayat will be pleased to see the grain you've brought. He's been in a bad mood the whole week."

When isn't *Sarpanch Vilayat in a bad mood?* Roshan thought as they left the house.

Things had been different when Vilayat's father was the village head. The old sarpanch was a forthright and principled man, one who'd despised Subedar Yazad as much as the clan did. But after he died two years ago, his son had been elected to lead the five-member village council. Neither Baba nor Roshan had trusted Vilayat's smooth voice and oily smile, finding both as slippery as freshly caught hilsa from the river.

Yet so far, Vilayat hadn't given them away to the Brights.

The village square was quieter than it had been years earlier, the only sound coming from a rat scrabbling in the yard of a neighboring house. A boy of about four or five sat by the door, his limbs oddly long and thin in contrast to his belly, which was swollen and protruding under his rib cage.

"What . . . what's wrong with him?" Navin asked quietly.

"Malnutrition," Roshan replied, equally quiet. "His father died of a heatstroke tilling the fields. His mother has four other children. We deliver food whenever we have it and the villagers help as best as they can, but it's not enough." She didn't mention how she'd tried healing the boy once. Or how badly she'd failed. Magic, she'd realized then, couldn't cure every illness. Could certainly not replace food.

A furrow etched itself between Navin's brows. "Can't food be conjured?"

"Have you ever eaten conjured food, Navin?" His name slipped out of her—partly out of contempt, partly weariness. "Do it. Then try to work in the fields the way these children do."

Beneath the fabric of his mask, she thought she saw his mouth move, heard an indecipherable mumble. But he said nothing more and Roshan turned away, her stomach curdling. What had she expected from him? Empathy?

They walked to the center of the village, where a bamboo fence had been set up around a small stone building shaped like a perfect square— unremarkable except for its dome and the fragrant sandalwood that burned red in the polished silver vessel beneath. The eternal flame. Visible through each of the four arched doorways, it was the fire that centered each of the fire goddess's temples—a fire that was never allowed to burn out. Except, here, there was no proper temple. Nothing, save the sanctum consecrated in the open air, a single bell hanging at the center of each arched doorway.

"The temple's coming along nicely," Lalit commented.

"Praise the goddess," Roshan said sarcastically. "You can bet the village spent every bit of coin that didn't go into paying the blood tithes into building this thing."

"Chhe! Don't be blasphemous. Sometimes faith is the only thing that keeps people going."

A pair of figures stepped out from behind the sanctum: a widow in mourning grays, helped along by a familiar man in a yellow turban, a long bamboo staff in his left hand.

Roshan noted Navin staring at the woman and then, as they got closer, release a curse under his breath.

Where the woman's eyes should have been were two scarred hollows: wounds on a pale face that was both old and lovely. The man, on the other hand, was no older than thirty, his smooth brown cheeks covered with auburn wisps of a beard. He halted on spotting the bandits, his upper lip curling.

"Who is it?" the widow called out, her voice high. Tremulous.

"Sultana Bibi, it's me. Roshan Chaya." Roshan forced herself to sound as cheerful as she could. "We came to see you today."

"Shubhdin, Sultana Bibi. Sarpanch Vilayat," Lalit addressed the man. "How are things?"

"They could be better." There were shadows under the village head's eyes. They skirted each of the bandits and focused on Navin. "Who—" he began to ask before Sultana Bibi tugged on his arm.

"Has anyone seen my Kaifi?" she demanded. When no one answered, the old lady repeated her question, her voice ringing in the silence.

Roshan's heart squeezed. "No, we haven't," she said. "Sultana Bibi, did you sleep last night?"

"He was here, my Kaifi." Words turned to sobs. "He came in the night, in my dreams. They took him away."

"It's fine." Roshan curved an arm around Sultana Bibi and pressed a glowing hand to her wrinkled forehead. "It's fine."

"Roshan, be careful," Lalit warned. But he didn't make a move to stop her. There were no hakims in this village, no healers around for miles. Roshan's gift not only helped the villagers in the valley, but it also kept the Shadow Clan safe. Thanks to the stolen grain and Roshan's healing, no one in Jyoti would willingly give up a clan member to a Bright.

Roshan braced herself against the pain, the maze of thorns that was Sultana Bibi's mind. Navigating it was a challenge, escaping it, even harder. This time was more difficult than usual to calm the old lady.

Don't go, Kaifi. Sultana Bibi's words clawed at Roshan. *Don't leave me.*

For some reason, to the blind woman, Roshan and her lost son were the same—always the same—even though Roshan knew she looked nothing like the garlanded portrait of the man on Sultana Bibi's wall.

"Roshan." Lalit's voice cracked through.

"I'm fine." Roshan carefully withdrew from Sultana Bibi's grip on her mind and stepped back. *Don't faint, don't faint, don't faint.* She nearly did, the world tilting for a moment before righting itself again. Blinking several times to clear her vision, she said: "Lalit—will you take her home?"

He nodded and, with a last wary glance backward, carefully escorted the old lady to her hut a short distance away.

Roshan turned to the head councilor, who was watching them the way a hawk would a group of rats. "Sarpanch Vilayat," she said, bowing her head slightly. "We've made our delivery today. The bags are at Dinamai's house, as usual."

The head councilor merely joined his hands together before saying curtly: "You're late. This delivery should've been here two days ago."

"Apologies. We were preoccupied," she said smoothly. "But there's good news: We have nine bags of grain for you."

"Nine?" Vilayat wrinkled his nose. "That's much less than what you brought us last month!"

"The haul wasn't as large this time. But your bags are much bigger."

Vilayat made a noise—something that sounded a lot like a distasteful *chhe*.

From the corner of her eye, she saw Navin fidgeting, shifting his weight from one heel to the next. Roshan frowned at him in warning. But it was too late. Vilayat had noticed the movement.

"Who's the tall one?" the head councilor asked. "Don't think I've seen him before."

"His name's Dildar," she lied. "He joined up after the Brights raided Raigarh a few months ago. He just finished his training, so we brought him out for deliveries today."

"Training, haan? Much to learn in looting, is there, Dildar?"

"Much," Roshan said acidly, "since it feeds more than just us, doesn't it, Sarpanch ji?"

"Apologies, Sardar." Vilayat bared a set of pale yellow teeth: more sneer than smile. "As you know, I'm worried. Our villagers are starving. With the badlands expanding so quickly, it is likely we must move again. Not that there *is* anywhere we can go where we do not pay the subedar for it," he concluded bitterly.

Baba would have told Roshan to use this opportunity. To commiserate with the man and bond over a common enemy. But before she could, Navin began moving again. Heel to heel, faster and faster, like a child desperate to get in a word.

"I'm sorry," the prince blurted out as she—and everyone else—turned to look. "But I really need to use the bathroom!"

16

NAVIN HAD FOUND HIS CRACK. THE WEAK SPOT IN THE SHADOW Clan's alliance with this village. A man named Sarpanch Vilayat, who was now staring at Navin along with the others.

"Maafi, Sardar," Navin addressed the Shadow Bandit, his apology a perfect blend of meek as well as desperate. "I didn't mean to interrupt."

Roshan's eyes had turned to slits above her mask. "Lalit." She turned to face the man, who had quietly returned to watch the proceedings a moment ago. "Could you take Dildar back to Dinamai's and—"

"Or Sarpanch Vilayat could direct me to an outhouse," Navin interrupted. He glanced at the village head, whose gaze had now turned curious. "I don't want to trouble Dinamai," he added. Part of this was true. Fond as Dinamai seemed of his captors—she'd called the Shadow Bandit "daughter" for goddess's sake!—Navin hadn't been able to ignore her obvious poverty. The old woman didn't need to worry about cleaning up after him—even if Navin had no intention of using her bathroom.

"Looks like you found yourself a gentleman, Sardar Roshan," the sarpanch commented, his voice too smooth to be kind.

Roshan said nothing, her eyes still dangerously narrow.

Navin was sure he'd pay for this later. But right now, he sensed it was the Shadow Bandit who was in a dilemma. Would she believe Navin and send him off with the sarpanch alone? Or would she send Lalit or someone else along with them—raising the village head's suspicions about her new recruit?

"If it isn't too much trouble, Sarpanch ji," she spoke at last.

Navin's shoulders loosened infinitesimally.

Vilayat wrinkled his nose. "Come, Dildar. This way."

Navin followed, keeping his shoulders hunched, his gaze lowered as they made their way toward the temple. His mind, however, raced. The contract Roshan had forced him to sign didn't allow any avenues of escaping the clan on his own. But what if Navin could share information about himself? Especially with someone who might also dislike the clan?

Navin's instincts told him that Sarpanch Vilayat would be loyal to the clan for only as long as he found it useful. Once they passed the sanctum and the bandits were out of sight, he decided to ease the sarpanch into conversation.

"That old lady," he began quietly. "What happened to her eyes?"

For a moment, the sarpanch didn't answer. "She claims they were extracted by the subedar's soldiers," he said.

An interesting choice of words. "She claims? Does she have proof?"

"Who knows?" Vilayat's response was cryptic. "Sultana Bibi was never right once her son, Kaifi, died."

"What happened to the son?"

"I don't know much; I was only a boy when it happened. But I know Kaifi started working for the subedar when he was twenty. He was clever, educated, and handsome. Everyone loved Kaifi. Including the subedar's daughter, Laleh."

Surprise jolted through Navin. This was the last name he'd expected to hear. "Subedar Yazad had a daughter?" he continued, pretending ignorance.

"You wouldn't know—young as you are. But yes, around twenty years ago, Subedar Yazad had a daughter. Laleh was a lovely girl. Gentle, kind. And she fell in love with a poor, handsome boy from a village. Her father didn't like it. He thought Kaifi was after Laleh's inheritance. Things get muddy from here on. Some say the subedar got rid of Kaifi. Some say the boy tired of Laleh and left the village. Either way, Kaifi disappeared. A year later, Laleh died. There are rumors that it was from an illness, but no one knows for sure."

Not even Shera, Navin thought with a pang. Shera had been born eighteen years after Laleh, a couple of years before she died. Like Navin, Shera, too, had grown up perpetually overshadowed by an older sibling. Unlike Navin, though, whose brother was still alive, Shera had to contend with a ghost—an older sister Governor Yazad never talked about, no matter how many times Shera had asked him.

"Sultana Bibi claims her son was murdered, of course," Vilayat continued. "She registered a case against the subedar in one of the big cities upriver. But a day before the hearing, we found her wailing in her house, her eyes gone."

They'd now turned into an alleyway, where a small outhouse was located, a mud-brick hut not unlike the others, distinguished only by the sign on its stained wooden door.

Navin tasted something sour at the back of his throat. "Could it have been robbers?" he asked, pausing outside the door.

"Perhaps. But those *friends* of yours wouldn't agree, would they?"

Vilayat tilted his head. Navin didn't miss the flash of distaste on his face, the obvious emphasis on the word *friends*.

Time for the truth. "They're no friends of mine."

"Ah." A pause. "Who are you, then?" the sarpanch asked.

Silently undoing the top front of his jama, Navin let the flaps fall to the side, revealing the gold tattoo of the homāi on his chest. His tattoo was the one distinguishing part about him that had remained consistently out of sight. So naturally, the Shadow Bandit had forgotten to disguise it.

"Who do you think I am?" he asked.

The sarpanch's mouth grew so thin it resembled a crack in the earth. "I'd heard about . . . but your eyes . . ."

"She changed them." No question about which *she* Navin was referring to. "You don't like her, do you?"

The village head grunted. "She and her bandits say they help. And they do, somewhat, I won't lie. But once they leave, the Brights come and harass us for information about them. I tried to trap her once, get her arrested by local darogas. But the other villagers helped her escape." A pause. "The Brights were here yesterday. Asking about you. Do you know where you're being kept?"

"The ravines look the same to me." Navin racked his brain. "Wait. There's an old ruin nearby. A—" His voice cut off abruptly, throat tightening as if in a choke hold, his tongue unable to form the words. That cursed contract. He'd pushed the magic too far.

"What ruin? A prayer house? Tell me," the sarpanch prodded. "Is it Zaalian?"

But Navin couldn't speak or nod. He took deep breaths, hoping he wouldn't be sick.

A second later, he heard footsteps, a voice calling out his false name.

"Aye, Dildar!" Lalit shouted. "What's taking so long? Are you dumping a castle in there?"

"Don't worry," Vilayat whispered. "Do up your jama. And try to come back during the next delivery. Quickly, Jwalaratan."

Jwalaratan. The term, which translated to *Jwala's gem*, was a title used for his brother, the crown prince, not the spare. But right now, it didn't matter. Navin did up his jama in record speed, opening and slamming the door to the outhouse a second before Lalit, Roshan, and two other bandits appeared around the corner.

They glowered at both Navin and Sarpanch Vilayat. "We're running late," Lalit said. "Come, Dildar."

"Haan ji," Navin managed to say, lowering his head. His mouth was raw, his throat still tingling from the contract's spell. He didn't look at the sarpanch.

"So, Sardar? When are you coming back with more grain?" Vilayat demanded, addressing Roshan. "This won't last us long."

"In a week—maybe less—if the raid we're planning goes well," she said stiffly.

"I hope it does," Sarpanch Vilayat sidestepped them. "For your sake, Roshan Chaya, I hope it goes as well as your father's raids used to."

A week, Navin noted. He'd have to return here somehow. He could feel the bandits watching him as they headed back to Dinamai's house, picked up the grain meant for the next village, and slipped through the gap between the rocks, leaving Jyoti behind.

Barely a moment went by before Navin found himself caught by the scruff and slammed against a rock wall, something cold and sharp at the back of his neck.

"What," Lalit growled in his ear, "did you tell the sarpanch? Were you trying to escape?"

In the background, Navin heard the Shadow Bandit urging Lalit to let him go.

"N-n-nothing," Navin gasped out. "I couldn't do anything like that. Your sardar made me sign that goddess-forsaken contract, remember?"

"Lalit!" Roshan's voice rose. "This is an order!"

Lalit swore furiously, but a moment later, Navin found himself freed. He turned around, the feel of the atashban still lingering against his neck.

He had to fix things. Fast.

"I asked him about Sultana Bibi," he said, forcing himself to lock gazes with both Lalit and Roshan. "About what happened to her eyes."

Silence. Lalit's fingers tightened on the grip of his weapon but otherwise didn't move.

"He told me about her son and his affair with Subedar Yazad's daughter," Navin went on. "And how Sultana Bibi thinks the Brights destroyed her vision."

"She doesn't think—she knows!" Lalit shot back. "She's not mad!"

Navin couldn't see Lalit's aura. But he could feel the air around him shift from hostile and suspicious to merely hostile. He'd take it.

"I didn't mean to imply she was mad." He released a breath. "I'm merely reiterating what that sarpanch told me. Besides, *you* lot offered to show me the real Ashvamaidan. How can I, without knowing what the people are like? What troubles they're facing?"

Pompous as the words sounded, they weren't false. Navin had been caught up by Sultana Bibi's story despite himself, had felt his own ribs ache on remembering her wails.

A thimbleful of truth for a barrelful of trust. The sentence was inscribed in every soul magic book and scroll he'd been forced to read by his tutors, a saying he'd never given much credence to until now.

"Besides," Navin added, raising an eyebrow, "if I *had* tried to escape, do you think I'd be standing before you in one piece?"

Lalit scowled but didn't answer.

It was Roshan who finally spoke: "Let's get moving. We've wasted too much time here."

She shot Navin a final glare. "And next time, Rajkumar, if you have questions, you direct them through me."

17

SOMETHING CRAWLED UP ROSHAN'S LEG UNDER HER TROUSERS—
a bloodworm that she pulled off her skin, red drops scattering across
the ground. Though the small bite on her calf began healing at once, she
could still feel the insect, its many legs climbing up her thigh and spine,
all the way into her belly, where a single thought had been festering for
the past two hours. *Danger.*

The feeling had nagged at her ever since they'd left Jyoti. There was
no trace of the Brights. Nothing except for the occasional field crow
and, once, a shvetpanchhi, white-feathered and carnivorous, soaring
over their heads. Navin, for what it was worth, seemed to be behaving
himself. Though Lalit had, at one point, suggested that Roshan freeze
his voice again. Or at least stuff his mouth with a gag.

"*You* told me to show him everything," she'd reminded Lalit. "Now
you're saying you made a mistake?"

"He could put us in danger!"

"So could Vilayat and Dinamai. They haven't. At least not so far."

It was true that survival was important in these parts, that alliances
could shift with the turn of the wind. But Roshan had to trust the
people she'd known since she was small, to keep faith in the relation-
ships Baba had built over so many years.

Not only Baba, Roshan reminded herself. You *helped, too.*

It was why Bhim Chaya had insisted on taking a younger Roshan along with him on these deliveries—why he'd encouraged her to mend bones, seal wounds, and help people sleep with only a touch of her hands. She glanced again at Navin: her only chance at getting back their lands and proving herself to the clan, a boy who was both asset and liability.

Why not turn him into an ally? The idea, originally suggested by Lalit, had made her laugh a week ago. But now, as she recalled Navin's genuine curiosity about the villagers and their lives, she wondered: *Could it be possible?*

As if sensing the turn of her thoughts, Navin glanced over at her. His eyes were still brown, her magic holding strong.

"Where to next, Roshni?" he asked her. "Or are you not going to bother telling me?"

"That depends," she said, looking up at the sky, where the clouds had shifted, mercifully blocking the sun. "*Do* I bother telling you anything if you don't believe me?"

A hundred yards away, a herder rounded ten ragged-looking goats, leading them toward an outcropping of rock that probably obscured another village. Navin paused, watching them.

"You were right about the poverty," he said. "There is much of it here. Though there are still some things that make little sense to me."

"Such as?"

"Such as why Subedar Yazad would intentionally allow the valley to turn to *this*." He gestured to the ravines. "Why not let the villagers prosper if he wants them to pay more tithes? Why drive them away?"

"Because he wants the land himself."

"But *why?*" Navin questioned. "Ashvamaidan is largely an agricultural province from what you've described, and I personally know that its governor is an earth magus. What use would nonarable land be to him? He'd need to make these badlands habitable again, which would be incredibly difficult, not to mention expensive, even with magic."

Curse the gods. Though mostly, she wanted to curse the spare prince for stumping her with his logic.

"I don't know," she said at last. "I'm only telling you what I—wait!" She held up an arm, holding him back. She could feel it again, that sense of danger. Traveling up her limbs, the tremors coming from right underneath her feet.

"It's a quake. Stay back!" she told the others. To the prince, she said: "Get to your knees and cover your head and neck."

"What—"

"*Now,* Navin!" she yelled as a violent thundering overtook the earth, forcing them into a crouch. The quake lasted maybe less than a minute. But when the land steadied and they rose to their feet, everything before them had changed.

Fissures pierced the earth that, only seconds earlier, had been relatively flat and walkable, along with potholes nearly a meter deep. The land ahead of them had been hit even worse, no sign of the herder or his goats.

"I'll go check on the herder," Roshan told the others quietly.

But when Roshan approached the area, she could see nothing except rocks littering the land, rocks and—a jolt went through her—a single, bloody human hand underneath.

"Lalit!" she shouted. "We need to move this!"

Lalit came running, along with two others. "There's no point," he said, slightly out of breath. "He's gone."

"*Do it.*"

Lalit sighed and nodded at Vijali Fui, who pressed her hands to the rocks, sending veins of light through them, turning them into ash. Underneath lay the herder, a gray film coating his brown skin, his mouth parted, his light blue eyes wide open.

"His spine's broken," Roshan whispered. "Organs punctured by bone."

Lalit was right. There *was* no point.

Roshan wanted to bury her head in her hands. To wail.

When she looked up, she found Navin staring at the man. Looking like he was about to puke.

"There's a village nearby," Vijali Fui said in her clear, no-nonsense voice. "I'll make sure someone's here to get him. See you back at the hideout, bitiya."

Roshan nodded. As Vijali disappeared between a gap through the rocks, she forced herself to speak.

"Let's get moving. We still have another delivery to make."

Once they put some distance between themselves and the corpse, Navin sucked in a deep breath. "I didn't know there were quakes in this region," he said. "I thought those only happened in the north. Near Atash Koh and other volcanic mountains."

"There weren't," Roshan said. "At least not twenty years ago." *Not before Governor Yazad took over Ashvamaidan.* Though Roshan didn't say this out loud, the implication was clear. She wanted to add more. How it wasn't natural for gullies or even potholes to form without running water—and that, too, within seconds. But she didn't. Her throat squeezed, images of the herder still flashing through her head.

She sensed Navin was thinking of the same. Even disguised, the spare prince looked stunned. She glanced up at Lalit, who was also watching Navin.

"This . . . isn't normal," Navin whispered. "No quake I've heard of has ever done this before."

She should've been triumphant. But all Roshan felt was resignation, a bone-deep ache that spread over her limbs. She stepped close, gently tugged the prince's mask back in place.

"I know," she said.

THE SUN CRESTED THE SKY AS AFTERNOON SET IN, ITS HEAT burning any bit of exposed skin. Field crows followed them to Firozgar, eerie sentinels watching over a silent village. But while most doors were closed, they weren't locked. Roshan's heartbeat eased when she spotted the milkman sleeping on a cot next to his hut.

The quiet of afternoon naps, she told herself. *Not the aftermath of a tithe collection.*

She nodded to the three bandits who carried the last gunnies. "Take those to the sarpanch. We'll see you at the temple."

Unlike many other villages, Firozgar hadn't had to move in the past ten years and its temple was still intact, its brick walls painted in whites and yellows, terra-cotta reliefs of the fire goddess and the flying mare rising from the thick columns at its entrance. Some of Roshan's earliest and happiest childhood memories were linked to this place and to Ervad Faridun, the priest who lived here—even though she no longer prayed to the goddess.

She watched Navin pause, staring at a sculpture in a corner of the arch. She followed the direction of his gaze, which had, unsurprisingly, landed on the bird there—the homāi, made distinct by the feathered crown on her head, nearly hidden among a branch of fireblooms.

A shiver went down her spine. *It's only a carving, bitiya,* Baba used to tell her. *Not a curse.*

"Didn't expect to see this here," Navin said. Roshan thought she heard a tremor in his voice, but if so, it was quickly controlled. "Don't people here in the west call the homāi a curse?"

So he knew that much about Ashvamaidan at least. "Some do," she said with a shrug. "But my baba used to believe she can be a blessing, too. So does the priest who runs this temple."

"What about you, Roshni?" Navin turned around to watch her, his false brown eyes nearly as probing as the bird's. "What do you believe?"

She could tell him she thought of the homāi as a curse as well. That she was no different from the others. But it wouldn't be entirely true.

"I'm not so sure anymore," she said. After seeing the homāi tattooed on Navin's chest, everything had changed, opening a new path for the Shadow Clan to free their lands. Of course, Roshan's opportunity had also resulted from Navin's misfortune. Heat pooled her cheeks. Glad that her complexion didn't allow for blushes—and that she was still masked—Roshan forced herself to hold his gaze.

I have no other choice, she wanted to tell him. And maybe she would have if she thought he would believe her. If her own insides didn't curl in on themselves—raising doubts where there were none before.

A beat passed before Navin changed the subject. "You're familiar with this temple?"

"Have been coming here since I was a little girl."

They took off their shoes and placed them in a corner and then, as custom dictated, stepped in, right foot first, onto the worn paisley carpet of the empty prayer hall. Dust motes danced in the sunlight pouring in through an open window. But apart from that, the temple was dark, the only other light coming from the eternal flame inside the sanctum, tall stone pillars forming a perfect square around the great brass vessel holding the fire. Scents lingered: lemon and salt, smoke and frankincense, the sweet, nutty aroma of malido and halwa from morning prayers. Roshan's mouth watered.

As always, Lalit and the others approached the sanctum and took turns prostrating before the flame, one after another, their foreheads pressing the cool stone threshold. They would eventually sit cross-legged on the carpet a few feet away, rocking gently as they murmured prayers.

"After you," Navin told Roshan.

She shook her head. "I don't pray. Not anymore, at least."

Not after Baba, whose utter devotion to the goddess should have earned him her protection but didn't.

"Apologies," she said offhandedly. In Ashvamaidan, there were people who believed in the various gods of Svapnalok or in magic, and also people who didn't believe in either. No one really cared. But in cities like Prabha, she'd heard that people frowned upon those who did not worship the fire goddess.

"No need to apologize," Navin said, shrugging. "Faith is difficult to hold on to. And the gods can be fickle."

"Some would call you blasphemous for saying so." Roshan, for her own part, would call him rather interesting. But she didn't say that out loud.

"It's true, though," he said. "The sky goddess of Ambar, the earth and sea gods of Prithvi and Samudra—they do as they please. Even raw magic as worshipped by the Zaalians has a mind of its own. Our fire goddess is more temperamental, ever-changing like the flames that make up her hair and form. A single wrong move and she turns to ice, every blessing disappearing." He snapped his fingers. "Why else do you think we stoke the eternal flame every hour? It can get a little exhausting."

She bit her lip, trying to curb a laugh.

"Ha! You think so, too, Roshni! Admit it."

"If she's so exhausting, why worship her?" she asked, genuinely curious.

"I can't help it. I've always been fond of difficult women."

The sparkle in his eyes told Roshan that his words weren't for the goddess alone. "You're ridiculous," she said with a snort.

"And you like that," he whispered.

Where in Svapnalok had *that* come from? Before she could retort or—*curse the gods*—stop a blush, the prince spun around to join the other bandits and prostrate before the holy flame.

Roshan was shaking her head at the conversation—and her own silliness—when someone called her name. Ervad Faridun emerged from the shadows behind the sanctum, the hem of his white jama brushing the ground, a matching turban covering his long gold hair. He trudged toward her with the help of a cane, his wrinkled face beaming.

"It's good to see you, bitiya." He enveloped her in a hug that smelled of frankincense and sandalwood, one so reminiscent of Baba that Roshan blinked back unexpected tears.

"It's good to see you, too," she whispered. She led him to a pile of cushions at the back and helped him settle down. "How is your leg doing?"

"Perfectly fine."

"Are you sure? You weren't relying on your cane so much the last time I saw you. Let me have a look."

"There is no need . . . Oh, all right." The priest smiled slightly when Roshan glared at him. "You're worse than my mate was, goddess bless her soul."

She waited for Ervad Faridun to lift the hem of his jama to his knees before lightly pressing her fingers to his socked feet and the loose cotton trousers covering his shin. Within seconds of touching him, she sensed pain's icy claws clinging to the ruined muscle of his calf, the result of an old atashgola wound. Roshan had been around eight when she'd first felt the scarring. She couldn't do more to heal the wound than what her magic told her to, which was mostly leeching away the priest's pain and taking it as her own. It had been the one and only time Baba had cautioned her against using her magic for every possible injury.

Taking a deep breath, Roshan allowed herself to close her eyes, her mind mapping through bone, muscle, and vein. Her hands moved across the calf, paused again on the badly healed scar tissue. As she'd grown older, she'd been able to reduce the scar somewhat. But healing with magic wasn't perfect. The older the wound, the more difficult it was to heal properly, as if the body itself found ways to repel any good magic.

Today, it was much the same. Roshan was about to release the calf when, amid the scars, she noticed something else. A mass of tissue that hadn't been there before. The tumor pulsated red in her mind, an awful thing that made her want to pull away at once. Years ago, she'd over-heard a group of hakims talking about something like this in a Prabha tavern—*an abomination untreatable by magic.*

Carefully, Roshan forced herself to withdraw. To pat the priest on the knee and nod reassuringly.

Ervad Faridun exhaled. "So? How long do I have?"

Two years? Maybe three?

Roshan's head pounded. She hadn't known of anyone with an abomination living longer. The truth, however, only made her choke. She forced a smile. "You'll probably outlive the rest of us, Ervad ji," she said.

The priest gave her a small smile in return. One that told her he wasn't fooled. "I suppose I feel a little better already." He slowly rose to his feet. And perhaps he was, because he'd left the cane leaning by the wall. "Are you hungry? Wait here. Let me get you something."

Roshan sagged against the wall as the priest trudged away, her head pounding, only long hours of training with Lalit and Navaz Didi still holding her upright. Her body would soon use its magic on itself, heal-ing from the inside out. Her heart, however . . . Roshan closed her eyes.

"What's wrong with the priest?" a low voice asked. She opened her eyes to find Navin crouched beside her.

"A tumor in his calf," she said. "It felt . . . wrong when I touched it. Untreatable. I guess a hakim would call it an abomination."

Navin winced. "Oh."

"He *could* be treated in a big city," she said, feeling bitter. "In a hospital, with real hakims and apothecaries and equipment."

"I don't know if that's true, Roshan," Navin countered, his voice serious but not unkind. "I've had relatives lose limbs or die of abominations within days of discovering them. If that priest is walking right now with a tumor in his leg, then you've done as much as any so-called real hakim at a big hospital."

Roshan's breath wedged itself between her throat and her mouth. She'd received compliments in the past for her healing magic. Even curses for the pain she'd caused. No one, however, had told her that what she'd done was enough. *Can you do it again? Can you do more?* were questions she'd been fielding since she was five. More for Baba. More for the clan. More for the villagers. More and more—until she had little left to give.

"Wah!" she spoke, infusing the phrase with sarcasm instead of delight. "I'm flattered. Didn't expect such a high compliment from you."

The prince's gaze warmed the side of her face. Roshan kept her eyes forward, focused on the cross-legged bodies before them, the hums rising in prayer.

"I mean it," Navin said. "Though, should I bother giving you compliments you don't believe?"

Clever bastard. Trust him to twist her words and throw them back at her. Reluctantly, she turned to look at him. And noted that, for the first time since they'd met, he appeared sincere. Even with those false brown eyes and that cursed mask covering most of his expression.

"I believe you," she said. And nearly laughed when he started. "What? I don't need to be a soul magus to know a real compliment."

"I wouldn't be so sure if I were you, Roshni." He leaned back again. The drawl had returned to his voice.

Yet, somehow, Roshan didn't mind it this time.

18

WHATEVER PEACE HAD SETTLED OVER THEM AFTER THAT moment in Firozgar's temple dissipated the moment they returned to the hideout.

"You took him *out?*" Hemant shouted at Roshan. "Who is he—your pet? Or are you screwing him now?"

Navin took a couple of steps backward. Hemant was waving his atashban in a particularly threatening way, sparks emerging from its tip. Roshan, however, seemed to have expected the outburst.

She merely crossed her arms and replied mildly: "Neither. He *is*, however, my responsibility. And he was watched at all times. Wasn't he?" The last question, addressed to the other bandits, was met with a staunch "Haan, Sardar!"

As Hemant stalked off, Lalit turned around and looked directly at Navin. "Well, not all the time. There was that time you went to the out-house with Sarpanch Vilayat."

"I told you everything there was to say about that," Navin spoke, without missing a beat. The other man still looked suspicious, but Navin also knew that lying was a game of who stood their ground. Who looked away first. In this case, Lalit did, carefully unraveling his mask. Navin undid his own as well, allowing his lungs to fill with the stale cavern air.

"So," Lalit said. "What did you think of our valley?"

"You were right," he forced out. "It's pretty bad here. Though, to be fair, I've only seen two villages."

"You want to see the remaining eighteen?" Lalit's voice was cool, disapproval bracketing his thinned lips.

"I wouldn't mind." Navin's mind raced, struck by sudden inspiration. "If I did, I could write to the queen and tell her about what's really going on in your province. Subedar Yazad's well liked in Prabha—in the whole province of Tej, in fact. But if *I* wrote to my grandmother, as a firsthand witness, she might listen—if only to launch an investigation against him."

Sarcasm edged Lalit's laughter. "Look here, Roshan," he announced. "Our prisoner wants to help us with our cause."

A couple of others who'd overheard the conversation chuckled as well. Roshan, who was speaking with Chotu, smirked when Lalit filled her in.

"Are we allies now, Rajkumar?" she asked.

"Navin," he corrected. "I'm not sure I'm your ally, yet. That requires trust on both ends. But I do know you won't hurt me. And that I'm not your enemy."

Silence punctuated the end of this speech. Lalit and Roshan exchanged glances. The sort that carried messages without speaking. It made Navin's stomach twist despite himself. To have a friendship like that. To have *anything* remotely like that.

"Your friend, Hemant, on the other hand," Navin went on. "He seems to be someone who needs watching. He might very well tell someone."

"He can't," Roshan said. "It's part of the magical contract he and everyone else signed when they accepted me as sardar."

Navin experienced a flare of reluctant admiration. "You seem to have a lot of contracts for a family," he said, raising an eyebrow.

"What do you think happens when people bind together to *start* a family, Navin?"

A corner of his mouth curved up. "I don't know," he said, pretending ignorance. "Of course, there's the food, the multicolored lightorbs, the dancers, and the music. The binding night, too, which *everyone* seems to look forward to."

She laughed. It was a nice laugh, the sort that could fill a room, the empty spaces of a heart. *Curses, where had that last thought come from?* It wasn't like he hadn't heard her laugh before.

Navin shook his head, focusing on the question she asked next. "Do princes even get a say in bindings?"

"To some extent. But not always. The crown prince's mate is voted on by the whole council." His ribs squeezed. He wondered what Farhad was doing now. If he was thinking about Navin. "In that instance, I think I'm lucky. I don't matter as much as my brother does."

"I think you underestimate yourself," Roshan said, surprising him. "Write to the queen. But mind you, we'll be checking your letter. Analyzing it for secret codes first."

Navin found his mouth go suddenly dry. *Was this a chance?* Roshan's warning and magical contract notwithstanding, a letter *might* give Navin an opportunity to hint to the queen about where the Shadow Clan's hideout was. "I don't have parchment," he said.

"Not so quick, Rajkumar." Lalit shook his finger as if Navin were an errant child. "As you said, you haven't seen everything. So we'll show you. You can come with us on more deliveries. You will write to

Parasmani Bhairavi when we feel you've seen enough. Until then, the negotiations will continue."

Navin's jaw hurt from grinding his teeth. *Patience.* "As you wish," Navin said, lowering his head. Asking them about the next delivery would be too suspicious. Any mention of Jyoti even more so. So he went back to his old routine. Washing dishes. Humming softly. Allowing himself to study the bandits and their auras before they dissipated. Talking to Roshan—though, after those deliveries to Jyoti and Firozgar, she rarely stopped to chat with him, keeping their talks limited to how he was doing and if he'd had enough to eat.

Maybe Hemant's comments had affected her. Maybe Lalit had said something. Or maybe she was thinking of something else altogether, her gaze distant, her forehead perpetually furrowed, her aura fluctuating between a collected brown to a worried blue.

It's fine, Navin assured himself. Not everything was about him. Certainly, he didn't *miss* their nightly chats. Or the laughter that heaved his chest at times, almost making him forget where he was.

Five days later, the bandits left Navin behind in the cave as the fourth torch went blue, disappearing with their weapons in tow. *Another raid,* Navin realized from behind his confinement barrier. It was also the first time during his captivity that Navin was entirely alone.

His fingers fluttered to his throat. *The first step to a good song,* his father had always said, *is to pay your respects to the stage, the great animal spirits, and the gods. If you don't respect where your gift comes from, hatchling, then do not expect it to work for you.*

Navin stared at the gunnysack hanging nearby, the symbol inked onto it slowly coming into focus.

Wasn't Ashvamaidan's flying mare an aspa? A great animal spirit?

Navin wondered how he could have forgotten the legend of the fire goddess setting the land that would become Jwala alight. Of the great horse spirit that had soared down from the skies, trampling out the flames, purifying the soil. It was how this province had gotten its name—Aspamaidan in Old Paras, Ashvamaidan in the modern dialect. Navin didn't know how true the legend was—if any living person had seen the aspa. Yet faith, nebulous as it could be at times, comforted him now. Gave him hope where there was none.

It would do, he decided, staring at the faded ink. As for the gods—or at least the fire goddess—he needed a source of light. Such as one of the seven torches flaming against the walls.

Keeping one ear cocked for returning bandits, Navin took a deep breath. He rose to his feet, touched the floor—his stage—and brushed its earth lightly over his forehead. He knelt, prostrating before the mare embossed on the gunnysack, and then before the midnight torch, which had yet to go blue, pretending it was the eternal flame.

As he sat cross-legged on the ground, Navin threw back his shoulders. Imagined a pair of invisible talons delicately nudging his back, correcting his posture.

He raised his hands, the palms cupped in offering, exactly the way he would during prayer. "With blessings of the great aspa and the goddess of flame, I offer you this song," he spoke aloud.

Even when there is no audience, you must pretend there is one, his father used to say.

Navin spotted a pair of moths braving one of the blue torches, translucent wings fluttering. He began with a *Sa*.

A note as still as water in a well, beating deep within his chest. Then, a *Re*. Ascending steadily like feet up a set of stairs that suddenly turned and curled and shifted. Rippled like the river Navin now sang of, along with the sharp tang of eucalyptus, the smoky sweetness of fireblooms in the air.

He'd forgotten how it felt to sing. How a melody, when rendered perfectly, could encompass him in vibrations that buzzed against his skin and filled his bones, that fluttered like a bird that had slipped into his mouth unseen and now lived in his throat, tucked between the vocal cords.

A buzz by his ear made him jerk back. His voice faded as he spotted the fly hovering nearby—an insect he'd certainly not seen moments earlier. The sixth torch glowed blue against the wall.

The bandits had returned.

He could hear them now, shuffling footsteps and indistinct voices—sounds that grew louder, more boisterous as they entered the cave, their backs bent over, loaded with sacks of grain and some with what appeared to be crates of liquor—if the clinking glass within was any indication.

Their auras were visible. Not only so, they were vibrant. Especially those of the two bandits that entered the cavern toward the end, one tall, one short. One with hair like copper, another with a mane that resembled blood gleaming in the dark. Navin stared at the short bandit, the glow on her face revealing nearly as much joy as the unadulterated silver of her aura.

"Good raid?" he asked. Roshan beamed at him and nodded.

"The best. I first thought it was a trap—the defenses were so poor!

Well, it doesn't matter. We got everything for the most part. Enough food for each one of our allied villages."

"So will you be making a delivery soon?" Navin kept his tone casual, indifferent.

"Maybe." Roshan smiled, but Navin could tell she hadn't been entirely fooled. "When would you like to go, Rajkumar Navin? Tomorrow?"

Tomorrow would be perfect. But saying so might also bring in a trace of blue to her aura, bruising the silver.

"Whenever you like." Navin nearly laughed at the way his comment made her aura glow. "You're sardar of the clan, right?"

"Let's make it tomorrow." She nodded decisively, then took a swig of liquor from a bottle being passed around. "Why not?"

"Yes," Navin whispered, still watching her. "Why not?"

Tonight, she chatted freely with Navin. Told him about the raid, her tongue loosened by the drink, her brown eyes luminous under the torches.

"How does the rest of the clan feel?" Navin asked. "They must be happy with everything you've done."

Her smile flickered. A trace of teal veined her aura: sadness. "Not entirely. I might have earned a bit of their trust today, though." She settled cross-legged next to him, outside his confinement barrier. Though she hadn't spoken, Navin saw the shift in her aura, the blue of suspicion mingling with green and silver. *What about you?* she was probably thinking. *What have you done to earn my trust?*

He decided to offer another thimbleful of truth. "When I was seven and Farhad nine, our grandmother set us a challenge to build a fort out of wood in the palace garden," he said. "No magic was to be used.

The prize would be a full day out in the city or any town of our choice. You might think that as princes, we went everywhere in Jwala with our grandmother. But back then, we were cooped up in the palace. No one was allowed to see us except our tutors and the sipahis guarding us."

"Isn't the palace beautiful, though?"

"A cage is a cage." He shrugged. "We were both desperate to get out for one day at least. So we competed. Farhad was getting ahead of me. But his designs for the fort were boring. Uninventive. There wasn't even a magical moat with stone makara to spew pitch at one's enemies!"

Her laughter warmed his skin.

"I suggested we work together," he went on. "I'd give Farhad ideas, and he'd come up with a way to execute them. This way, we could both go out together. Farhad thought the plan was great. We both worked on a big fort, building it right in the center of the garden. Of course, our exalted Parasmani ji didn't agree." Navin's throat felt as if it were clogged with pebbles.

Goddess's hair. Why had he chosen to tell this tale?

The scent of cloves wafted over: Roshan had leaned close, holding up a dusty glass bottle.

"Have this," she offered. "Makes talking easier."

His brain warned him against intoxication, reminding him of its effect on his soul magic. But refusing would make him look suspicious.

Navin accepted the bottle. It was mahua, a liquor made from the white flowers of the madhu trees found in the forests of eastern Jwala. The sweet, surprisingly cool liquid seared Navin's mouth when he took a swig, leaving behind a smoky aftertaste. The burn also loosened the ache in his chest.

"My grandmother said that we'd broken the rules and that it was a *competition*," he said. "That we'd not always have each other for help. When she found out that I was the one who proposed the plan, she rebuked me. Called me lazy for trying to get out of doing the hard work myself."

"That seems . . ." Roshan paused. "No, it actually is ridiculous."

"The parasmani decided that Farhad was the winner and that I would stay home," Navin went on. "My brother didn't accept the prize. Said he wouldn't go if I couldn't. But it didn't matter." He took another swig of the mahua. "Ever since that day, my grandmother never saw me the same way again. You're lucky in that sense, Roshni. At least your clan gives you chances to prove yourself."

Roshan was frowning. Her aura, which had started to fade again, was shifting color from blue to what looked like ebony. Belief. Certainty. Navin's tongue brushed the blister that had formed inside his cheek.

"We'll go on a delivery tomorrow," she said. "Give you something to write about to the parasmani. Maybe you can change things. Prove yourself as well."

It was an effort not to use his magic right then and nudge her into going back to Jyoti. But Navin's instincts told him to wait. To hold back for now.

"Are we going back to the same villages?" he asked casually. "Or somewhere else?"

"Somewhere else. Though we might quickly stop at Jyoti. Appease the sarpanch there." Red bloomed across her aura. An anger that Navin sensed was directed toward Vilayat.

She rose to her feet. "Sleep well, Navin."

The blister burst. Blood swirled in his mouth along with the last bit of the liquor. He swallowed it, new pain burning away with the old.

"Sleep well, Roshan."

19

THE VILLAGE OF ALIPORE LAY ACROSS THE RIVER, A FEW MILES west of their new hideout. Since it was a larger village with more deliveries, Roshan decided to go there first.

There was no bridge connecting the two shores, forcing them to wade across the river on foot. There were fourteen clan members this time and Navin, who followed Roshan closely, making sure to step exactly where she had. Behind them, Roshan heard Vijali Fui's soft murmurs: spells cast behind them to remove any footprints. From the side of her eyes, she kept track of Hemant and two of his cronies, who carried gunnies on their backs, their comments occasionally reaching her ears.

"...again she gives away too much grain to the villages, Hemant Bhai."

"Chhe!" There was another murmur, followed by "...idiots!"

"They don't seem very happy," a voice spoke in her ear. Navin, his eyes shaded brown in disguise, a frown between his brows.

The sun remained mostly hidden that morning, and clouds floated overhead like tattered flags, casting shadows over thatched roofs in the distance. She exhaled, readjusting the sack over her shoulders.

"Haven't you heard of the old saying?" she told Navin in response. "Where elephants stroll, wild dogs bark?" *Or something of the sort.*

Navin laughed. "My brother would say that whenever people get too abrasive at court. 'Ignore them, Navin,' he'd tell me." He paused. "Never thought I'd miss the uptight prick."

Guilt pinched Roshan's insides. Two weeks ago, she'd have laughed if someone had told her she'd feel anything of the kind over Jwala's spare prince. She shook her head hard. She couldn't afford to feel this way. Not when their lands got swallowed daily by ravines. Not when Roshan's own future with the clan remained at stake.

More worryingly, Khush had yet to return from Prabha with the queen's answer. The living specter had never taken so long before. Even Khizer was surprised by his brother's absence, but he'd tried to reassure Roshan with a simple reminder: Khush was already dead. No one could kill him again.

Roshan heaved out another breath. They'd reached the shore, their clothes splattered with water, their boots trailing mud. Pausing for a moment, they sipped water from skins. She stuck another clove between her teeth and chewed. Last night the clan had had one of its most successful raids yet—at one of the governor's older warehouses on the outskirts of Surag, guarded by a pair of Brights who'd run for cover the moment they spotted the bandits. The clan had found grain and alcohol at the warehouse, and spices as well—so much bounty that Roshan had wondered if a trap had been laid. But no one had stopped them. Nor given them a fight on the way back. She and Lalit had even kept watch as they returned, making sure no one was following them back to the hideout.

No one had.

Roshan brushed off the strange, inexplicable sense of unease. It was fine. Even she was allowed to get lucky sometimes. She glanced at Navin again, wondering if he would speak, but for the most part, he'd gone quiet and was now staring at the ravines that surrounded Alipore village like towers, caging it into a near perfect oval.

Sarpanch Sohail, the village head, lived near the front of the village, in a thatched house with a well. Roshan and the others dropped eleven sacks at the front. A small boy peered out. The sarpanch's son—who had a terrified look on his normally cheerful face.

"What happened, Shapur?" Roshan asked gently. "Where's your baba?"

"He's by the temple, Sardar Roshan." The boy chewed on his lower lip. "Some people brought in Jaya Didi. Her face was so bloody."

Murmurs broke out among the clan. Roshan had the sensation of having tasted something rancid. She straightened, and though Shapur couldn't see it under her mask, she forced a smile so that her voice would sound calm.

"It's all right. Blood can simply cover up a small injury. I'll go by the temple. Check to see what's happening. Tell your baba that we dropped off the grain here, would you?"

The boy called out to her again when she began to turn. "You'll be able to cure her, won't you?"

"I'll try."

Though even trying might be a stretch, Roshan realized when they approached the temple and saw the girl in question. Around fifteen or sixteen blue moons in age, her eyes and mouth oozing blood.

"What happened to her?" Navin whispered. "Her eyes—"

"They've been gouged out," Sarpanch Sohail, who was kneeling beside the girl's still form on the floor, answered the question wearily. "Her

tongue has been cut, too, so she cannot speak. She can still hear, at least."
He looked up from underneath his ochre turban, pale brows forming a V
over a broad, sun-browned forehead. "Can you help her, Sardar Roshan?"

Roshan released a breath. She pressed a hand against the amulet at
her throat. This would be difficult. She doubted she could grow back
those eyes. She knelt next to the girl. "Where did you find her?"

"By that abandoned firestone mine outside the village. She and her
sister were missing for three days. Well, her sister is still missing. Though
of course, Jaya may know what happened."

"It's those Brights," a voice sobbed—a woman who shared the girl's
softly pursed lips and curved nose. "It has to be."

"Shhhh, Bibi ji," the village head soothed. "We cannot say such
things without proof."

"Proof!" The woman wiped her eyes with a soiled hand. She spat on
the ground. "That's what those fiends always want. There is no justice
for the poor."

Roshan looked up, her gaze finding Navin's. Under the mask shielding his face, his neck had grown taut, a vein roping its side.

"The village hakims," he addressed Roshan directly, remembering her
instructions to not talk to the villagers. "Can't they help? These injuries
are . . ." His voice trailed off as Roshan vehemently shook her head, urging him to be silent.

Jaya could still hear and Roshan didn't want to dishearten the girl
completely by letting her know that such injuries would need not one, but
several healers working their magic in tandem. Preferably at a hospital.

"Sadly, we don't have any more hakims left in our village, child," the
sarpanch spoke again, slowly rising to his feet. His long gray jama was

patched over with blood. "The nearest hakim lives in Surag. I hawked an urgent message, but it may still take him a few hours to get here. We wanted to take her to a hospital, but . . ." The sarpanch gestured to the scorch marks on the temple floor—the chip on one of its pillars. "She didn't want to."

A protection spell, Roshan realized. When children were small, their powers not quite developed, magic could explode out of them in fiery sparks whenever they were scared or feeling threatened. It was the sort of thing that also happened to sipahis who went to fight wars and then returned, not quite themselves.

"Why should she want to go?" an old woman demanded. "The subedar owns that whole city, every hospital there. She—" The woman's voice cut off briefly as a few others spoke, urging her to be silent. "No, I will not!" she exclaimed, her voice rising. "To the highest of hells with the subedar and Shera Aspa! To—"

Jaya made an indecipherable sound and thrashed on the floor again.

Roshan placed a hand on the girl's arm, feeling the tremors under her sweaty skin. "Silence," she commanded. Though her voice wasn't loud, it cut through the others' arguments. The villagers quieted, with the exception of Jaya, who softly continued to wail. "I need everyone to clear out. Except for the sarpanch and the girl's mother."

"Do you want us gone, too?" Lalit asked, gesturing to the clan.

"You lot can stay. But keep quiet. I want her to remain as calm as possible." Roshan lightly brushed the backs of her fingers against the girl's forehead. This was going to be painful—for them both.

Once the temple had cleared out, Roshan sat cross-legged on the floor. Magic slowly flooded her limbs, sending a wave of ice and heat through them. She stroked the girl's forehead again. Jaya's mind was even more barbed than Sultana Bibi's. Soothing her would take ages—and also be a waste of healing magic. Roshan would have to try to directly heal her injured eyes and mouth.

"Jaya, you will need to be brave, all right?" Roshan said. "It will be painful, but I'm going to try to do this as quickly as possible."

She gently tugged on the girl's mouth, opening it to get a closer look. A dagger had been used to do the damage. Perhaps the sharp end of an atashban.

Butchers.

Roshan straightened her tensing spine, controlling the urge to vomit. Regrowing the girl's eyes or tongue might have been possible with several hakims working in tandem, one simply working to keep Jaya calm. But right now, the only thing Roshan could do was stop infection and cauterize Jaya's wounds before fever set in.

She began with the eyes first, lightly, then more firmly, pressing her thumbs below the sockets. Focusing on the magic alone, on the network of blood, veins, and sinew, she began to slowly seal the wound. It was a difficult process, made slower by the warm blood seeping from the girl's sockets. The wound wasn't even halfway sealed when a headache began creeping up Roshan's skull, her vision beginning to blur.

Jaya writhed underneath. Her hands, hardened by working the fields, dug into Roshan's forearms. Again, Jaya cried out, attempting to speak. Her face began to burn. Roshan had only seconds to detach herself before sparks exploded from Jaya's hands, one singeing the sleeve of Roshan's red jama.

"Roshan?" she thought she heard Lalit say from a distance. "Are you all right?"

"I'm fine," she managed. Sweat trailed down the sides of her face. The heat from her healing magic made Roshan's own body feel like a tandoor. "It's normal for anyone being healed to feel pain."

She didn't tell Lalit that if this went on, it would be difficult to even cure any infection, let alone quicken healing.

Behind her, she heard a throat clearing. "I can help, maybe?" Navin offered quietly. "I . . . I was good at singing as a boy. Maybe I could distract her with a song while you work."

"Singing? What—are we at a recital?" Hemant sneered. "This isn't your pa—"

"Enough." Roshan glared at the man.

Hemant glared right back at her. "This isn't a joke," he told her. "This is someone's life."

"I'm not joking," Navin said, again addressing Roshan and not Hemant. "I . . . I used to sing my brother to sleep."

"Let's try," she said. "If it doesn't help, then you stop at once. Understand?"

He nodded and then sat next to Jaya, facing Roshan.

"Suprabhat, Jaya ji," he said, as sweet as honey, his hand curling delicately around the girl's shaking one. "I'm going to help you and Sardar Roshan, all right? Just focus on my voice." He paused a moment as the girl let out a moan. Then, locking eyes with Roshan, nodded.

Roshan pressed her thumbs below Jaya's eye sockets, her body glowing again. Trembling with effort. In the background, Navin's voice rose, soft and melodic, in a hymn that Roshan recalled priests singing at temples during the Hashtdin festival:

What are light and shadow but twin spirits?
What are day and night but a single soul?
You venture seeking evil everywhere, mortal,
Yet forget to look in your own heart.

As he sang, Jaya visibly relaxed. The sweat lining her face and neck cooled. Roshan moved quickly, sealing off the open wounds in and around Jaya's eyes, and then pressed her fingers to the sides of the girl's mouth, siphoning away the dried blood, cauterizing the wounds on her tongue. Jaya trembled, again catching hold of Roshan's arm. But there was no feel of being burned by her fingers now. Only the bite of nails digging into Roshan's skin.

Navin kept singing the hymn. Over and over, his hand tightly clasped in Jaya's, his focus entirely on the girl's face.

"It's done," Roshan whispered. Then, louder: "Na—Dildar!" she corrected, mentally cursing herself for the near slip. "I've done everything I can. Can you hear me?"

He nodded hard. Moisture beaded the skin above his brows. He slowed the verse, softened the words to a hum. Tremors racked Jaya's form. But her breaths had slowed, grown more even.

As he sat back, Navin met Roshan's gaze. Around them, everyone had fallen silent. No one spoke. Not the sarpanch, nor Jaya's mother. Not even Hemant.

When Roshan was nine, she'd sneaked out of the clan's hideout after her first and only fight with her father. Her temper had been so bad that she'd not paid attention to where she was going and had tripped and fallen in the ravines nearby. She'd landed at the bottom of a hill, her ankle twisted so badly that she'd fainted from the pain. When she'd finally come to, her body sore and healing, a figure stood over her. Not Baba nor Lalit as she'd expected but a stallion with a mane as red as blood, his coat glowing like flame in the setting sun. It was the first and only time Roshan had seen a wild Ashvamaidani horse in the badlands. The stallion had watched her curiously and then cantered away before she could do little more than breathe.

Right now, she felt as bereft as she had in that moment. As if she'd witnessed something incredible—only to have it snatched away.

What would it have been like, she wondered, watching Navin, *to have met him like this?*

Where they were not bandit and prince, but merely healer and singer. Two ordinary strangers brought together by talents that seemed incompatible, yet somehow worked in perfect sync.

She imagined Baba's sad smile—the same smile he'd given her when she was five and had asked for one of the two moons. *O, bitiya. Don't wish for things that don't fit in the palm of your hand.*

Roshan released a breath that was at once sharp and painful.

It was only his peri blood, she told herself. *Lending him a magic where there is none.*

Even so, it seemed wrong to stay quiet.

"I don't believe in the fire goddess," she told Navin. "But if I did, right now, I'd thank her for you."

20

NAVIN DIDN'T KNOW WHAT WAS WORSE: BEING TOLD HE WAS A blessing by a girl who was his captor—or never being told anything of the sort by his own family. Under the mask, his mouth felt full. Throbbing with a particularly painful blister that had formed under his tongue. He wanted to break away from Roshan and her intense gaze, the dark aura of truth surrounding her turbaned head.

But he couldn't. No more than he could stop himself from reaching out to Jaya moments earlier. Navin's former lovers had accused him of lacking empathy. Of being cruel, even. It had been Farhad who had pointed out the real problem: *You do not like facing anything that causes you discomfort, little brother.*

It should have been easy for Navin to ignore Jaya, to block his ears to her heart-wrenching cries. No one—not the villagers, nor the bandits—would have judged him for it. *I would have judged myself*, he realized now. Queen Bhairavi might be indifferent to his capture. He might remain stuck in Ashvamaidan for the next week or month—or maybe get killed if the bandits grew tired of him. But Farhad might've had a point about facing one's discomforts, because it was here, in this temple, in a bandit's borrowed clothes, that Navin had discovered something he could do. Something even his upstanding brother might consider worthwhile.

Jaya's aura had appeared within the first few notes of the hymn—yellow and green like a bruise. Initially, Navin didn't know if he'd be able to influence her emotions; he'd never attempted this aspect of soul magic without verbal commands. But necessity allowed his instincts to take over, and instead of using direct orders, Navin had used the melody of the hymn itself, finding spaces for his thoughts in the breaths between each note: *You are safe. No one can hurt you now.* As he'd repeated the hymn several times, Jaya's aura had shifted, its angry hue deepening to a rich, soothing brown.

The warmth of Roshan's life magic still emanated from Jaya. While singing, Navin had sensed flashes of it against his skin—an energy that, unlike his consistently warm soul magic, pulsed between ice and fire, a magic that could easily kill someone if it spiraled out of control. Not with Roshan, though. She'd remained steady, her gaze focused on Jaya's eyes and mouth, unflinching, even when the latter gripped her forearm, indenting it with crescents. Untrained though the Shadow Bandit was, Navin suspected that she was as capable as, if not more than, most hakims at a big-city hospital.

"Meherbani, Sardar Roshan," Sarpanch Sohail spoke, his voice making Navin start. "Meherbani, Dildar. You both have done more for us than we can express."

"No thanks needed, Sarpanch Sohail," Roshan said. She shook her head as if clearing it of clouds. "I didn't do much, really. And I couldn't have done it without Dildar."

A heat that had little to do with the temperature rose to Navin's cheeks. "She's being too modest, our sardar," he told the village head. "She always feels like she doesn't do enough."

Roshan glanced at him again, her eyes narrowing with something that he might have thought was anger—if he couldn't see the pale, shimmering residue of shock mingling into her aura.

"The sarpanch is right, Sardar Roshan," Jaya's mother chimed in, her voice hoarse from crying. "You saved the only daughter I may have left now." She wiped her eyes. "Goddess keep you safe. You, too, young man," she told Navin.

"Goddess keep you safe, Kaki ji," Navin replied, years of ingrained courtesy springing to action. It took him a moment to register the acid burning his gut. He didn't bother asking who could have done something like this. The villagers had already voiced their suspicions about the Brights, and the Shadow Clan would merely agree. It was only more conjecture, of course. But then . . . Navin thought back to Sultana Bibi's very similar injuries. Her assertion that it was the Brights who'd done her wrong.

His head spun.

Abruptly, he rose to his feet and announced: "I need air."

Without waiting for a response, he stalked out, ignoring the multiple gazes now burning holes into his back.

He sat on the stairs outside the temple, next to one of the statues of the flying mare flanking its entrance. Here, he loosened his mask slightly, inhaled and exhaled several times over the flap of dark fabric. A breeze lingered, cooling his overheated skin.

". . . you listening to what I said?" a voice floated to his ears from somewhere behind the statue. "They found the girl out near the old firestone mine. I bet she and her sister saw something there. Something they shouldn't have."

"The mine's been shut for over fifty years," someone else argued. "There are no firestones here anymore."

"So you think."

Navin frowned. Firestones were versatile and powerful amplifiers, used for magic that required expending high amounts of energy. They were also rare and, resultantly, restricted to hospital use for complex magical surgeries and the manufacture of atashbans and other weapons powered by death magic. Centuries ago, Jwala had been famous for its firestone mines, exporting the amplifiers across the four kingdoms of Svapnalok and to empires across the Yellow Sea, where they were in high demand. Over time, though, wars and excessive mining had depleted the mines, shutting them down. To Navin's knowledge, there were no active firestone mines in the kingdom anymore. If there were . . . then the owner of the mines would be more powerful than anyone else in Jwala.

Including the queen.

"Dildar?"

Navin nearly leaped out of his skin when a hand touched his shoulder.

"Where are you off to?" Roshan asked, her soft voice doing little to hide the steel underneath.

"Nowhere." He paused. "What do you know about the firestone mines in this area?"

"There used to be some, I think." She frowned. "Where we're staying now—that was some sort of old mine, too. Probably had firestones. But that was over a century ago. Why?"

So much for that theory. "No reason."

Another pause. "I wanted to thank you," Roshan said. "For what you did there."

"You're welcome." He shrugged. "I *was* a little worried I'd gone tone-deaf, but bless the goddess, I haven't. Still perfectly pitched."

She snorted. "Not very modest, are you?"

"Why should I be? I'm all for artifice and posturing, but false humility can be such a bore." *Especially when you get so little praise from anyone else.* He bit back the last thought and turned to face her. "You should try it, Roshni. It feels *so* good."

"Right," she replied in her usual dry tone.

But the skin around her eyes crinkled and he knew she was smiling even before glancing up to confirm the silvery tint in her aura. It made the corners of Navin's own mouth turn up before he realized what he was doing.

Footsteps marched in from behind and Roshan rose to her feet, dusting off the back of her jama. "We need to get moving."

After nearly a week of waiting for this moment, the trek to Jyoti felt tedious, less exciting than Navin had imagined.

At the village, Sarpanch Vilayat took ages to come and see them when called. He didn't look at Navin—not even when the latter announced he was going to use the outhouse.

"I'll come with you, Dildar," Lalit said. "I feel the sudden urge to piss, too."

The comment made the others chuckle. Roshan, who was arguing with the sarpanch again, didn't hear. Navin wanted to sink through the ground. Maybe the sarpanch hadn't seen Shera after all.

"You did a good thing back in Alipore," Lalit told Navin as they made their way past the temple and into the gully that held the out-house. "Where'd you learn to sing like that?"

"From my father."

"Your father's a peri, isn't he?"

When Navin said nothing, Lalit took two steps forward and blocked his way. "You didn't answer me, Dildar." The other man's voice was a purr.

"He is." Navin inhaled deeply, hoping he didn't sound belligerent. "So?"

"So it's a wonder his Pashu magic didn't pass on to you."

Navin's heartbeat kicked up a notch. There was a trace of blue in Lalit's fading aura. Suspicion. Using soul magic on the bandit now wouldn't be wise. Especially since Navin hadn't bothered bonding with him as he had with Roshan.

"If it had, I wouldn't be standing here with you, would I?" Navin asked calmly. He wanted to add more. Something along the lines of *If I had a peri's magic, I would have flown away, would have sung until your eyes and ears bled out*—if not for the glint in Lalit's eyes, the flushed whites of his knuckles gripping the atashban.

Patience.

"Please, Lalit ji." Navin almost smiled when Lalit started at his use of the honorific. "I'd really like to use the bathroom."

A beat passed by. Another. Lalit's aura teetered between red and blue before settling into a dull maroon. Irritation. He moved aside, letting Navin pass through the door.

The inside of the bathroom was small but clean, a clay ewer placed by a large brass pot full of water near an oval toilet dug into the ground.

Light poured in from a small window overhead. Navin hadn't seen a real, working bathroom—with pipes, the river water gurgling through them—for so long that he might've just stood there staring at it. Entirely missing the tiny scroll propped up on the ledge.

Glancing back to ensure the door to the outhouse was still shut, he picked up the scroll and pulled off the string holding it together. The note was short and written in Shera's familiar slant: *Get the Shadow Bandit to the Zaalian ruin at midnight. Make sure you both are alone. I'll keep coming there every night until you do. Destroy this note.*

Heart pounding, Navin ripped up the paper, chucking the pieces into the toilet. He then poured water over them from the brass pot, which kept magically replenishing. His heart didn't slow to a normal rhythm until the parchment flowed out of sight and into the drain.

Lalit didn't use the bathroom after Navin emerged. "Let's go," he said briskly. "After you, Dildar."

Navin said nothing, noting that Lalit's atashban was still glowing a dull red. Sarpanch Vilayat glanced at them as they returned. Slowly, deliberately, Navin blinked at the man. He received an equally slow blink in return. But apart from that, neither gave any sign that they'd seen each other, and soon enough the bandits left the village, heading back to the hideout via another route that Navin didn't recognize.

Get the Shadow Bandit to the Zaalian ruin at midnight.

Shera's instruction simmered in Navin's mind. It was easy enough to get Roshan to take him to the bathroom these days, even let him stay longer in the kitchen area as he washed the dishes. But to trick her into taking him outside without anyone else would be a challenge—if not impossible.

Logistical issues aside, there was also the matter of Navin's own gut. Of the slow, uneasy flip in his belly at the thought of having to trap Roshan after helping her heal that girl at the temple. After having seen bone demons, the badlands, the villagers who were clearly starving, even terrified of Governor Yazad, Shera, and the Brights.

Roshan and the Shadow Clan might be criminals. But Navin could no longer definitively call them liars. Something *was* amiss in Ashvamaidan: something his oldest friend and his father might be responsible for.

Navin's head ached. *Farhad would know what to do.* Unlike Navin, Farhad always had a plan. Was it any wonder the parasmani trusted him more?

The thought continued festering in Navin's mind after they returned to the underground hideout, well into the night, when nearly everyone else had fallen asleep. His sore mouth craved the palace hakim's potion: a mix of raw shvetpanchhi egg and herbs that he'd normally despised taking to soothe his blisters. The bandits' auras had disappeared again. The only exception remained Roshan, whose aura was faded but still visible.

He saw her now, a few feet outside his confinement barrier, pausing next to Lalit, who'd emerged from somewhere within the mines. Navin squeezed his eyes shut and pretended to sleep, his chest rising and falling. He did this sometimes to eavesdrop on the bandits and their conversations. Though he'd never really heard anything useful so far, apart from Hemant's obvious distaste for Roshan and her leadership.

Today, however, the word *rajkumar* floated his way.

"No one likes Hemant, but he has a point," Lalit was saying. "You *are* getting too close to the rajkumar. He's your hostage, remember? Not your friend."

A familiar huff that Navin now recognized as Roshan's laugh. "Of course I remember. Do I look like one of those simpering fools at court who throw themselves all over the spoiled brat?"

Navin's breath caught. His throat tightened painfully.

"I'm worried about Khush," she added. "He hasn't returned yet with an answer. We'll need to add more pressure on Parasmani Bhairavi. Maybe . . ." Her voice softened to a murmur, fading from Navin's ears.

It didn't matter. He should've known better than to feel bad for her. For any of these crooks. Perhaps the villagers were truly in trouble. But to the bandits, Navin was no more than a tool to get exactly what they wanted from the queen.

Good luck with that, Roshni, he thought.

By the time he was done with her, she would not only be simpering exactly like those fools at court but also crying.

As a child, whenever Navin grew angry, his tutors would advise him to breathe. In and out, repeatedly, until his body calmed. He did the same now, his inhales deep, the exhales slow and nearly soundless.

The time for patience had come to an end.

21

"WE'LL NEED TO ADD MORE PRESSURE ON PARASMANI BHAIRAVI. Maybe we could have Na—the rajkumar write to her?" Roshan added, lowering her voice as they walked out of the main cavern and toward her room. "It would be risky, I know, but—"

"No," Lalit said firmly. "Let's give Khush a couple more days."

"If he doesn't come? Then what?" Roshan demanded. "I am not cutting off the rajkumar's ears."

"I didn't say you should." Lalit paused. "Give me some time to think."

Roshan bit her tongue. A part of her knew Lalit was right. But what other choice did they have? She couldn't keep the prince here forever. The others would be furious, for one. Already she'd heard Hemant making comments, trying to stir mistrust about her. But also, there was the matter of Navin himself. Of the guilt Roshan had been feeling ever since he'd talked about his dysfunctional relationship with his grandmother, or how he'd missed his older brother. The fact that Navin *wasn't* merely the spoiled brat she'd said he was. Or that, in another lifetime, Roshan may have liked the prince, may have been friends with him, too. She was glad Lalit wasn't watching her now—hot-faced and agitated, the truth plain on her face. Their conversation had already soured her night and wouldn't let her sleep. When tossing and turning got to her, she rose up and decided to make herself a cup of chai.

In the cavern, she found the prince awake as well. Sitting on his rock and staring off into the distance at one of the flickering torches on the wall. On spotting Roshan, he straightened. "Can't sleep?" he said, his low voice carrying in the silence. She nodded, then raised a finger to her lips. He nodded, his gold eyes scanning the sleeping bodies wrapped in blankets around the cavern. Most of the bandits were deep sleepers, but Roshan didn't want to accidentally wake anyone.

Filling a small clay mug with water and crushed tea leaves, she carried it with her to Navin's confinement barrier. He slid aside, patted the rock with his hand. She hesitated. Lalit's warning was still fresh in her mind.

"I don't bite, Roshni," he said, his voice so quiet only she could hear. "Or maybe I do—if you're lucky."

Roshan rolled her eyes. But somehow she didn't find his antics annoying anymore. She sat next to him and conjured a small lightorb that floated between her knees.

"What happened?" She held the clay mug over the lightorb, waiting for the water to catch heat. "Can't sleep, either?"

"I keep thinking about that girl, Jaya," he said, growing sober. "About what will happen to her. In Prabha, there are special schools with teachers who could train her to live independently. Even Surag has such a center, I believe."

"Her mother wouldn't be able to afford it." The cup in her hands was already steaming. Roshan drew it back, allowing the lightorb to flicker out. "Special schools need lots of coin, Navin." With Lalit gone, it felt safe to return to a first-name basis.

"Maybe." He frowned. "I could help. I have coin of my own at the palace."

She would have laughed—if not for the look on his face. The utter seriousness of it. Flames danced against the wall, reflected in his eyes, turning them amber.

"Jaya is only one person. There are many others like her across the province. You can't save everyone." Baba's death had taught her that much, at least.

"That's what you're trying to do, isn't it? Be Ashvamaidan's savior?"

The tea scalded Roshan's tongue. Or maybe Navin's words. "I only fight for what is mine," she said, gesturing around the cave with her free hand. "For what is rightfully theirs."

"And clearly there's no other way to fight except to loot, murder, and kidnap."

Roshan gritted her teeth. A part of her was tempted to get up and walk away. But she knew Navin better now. Knew that the posturing and sarcasm were merely a way to hide his own fear.

"Tell me something, Rajkumar," she said. "What would *you* do if you came across Jaya's tormentors?"

He looked annoyed now. "There's a Ministry of Justice. There are courts—"

"And how long on average does it take a court to try a new case? Five years? Or have things improved and is it four now?"

He opened his mouth, as if to speak. Nothing emerged.

She suppressed a sigh. "I don't say that my methods are right. Or legal. But whatever happens, I will not hurt you. Neither will I let anyone else." She could promise him this much—if nothing else.

He wasn't looking at her face, but somewhere above her hairline. He shook his head. "There are times I don't know what to believe," he said.

"Sometimes it's impossible to accept the truth that's right before us." Roshan paused. "When I was nine years old, I overheard some of the bandits talking about me, mentioning I was adopted. I didn't know what the word meant. I went and asked Baba. And that was when he explained to me that he wasn't my real father. I was angry with him then. I thought he'd lied to me by omission—that he'd kept me from my real parents. I even tried to run away once—to go look for them."

From the corner of her eyes, she noticed Navin straightening. As if interested.

"I wasn't as good at navigating the ravines then. I slipped and fell over a hill. Fainted, too. Now thinking back, I could have easily broken my neck instead of twisting my ankle. There's no recovering from that—even if you have life magic." A soft laugh. "Or maybe I would've been eaten by a tusked jackal. But when I woke up, there was a wild horse nearby. Keeping watch."

"A wild horse?" Navin's voice was equally soft. Wistful. "I've heard of those. Never seen any roaming the plains, though."

"Most disappeared decades ago." *Around the time Yazad Aspa took over Ashvamaidan's governance.* But Roshan didn't say the last sentence out loud. A peace had fallen over them now: as fragile as a feather balanced on a ledge. "Seeing that horse made me realize how scared I was. How I missed Baba already. He wasn't the father who sired me, but he was the only one I'd known." Pain traveled down the backs of her hands. She loosened her grip on the cup, quickly gulped her tepid tea. "Baba, the Shadow Clan—they raised me. They're all I have now."

Freeing their lands from the governor's grip was the last—perhaps the only—way Roshan had left to show herself capable of leading them. To prove that she belonged.

There was a long pause. "Do you have a backup plan if the queen doesn't agree to your demands?" Navin asked.

"To modify them," she said, shrugging. The truth wasn't something she liked to admit—especially to the prince. But it might help get him on their side. "I don't intend to rule the province. I only want Subedar Yazad gone."

"I see." Navin's forehead wrinkled for a split second before smoothing out again. "Let me know if I can do anything for you."

"Really? What about your friend Shera? What'll he think if you go against his father?"

He rolled his eyes. "Roshni, do I look like I'm made for a life in a cave? If helping you means I can go back to a place with a usable gusalkhana again, I'm all in."

She snorted, even though the mention of his wanting to leave unspooled something within her. Something she forced herself to ignore.

"Very well, Rajkumar—"

"Navin," he corrected.

"Naveeen," she drawled. His laugh made her heart skip a beat. "We'll see what happens tomorrow."

22

TOMORROW CAME AND WENT. SO DID THE NEXT DAY, AND THE day after. Navin's stomach roiled each time Lalit shook his head at Roshan's query: *Has Khush returned with Parasmani Bhairavi's reply?*

Khush, Navin had guessed by now, was a living specter. The sort of messenger his grandmother despised. Chances were she'd locked herself in her suite of rooms, which were imbibed with enough spells to keep out anyone she didn't want. Living or dead.

Softly humming as he did the dishes, Navin glanced at Roshan, spotting traces of blue around her hair. Though, after so many days of talking with her, he could have easily guessed she was worried from body language alone. At least she didn't appear angry. Plus, she *had* come to talk to Navin every night for the past three nights.

Yet, for all of Roshan's promises to keep him safe and let him write to the queen, there was no guarantee she could live up to them. Or be persuaded by someone else to change her mind. Navin hadn't missed the hard looks he kept receiving from the other bandits. Hemant. Lalit. Even the otherwise calm Vijali Fui. Only Chotu's smiles appeared guileless, his laughter echoing in the cavern as Navin applauded his somersaults through the air.

No, if Navin intended to escape, he had to do it soon. Tonight, if possible. It would be tricky. If he pushed too hard, Roshan might sense his soul magic trying to penetrate her mental barriers. He only hoped that the bond they'd formed by now was strong enough to defuse any questions that cropped up in her mind. He'd have to risk everything the way he had once at rowdy gaming tables at the university inn and expensive Prabha taverns—only this time the stakes involved more than a few coins or nudity.

As Roshan approached him that evening, an hour before the midnight torch, Navin slid his last piece into play, beginning with casual small talk, before slowly, carefully directing the conversation to his singing.

"As a boy, I'd sing frequently," he said wistfully. "Everywhere in the palace. I'm sure the servants grew tired of the racket I made."

A small smile flickered across her pretty face. "Yuvraj Farhad's lucky," she commented, "to have had you sing him to sleep."

Goddess be praised. It was the perfect opening.

Navin let his own smile slip. Waited for a swirl of confusion to enter her aura before saying: "It wasn't Farhad I sang for."

"Oh." She paused. "I thought you mentioned your brother in the temple."

"Farhad isn't my only brother," he said, careful to keep his voice low. "My father . . . he has another child. A peri child."

"But you're peri, too, aren't you?"

"It's not the same without wings." There was an ache inside his chest, one that had been brewing since the night he'd sung alone in this cave. Since he'd sung again for Jaya. "The Pashu . . . they don't see you the same way. In the kingdom of Aman, I was the human hatchling with peri eyes. My first time there, my father had to save me from being eaten by a makara. Pashu with crocodile heads and human bodies," he explained when he saw the bemused look on her face. "I didn't know enough to be afraid of them."

"Why would you? You were a child!"

"Yes, but I am also more human than I am Pashu. After my mother died, my father brought me with him to Aman for a month each year to stay with him. Everyone was kind to me, but they'd always refer to me as the human hatchling. I wasn't winged and did not have their instincts. Then came the year I turned nine. My father had had lovers among the peri, none who'd lasted too long. But earlier that year, one of them had given birth to a child. A peri child with little wings already budding from his shoulders. He'd be ready to fly within weeks.

"That month, I might as well not have existed for my father. I was jealous, starved for his attention. So I drew my half brother to me with pretty words, treats, and singing. I didn't even need to use soul magic to make him follow me to the river. I sang with him, taking him right to the makara's watering hole."

For long moments, Roshan didn't speak. Navin turned away from the shifting colors of her aura: shock and sorrow competing with befuddlement and anger. He didn't want her to confirm the truth. That what he'd done was worse than anything the Shadow Clan had dared plan.

"What happened?" she asked at last. "Did your brother . . . ?"

"My brother survived. Barely. I didn't know that my father had put a tail on us both—another peri whose job was to make sure we didn't get into trouble. Which I did, of course. But I got my father's attention. Every bit of it—for one brief moment."

A tremor went through him, one that he had to grip both arms to control. "He should have screamed at me, scratched my face out with his talons. But instead, the only thing I got from him was disappointment. A feeling of deep sadness. I begged him to forgive me. To not send me back home to Prabha. When he didn't agree, I tried to use soul magic on him. Tried to convince him of my lie. It made him furious. I knew then that I wouldn't see him again—and I was right."

There was a long silence, which both terrified and relieved Navin. He hadn't understood how much it would hurt to tell the story. Or that the hollow his father had left behind would still feel like a wound, bleeding raw over his chest.

"Navin," Roshan said. "Navin, please look at me."

Her aura had shifted again: this time to the clear sparkle of the night sky. "As you know, I'm not a saint," she said. "So I can't really judge anyone. But what you did in that temple for Jaya was the exact opposite of what you did when you were nine. There are moments in life that define us. Then there are other moments where we turn things around, changing that very definition. Not even rocks stay the same across a lifetime. Who are we, then?"

"Did you just compare me to a rock?" A sound that might have been a laugh tumbled out of him, loosening some of the tightness in his chest.

"Maybe." She sounded amused. There again was the midnight certainty of her truth: an aura that both comforted and allured.

He examined her full cheeks and speckled chin, the firm, shapely mouth that could soften unexpectedly with a laugh or a grin, the dimple that occasionally cleaved her left cheek. Her breath caught before he realized his hand had risen, paused inches away from touching her face.

Fire and ashes. He dropped his arm hastily.

It was the bonding. Sharing his emotions and feelings could give him more control over Roshan, yes. But doing so could also affect *him*, drawing him closer to her. Bringing in confusion where there ought to be none.

He released a breath. His magic delicately pulsed in his throat.

"Want to hear me sing?" He delivered the words with a sheepish smile and the tiniest hint of a challenge.

"Here?" Her aura was flushed with embarrassment and confusion. "Now?"

"Well, if not here, then somewhere else." He shrugged, allowing some of his magic to seep in. "These tunnels carry echoes and sound, though. We wouldn't wake up anyone if we stepped outside for a few moments."

Again, the suggestion was far too bold. But the midnight torch was already turning blue. Navin had maybe an hour before his soul magic faded again. If that. Of course, if Roshan was thinking clearly, she would have simply put up a sound barrier around them both, which would do away with the necessity of leaving the cave.

But right now, there was no trace of suspicion in her aura, which had lightened from black to a rich mahogany, marbled with rose and silver. Slowly she rose to her feet.

"We'll have to be quiet." Her eyes appeared glazed, her voice soft, almost dreamy.

Heart in mouth, Navin clasped the hand she offered. The barrier tickled his face as they stepped out of it, then tiptoed past the sleeping bodies on the floor. He half expected her to pause at the staircase. To come to her senses when they were facing the open sky.

Stars glimmered around them. Chills crept up his skin. He'd forgotten to account for the weather. Roshan looked at him. In the semidarkness, he could barely make out the colors of her aura.

"Are you cold?" she asked.

He shrugged. Tried not to let his teeth chatter. "O-only a l-little."

Was that a smile on her face? If so, it disappeared even faster than it had arrived, like a rainbow in the dark. She held up their clasped hands, her own glowing with magic. Within seconds, his skin began to thaw, from his earlobes to the tips of his toes. There was something else, too. Hinted by the slight flare of Roshan's nostrils, the unconscious way she licked her lips, the tinge of pink in her aura.

It wasn't unusual, Navin knew, for soul bonding to be mistaken for attraction. A few weeks ago, he might have encouraged the Shadow Bandit's lust. Might have pretended to shiver and inch closer, first grazing, then pressing his body to hers. It wouldn't have mattered to him. Roshan was more than pretty, her hair smelling of salt and cloves, her body a prelude to flame itself. But tonight, something held him back from indulging. A feeling of *wrongness* he didn't quite understand.

"Why don't we go to that old Zaalian ruin?" he asked, keeping his voice soft. Then he hummed a line of melody, as if testing it out loud. "The acoustics might be better there."

Another blink. Her body stiffened slightly and Navin wondered if he'd gone too far by being so specific about the location. But her aura remained visible. Dark, streaked with light. She sighed. "All right," she said.

She stepped back, letting go of his hand, and almost at once, his body rebelled against the chill in the air. He followed her across the nooks and crannies of the land—a thing that might have been difficult in the dark but wasn't anymore, thanks to his recent excursions with the bandits.

The shadowy dome of the Zaalian prayer house rose up ahead. Navin's tongue grazed a scar on the roof of his mouth. The remnant of a blister that had healed from the last time he'd performed soul magic. New ones had formed by now, of course, but he barely felt them. His whole being was focused on Roshan, who conjured a small lightorb that floated above their heads.

A cracked staircase led into the prayer house, which was no more than a single square room, its stone walls plain, no carving nor paint marking their cracked surface—in line with the teachings of Prophet Zaal, who'd claimed there were no gods in this world, only magic. Starlight poured in through the door behind them, but the lightorb illuminated every corner of the empty room.

Where were *they?*

Navin hoped he didn't look as panicked as he felt. It *was* midnight, wasn't it? Or had he read Shera's note wrong? Goddess help him, he hoped not. It had been hard enough to bring Roshan here without activating that goddess-forsaken contract she'd forced him to sign.

I, Rajkumar Navin of Clan Behram, will not escape nor try to escape the Shadow Clan in any way.

The words now hammered his skull as he glanced at Roshan's profile, the soft curve of that small, stubborn chin. Her aura had begun to fade. A frown overtook her smooth brow.

"What am I doing . . . ?" Her voice trailed off, her eyes sharpening as they focused on Navin.

Outside the earth thrummed with the sound of boots. Shouts rose in the air, one that distinctly sounded like Navin's name.

"Bastard," Roshan said.

23

He'd trapped her.

Conned her like the fool she was by finding a way to amplify his soul magic—maybe with an object he picked up while out with them? Or maybe with something else. Who knew? And who cared anymore?

As a child of four, Roshan had come across a wounded field crow in the forest near the clan's hideout. She'd not known much about healing then. Only that she wanted to help the bird and make it fly again. And then, before she knew what she was doing, life magic began pouring out of her, draining from her like blood, turning the whole world fuzzy and dark.

Colors and shapes swam before Roshan now as they had that day, a sour taste flooding her mouth. To think she'd begun feeling sorry for the spare prince. *Liking* him, even. She pinched the inside of her arm, her mind clearing from the pain, alert in a way it hadn't been for the past hour, maybe even in the past seventeen days.

Rapidly, she evaluated her options. She could use Navin as a shield, forcing the Brights to let them pass. But there was a risk of the prince doing soul magic again and trapping her further. Also, who knew how many Brights were waiting outside?

No. She was best off fighting alone at first and dispatching as many

Brights as possible. There *was* the risk of losing the prince to the other side, undoing her and the clan's efforts, but then . . . she shook her head.

She had to get out of this alive first.

Tremors snaked through the floor and the walls of the prayer house. "We know you're in there, witch!" a magically amplified voice boomed inside, pounding her eardrums.

Shera Aspa.

Instinctively, Roshan reached for the edge of her turban, grasping strands of her own hair.

You cannot be seen. Baba's old warning hammered her skull. *Nor recognized.*

As Navin watched, ashen with fear, Roshan held a glowing hand to her face, pinching her nose and mouth until her eyes watered. Shapeshifting her own features was difficult—especially without a looking glass. But already she could feel her nose curving, then her mouth stretching painfully as her lips thinned. She tugged at her hair, her scalp feeling like it were peeling off: a sign that her hair had turned color. Lightened to a dull brown.

She unsheathed her katar as the Brights began pouring in, their gold armor reflecting the lightorb, smarting her eyes. Four, five, ten. They instantly formed a semicircle of sorts, converging on her, forcing her to step back, farther and farther, until she hit the wall. Behind the Brights, she spotted two figures: Shera, gilded like his men, his long red hair and beard vivid even in the dark. Next to him stood Navin, his eyes trained on her.

He'd pay for this. How and when, she didn't know.

But first—she raised her dagger as one of the Brights bared his teeth—*let's break up this merry group.*

Ducking a spell that singed her elbow, Roshan spun sideways, her katar piercing the Bright at one end of the semicircle, his blood splattering her face. Ignoring his howls, she ducked another spell and spun again, her fingers pinching one Bright by the neck, using magic to immobilize him, right while her dagger sliced open the cheek of another.

It was hard. More brutal than any fight she'd been part of before. Her head, which still felt a little disoriented from being exposed to Navin's soul magic, began to ache, the pain climbing more rapidly than ants on a wall.

In the background, she heard Shera shouting instructions at his men. Telling them to corner her. They couldn't. Not even when four shot their atashbans at her at once. Nothing happened until a burly Bright pushed forward, a brute with shoulders as broad as an ox, parrying every one of her attacks until he managed to find her unprotected belly and bury a giant fist in it.

Her eyes watered. *Don't fall!* Once she was down, it would be much harder to fight back. On another day, she wouldn't have even considered using magic. But with no clan, no Lalit for backup, she had no choice.

She lunged at the Bright, hoping to take him by surprise and sink her burning fingers into his unprotected neck. It was a mistake. The man grabbed her by the hair, twisting her head sideways until something snapped. A bone? Maybe her spine. The world began fading at the edges. Roshan's bones screamed in agony, her body feeling like an open wound.

Stop, she thought she heard someone say. Maybe it was even her.

It was the last thing she'd remember as the big Bright kicked her in her face—over and over with his steel-toed boot—until blood poured from her mouth, and she finally lost consciousness.

FIRESTONES
AND FATHERS

The city of Prabha

DAY 1 of the Month of Tears
YEAR 40 of Queen Bhairavi's reign

24

Navin woke with a start.

Sweat soaked through his tunic, and he was gasping for air the way he often did after a nightmare. On instinct, he glanced sideways, expecting to see dark red hair, a bruised cheek. But the other side of his bed was empty, except for the unraveled ropes of his turban—a side that had remained empty ever since his return to Prabha from Ashvamaidan eight days ago.

Roshan—*the Shadow Bandit*, he corrected—was now awaiting trial in the towering lapis-and-sandstone bandikhana bordering central Prabha, a fortress so enchanted that no prisoner had been able to escape it for centuries.

To Navin's shock, his grandmother had enveloped him in a crushing embrace seconds after he entered the palace. It was perhaps the fourth time in nineteen years that she'd hugged him of her own accord. "Goddess be praised," she'd whispered in his ear. "Now we can celebrate instead of mourn."

Mourn? he'd wondered then—only to learn later that the queen, who'd been secretly working with Governor Yazad and Shera to rescue Navin, had also planned a contingency state funeral in case things didn't work out. There had been no plans to give in to the bandits' demands.

"Don't be unreasonable, brother," Farhad had told Navin yesterday, his voice taking on the forced calm it always did when Navin grew enraged. "The Aspas didn't even know if you were still alive. Those bandits could have done anything to you. Besides, Ashvamaidan valley makes up nearly a third of that whole province. The parasmani couldn't have simply conceded."

Perhaps not. Perhaps, when it came to political matters, Farhad was right. But it still didn't make Navin feel any better to know that his own grandmother had willingly wagered his life for a piece of land.

His mouth was raw now, soured by whatever concoction he'd used to drown his fury last night. Spiked maces pounded the inside of his skull: a sign that he'd, in a moment of sheer stupidity, decided to consume rang ras, a deceptively milky potion that a distant cousin had sneaked into the stuffy palace dinner in a jade bottle. The drink, used by scryers in Tej Forest to enhance their visions of the future, was also consumed by bored palace courtiers to escape their own tepid realities. And clearly, it had worked, for Navin no longer remembered what he'd done last night.

From the window, sounds began filtering in, temple bells and drums accompanied by chanting beyond the palace walls.

"From fire and ash, let her be born! From fire and ash, let her be born!"

High hell. He'd forgotten it was Hashtdin, an annual spring festival that spanned the first eight days of the Month of Tears. Any other day—or any other festival—Navin could have begged off attending. But Hashtdin commemorated the birth and rebirth of the fire goddess. Nothing short of death—or a kidnapping—would have been an acceptable excuse to ignore its rituals and prayers, which began as early as the sixth hour of the morning.

As if to punctuate this, three sharp knocks sounded on the door.

Navin groaned and clutched his head in his hands.

"Apologies, Rajkumar." A serving boy bowed. "The parasmani and yuvraj wish to see you before morning prayers."

Of course they did. His grandmother and brother both were alike in that sense. Always waking at the crack of dawn, without a servant's prompting. Navin forcibly scrubbed his eyes with his fists. "I'll be there in a moment, Sushil."

"The parasmani said not to leave you alone. Not after what happened last night."

Curses. Had he tapped out tabla rhythms on the Minister of Food's bald head again? Navin forced himself to think, but his memory was a blur of color and sound.

"She also asked you to drink this." Sushil held out a jade cup full of bubbling red potion that smelled of eucalyptus and what Navin suspected was freshly fed leeches. The palace hakim's morning brew. Designed to cure any hangovers—even if it did make Navin want to vomit.

His mouth still holding the medicine's rancid aftertaste, Navin slid off the bed, nearly falling off in his attempt. *Never again*, he promised, as Sushil guided him to the adjoining bathing chamber, where a pair of servants waited quietly with steaming, floral-scented buckets of water.

An hour later, his head no longer pounding as much, Navin stood before a giant looking glass in a soft blue undervest and scarlet trousers, clean-shaven, his black chin-length curls dyed a fresh red-brown. His black hair, his grandmother had once said, made him look too much like his "wastrel peri father."

With Sushil's help, he slid his arms through a diaphanous sapphire jama that was tied at the left shoulder and cinched at the waist with a red patka embroidered with fireblooms. Bloodred slippers made of velvet and a blue turban completed the outfit, along with pearl hoops, a matching necklace, and new bracelets of white jade to replace the amplifiers the bandits had stolen, copied perfectly by the palace jeweler, right down to the shackle-like feeling around Navin's wrists.

"Rajkumar, please," Sushil pleaded. "Only a small hint of the flames on your face and neck. It's inauspicious to go unpainted during Hashtdin."

"No, Sushil," Navin said, his voice patient but firm. The boy was new to the palace, having replaced Navin's former valet, and fairly young: only fourteen blue moons. His aura was also tangibly yellow with fear, which meant he was probably worried about getting into trouble with a supervisor. "Don't worry." Throat tingling with magic, his voice poured over Sushil like cool water down a parched throat. "You will not be blamed for it. I will take full responsibility."

The fear in Sushil's aura diminished, deepened to gray—relief.

A pair of sipahis detached like shadows from the walls as Navin left his suite: tall, pale-skinned mountain women who'd been following him everywhere ever since his return. He'd tried talking to them a couple of times, but the women mainly spoke Atashkohi, a dialect native to northern Jwala—one Navin now regretted not having paid attention to as a boy.

A memory surfaced: *You're like every other rich city brat who hasn't bothered to glance beyond his own nose.*

Navin pushed it aside.

He wasn't in Ashvamaidan now, but in Kiran Mahal. The parasmani's official residence in the capital, a palace built to resemble the sun, with a gilded central dome housing the throne room and seven long buildings that extended outward from it like rays, each designating a separate wing.

Navin's quarters lay in the Baag, a section named after the gardens surrounding it. The long passage outside his room occasionally opened to marble verandas on both sides, revealing verdant green or riotous orange from the firebloom and mango trees, the bamboo blinds rolled up to let in cool, rose-scented air that would flow through the rest of the palace through ancient, cleverly designed wind catchers within the walls.

The sipahis grew in number, stationed closer together as Navin's party approached the much larger Royal Wing, where the queen and the crown prince lived. The Baag's elegant but plain mahogany floors gave way to thick paisley carpets and gold-veined marble tiles. High-hanging torans made of volcanic glass beads glittered over every arched door, their wide, flat panels depicting everything from ancient human and Pashu wars to tranquil village scenes. Life-size paintings graced the walls—from Jwala's first monarch, Behram, on a flaming throne to its current ruler, Bhairavi, atop a gloriously caparisoned thoroughbred, the armored stallion's sable mane tamed into neatly spaced button braids along the neck.

As a child, Navin had not known that his grandmother had never ridden to war, that the painting was merely the product of an atelier. He'd spent hours studying Bhairavi's face, picking out parts of her features that most resembled his own: the thin, finely arched brows, the firm chin that gave them both a stern countenance when they didn't smile.

She wasn't smiling in the portrait. Unlike her more lavishly dressed predecessors, Bhairavi appeared almost austere, her hair in a single auburn plait down her back, her long jama and billowing trousers made of simple white muslin, embroidered at the hem with starblooms to reflect her northern mountain heritage. The ceremonial Jwaliyan taj circled her head: leaves of gold and iridescent indradhanush hammered and shaped to form the homāi's distinct, flame-like feathers, encrusted with shimmering red and white firestones.

Today, Bhairavi was seated behind a desk instead of on a horse. Her red hair, after thirty-five years, was streaked with bronze and held back with an embroidered dome cap made of red velvet. Painted yellow and red flames crept out of her hairline and onto the warm brown skin of her temples, but apart from that small festive concession to Hashtdin, the queen was garbed, as always, in the purest white.

"I'll be another moment," she said, still poring over a scroll, as Navin entered the room alone, his guards remaining outside.

Next to the queen, much like the crimson sunbirds that continually hovered beside the garden's ornamental banana flowers, stood Crown Prince Farhad, his sandalwood attar infusing the room. He was dressed identically to Navin, except for the upper part of his handsome face, which was painted over with flames yellow, red, and blue, as if he were wearing an elaborate mask.

His older brother grinned. "Shubh prabhat, little brother. You look well this morning."

Colors floated behind Farhad's head: blue for worry, purple for guilt.

Though they'd both inherited their magic from their late mother, normally, Navin wouldn't have been able to see his brother's aura. Soul magi were trained to hide their auras from other soul magi for their own protection—it was the first lesson they'd been taught at the palace. But Farhad was probably feeling bad about what he'd said last night. *Don't be unreasonable, brother.*

"Suprabhat." The morning greeting, spoken the Ashvamaidani way, slipped out before Navin could hold it in.

The queen looked up from the papers she was studying, her dark gaze pinning Navin in place. "Your face isn't painted," she said bluntly.

On another day, he would have apologized. Would have claimed to have forgotten and rushed to fix his face again.

"I didn't feel like it," Navin said with a shrug. From the corner of his eyes, he noted his brother stiffening. "Paint clogs my pores."

"Do you think this is funny?" Queen Bhairavi asked, her voice soft, deadlier for it. "Tradition does not care about your feelings. Nor do our people. Your brother and I have struggled as is to undo the damage your kidnapping has done."

Navin's throat tightened. Looked like his warm welcome was at an end. "What do you mean by damage? Getting kidnapped wasn't my fault."

"Parasmani ji—" Farhad began.

"Not your *fault?*" Bhairavi rose to her feet and leaned forward, making Navin automatically take a step back. "Not your fault that you consistently broke protocol for *years* to do whatever you pleased? Do you know how terrible it looks when one of the princes gets stolen away by provincial bandits—how badly it reflects on my reign? We must thank the goddess you are still here and not dead in a pool of your own vomit."

Neither prince dared to speak. Farhad had once equated a reprimand from the queen to having one's skin peeled off—and Navin couldn't find it more accurate than he did now.

Bhairavi straightened, folding her spectacles with a gentle *tap*. Her aura, as always, remained blank, every emotion carefully shielded behind a wall neither Navin nor her favorite, Farhad, had been able to breach.

"You will apologize to Minister Babita, whose sari you ruined last night with that pitcher of wine," she told Navin. "Also to poor Steward Dharmdev, who faced the brunt of your inebriated curses."

So that's what had happened. Navin felt bad about the minister, who'd always been kind to him. Old Decorum Dharmdev, on the other hand, could go fly a kite. Navin had little sympathy for the man—especially after years of his snide remarks, the taunts that had been made to humiliate Navin whenever he got the chance.

"Yes, Parasmani ji," Navin said.

She frowned, likely not appreciating the flat tone of his voice. But she didn't say anything else.

Navin followed the queen and Farhad out into the hall, and their retinue of guards trailed them down the stairs leading to the grounds and into the palace temple. His head pressed against the marble floor of the sanctum, Navin was reminded briefly of another temple in the village of Alipore, of a girl bleeding onto its floor.

"Navin," a voice murmured. Farhad. "Do you need more time?"

He rose to his feet again, curbing the tremors that threatened to overtake his limbs.

"What's wrong?" Farhad asked, staring at him.

"Nothing. I'm fine."

Bhairavi, whose magical gifts included truth seeking, would have instantly caught the lie if she was touching Navin. But the queen was holding on to Farhad's arm. Her cold eyes assessed Navin, as if testing him for weakness. Navin couldn't let it show. Not to her. Not even to his brother, who clearly appeared worried.

Later, they stood on the viewing balcony at Kiran Mahal, a perfect little family of three, clothes smelling of sandalwood, foreheads marked with ash, palms joined in greeting before a crowd of over ten thousand citizens gathered outside the palace since dawn, a sea of fiery faces painted in different hues of red, yellow, and blue.

"It's a nice, clear day, isn't it?" Bhairavi said, addressing Farhad.

"Better than last year, when everyone was soaked to the skin," Farhad agreed.

Navin said nothing. Celebrating a festival of fire during a month known for its monsoons was always a challenge. But Jwala was a stickler for tradition where the fire goddess was concerned. Navin spotted several colorful umbrellas and glowing blue deflector shields in the crowd—though rainfall didn't appear likely today.

The queen addressed the crowd, her voice amplified with magic: "From fire and ash, let her be born!"

The high, reedy pitch of the shehnais, expertly played by palace musicians stationed under the balcony, mingled with the drumming of dhols. The crowd erupted into cheers that vibrated the tiles under Navin's feet.

"With blessings from the fire goddess, we stand before you today—two more generations that will continue the legacy of Jwala's first king, Behram."

More cheers from the crowd, though this time, they were accompanied by a chant that slowly grew in volume: "Raj-kumar Navin! Raj-kumar Navin!"

Navin stilled. Was he dreaming? Or was the rang ras still messing with his head?

He pinched his arm—hard enough to leave a bruise.

It was no dream. The crowd continued its chants throughout the queen's droning speech, refusing to shut down, even when sipahis fired warning shots in the air with their atashbans.

"Looks like you're rather popular, little brother," Farhad murmured. "Maybe I should get kidnapped the next time."

Navin frowned. Was Farhad serious? Without seeing his aura, he couldn't tell if his brother was annoyed or merely amused.

"Maybe you should," Navin replied. "Maybe you, too, will then wake up each night feeling like you can't breathe. Like you're still trapped underground."

Farhad's mouth opened. Closed.

The smile on Navin's lips tasted bitter. What did he expect? An apology from Jwala's perfect crown prince?

He turned and waved at the crowd, whose cheers grew louder.

"What are you doing?" Farhad's whisper grew harsh. "The parasmani is still speaking."

She was. And, from the way her back had stiffened, it was clear she was furious.

But for once, Navin didn't care. He might be expendable to his grandmother. Might not mean much once Farhad took the throne. But to the people of Jwala, Navin still meant something. A banner unfurled at the back of the crowd: WELCOME HOME, NAVIN. OUR PERI PRINCE.

"Don't be unreasonable, brother," Navin replied. His smile widened, and he blew a kiss in the banner's general direction. "I'm merely acknowledging our people."

25

THE CROWD'S EBULLIENCE BUOYED NAVIN THROUGH THE REST
of the morning. Through the tongue-lashing his grandmother gave
him for "usurping the royal address," through the brief, uncomfortable
lunch, and through the long-winded prayers that swallowed the rest of
the afternoon in the palace temple. By sunset, Navin's shoulders were
sagging again, his body nearly as drained as it would have been after a
long trek in the ravines. He'd forgotten how exhausting it was to smile
constantly, to put on a perpetual front before the courtiers, and to match
them wit for barbed wit.

Was *this* the life he'd missed in captivity? His mouth watered already
for another drink. Something that numbed him to his surroundings—
though perhaps not as potent as rang ras.

Navin was so tired that he didn't even argue when Sushil adorned
his face with blue and yellow flames to match his dinner outfit: a bro-
caded ochre jama and trousers and a midnight-blue turban festooned
with strings of golden seed pearls.

The first Hashtdin dinner was held in the palace gardens, bedecked
with hundreds of floating lightorbs. Appetizers floated by on trays for
the hundred or so guests to partake in—cubes of freshly caught rawas
grilled to a char, fried turnip bhajias, and zardalu balls in firebloom

syrup. Children gathered by the fountain, splashing water that changed to reflect the sunset or the night sky with a touch.

Nearby, a musician played the sitar on a small stage, an elderly woman in a pale green jama, her entire being captured by the evening raag. Navin stood watching her for long moments, wondering what it would be like to submit to music like this again—without a care for the world, without being reminded each time of everything he'd done wrong.

What you did in that temple for Jaya was the exact opposite of what you did when you were nine.

The voice echoed through Navin's head even as he forced himself to focus on the song. A moment later, he sensed a presence by his side. One fragranced with sandalwood and vetiver.

"I miss seeing you play the sitar like this," Farhad said quietly. "And sing, of course."

"I played the tanpura," Navin corrected after a pause. Maybe it was petty, but he was still annoyed by Farhad's comment on the balcony earlier. "It has only four strings and is used to accompany singers and musicians. A sitar has frets and more strings." *And it could be played on its own.*

"I see."

A pause as the musician completed her piece. The princes clapped, their applause sending a silver rush of pleasure through the old lady's aura. Navin was about to turn away when Farhad caught hold of his arm.

"Navin," he whispered. "Please talk to me."

Tempted as he was to ignore Farhad, Navin was also aware of the gazes on them right now. If he walked away, there would be even more whispers of "new tensions" between the crown prince and his "peri brother." The *Jwala Khabri* would have a field day with that.

"What's there to talk about?" he asked.

"I want to apologize." Midnight wisps of his aura curled around Farhad's gold turban. "What I said on the balcony was reprehensible. Please. Forgive me, little brother."

Navin's insides contracted. This was the second time that day his brother had let him see his aura. His truth. He faced the musician again, who was beginning another song.

"The last time I sang was in the badlands," he said quietly. "It was the only way I could do magic without my amplifiers."

"What? Are you sure?"

"Either that or the Shadow Bandit was far too gullible." And Navin doubted that was the case.

Farhad frowned. "I wrote to your father, you know," he said. "When you were kidnapped. He wrote back, wanting to know if he could help."

A curse rose to Navin's lips. He bit his tongue. "What do you mean you wrote to him?" *And that he wrote back?*

"News about your abduction was spreading everywhere—even to kingdoms outside Jwala. It was better he found out from me than another source. Don't glare at me that way, Nav. If something like this had happened to me and my father were still alive, I'd want him to know."

"Well, mine *did* know, according to you. And he didn't do anything." Navin wondered why that continued to hurt him.

"That was because the parasmani refused his help." Farhad glanced both ways to make sure no one was listening. "She said she didn't want the peri flying all over Jwala. It would equate to external interference in our domestic affairs. She was furious that I wrote to him. Navin? *Navin!*"

But Navin didn't want to listen anymore. Didn't want any more explanations about his grandmother, his father, or his so-called *family*. Farhad's voice faded from his ears. Everything faded, except for the tinkle of jade and rock crystal goblets magically floating on trays around the guests, filled to the brim with spiced wine. Navin picked up one and downed the drink in a few gulps. Throat burning, he passed the empty goblet to a serving boy, reached out a hand to lift another.

"Trying to upstage the rest of us again, are you, Peri Prince?" someone said.

Navin spun around, ready with a cutting retort when he recognized the grinning face under the wild swirls of red and blue paint. Shera. Appearing like an unexpected blessing at the end of a prayer.

Navin exhaled. "You're here," he said.

"Where else would I be?" His friend lightly punched his shoulder. A cloud of silver aura floated around his black brocade turban and long red curls. "It's Hashtdin, remember?"

Hashtdin, when they'd pretend to be good for the day, then feast and drink away the nights, finding girls, boys, and taverns to slip off to in secret, when the stars came out. Behind Shera, he spotted a pair of ministers talking to Queen Bhairavi and Farhad. His brother was still glancing at Navin from time to time, trying to catch his eye.

The knot in Navin's throat tightened. "Can we get out of here?" he whispered.

Shera laughed. "What? The party's too tame for you?"

More like it was too much.

But Navin wasn't in the mood for the gaming tables or pleasure houses his outings with Shera usually entailed. "I . . . need air."

The best part about Shera Aspa was that he knew Navin well enough to not ask any questions. Even though a shade of blue entered his aura. Worry.

"Premchand's a few miles from here," he said simply. "It's quiet and the owner's pretty discreet. Serves an excellent firebloom madira, too. What about the parasmani? Will she be comfortable letting you go out so soon?"

She'll be glad to see the back of me after this morning. But Navin didn't say the words.

He gestured to his guards, waiting a few paces behind him in the garden. "Don't think she cares as long as *they're* with me."

"All right, then." Shera grinned. "Let's go."

THE FIREWORKS HAD BEGUN BY THE TIME THEIR CARRIAGES pulled up to Premchand's, a small inn on a hill, away from the bustle of central Prabha. The proprietor was Pashu—a yima named Saam Premchand, his bulk squeezed into a small chair behind the reception desk. He raised his horned head, taking in Navin and Shera with a single glance.

"Please follow me," Saam murmured with a bow before either man could say a word. A long tail peeked out from under his jama as he walked ahead, cut cleverly by a tailor to accommodate the human and bovine parts of his large form. "We will ensure that you are not disturbed by anyone."

A door slid open to reveal two large beds, a sitting and eating area, and thick silk drapes to close over large windows that gave them a view of the sparklers bursting over the palace's giant golden dome.

Some of the tension left Navin's body. Behind him, he could hear Shera whispering to a servant along with the tinkle of coins. When he turned around, he saw that the low table by the sitting area had been set with food: a fragrant vegetable pulao, steamed pomfret encased in banana leaf jackets, a saag of fresh green riverweed and crumbly paneer accompanied by folded squares of muslin-thin roomali roti.

Navin's eyes widened. "How come we've never been to this place?" He ripped open the banana leaf, digging into the pomfret with his hands.

"It's more my father's style, that's why," Shera remarked dryly. "He comes here whenever he has business matters to deal with. Of course, tonight, he couldn't be here. Laleh beckoned," he added bitterly.

Navin felt a twinge of guilt. He'd forgotten that Shera's sister had died sometime during Hashtdin. It was why Governor Yazad never celebrated the festival, why he remained, according to Shera, cloistered in his haveli in Ashvamaidan, mourning before a framed painting of his favorite child.

Navin handed Shera one of the goblets of bloodred firebloom madira from the northern mountains. "To friendship," he said.

Shera's lips curved slightly under his beard. "To friendship."

By the third cup, Navin was feeling a pleasant buzz, the sort that accompanied a particularly excellent wine.

"How about this?" Shera withdrew a small, familiar-looking jade bottle from his pocket. "Bought it off one of your cousins. Guaranteed oblivion."

Navin snorted. "The remedy for that is ten times worse. I'll pass."

"Don't go old on me now, bastard."

But ultimately it was only Shera who emptied the contents of the rang ras in his glass. A part of Navin—the one that had always envied Shera's tolerance of liquor and most intoxicants—itched to join him. But he was still a little nauseated from last night's escapade and contented himself by watching Shera down the rang ras and a whole bottle of the firebloom madira. Shera's stories—about hunting shadowlynx in the kingdom of Ambar and bedding mermaids in Samudra—grew wilder with each peg, his aura a gleeful silver.

They moved onto one of the beds, lying flat on the mattress, watching the ceiling that mirrored the night sky.

"Aye." Shera poked Navin in the ribs. "Want to hear a secret?"

Navin smiled lazily. His liquor-induced buzz, though fainter, was still there. "Why not?"

"Wait." Shera sat up slowly and withdrew a necklace from inside his jama, holding it up to the light. Between four gold claws, a roughly hewn pendant hung. Uncut, the firestone would have looked like little more than a brown rock, if not for the nicks on its surface, revealing parts of its gleaming yellow facets, its magic glowing within like an ember. "Guess where I found this."

Navin blinked rapidly. "That's . . . that's a—"

"Firestone," Shera confirmed, his voice slurring slightly. "From Ashvamaidan, no less."

They found the girl out near the old firestone mine.

No, Navin told himself. There had to be another explanation. Aloud he said: "That must've been excavated centuries ago."

Shera giggled, a sound Navin was certain he'd never heard his friend make before. "Try two weeks ago."

Pain shafted through Navin's jaw. On a hunch, he did something he'd never done with Shera before. "Tell me the truth about the firestone," he commanded, magic both warm and prickly on his tongue.

There was a pause as Shera's aura shifted, its hammered silver hue changing to ebony. He yawned. "My father found the first one twenty-five years ago," he said. "It was in Alipore—the abandoned mine there. He figured there might be more mines, but most were underground and overlaid with villages." Another yawn.

"What did the subedar do?"

"He tried to buy the farmers out initially. They wouldn't agree, the bastards. They wanted more coin. So eventually, with the queen's permission, my father introduced the blood tithes. That was when things began to cha . . . ange . . ."

"There were a pair of girls," Navin urged, forcing his words through the sleep-induced fog surrounding the other man. "From Alipore. What happened to them? Were they in the mines?"

"Stupid w-witches," Shera sputtered. "Thought they could outsmart us. Steal . . . steal from us. We showed them. We . . . showed . . ."

A thud followed as Shera fell on the bed, snores emerging from his fluttering mouth.

Carefully, Navin slid off, his bare feet sinking into the grassy rug. His mouth was sore from having accidentally bitten a blister on his cheek. But his stomach felt worse. As if every bit of his dinner was going to expel itself from his body.

Shera wasn't a truth seeker like Queen Bhairavi. Nor a soul magus like Farhad. Yet, somehow, for all these years, he'd managed to keep parts of his emotions hidden—a partial shielding of sorts that other magic wielders could learn against the influence of soul magi, if they tried hard enough.

Moreover, this much was certain: Roshan Chaya hadn't been lying about the blood tithes. It was also clear that Governor Yazad was forcing the farmers off their land to excavate it for firestones.

Did his grandmother know about the mine in Alipore? Did Farhad? Navin wasn't sure. Shera had asserted that the queen knew about the blood tithes, but no one had spoken of them to Navin. No one except the girl now caged in Prabha's central prison and her marauding clan.

The room spun. Navin took deep breaths, steadying himself.

Roshan had kidnapped him, had held him captive for seventeen days. She was a thief, a murderer who'd been on the lam for most of her life.

But . . . she wasn't a liar.

She'd told him the truth about Ashvamaidan's badlands. She'd committed crimes, yes, but she'd done them for her clan. For villagers like Dinamai, Sultana Bibi, Ervad Faridun, and Jaya. For young children who edged the brink of death.

No, Roshan Chaya was no hero. Yet she wasn't exactly a villain, either.

Navin found his guards dozing outside the room.

He cleared his throat. Almost instantly, the women straightened, red flushing the tops of their pale cheekbones. "Rajkumar," they murmured.

"I need to go somewhere," Navin told them. "With discretion. No one must find out."

"Ji, Rajkumar." Their auras were clear of any deception. "Are we not going back to Kiran Mahal?" one of them asked in halting Paras.

"Not yet." Navin handed her the unraveled cloth of his turban. "First, we need to make a stop."

26

THE WARDERS WERE FLAYING SOMEONE ELSE TONIGHT. MORE specifically the prisoner in the cell across from Roshan's. They'd brought the unfortunate soul into the bandikhana earlier this morning, when Roshan had dozed off on the floor, her body only partially healed from the injuries the Brights had given her eight days ago. Instinctively, she reached out a hand to touch her firebloom amulet, pain stretching the tendons in her arm until she remembered it was gone. The amplifier that had been with her since she was a newborn—taken away by the prison guards—along with Baba's red jama and every other bit of clothing she possessed. The spare prince's teak ring was gone, too, the warders having ripped it off her thumb, leaving behind a scar. The prison hakim, who'd come into the cell later to examine her injuries, had simply declared that Roshan was "still alive."

Alive in time for today—her nineteenth birthday, not that Roshan had cared for birthdays. Alive like the other bruised and broken convicts on the floors below her, her gray prison jama stained with a former prisoner's blood. From eavesdropping on the guards, Roshan deciphered that she was on the bandikhana's eighth floor—one that housed the kingdom's most dangerous prisoners. She sensed it, too, from the confinement barriers around her cell, a sly and ancient magic that turned her dizzy whenever she got too close to the mottled stone walls.

Prabha's central prison was designed to heighten claustrophobia. To turn its prisoners into husks of their former selves.

Roshan rubbed the scar on her right thumb. It reminded her of the spare prince: why she was imprisoned here. And why she needed to break out. However, without a proper amplifier, she didn't know how she'd manage it. Most of her wounds still remained unhealed. Her poor recovery could also be attributed to the prison diet: a bowl of watery rice slid twice daily in her cell. If this went on, Roshan vowed, she'd catch one of the rats that bit her during the nights. Eat it raw if she had to.

"Stupid cat!" The warder's voice was like a whip against the ears. "Making me miss the fireworks on the first day of Hashtdin. Tell me now! Who's making you those permits?"

"What'd you think?" his companion asked, a leer entering his voice. "Do its lower bits work like a woman's, too?"

"If it doesn't fess up, we might have to check and see." Another crack, this time followed by a yowl that pierced the air.

Roshan's insides curdled. She had kept quiet ever since she'd been brought to prison. Had done as little as possible to draw attention from the warders. Yet whatever they were planning with this prisoner smelled fouler than the excrement bucket in her cell. Shoving aside her nausea, Roshan forced a laugh. A loud, hoarse cackle that echoed in her cell and the empty corridor beyond her barrier. The movement sent stings up her arms from the glowing blue shackles on her wrists.

"Aye!" One of the warders in the other cell shouted after a moment. "You! Shut it!"

But Roshan kept laughing, growing louder and more hysterical, until they exited the other cell and entered hers.

"Shut!" The first warder shouted, peeling away the flesh from her back with a whip. "Up!"

Roshan's laughs devolved into screams. "Baba!" she wailed. "I want my baba back! Please, brother! Take me to him!" She tried to clutch the second warder by his knees but was thrown back with a kick.

"Goddess's hair! This one should've gone to the madhouse," he muttered. "Screw it. Let's go up to see the fireworks as you said. We'll interrogate the wretched cat tomorrow."

The cell door rolled shut. What felt like hours passed by. When Roshan finally managed to sit up, she noticed that the other prisoner was sitting up. Staring right at her with large pale-green eyes that gleamed like seaglass in the torchlight.

Above the eyes were pointed gray ears and below, whiskers sprouting from furry gray cheeks. The catlike chin tapered to a smooth, human neck and bruised brown shoulders, the curve of a breast partly hidden by a long, ragged blue tunic. The prisoner was a bidaal—a Pashu who was both human and feline. Roshan had seen other bidaals on secret jaunts to the black market near Surag sometimes, usually dressed in long robes and saris, scrying the future with cowrie shells, while also secretly relieving wealthy merchants of their coin. This bidaal had been badly beaten, bruises blooming on her shins and swollen toes.

"Silly girl," she told Roshan now, her voice somewhere between a growl and a purr. "Just as I was about to sink my teeth into that soft, meaty flesh. The other one wasn't bad, either. A little lean, perhaps, but with the right amount of chew." She licked her lips, revealing yellow katar-sharp canines.

Well, fire and ashes.

"I'll remember to ignore you the next time," Roshan said dryly. She pressed her hand to her shoulder, where a whip scar burned. The glow on her body was dim. A false platitude of a magic that would not heal—not that Roshan hadn't tried.

The bidaal tilted her head to one side, a gleam of recognition dawning in those green eyes. "You're the Shadow Bandit," she stated. "The one who kidnapped the Peri Prince. Your face looks different from the one they published in the news scrolls, though. A veiling spell, I presume?"

Roshan stiffened. She glanced to her left, where a gap between the bars gave her a view of the far end of the corridor. A pair of night guards lounged against the walls, talking to each other. Too far off to hear any quiet conversation.

"I take it you disapprove?" she asked the other prisoner coolly.

"On the contrary, I'm indifferent." The bidaal's small, sharp teeth flashed in the damp light. "We may both be Pashu, but my kind don't get along with the peri. We bidaal have always had a taste for feathered and scaled things."

Human, too. Suddenly Roshan was very glad for the bars and barriers surrounding them.

"Don't worry, girl." The bidaal let out a purr. "You took a beating for me. Unnecessary as it was, the least I can do is not eat you."

Roshan got the sense the bidaal wasn't joking.

"What brought you here, uh . . ." Roshan's voice trailed off. "Sorry. I don't know your name."

"I am called Kamal. I was caught peddling prophecies with a fake permit." Another one of those purring sounds. One that sounded rather satisfied. "I decided to make the best of the situation by making one or both of those guards my snack." She licked her lips again. "Eating humans can be so satisfying after a long day of their badgering you for their fortunes, you know?"

Roshan paused, unsure how to respond to this unsettling bit of information, when the door at the end of the hallway squealed open, voices filling it.

"... can't let anyone go there!" one of the guards was protesting. They crowded the entrance, and Roshan couldn't see whom they were talking to.

But then she heard the voice. One that sounded like music. A voice that crawled up her skin and made her heart simultaneously sigh.

What was that silver-tongued bastard doing here? And why was *she* bristling?

"I ... no ... yes, Rajkumar." The guard's voice wavered from belligerent to suddenly accommodating. "Of course. Please go ahead. She's in one of the cells at the very end."

It took a few moments for the spare prince to get to her, even longer to spot her crouched in her cell, next to the iron bars. It gave Roshan enough time to see that he was dressed for Hashtdin, his broad shoulders nearly filling up the doorway, his vibrant jama brightening the gold of his eyes. Two female sipahis stood guard behind him and coldly assessed Roshan.

"Roshan?" The prince approached her cell cautiously. "Is that you?"

He was the first and closest thing she'd had to a mirror these past few days: the flash of horror on his face confirming what her own looked like.

He reached out to brush a hand against the bars and jolted back in surprise. The bars had turned blue like the shackles on Roshan's wrists—the shackles Navin had worn himself in captivity.

"Come here to laugh?" she forced herself to drawl, mocking his usual tone.

He was staring at her swollen mouth. He didn't mock her back. When he turned to look at Kamal, his back stiffened even more.

"Are there no healers here?" he asked, his voice sharper than she'd heard it before. From somewhere behind the prince's forbidding sipahis, the prison guard mumbled an excuse.

"Once I'm gone, make sure a hakim comes by these cells and heals these prisoners appropriately." Navin's voice took on a resonance that made Roshan's skin prickle.

"Yes, Rajkumar." The guard sounded uncharacteristically docile. "I'll put in those orders at once."

Roshan's head throbbed, reminding her of the pain that had forced its way into her skull when Navin had used soul magic on her. He was doing it again now—but for once, she didn't want to stop him. She didn't know what game he was playing, but healing would definitely help her regain her energy. Maybe even allow her to break out of here.

Once the guard was gone, Navin faced Roshan again. Torchlight danced across his painted face.

"I spoke to Shera Aspa a couple of hours ago," he said. "He confessed to me that there were firestone mines in Ashvamaidan. It's why his father is buying out the land from the villagers. He also confirmed the existence of the blood tithes."

Surprise, she wanted to say sarcastically. But pain jolted through her injured shoulder and for a long moment she couldn't speak.

"He had a firestone around his neck," the prince went on. She heard him swallow. "I saw it." He paused, as if hoping for an answer.

She didn't give him one. To be fair, she hadn't known about the firestone mines—even though the existence of an active mine could explain some of the things that were happening. Considering how rare—and coveted—firestones were, the subedar would earn ten times more for excavating and selling them than he did generating tithe revenue from the farmers. What puzzled her were the badlands themselves and why they were expanding so rapidly. Though this wasn't something she was going to share out loud.

"Shera might have mentioned Jaya. That girl from Alipore." Navin's comment took Roshan by surprise. "While I was in the village, I overheard a couple of people talking. They said she was found by an abandoned firestone mine nearby. That she'd seen something she shouldn't have. Maybe . . . maybe she saw the mining? Or the gems?"

Roshan hadn't intended to speak. But the memory of Jaya and her pain made the words bubble out hot and dark like pitch:

"So it took an innocent losing her sight to make the spare prince of Jwala discover his own?"

The prince winced. She expected him to defend himself. But instead, he said: "I was wrong. About you. About many things. I'll make things right. I promise."

Roshan stared at him for a long moment, then gestured for him to come close, waiting until he was crouched the way she was, his face only breaths away from her own. The lines around his irises were so clear she could count them, along with the individual shades of amber and yellow that made up the gold.

She spat, a wad of blood and saliva sliding down the invisible barrier that kept her confined to her cage as if it were no more than a pane of glass.

"This," she said, "is what I think of you and your promises, Rajkumar."

"I WOULD NOT HAVE DONE THAT," A SOFT VOICE SAID ABOUT AN hour after Navin was gone.

It was Kamal, her green eyes twinkling at Roshan through the bars. "He sounded sincere to me," the bidaal continued.

"He's good at sounding sincere," Roshan said dismissively.

"Not to me. I am Pashu," Kamal elaborated when Roshan looked at her askance. "Our kind cannot deceive one another as easily as we can humans. You helped me today, Shadow Bandit, so let me help you. To know a Pashu's truths, you need only look into their eyes. They are the clearest then, every line and curve around the pupils visible."

Roshan's stomach flipped. "You're lying."

"Why would I have need to lie?" The bidaal's eyes were so clear that Roshan could, indeed, see the rays of her irises, the starburst of pale yellow around dark, elliptical centers. "I owe the rajkumar nothing. Rumor suggests that he dislikes, even denies, his Pashu heritage. I don't know how true that is, but—"

"It's not." The truth slipped out before Roshan could bite it back.

Kamal watched her for a moment, but Roshan didn't elaborate.

"Even if he did," the bidaal went on, her voice gentling, "I don't blame him. Some Pashu may live among humans. May even birth children with them. But many of your kind still see us as animals, not people."

A pang went through Roshan. It was true. The Pashu might be powerful as far as their magic was concerned, but the years had not diminished human prejudice against them—even though Roshan, herself, didn't agree with it. For a moment, she wondered if that was part of the reason Queen Bhairavi had been so furious with her daughter's decision to give birth to Navin, why despite being his grandmother, she'd been so reluctant to negotiate with the Shadow Clan for the prince's release.

Footsteps sounded in the corridor. A guard followed a small, diminutive figure, whose flat, white turban looked like a beacon in the torchlight. The scent of herbs and something astringent stung Roshan's nostrils as they paused before her cell. A badge shaped like a mortar and pestle was pinned to the man's blue jama, a thick white satchel hanging from one shoulder. His eyes, unlike those of the prison guard, were kind.

"Hakim Kersi of Clan Nusserwan," the man announced. "Here to heal the prisoners by order of the rajkumar."

27

"WHAT IS IT?"

The queen murmured the words, barely glancing up from the scroll she was reading the next morning. That Navin was up and in her study before the sixth temple bell, perfectly attired for the second day of Hashtdin, face paint included, was entirely wasted on her. It didn't help his frayed nerves that Farhad was there, too, looking twice as fresh.

"I want to talk to you about Subedar Yazad Aspa," Navin began his carefully rehearsed speech. "About what he's doing in Ashvamaidan. Did you know he's imposed blood tithes on the villagers? More recently, I learned there were still firestone mines in—"

"Is there," Queen Bhairavi interrupted, "a point to this?"

Her expression reminded Navin of a time last year, when he had, in an effort to impress her, put forth a proposal to improve her security. After months of research, Navin had suggested the purchase of new atashbans for the royal sipahis or—at least—stabilizing their old Lohar-era atashbans by tipping the arrows with white marble. New or improved weapons, Navin had asserted, would help the queen's soldiers protect her better.

At the end, though, Queen Bhairavi had only stared at him before tossing his report aside. "Please," she'd said coldly. "Don't waste my time again on such trivial matters."

Navin suspected—no, he *knew*—she wouldn't have been so dismissive if the idea was Farhad's. It should have been easy to hate his brother for being crown prince, for being so irritatingly perfect. But it wasn't. Not since Navin was four and Farhad nine, when the latter falsely took the blame and punishment for imprinting muddy fingers over an expensive tapestry in the palace. For each time he'd tried to protect Navin in the years that followed.

He could feel Farhad watching them now from behind his own table in the corner of the study, silence having replaced the rustling of parchment.

Navin steadied himself. "I understand you're angry about what happened yesterday, Parasmani ji—and rightfully so. I am deeply sorry for my behavior and I cannot express how much I regret it. But this is important. Last night, under the influence of rang ras, Shera Aspa told me that his father—"

"Anything spoken under the influence of rang ras is pointless, Grandson," Bhairavi said coldly. She held her body straight, its every line taut with irritation. "Farhad. Deal with this, please. I've much to do before afternoon prayers."

This. As if Navin were not even a person, let alone the grandson she'd called him.

Fury rose, as sharp as ice on his tongue. "If you'd only *listen*—" he began, when the parasmani snapped her fingers. A buzzing sound filled Navin's ears, the shock of being blocked by the sound barrier so intense that it did silence him.

"Come on," Farhad's voice was soft. Under the festive face paint, his face was ashen. "We need to talk."

Still numbed by what had just happened in the study, Navin followed the crown prince out into the hall and farther ahead to a large suite of rooms.

Farhad's private quarters were decorated much like Navin's: a large four-poster bed with mosquito netting and curtains, deep wood furniture, and thick paisley rugs. The only exception was the homāi embroidered on the linens and engraved over the bed frame, the word *Jwalaratan* etched beneath in Paras.

"She *silenced* me!" Navin's voice was loud in the quiet room. "She threw up a cursed sound barrier! On her grandson!"

"Leave us," Farhad commanded, which was when Navin grew aware of a serving girl still in the room, polishing the side table. Next to her stood Navin's new valet, Sushil, his face and aura flushed with guilt.

"Apologies, Yuvraj." They both exited rapidly, closing the door behind them.

Farhad turned to Navin. His aura, a surprise yesterday, felt like a rebuke this morning, with its shades of blue, green, and red—like an ocean tossed with blood.

"Now," he said, voice outwardly calm. "Say whatever you need to first. Start at the beginning."

Navin did, first recalling his kidnapping by the Shadow Clan, Roshan Chaya's seemingly outrageous claims about Governor Yazad and his blood tithes. Then he talked about the badlands, the quake that formed gullies before his eyes, the destitution of Ashvamaidan's remaining villages, the deaths, the terrible injuries.

"I didn't believe Roshan," he said tightly. "I didn't *want* to believe her.

But she was right. About everything. Last night, Shera told me that there's an active firestone mine near—"

"Alipore. Yes, we know," Farhad said, stunning Navin into silence.

There was a tinge of sadness, even pity, in the crown prince's smile. "The parasmani knows, too. We've known for a long time now."

For several moments, Navin couldn't speak. Couldn't process what he'd just been told.

"You knew?" he whispered. Then, his voice rising: "You *knew* the subedar was torturing those villagers?"

Farhad's face remained expressionless. The red in his aura deepened. "It's not as simple as you think."

"What's complicated about protecting your own people from starvation?" Navin demanded. No wonder Roshan and the Shadow Clan had resorted to banditry, kidnapping, and murder. What choice did they have in the face of this?

"Our grandmother is parasmani of Jwala," Navin continued. "Why can she not remove Subedar Yazad from governing the province?"

"The subedar remits the palace our required share of land tithes exactly on time. Also, the subah of Ashvamaidan was promised to the Aspas by the first king himself. You cannot simply remove Subedar Yazad from his ancestral land."

"So because our treasury is sufficiently full, we must avert our gazes from everything else?"

Navin couldn't believe he was talking to Farhad. Upright, uptight Farhad, whom Navin had often, derisively, called too noble for his own good. "Surely exceptions are made if the people of a subah are being oppressed! The subedar's job is to govern them, not crush them under his heel. Also, *you're* the yuvraj of Jwala. Where's *your* sense of justice?"

"The yuvraj doesn't have the powers of a monarch," Farhad retorted. "You know this as well as I do. I can advise the parasmani on policy, occasionally influence her decisions—"

"So why not do the same for Ashvamaidan? Why not suck up to her the way you have your whole life for everything else?"

"Because I *can't!*" Farhad shouted.

Silence. Navin stared at his brother's face, the scarlet cloud around it. He couldn't remember the last time Farhad had lost his temper like this.

Farhad exhaled now, exerting that same rigid control over every muscle that had grown tense over the past few minutes, his aura deepening to a soft brown. Mostly. Traces of red still lingered. Along with purple. Guilt.

"When I was made yuvraj four years ago, I tried to bring about some land reforms for the tribes in the forests of the southern provinces," Farhad said. "They're mostly non-magi who live off the land—simple people with simple lives. But their home is now being encroached upon by magi city dwellers in the south. I wanted to stop that. To give the non-magi their forests back. Our grandmother told me in no uncertain terms that if I tried anything, there would be a revolt against us."

"What do you mean, a revolt?"

"Did you pay no attention to our tutors during history lessons?" Farhad asked, sounding more weary than sharp. "Think, brother. Why does Subedar Yazad have so much power over Ashvamaidan? Why can the subedar of the southern province do much the same? Years before we were born, Jwala was impoverished. There was a threat of rebellion against the parasmani by our kingdom's most powerful provincial governors, who had their own armies. Guess which provinces these were."

"Ashvamaidan and Dakkin," Navin said slowly, realization sinking in.

"Exactly. The governors of those provinces promised the parasmani that she would hold her throne as long as they supported her—and as long as she never interfered in their provincial matters."

Navin's knees trembled. He walked over to the bed and plopped down on it. Farhad sat next to him, his weight sinking into the mattress with a soft hiss.

"The parasmani would need strong reasons to launch any investigation into Yazad Aspa's activities. Perhaps she could be swayed by a protest by Ashvamaidan's farmers that also garnered attention and sympathy from the rest of Jwala. Or we would need irrefutable proof that the subedar was engaged in criminal activity. Like a murder."

"Or making bone demons?" Navin asked quietly.

"Bone demons don't exist anymore."

"What if I told you they did? That I saw them?"

Farhad stared at him, his aura turning blue with confusion and worry. Navin's heart sank. The terrible part was that he couldn't even blame his brother. Had Navin not been nearly killed by them in the Maw, he wouldn't have believed bone demons existed, either.

"There is nothing I can do, brother," the crown prince said. "Nor the parasmani. Not against one of her strongest allies. I'm surprised, in fact, by your vehemence at wanting an investigation. Whatever his flaws,

Shera is your best friend. He risked life and limb to rescue you. Instead, you're defending the bandits and their actions?"

Navin swallowed. Was he being ungrateful to Shera? Perhaps. But then ...

He thought back to Sultana Bibi in Jyoti. Her eyes reduced to sockets, allegedly taken by the Brights. He thought of Jaya, who'd lost both sight and speech, her injuries eerily similar.

Yes, Farhad was right. Shera had risked himself to rescue Navin.

But Roshan, too, had risked herself. For her clan, for the villagers, many of whom were strangers. She risked herself every time she healed someone, her magic making her break out in a sweat, or even making her collapse. His mouth still sore from last night's blisters, Navin gained a new understanding of the sacrifice it took. The enormous heart it required.

"You're saying that because Shera is my friend, I ought to treat him differently," Navin said at last. "You want me to evaluate him by a different standard than I would Roshan Chaya or anyone else who committed a similar crime."

"Navin, you don't even know if Shera did any of these awful things!"

He could have. The thought had kept Navin up the whole of last night and made his insides curdle now. "The villagers insinuate that the Brights were involved in brutally injuring a young girl and her sister's disappearance. Shera *leads* the Brights."

"But there's no proof against them, is there?" Farhad's tone reminded Navin of the one he'd used on Roshan. Cold and ruthless.

"I see." Navin didn't bother hiding his sarcasm. "Well then, Yuvraj, I'm sure you'll follow right in our parasmani's exalted footsteps."

"Wait. Navin!" Farhad caught hold of his arm, forcing him back down onto the bed. "Look," he said, his voice softening. "I don't deny your truth. But no investigation can be opened without evidence or without the approval of the queen and two-thirds of the courtiers. A few are even related to the Aspas."

Navin's shoulders sagged. He hated his brother right now. Even more so because whatever he said was true.

"I love you," Farhad said after a pause. The words sent a jolt through Navin. He wondered if Farhad had guessed his thoughts, but no—Navin's aura wasn't visible to him right now. "I've loved you since the day Ma put you in my arms, terrified I'd drop you somehow. I felt that same terror the day I found out about your capture. But instead of fighting our grandmother to send more troops to the area and doing everything possible to negotiate with the bandits, I held back. I failed you as a brother." Bitterness crept into his tone. "And now I'm failing you and our people as their crown prince."

He was. But for once, Navin said nothing. His brother's emotions were muddled with sorrow and self-loathing. It was a feeling Navin had experienced often enough to know how terrible it was.

"You're not infallible," he told Farhad. "Even perfection screws up on occasion."

Farhad's mouth twisted. "I've always envied you, you know. People call you reckless, but they fail to see your courage. Or the brilliance of your solutions."

Navin snorted. "You don't need to lie to me."

"I'm not lying. If I were parasmani, I'd have accepted your suggestion to use marble arrow tips for the sipahis' older atashbans. It would certainly prevent the backfiring problem."

"You would have?" Navin wondered if he was dreaming right now. "Truly?"

"Truly." Farhad's black aura reflected his sincerity. "Believe me."

There was a pause. Navin said nothing for long moments and merely watched as Farhad took a step back. His brown eyes widened upon seeing the aura Navin had never revealed to him since they were boys.

"I believe you," Navin said.

28

THE LIGHTNESS LEFT NAVIN THE MOMENT THEY BOTH STEPPED out of Farhad's suite—and nearly slammed into Sushil.

"Apologies, R-rajkumar, Yuvraj," the boy stuttered. "But the parasmani is calling for you both. She expects to see you at the temple at once."

Farhad smiled at Navin. *Showtime*, he mouthed.

And what a show it was—again a drudgery of ritual and prayer and parades, but this time of black-helmeted sipahis riding horses and chariots, their weapons glinting in the distance, of giant, ten-foot-long atashbans being pulled down the street on wheels by elephants from the southern forests.

There were more people on the palace balcony on the second day of Hashtdin—ministers, court advisers, and relatives vying for the attention of the parasmani, hoping for positions at court. The parasmani ignored mostly everyone, deep in conversation with the Minister of Treasure.

Is she counting the coin she'd earned off the backs of peasants? Navin wondered. *Or is she planning to extract more?*

Even if she was—what could *Navin* do about it? A second prince, whose words and title carried little meaning, even when he wanted them to.

Farhad, the only person who might have been able to influence the queen, was on the opposite side of the balcony, chatting with their younger cousins. He gave Navin a smile. Navin would have smiled back if not for the exhaustion in his limbs, the reminders of Ashvamaidan in the sipahis' ancient, glinting atashbans, the false dye on an aunt's braid mimicking Jwaliyan red hair.

Excusing himself from a bland discussion about the weather, Navin made his way to the edge of the balcony and breathed in the scents of damp earth and sticky, fragrant air. A light drizzle had begun midway through the parade, one that now was increasing in fervor, threatening a downpour. Somewhere nearby, a bamboo pipe had burst, the putrid stench of waste mingling with the fireblooms.

"Goddess save us! What a terrible day!" said an aunt—one of Farhad's late father's many sisters—her bright mango sari making her look like an overripe version of the fruit. "The rain makes things worse—uff, that smell!"

"I've heard that the peri can sing away the rain," a distant cousin said. "It would be so useful right now. Look how it's ruining the parade with all that mud!"

"The peri don't influence the weather!" the aunt scoffed. "Their singing only affects people!"

"Naturally. Did you not see how our rajkumar affected them yesterday?"

"You mean, the one time he had an effect?" she questioned, raising her voice with the taunt, probably so that Navin could hear.

Normally, Navin would have ignored the comment. Today, however, he'd had enough of being made to feel powerless. He thrust his face into the rain so that his head and shoulders were completely drenched. As expected, a servant came rushing at him.

"Rajkumar, your clothes!" Sushil sounded harried. "Your makeup! Please come under the parasol!"

"Don't worry, Sushil." Navin made sure his voice was as loud and carrying as Farhad's aunt. "The peri may not control the rain, but at least we don't fear it like overbearing aunts."

The laughter behind him abruptly stopped. Scandalized whispers melded with the rustling sound of rainfall, the pound of boots against cobblestones and earth. Navin's attention snagged on a sipahi adjusting his dagger belt, the ornamental katar hanging from it. He thought again of Roshan, for perhaps the hundredth time that day, and how he'd promised to make things right for Ashvamaidan.

But how?

He didn't have the answer when he returned to his quarters to change out of his wet clothes. Instead, he found a scroll waiting for him on his bedside table.

You disappeared last night. What happened? See you tonight at the dinner.—Shera

Navin tossed the parchment aside, stomach roiling. He didn't want to see Shera right now. But refusing to meet him would only make the other man suspicious. So, once evening prayers were complete, he entered the banquet hall, arranged with rows of low tables—a much larger dinner that would only grow larger as Hashtdin progressed, culminating in an enormous feast in the town of Khwabganj, offered to the public and paid for by the queen.

Tonight, Shera didn't imbibe on intoxicants. "My head still feels like it's spinning," he informed Navin. "What about yours?"

"It's no better," Navin lied quickly.

"Hmm." Shera took sip of water from his goblet. "Where did you go last night? Don't tell me you made off with one of your guards." A wink.

Navin forced himself to wink back. The whole conversation was making his head ache. "Naah. I was just feeling a little sick, so I decided to head home."

There was a pause.

"Did I say something last night?" Shera asked.

The water in Navin's goblet sloshed. Dribbled down his chin. He wiped it away with a hand. "N-no. Why?"

"You're acting funny."

"I had a fight this morning with my grandmother." A thimbleful of truth. "And it's been a long day."

Shera said nothing. He was watching him with an expression Navin couldn't figure out. His aura, normally so clear to Navin, was faded and milky, no distinct colors visible.

They didn't speak through the rest of the dinner, rising to their feet once the parasmani did, signaling its end.

Navin swallowed. "I'm going to call it an early night, too. If you don't mind."

"I don't." Shera squeezed Navin's shoulder. "Rest well, yaara."

His friend's calmer tone and affectionate address at the end mollified Navin somewhat. Parting from Shera outside the banquet hall, Navin decided to approach the queen again. His guards quietly following him to the Royal Wing, Navin quickened his pace as he caught sight of his grandmother in the hall. "Parasmani ji! A word, please."

Queen Bhairavi turned to one of her guards and murmured something. They turned around and walked to Navin, blocking his path.

"The parasmani is tired. She is not seeing anyone, Rajkumar," he said flatly.

"What do you mean, blocking me like this!" Navin demanded. "Move out of my way!"

But the guard simply clapped his hands together and a shimmering barrier went up between them, barring Navin from entering the Royal Wing altogether. Navin stepped back, stunned.

The barrier remained the next day and the next. The queen was always surrounded by guards or her own ministers, leaving no room for Navin to approach her privately. On the fourth day of Hashtdin, he caught Farhad outside the temple.

"I need to speak to the parasmani. Urgently!" Navin insisted.

"This is a lost cause, Nav. Don't push it."

"Oh, but I *am* going to push it. I made many mistakes when I was in Ashvamaidan." This time Navin ensured that Farhad could see his aura. His anger. "My biggest mistake was my ignorance about my own people. But you? You and the parasmani *know* what's going on. And you don't care what happens as long as the royal coffers remain full."

"Enough." Farhad's voice was low, sharp. "I've told you. I can do nothing. Neither can the parasmani."

"You *choose* to do nothing!" Navin retorted. "We all have choices, brother. You've merely decided to make the easiest one."

"If you feel that way, go do something yourself, little brother. Show me how a kingdom should be ruled."

"Rajkumar?" a voice interrupted. Navin spun around to see Sushil eyeing them both warily. "A messenger came to give you this."

Navin took the scroll and ripped it open.

Urgent matters came up back home. Leaving at once.—Shera

He sighed with relief. At least he wouldn't have to deal with Shera right now or think up excuses to avoid any parties after the mandatory state dinners. Last night Shera had not invited him out, saying he had urgent business to attend to. Perhaps this was it. Perhaps it was something else. By the time Navin's head rose from the parchment, Farhad had walked away, the sight of his retreating back as much an answer as anything that could have come from his mouth.

29

ON THE LAST DAY OF HASHTDIN, THEY ALL WORE WHITE. THE morning dawned clear and blue, wet and muddy roads gleaming ahead of the royal procession marching slowly to Khwabganj. A pomposity—Navin privately called it—of 320 humans on foot and horseback: wand bearers, sipahis, servants, courtiers, and royals.

Queen Bhairavi sat at the center of the line, atop an elephant painted over with flames, the animal and her howdah protected with a glowing orange shield. Farhad and Navin followed her in carriages pulled by finely groomed redmanes, the horses similarly hedged by their own barriers and an increased number of sipahis, long, thin spears pearlescent in the sun.

Once a small market named for the dreams hawked on the river by tribespeople from Tej Forest, Khwabganj was now a town bustling with oddities, wonders, shops, inns, and taverns—a place that Navin had ached to escape to as a child.

Copper lotuses, made of thinly hammered metal, had been planted by the riverside for the last day of the spring festival. When the royal procession arrived, the flowers rose about twenty feet, unfurling to reveal miniature suns at their centers. Lightorbs smoked and flamed, rising to form an image of the fire goddess, her hair the first to immolate, followed by her body, the effect nearly blocking out the real sun.

"Praise be!" voices cried.

"What a wonder!"

A wonder made possible by over a hundred levitators and their magic, Navin noted, watching several figures in sequined blues and reds floating the lotuses back to earth. The sight of a young boy hovering a foot in the air next to the levitators made several people laugh. But Navin thought of another boy of around the same age miles away from here, his brown eyes dancing whenever Navin shared some of his food.

Was Chotu getting enough to eat? he wondered guiltily as they passed through a long lane of sweet stalls. Flaming gulabjamuns on sticks, fire extinguishing the moment the hot, syrupy dumplings entered your mouth. Frothy glasses of firebloom falooda. Suterfeni as light and fluffy as a priest's beard. The juiciest jalebis you could find in Jwala, their bright red spirals bigger than Navin's face. The sight would have made his mouth water once. Now it only made him sick.

The queen and Farhad were farther ahead, chatting with the governor of Tej. Queen Bhairavi had ensured that she didn't come into contact with her least favorite grandson all week, and now she'd further ensured that they were separated by sipahis and groups of relatives.

As the hour went on, the crowds only seemed to grow. Touts with oily grins latched onto unsuspecting royal cousins, drawing them into shops and taverns. Navin, with his formidable mountain guards, managed to shake everyone off and slip into the maze of shops behind the sweet sellers' lane.

Here, Navin spotted two men lounging by a cart of marigold garlands, dressed in white jamas like everyone else, their eyes skirting sideways the moment his gaze fell on them. With his gold eyes and royal clothing, it wasn't unusual for Navin to draw stares in public. But his skin prickled at the sight of these flower sellers; and sure enough, when he glanced back, they were watching him again.

"Stay close," he warned his guards. *Where was everyone else?*

Plenty of strangers were around him, but no one from the royal party. Navin tried to calm himself. He knew that everyone would eventually cross the bridge over the river for the final Hashtdin prayers. Plumes of smoke now rose over the thicket of trees that swallowed the bridge. On the other side, priests were already preparing for the final ritual.

Navin glanced back and, again, spotted the men. Abruptly, he darted sideways through a lane snaking between two havelis, paint curling off their mud-brick walls. Another lane. Then another. A stitch ran up his side. His guards, too, were gasping behind him, but they didn't stop to ask questions, and Navin didn't pause until they reached the front of the bridge.

Underneath, the Behrambodh flowed—jammed with tribespeople in slender boats, the musky sweetness of green pear-shaped dreamfruit pervading the air.

"Dreams, nightmares, babeslumber, and waking rest!" their voices cried out. "Rajkumar! Rajkumar! Would you care for a daydream?"

"No, than—" Navin was saying when screams echoed behind him.

He rounded on his guards, who were pummeling the two men from the flower garland cart, blood already sprouting from the latter's nostrils.

"Tell!" One of Navin's sipahis was shouting. "Tell why you follow us! Who do you work for?"

But all of a sudden, four others emerged from the crowd: men who converged on the sipahis with atashbans and spears—the tips of their weapons glowing red.

"Stop!" Navin's throat tingled, his command filling every pair of ears within a few feet. "Drop your weapons!"

Yet, while other bodies around him jerked, small daggers and other weapons raining on wood like anklets, the brutes beating up his guards merely looked up.

Cotton, Navin realized sickly, spotting tufts of it in his attackers' ears. A simple, yet effective way to block his voice—and his soul magic.

Navin ran, sidestepping the temporarily frozen bodies, over the crest of the bridge, down into a thicket of trees, and jumped, his feet finding swaying ground.

As boys, Navin and Farhad had occasionally run onto the Bridge of Lights to escape their tutors: a long series of wooden planks hung with ropes between a passage of giant neem trees, the canopy so thick that it blotted out the sun. The bridge and forest, magicked into existence by Jwala's first king, were supposed to symbolize a soul's journey through darkness into the fire goddess's flame of eternal light.

Over time, however, more monarchs had come and gone and some, like his grandmother, had added more magic to the bridge, securing it against accidental deaths—and assassins. Navin spotted Queen Bhairavi's tree, bedecked with glittering, glass-beaded torans. "Save me, Goddess!" he whispered, and then jumped—

ten

twenty

forty feet through the air—

his body weightless, the closest he'd come to imagining wings of his own.

This, however, was only possible because of the ancient magic of the Bridge of Lights that protected those of royal blood. No one other than Navin, Farhad, or the queen could have made the jump safely—not even with levitation magic. At about sixty feet, Navin began slowing to a float, which was when he pricked his thumb with his turban pin, pressing the bloodied digit to the bark of the tree. The wood glowed on recognizing his blood and opened a portal. Torans rustled overhead, muffling his attackers' shouts.

Navin clambered into the portal, which closed behind him at once, and crawled through a short, glowing tunnel that led into the dark storage room of a bookshop.

Gasping, he leaned against a shelf of scrolls for several moments, their hollowed ends digging into his spine. Dust floated quietly in a cube of light that poured in from an overhead window. No one else appeared. Not even the bookseller, who was probably out front serving customers.

Who were those men? Navin wondered. *Kidnappers? Or merely thieves?*

They didn't appear to be from the Shadow Clan. For one: They weren't masked. And after over two weeks of living with the bandits, Navin had a good idea of what most of them looked like.

Slipping out the bookshop's back door, he trudged through an alleyway, past musty heaps of garbage and flies, and a lone monkey stalking a clothesline overhead. Pain shot up Navin's thigh: Under a rip in his jama, he'd begun to bleed.

"Idiots!" The sharp, familiar voice made Navin instantly flatten his back against the door of a shuttered apothecary. "Didn't I tell you to keep your distance? To follow them *discreetly?*"

Shera? Navin's heart thudded in his chest. *Shera was still here?*

"Those two mountain witches were beating our brothers!" a voice snarled. "Am I such a coward that I'd watch that happen and do nothing?"

"It would have been better than chasing the rajkumar right across the bridge. In public, no less!"

Silence filled the gap, congealed like tar.

"So what do we do now?" another voice asked, sounding hesitant.

"Keep going to the palace," Shera instructed. "The rajkumar has a valet, Sushil. He's given me the most accurate information about the prince's movements so far. Pay him ten coppers. A silver if you must. I leave for Ashvamaidan tonight. Any conversation, anything at all—I need to know. Understand?"

"Haan ji," the man demurred. A pause. "What if the prince catches on to us? Finds out who we work for?"

Navin's fists clenched, his body digging now into the rock surface of the wall.

"Get rid of him," Shera said coldly. "Make sure it looks like an accident."

30

MAKE SURE IT LOOKS LIKE AN ACCIDENT.

The words tumbled over themselves in Navin's head, his brain unable to process the meaning for long moments. Had Shera—his best friend, Shera—given orders to kill him?

What else did you expect? The voice in his head sounded a lot like Farhad's. *Shera rescued you. And you repaid him by trying to get his father in trouble.*

Something wet trickled down Navin's chin. Blood from a blister that had burst in his mouth. His head was clogged, as if full of stagnant water. Minutes passed by. Perhaps an hour. He stayed pressed to the wall long moments after the prayer ceremony was over.

The sound of horses clopping down the alleyway made him finally move forward. A pair of black-helmeted sipahis on redmanes paused about a foot away from him. One leaped off his horse to approach closer.

"Rajkumar?" the sipahi asked hesitantly. Sweat beaded the exposed red skin of his forehead below the helmet. "Are you all right?"

"Fine," Navin managed. "My . . . my guards," he added, suddenly remembering. "They fell into the river. There was a scuffle on the bridge."

"They're fine. We found them washed ashore." The sipahi sounded disgusted. "They will be removed from their posts."

"No!" Navin shouted, making the sipahi jump. "It was my fault. They were only trying to keep me safe!"

"But, Rajkumar, our witnesses said—"

"No one will be removed from their posts," Navin cut in. "Is that understood?"

"Yes. Yes, Rajkumar." The sipahi bowed.

His guards were waiting for him near the dinner area, their red braids matted and frizzy, their armored hands pressed together, mouths moving in ashen-faced apology.

"No need," Navin told the women gently. "You were protecting me, remember?"

A hakim came over to examine the prince. From a few feet away, Navin watched others in the royal party observing him. No one made a move to approach, not even Farhad, whose aura was bluer than Navin had ever seen it before. The healer made some quick examinations and, after magically healing a couple of mild bruises, pronounced Navin "as taut and firm as a new tanpura string."

The dinner at Khwabganj and the journey back to Prabha happened in a haze. For some reason, Farhad decided to accompany Navin in his carriage.

"What happened to you?" his brother demanded. "And don't say it was nothing. The hakim repaired your body, not your clothes."

Navin longed to tell Farhad to shut up. To drop the concerned sibling act. But a moment later, he adopted the lazy, wastrel smile his brother hated. Imagining a shadowy figure and a warm laugh, he allowed his aura to emerge, pink and sated. "A roll in the hay. You know. We might've gotten carried away."

Farhad frowned and Navin wondered if his brother had caught the lie. But then the crown prince rolled his eyes. Disgusted. "You'll never change," he said, leaning back in his seat.

Neither will you. Cold seeped into Navin's bones though the night was humid.

What would Farhad have done if he'd known about Shera having Navin tailed? Probably scolded Navin again, telling him it was *his* fault—that *he* ought to apologize to Shera or simply stop pushing for an investigation into Ashvamaidan.

There was no solution here—*nor safety,* Navin realized with growing dread. He and Farhad spent the rest of their ride in silence, parting ways at the palace lobby that branched off into separate wings. Sushil wasn't valeting tonight, and for this, Navin counted his blessings. He still didn't know how he'd deal with the boy right now.

Two months ago, Navin would have reprimanded him, perhaps, then dismissed him from his post. But the Navin who'd experienced hunger with the Shadow Clan and seen its effect on others understood a little more about poverty and desperation. Despite everything that had happened today, Navin had more sympathy for someone like Sushil than he did for his grandmother or Farhad.

Twenty-four bells tolled in the palace temple. Midnight. Unable to sleep, Navin walked out onto the balcony. In the distance, more fireworks bloomed across the city. Prabha would not sleep on this last day of Hashtdin. Normally, neither would Navin.

"Goddess help me," he whispered. "What do I do?"

Pray. The voice was soft. Came from somewhere deep within.

Navin closed his eyes and hummed the beginning of the hymn he'd sung for Jaya. He slowly sang the words, over and over, not stopping until the last fireworks fizzled to smoke.

Silence had fallen over Prabha. Dawn would be here in a few hours.

A sharp trill pierced the air, drawing Navin's gaze. He blinked hard once. Twice.

Was he drunk?

No. For once, Navin was stone-cold sober, not even the taste of wine lingering on his lips.

The bird hovered over the marble ledge of his balcony, bigger than a bulbul, smaller than a hawk, its golden feathers glowing in the dim light of the moon.

Years ago, Navin had heard someone say that the homāi had no legs—that she remained forever in flight, never touching anything on this earth. But he saw now that it wasn't true. The homāi's feet scratched the ledge of his balcony as she landed. She tilted her head sideways, black eyes bright with humor.

"Are you real?" Navin whispered. "Or a dream?"

In answer, the homāi began to sing the same hymn, her trilling voice filling his ears so completely he wondered how they could bear any other sound:

> *What are light and shadow but twin spirits?*
> *What are day and night but a single soul?*
> *You venture seeking evil everywhere, mortal,*
> *Yet forget to look in your own heart.*

Navin wasn't sure when the homāi had begun rising in the air again, or when exactly she faded: a lantern swallowed by the breeze. A feather floated below, landing at his feet. He picked it up.

It wasn't gold as he'd expected, nor small. Had Navin not seen one before, he would have thought it a cleverly wrought metal quill made of rainbow-hued indradhanush from the Brimlands. But no. This was a feather, soft with a springy vane, its ends black as if dipped in ink.

A peri feather. His father's to be precise.

Navin had never forgotten the pattern of his father's wings. Or the way they'd felt against his skin. Like a rebuke and a homecoming all at once.

Overhead, clouds had begun gathering again, dark with rain, a light drizzle erupting over the garden. Navin held up the feather and closed his eyes, singing a song about spring—one of the very first his father had taught him. He allowed the music to fill his veins, the lyrics teasing the sun for being a shy lover, for hiding its brightness behind the clouds.

The rain stopped. When Navin opened his eyes at the end of the song, there was no sun. But on the balcony ledge before him sat a figure. Long limbs and gold skin, enormous, iridescent wings held eerily still. A quiver hung across Peri Tir's back, full of glistening arrows.

"So the rumors were true," the peri said, his voice both human and oddly birdlike, a voice that had never failed to send shivers down Navin's spine. "You haven't really sung much in these ten years."

Navin would've snapped at the criticism if his father hadn't sounded so sad.

He cleared his throat, but stuttered anyway. "Pitaji. I . . . I d-didn't think you would c-come."

"When the great firebird appears in my dreams singing in my child's voice, do I have a choice?" Peri Tir held up a feather—smaller than his own, soft and golden, its tip like the end of a flame. "I figured now was as good a time as any to ignore Parasmani Bhairavi's edict."

"Edict?" Navin asked, bemused.

"Warning me to stay away. Banning me from visiting you. She said that I was a bad influence. That Jwaliyans watched you with enough suspicion as is for your Pashu heritage. But magical barriers can last for only so long. And, from what I've heard, Bhairavi has made a mess of her own kingdom."

Navin studied his father's smoky black aura, fainter than any human's—a natural protection Tir's Pashu blood had built around his mind. The only reason Navin could see the aura today was that Tir wanted him to. His father studied Navin in return with sun-bright eyes, feathers scaling the sides of his neck and shoulders, forming the wings Navin had desperately wanted as a child.

"I'm sorry." The words, held in for so long, spilled out of Navin. "For lying to you that day in Aman, for trying to magically convince you about my lies. I've regretted that my whole life. I regret even more what I tried to do to my own brother. Adi must have grown up hating me."

"Adi doesn't hate you. Neither do I, for that matter." The hard lines of Peri Tir's face softened. "I went wild with fear when I found out you were kidnapped. Even tried to go to Ashvamaidan and look for you. But one of your sipahis spotted me flying over Khwabganj. They reported the news to Parasmani Bhairavi, who immediately hawked the Pashu queen, Sarayu.

"Rani Sarayu wasn't happy with me. She insisted I come back with her. She didn't need another Pashu and human war. I listened. And then stalked the border between Aman and Jwala for weeks, waiting, watching for news about your return. It was a mistake on my part. I am sorry for it, hatchling."

I would not have sat around waiting if I was in your place.

Navin was tempted to say the words aloud, to give in to the blood rushing through his veins, loaded with old feelings of rage and resentment. But then he bit his tongue.

His father had apologized for his behavior. And Navin, in turn, was no saint.

"I'm surprised that despite everything I've done, you sang for me." Tir's words held a question in them. "And that you have my feather. Did the homāi appear in your dream as well?"

"She appeared while I was awake," Navin said. "Or . . . I think she did. She sang with me and dropped your feather. I'd been praying to the fire goddess for help. For Roshan Chaya."

"The bandit who kidnapped you and held you captive for seventeen days?"

"Yes," Navin replied. "But it's not that simple."

Tir remained silent as Navin told him about the poverty-stricken villages, the ravines, and the treacherous quakes. About helping Roshan heal a village girl and then betraying her to the Brights. About Shera's startling confession under the influence of rang ras and soul magic.

"My singing," Navin paused. "It amplifies my soul magic. Makes it stronger. Is it because I'm part peri?"

"Perhaps," Tir said. A sad smile lingered on his lips. "I wish I could tell you more, son. But unions between humans and peri have not resulted in any offspring for the past hundred years. It's why I don't know much about your powers. But if you were able to see Roshan Chaya's aura . . ."

"I was. And now I found out she may have been right about Subedar Yazad." Navin's head ached. "I've been trying to get both Parasmani Bhairavi and Farhad to do something about it—to open an investigation into the Aspas. But Farhad insists they can do nothing. He implies that the parasmani is trapped by a bad deal to keep the throne. And now, the other problem is that Shera knows—or at least he suspects—what I've been trying to do. I spent a good part of my morning running from his men in Khwabganj."

Fury turned Tir's aura red. "What do you want to do, Navin?"

"I don't know. I've never known what I was supposed to do in life, let alone something like *this*!" Navin spat out the last word. "But now . . ."

"Now you are faced with something truly wrong that no one else wants to make right," Tir said gently.

"Yes."

There was a pause.

"So back to Roshan Chaya," Tir said. "You feel you've wronged her. Are you sure there's nothing more to it?"

Navin's heart skidded in his chest. "What do you mean? Why would there be?"

Tir shrugged. "I only asked. Are you . . . attached to her? These things do happen sometimes, you know."

"*Attached* to her?" Navin didn't understand why it felt like stones were lodged in his throat. "She kidnapped me. I'm under no illusions about that, Pitaji. Are you saying that I'm wrong about wanting to help her? That my mind is playing tricks on me about what I'm feeling now?"

"I am no soul magus and cannot talk to your emotions, but from what I can tell, your mind is perfectly sound, beta." The Common Tongue word for *son*, added softly at the end, surprised Navin as much as it warmed his insides. "You did what any reasonable person would have when captured. You escaped and had your kidnapper arrested and imprisoned. Yet now, in the face of new evidence, you're questioning yourself. I don't see anything wrong with that. The Pashu have always believed that it is far worse to imprison one innocent than to let a hundred criminals roam free."

"Roshan's not exactly an innocent."

"Who among us is?" Tir asked softly. A soft whistle left his lips. "Did you know that when I first began an affair with your mother, it was for political reasons?"

Every bit of Navin's body grew still.

"I'm not proud to admit it." Tir's aura reflected his shame. "The Pashu wanted to free some of our own, who had been indentured in Kiran Mahal for generations. My queen asked me to befriend your mother. To have her persuade Parasmani Bhairavi to pass a law freeing them. It worked. No Pashu can now be magically enslaved in Jwala—at least not legally."

"Did . . ." Navin cleared his throat. "Did Ma know? About what you were doing?"

"She did. She was the crown princess. A woman much too familiar with people wanting to use her." Grief etched Tir's face. "The trouble with Pashu, with humans, too, is that we always want everything to unfold cleanly—in ways society calls unambiguous. But love is a strange thing. Fickle, fussy, older than the gods, more unpredictable than magic itself. When I first met your mother, I told myself I didn't love her, repeated the same thing to myself over and over again, even when I took her to my bed."

Navin's breath caught.

"I took her because I wanted her," Tir went on, his voice hard. "I took her because unions between humans and Pashu rarely last and never resulted in love. I was wrong. On both counts. I did fall in love with Athiya. I wanted to elope with her, to bring both you and your brother Farhad with us. But Athiya refused. She said she could not leave Jwala, nor the path she was born for. I didn't know whether I hated her for her determination or loved her even more for it."

A short silence fell between them, one Navin didn't dare break.

"Athiya didn't survive the birthing. And your grandmother refused to give you to me." His father's jaw was tight with grief. "I could have stolen you away, of course. But Parasmani Bhairavi was right about one thing: Aman isn't a kind place to a hatchling without wings."

"Nor is Jwala kind to a child with peri eyes," Navin said, wondering if he sounded as tired as he felt. "But somehow, I'm still here, aren't I? I'm surviving."

"More like thriving." His father gave him a smile, sudden and fierce. "The peri say that our children are grown when their wings are fully formed. Yet no child fully reaches maturity until they learn to ask questions of their own, to try to right wrongs the way you've been doing now."

"I'm not so sure about that. Farhad said that the only way to arrest Subedar Yazad is with proof about his criminal activity. Or to bring a protest by Ashvamaidani villagers to the capital. How do I get either of that to happen? I'm only the spare prince," he concluded bitterly.

No one spoke for a long moment.

"There is a way," Tir said at last. "But to make things right, you may have to commit some wrongs yourself."

"What kind of wrongs?"

"Breaking Roshan Chaya out of prison, for one."

Only hours earlier, the words would've made Navin recoil in disbelief. But Shera's voice still lingered in his head. *Make it look like an accident.*

"If you want proof about Subedar Yazad's criminality, Roshan Chaya may be your only key to unlocking it," Tir said. "She knows her province and its people. In fact, she may be one of the few individuals who can influence them to bring a protest to the capital. Isn't that what Yuvraj Farhad said? Tell me clearly. Try to recall the conversation word for word."

Navin racked his brain, telling his father everything he could remember. By the time he'd finished, a temple bell rang once, announcing a new day.

"This will not be easy, hatchling," his father said. "Are you willing to do what I asked . . . and incur more of your grandmother's wrath?"

"I think I already do that on a regular basis, Pitaji."

Tir's hard smile mirrored his own. "Good."

31

"Number forty-two!" Something rattled the bars. "On your feet!"

Roshan wearily raised her head. A warder stood outside her door, a man with a long bamboo staff in one hand, his shriveled face grim. Warders with whips meant torture. But warders with staffs probably meant the day of her trial had arrived. Or a sentencing without a trial. It had happened to Kamal only a few days ago. The bidaal had been taken out of her cell by a pair of warders, and Roshan had not seen her since. Perhaps she was free again, Roshan hoped. Prayed, even, in a moment of weakness. But her sinking heart told her otherwise.

Hashtdin had come and gone. Nine days had passed by since Navin had visited her in prison. Nine whole days during which her initial triumph at refusing his help had turned to regret, then worry. She'd wasted time thinking about what he was planning to do. *How* he would make things right. Fool that she was.

She should have been thinking of ways to escape. Now, it was too late. Or . . . maybe not. At least there was no pain in her limbs now thanks to the prison hakim's ministrations. Her face, too, felt normal to the touch, the magic from her disguise having long since faded.

The bamboo staff tapped the bars again, making them glow gold instead of blue. The warder stepped in, hauling Roshan to her feet. She tightened her shackled fists, readying a blow.

"I wouldn't do that if I were you, Roshni."

The name slid like ice down her back. "You . . . ? You came?"

"I did," Navin replied, the smile faint on his lips.

His hair was shorter, dyed a bright red and cropped like a sipahi's, his irises a dull gray. Only his pupils remained elliptical. As for that voice . . . Roshan suspected she'd recognize it in her sleep.

"Scream." Navin whispered now. "As if I've pulled your hair or twisted your ear."

It was easy enough to fake the right sound. She paused as Navin muttered something about her shackles being too difficult to break.

"No matter," he said. "We'll deal with them later."

They trudged ahead, slowed partly by the shackles jolting her wrists and ankles with each step. Roshan nearly froze when she saw a pair of bound-up men on the floor next to the ward entrance, their mouths stuffed with rags. The naked one—Roshan realized—had been beating up Kamal in the name of an interrogation.

"They're all right," Navin said. "Only unconscious."

"Too bad."

A grin flashed across his face, revealing the prince under the warder's disguise. They kept moving, passing cell after empty cell, Roshan holding her breath for some sort of magical trap to fall into place and lock Navin in with her.

Moments later, he paused before a wall in the quiet passage outside the ward and pulled out what appeared to be a feathered turban pin.

To Roshan's bemusement, he pricked his finger and traced a symbol on the wall—a bird with a feathered crown.

"Careful," he whispered as his blood seeped into the stone, which melted to reveal an open door. "Don't let go of my hand."

She soon understood why. A confinement barrier began squeezing her ribs—nearly crushing them—as they passed through the door and onto one of the prison's domed, open-air watchtowers, its warders lying trussed in a heap in the corner. A hundred feet below, the city thrummed, unnerving Roshan more than any raid.

Until she saw the figure perched on the sill.

Over ten feet tall, with enormous opalescent and black wings, the peri had golden eyes and shimmering skin of nearly the same color, his long black hair in a single braid. Tucked between the wings, Roshan saw more feathers—arrows, along with a sleek bow that looked like it was made of bone. The peri's face looked familiar: a harder, older version of Navin's own.

"This is my father, Tir," the prince said.

Roshan broke her gaze away from the peri to look at the boy who had arranged this, noting for the first time a darkened bruise on his chin.

"What are you doing, Navin?" His name slipped out like a bad habit she couldn't rid herself of.

He smirked in response, but his mouth trembled. "Not much. As I promised, I'm getting you out of here."

As Navin spoke, Peri Tir reached out, lightly brushing his gold fingers against Roshan's wrists. The shackles melted away, sending tremors up her skin.

Without thinking, she held on to Navin's arm for support as Tir did the same for her ankles. And then dropped it, as if it were on fire.

"Listen, Roshan," Navin said seriously. "You need to go back to Ashvamaidan and get evidence against Subedar Yazad's criminal activity. Maybe you can find witnesses, a group of villagers who will vouch for your truths. Alternatively, you must organize them in a protest group, bring it to Prabha, and get the public's attention. That will force the parasmani to listen to you."

"What . . . what are you saying?" Roshan's head spun. *A protest group? Was he serious?* "The parasmani won't listen to us. She never has!"

"She will if you get the rest of Jwala to your side."

Curse you to the highest hells.

Roshan wanted to punch that stupid, hopeful look off his face. And she would have if not for the peri looming over them both.

"And how do you expect *that* to happen?" she demanded. "If you think it's that easy to get public support, why don't you come along to Ashvamaidan and show me how it's done?"

"Yes," Tir spoke, his voice reminding Roshan of birdsong over a still river, of lightning before a storm. She looked into the cold depths of his eyes and failed to suppress a shiver. "Why don't you, Navin?"

Navin began to sputter something inaudible. Any other day, she'd have found this hilarious. Any other day when they weren't a hundred feet above the ground, Prabha's streets ribboning below, churning with a crush of carriages, fruit carts, Pashu, and humans.

Behind them, a bell clanged, a magically amplified voice echoing from inside the prison walls: *"Breach on Level Eight. Prisoner on loose."*

Tir's scaled ears cocked to the sides of his skull. But apart from that he gave no indication of having heard the alarm, his unperturbed gaze on his son. "When peri hatchlings grow their wings, we drop them from a cliff," he said, gesturing to the air. "We watch if they can fly. Those who do can survive the worst life throws at them. Navin, this is your cliff. Are you ready to test your wings?"

"Pitaji." Navin gritted his teeth. "I don't understand. What do you expect me to *do* in Ashvamaidan?"

"What are you going to do *here*?" his father countered. "Apart from rotting in the same cell that you freed this girl from?"

"They can't imprison me! I'm a prince!"

"Do you think princes can't be made examples of, child? Or do you truly believe Parasmani Bhairavi will let you off with an apology for breaking out a prisoner? And even if she does, do you think Shera Aspa will leave you be?"

Shera Aspa? The name surprised Roshan. *What happened there?*

Navin's throat bobbed. He said nothing.

"Parasmani Bhairavi isn't your only option to gain justice for these people, son. You must not forget Yuvraj Farhad, nor underestimate the strength of your bond with him. All that said, I will not force you. If you wish, I will take you back to the palace and Roshan Chaya back to Ashvamaidan, as promised. But you are wrong if you think yourself useless. You are more than just a spare prince."

Inside the prison, the bell was still clanging. Shouts rang in the air, mingling with the sound of the announcement. Roshan tensed, glancing below. If she were like Chotu, she would've risked a jump and attempted levitating to another building nearby. She *could*, of course, scale the prison walls like a cliff. But by then, the guards would already have congregated below, their death spells sinking into her back before her feet had a chance to hit the ground.

"All right." The words left Navin in a hush. "I'll go to Ashvamaidan."

He didn't look at Roshan. It was probably a good thing, because she was certain that anger was etched into every line of her face.

Patience, bitiya, Baba would have said.

She forced herself to think with a cool head, to mentally thank whatever was working in her favor for this stroke of fortune—this opportunity for escape. But even if they somehow dodged the guards here and reached Ashvamaidan safely, Roshan didn't know what the situation was like in her province. Eighteen days had passed since she'd been imprisoned. Enough time for the Shadow Clan to have turned on her or split into factions. Even if they were still together, there was no guarantee they'd accept her as their leader again. With Navin by her side, though, she *might* convince them otherwise. That she still had things under control and this colossal screwup on her part was part of the bigger plan to get back their lands from Governor Yazad.

Tir held out his hand. "Come," he told her firmly, but not unkindly. "We must move."

Roshan's hand didn't release its sweaty, death grip on the prison finial.

"Don't worry, child," the peri went on. "I will harness you with ropes so that you don't fall."

"Ropes?" She squinted at his shoulders—one holding the quiver, the other bare.

"Turn around."

Gently, he guided Roshan so that her back was to the side of his chest. Ropes emerged from the air, wound around her like snakes. She swallowed, feeling like a trussed bird, unable to move even if she wanted to. Tir did the same for Navin so that he was bound next to Roshan, the ball of his shoulder brushing hers.

"Hold steady," Tir whispered. "They're coming. Navin's royal blood will pull us through the barrier."

Roshan would take his word for it. The prison's barrier around the tower had locked out all sound, clawing at her face again as if hoping to hold her back. By the time they broke out of it, Navin's hair had grown out again, his magical disguise gone, his auburn curls tickling her ears in the gusts from his father's powerful wings.

"Don't kill me when we get to Ashvamaidan, will you, Roshni?" he shouted.

"Not making any promises," she yelled back. Something trickled down her stinging cheeks. Probably blood. "Also, stop calling me Roshni!"

She stilled as his fingers brushed the back of her hand, paused at the scar on her thumb. The one left behind by his teak ring. He yelled something else, but his words were swallowed by the wind.

A group of warders burst through the wall, their red spells webbing the air. Tir swerved sideways, through a layer of dark clouds that drenched them with rainwater. Next to her, Navin's mouth was open in what appeared to be a scream. Roshan couldn't hear it. Her teeth chattered and her ears rang with a high pitch. Whatever she wanted to say devolved into a whimper, the blinding sun filling her vision, its light swallowing her whole.

DEMONS, OLD AND NEW

The ravines of Ashvamaidan

DAY 10 of the Month of Tears
YEAR 40 of Queen Bhairavi's reign

32

His father dodged the warders' spells, weaving so quickly through the clouds that Navin felt every one of his inner organs lurch.

Blessed goddess, let me not vomit.

Eventually, they steadied over the layer of black clouds, and Navin's ears unblocked, some dormant part of him waking to the rush of air against his cheeks. A sudden laugh burst from his mouth.

Was this what freedom felt like?

Next to him, Roshan jolted, as if surprised. But she didn't ask questions, and Navin wasn't sure if he could explain himself anyway.

They flew for most of the afternoon over a thick layer of clouds, their bodies drying in the scorching heat, then growing chilled again as the sun set, the sky deepening to a starry mauve. Navin had lost most sensation in his ears, nose, and limbs, even though they'd dodged the worst of the rain and thunderstorms, his brain barely registering the silvery river shrinking into Ashvamaidan's fissured landscape. Pockets of light and magical fog hinted at the few villages they passed by. The air tasted like dust and copper, reeked of peat floating up from murky pools below.

"All right?" Tir asked as they began descending, so quietly that Navin barely heard the words.

Navin wasn't sure. His earlier lightness had diminished by now and a tiny part of him wondered if it was smarter to return to Prabha and its familiar pit of vipers. Yet, as he thought it, his insides squeezed, as if pushing through the prison barrier again.

He could die in Ashvamaidan. Or be seriously injured. Roshan hadn't spoken to him the whole journey, and he'd only occasionally been able to swivel his head to see her aura, which had now set into a mix of anger and fear. But staying in Prabha would choke the life out of him, too. One day at a time.

"I'm all right," he told his father.

If Roshan was worried about how the clan would react to their reappearance, Navin could use that to his advantage and talk her into forming an alliance with him. He was about to open his mouth, ready to propose this, when she announced: "Left from here, Tir ji. Off that Zaalian ruin there."

Navin's tongue stilled. From her hard tone, he sensed she was thinking about the time he'd trapped her in that very ruin.

"Meherbani, Roshan Chaya," Tir trilled. "Try not to kill my son. I do know where you live now."

"I won't—provided he puts his soul magic to use and ensures that the others do not murder us both," Roshan replied, equally sweet.

"I'm still here, you know," Navin retorted. "And I can't guarantee that soul magic will be enough to control your entire rabid clan."

"Well." The sneer was evident in Roshan's voice. "Then you'll have to charm them, won't you, Rajkumar?"

Tir's chest heaved against Navin's skull, and he had the strongest suspicion his father was laughing at them.

"Don't get too happy, Pitaji," Navin told him. "I might still die, you know."

"You won't."

Tir's words were confident as he alighted on the ground. The ropes binding Roshan unfurled, and she tumbled over the wet rocks.

Tir pressed a peri feather into Navin's palm. "Call if you need me. I will come, no matter what." Then he rose in the air, disappearing into the clouds.

Navin watched him go, his ears still unblocking from the descent, his heart full and aching from his father's last words. But he had the presence of mind to slip the feather into an inner pocket of his jama. Roshan hadn't noticed. She was on her feet again, staring into empty space.

"I sensed Khush lurking nearby," she whispered. "Our welcoming party will be here any moment. Ready yourself, Rajkumar."

Khush? The name was familiar to Navin, but he couldn't recall who it was. It didn't matter. There was no time to ask.

Bodies had slid out of the darkness, masks covering their faces.

The man at the front of the group lowered his atashban. "Roshan?"

"It's me, Lalit," she confirmed, her voice far brighter than normal. "I'm back."

"Me too," Navin said hesitantly, hoping he could get an explanation in first. "I—"

He found himself slammed to the ground, his clothes sticking to the mud, a hard knee wedged into his chest.

"What are *you* doing here?" Lalit was flint-eyed and furious, his rage confirmed by the faint aura of red around his head.

"Lalit, I think you ought to listen to him first!" Roshan said.

"You don't give Lalit orders anymore!" Hemant's atashban was aimed directly at Roshan. "You were the one who endangered the clan. You are worthless as our sardar."

Fire and ashes, were they going to kill Roshan, too?

No one defended her. Not Lalit. Not even Chotu, who hovered in the back, his gaze dancing from one face to another. Roshan widened her stance, her aura radiating calm. She had no weapons on her. Nor amplifiers. But Navin knew she wasn't afraid. She'd take on the clan the way she had the Brights—single-handedly. Even if she would lose.

"If it weren't for *her*, you wouldn't have garnered any royal interest in your dying province!" Navin forced out. Years of projecting his voice in speech training came into effect, his voice drawing several beats of silence.

"Is that so?" Lalit asked, still suspicious.

"Roshan was the one who convinced me that something is wrong with Ashvamaidan. She went to jail for it in Prabha. I didn't see any of *you* attempting to rescue her. I did."

More silence. Lalit's knee slowly moved off his chest. He held out a hand. Navin took it. Seconds after he was drawn to his feet, his teeth rattled again with a fierce punch. And then another.

"That," Lalit growled, "was for trapping and imprisoning our sardar in the first place!"

Navin waited, bracing for more blows. When none came, his coiled insides relaxed.

Lalit still appeared to be on Roshan's side. But the rest of the clan— Navin couldn't tell. It was impossible to gauge every aura in the dim evening light. He focused on Lalit and the wisp of navy aura emerging from the back of his turban. *Curiosity*.

"You've tried to get back your lands for over twenty years now," Navin told him. "You've failed each time because of Subedar Yazad's influence over Parasmani Bhairavi. And because of the parasmani's own corruption."

Lalit merely stared at Navin, which the latter figured was a hint to go on.

So Navin did. He told the clan about his night with Shera, the fire-stone mine that was still possibly active. He also outlined what Farhad had told him about the need for proof against the governor's criminal activities, or a public protest to bring Ashvamaidan valley to the attention of the Jwaliyan public.

"Why must we do this?" someone asked. It was Vijali Fui, a gold braid hanging over one shoulder. "Especially when you and Yuvraj Farhad already believe us, Rajkumar?"

"Neither Farhad nor I have the power to remove Yazad Aspa on our own," Navin explained. "At least not legally. I tried my best to talk to Parasmani Bhairavi when I was in Prabha, but she shut me out completely. If we're going to beat the subedar at his own game, we'll need to do it from within the confines of the law. We must persuade two-thirds of the royal court to open an investigation."

"So you mean you have no plan!" Hemant said. "You're going to lie around here and—"

"Do what exactly?" Navin cut in, his voice cool where the other man's was hot. "Why would I leave the palace and put myself at risk again by coming here to you?"

"Who knows?" Hemant sneered. "Maybe you're looking for some of those firestones. They're mighty powerful, aren't they? Also fetch pretty coin on the black market."

Navin's jaw tightened. He'd never had to argue this much with anyone before. But Hemant was only voicing what others likely thought. As an old tutor had once told Navin: The hardest part about soul magic wasn't using it, but knowing when *not* to use it.

Pressing a hand to his chest, Navin felt the smooth lines of his father's feather. Still intact.

"Hemant ji," he addressed the man. "I understand your concern. I didn't know much about your province when I was first brought here. And when Roshan tried to show me, I didn't believe her. I didn't *want* to believe the truth, even when it stared me in the face. I deserve your beatings," he addressed Lalit and the others now. "Your suspicion. But I promise I am here to help. To make things right."

"And what guarantee is there that you'll do it?" a young woman next to Vijali asked.

"I'll be his guarantee."

Everyone turned to face the speaker. Roshan turned her head sideways, her profile etched into hard lines. "I'll vouch for Rajkumar Navin," she said.

"You can't talk," Hemant said with a sneer. "Vouch for your lover if you like, but you're no longer sardar."

"Said who?" Lalit asked, his voice calm.

"Said me! And Fariyal, Saloni, and Khizer, and the rest of this lot!" Hemant gestured to about five other people.

"I didn't say anything," a man spoke, his voice soft. The one named Khizer.

"Lying bastard! You agreed that with Roshan gone, it was time for a new sardar!"

"When you said *gone*, you meant dead, Hemant Bhai." Navin marveled at Khizer's calm. "But Sardar Roshan is still here. Alive." The man glanced at Roshan, his smile tremulous. "Till death, Sardar."

"Till death!" Chotu cried out from overhead, drawing a murderous glare from Hemant. The boy's wide grin lifted Navin's spirits.

"Till death for our little hakim!" someone else announced.

Navin's skin crawled at the sensation of cold; now he remembered who Khush was.

"I also vouch for what Rajkumar Navin said about the parasmani blocking people out," the living specter said. "It was why I had so much trouble getting answers from her before. She'd barred her rooms to living specters with magical barriers and then refused to leave them for days."

"And now we'll have to wait more days, maybe years to get what we want!" Hemant cried out.

"No, we won't," Roshan said calmly. "It's why we've brought Rajkumar Navin with us. To quicken the process."

Hang on. What did she mean by quicken?

Before Navin could clarify, Hemant spoke: "We're not going to wait indefinitely. You and your pretty prince have a week. If you fail to live up to your promise and get us our lands, you are no longer sardar."

"A week's too short!" Navin snapped. "You'll need to give at *least* that much time to communicate with the palace. We'll need a *year* for any progress to happen."

"I agree," Lalit said, unexpectedly. "A year's fair."

"A year's too long," Hemant called out after consulting the woman next to him. "Two weeks."

"Two *months*," Roshan countered.

Wait a minute.

"One month!"

No.

"Done," Roshan said.

High hell!

A slow smile spread across Hemant's face.

Navin wanted to bury his head in his hands. Even twelve months had been pushing it. But one?

He glanced at Lalit, hoping he would talk some sense into his companions. But the bandit said nothing. His eyes were on Roshan, who finally turned to face them, her face shuttered of expression. Only Navin could see her aura, the blue and yellow veining the red.

Goddess help us, he thought.

33

THEY WERE DOOMED.

Roshan saw the verdict on Navin's horrified face, on Lalit's blank one. Behind them, others stared at her, some, like Chotu, blinking as if surfacing from underwater.

Only Hemant appeared pleased. His smile stretched from one corner of his face to another, tongue clicking behind his browning teeth. He made that sound whenever he thought something had gone his way.

Which was exactly what Roshan wanted him to believe.

Salute the wicked first, as the old saying went.

Roshan glanced at Navin. Hemant's earlier comment about the firestones was again making her question her original instincts about the prince. She was certain Navin hadn't used soul magic to influence any of her decisions. But had that conversation with his father on the prison tower been an act? *Was* Navin looking for access to the firestone mines—and using Roshan and the clan in some twisted way to free them from Governor Yazad's clutches?

A wave of exhaustion rolled through her limbs. Before encountering Navin on that dhow, Roshan had, to some extent, understood the world she lived in, including who her friends and enemies were. Now, however, she didn't know what to believe. Or whom.

"Do you want to take him to see a truth seeker?" Lalit murmured in her ear. He, too, was watching Navin.

She suppressed a sigh of relief. If she believed in the gods, she'd thank them for Lalit. For Khizer and Chotu and Khush.

"A truth seeker's a good idea," she said.

Truth seeking wasn't entirely foolproof against soul magi, who had stronger mental barriers than other people. But Navin couldn't outright lie to a truth seeker, and—if Roshan's instincts were right—his truths might keep Hemant and his minions at bay.

For now.

She watched the prince repeatedly tug on the sleeves of the gray jama he'd borrowed from the warder, probably attempting to keep his jade bracelets hidden. Roshan automatically reached up to touch her firestone amulet even though it no longer hung between her clavicles.

Was this how Navin had felt when she'd taken his bracelets away? As if he'd lost a limb?

The realization discomfited her, would have made her feel guilty even—if her position with the clan wasn't so precarious. Casually, she walked over to the prince. She could feel the rest of the clan watching.

"Rajkumar—" She leaned in close, her voice low.

"Navin," he corrected with a small smile. Luckily, he had the sense to mimic the volume of her voice. When she didn't respond, his smile faded. Those cursed eyes of his. So bright. So clear of deception now.

"I know you don't trust me, Roshan. But I—"

"Save it, *spare prince*," she emphasized the last two words, relishing the way he stiffened at them. "Don't make me regret saving your life."

Maybe he was telling the truth and *did* have a sudden change of heart. But that didn't mean Roshan wasn't still furious at having been tricked, beaten within an inch of her life, and imprisoned. She was angrier at herself for being fooled and nearly losing everything the clan had worked for these past two decades.

But now wasn't the time to show any cracks in this newly formed alliance with Navin—the only thing keeping the clan from expelling Roshan herself.

Without warning, she took the prince's hand, felt his pulse skid in response. "Walk with me," she whispered. "Let them think we're friends. Or lovers. You can pretend this much, can't you?"

A corner of his mouth tugged. Without taking his gaze off her, he raised their clasped hands to his lips and brushed a light kiss across the sensitive skin of her knuckles. A shiver ran down Roshan's spine, more from pleasure than from disgust. Fire and ashes, but the bastard was good.

Lalit and Khizer fell into step next to Roshan, Vijali and Navaz next to Navin. Chotu and Khush floated overhead, and for a few brief moments, Roshan could almost believe this was a real reunion. That they could defeat the governor of Ashvamaidan and a corrupt queen and that the mutterings behind her were only the wind.

Back in the cavern, Roshan, Navin, and Lalit broke away from the rest of the clan, making their way through a tunnel that led into the small space Roshan had claimed as her room. Her breaths eased, noting that it appeared more or less the same as she'd left it.

She dropped Navin's hand like a rock. There was no need to pretend in front of Lalit, who was watching them both with curious eyes.

"All right, Lalit." She nodded to her second-in-command. "Tell us everything that's happened here so far."

Being gone eighteen days from Ashvamaidan wasn't much to any ordinary person. But when you were the sardar of the province's most notorious clan of bandits, it could very well lead to anarchy. And, according to Lalit, it nearly had.

"Fariyal's sleeping with Hemant now," Lalit informed Roshan. "She's made all three of her siblings join his old group of seven. Ever since you were captured, they kept encouraging the idea that you were sentenced to death, that you were most likely dead by now. Nearly swayed the whole clan. Truth be told, I was getting worried, too." Torchlight flickered against the wall, revealing the hollows under Lalit's eyes. "I wanted to go look for you. Break you out of the bandikhana, if possible. But I didn't dare leave them alone here. In that, I failed you as your second, Roshan. I'm sorry for that."

"Don't apologize," she said. "If you weren't here, the others would've probably killed me and Navin."

Maybe things might've been different if Navin's father had remained behind to ensure their safety. But she still wasn't sure they'd have made it out in one piece. Moreover, Lalit alone would've had no shot at breaking her out of prison. Not without the royal blood needed to breach its barriers.

Speaking of which . . .

She turned to Navin. "On the tower. What was that talk about you and Shera Aspa not getting along anymore? Did he remember telling you about the firestones?"

"I don't think so. But he sensed something was off with me afterward. I was . . . not myself with him." Navin's frown deepened. "He left the Hashtdin celebrations, pretending he was going back to Ashvamaidan. But he was still in the city, getting information about my movements at the palace. On the last day of Hashtdin, in Khwabganj, his men beat up my personal guards. I later overheard him instructing them to get rid of me if I figured out his involvement."

Curses.

"So that's why you left the palace." Roshan ignored the sudden tightness in her chest. "Because you feared retaliation from Shera."

"Partially." Navin leaned against the rock wall, looking like he would collapse into it. "No one at the palace was willing to listen to me as far as the Aspas were concerned. The parasmani fears losing Yazad Aspa's support and her throne. Even Farhad told me he could do nothing—though maybe he'll pay attention now that I'm gone. My father will deliver a letter to him tomorrow about what I've done."

"Why come *here*, though?" Roshan did her best to speak calmly and not shout. From Lalit's wince and the buzz of the sound barrier that followed, she guessed she'd only partially succeeded. "Why not go into hiding elsewhere—with your father, maybe? Do you have a death wish?"

"Maybe." Navin made a sound that could have been a laugh—if it hadn't sounded so sad. "I've been hiding my whole life. From my brother's and grandmother's judgment. Behind bottles of wine and rang ras, in the arms of lovers I barely remember. Even if I went with my father to Aman, what would I—someone more human than peri—do there before I was trapped and eaten? The Pashu work by different rules, Roshan."

A pair of wide green eyes flashed in Roshan's mind. She suppressed a shudder.

"I'm not pretending to be noble," Navin said. "But Pitaji was right when he said I am not a hatchling anymore. I have to venture out and find my purpose in life. Even if it is to fix something I screwed up—among bandits who might kill me."

The boy who stood before her was different from the one she'd seen on the watchtower earlier that afternoon. That boy had looked like he'd shatter at a touch. This one stood firm, a glint of resolve in his clear gold eyes.

You are more than just a spare prince. Roshan would never admit it out loud, but Peri Tir's words seemed to ring true in this moment.

"The screwup isn't yours alone, Rajkumar." As the words left her mouth, she knew they were true. "Let's start over by declaring a truce. You help us free our province of its corrupt governance. And I'll make sure you don't die in the process."

Gold eyes narrowed. A smile flickered across his flattened lips.

"Deal," Navin said. "Do you want me to seal my promise with a magical contract?"

"Is there a point to it considering how successfully you circumvented the last one?" Lalit asked, raising his eyebrows. "We'll have to trust you—until you meet the truth seeker tomorrow."

If the news about the truth seeker startled Navin, he didn't show it. "Done," he said.

"Might also be a good idea to spread the rumor that you both fell in love along the way or something." Lalit grinned when they both turned to stare at him. "What? Most of the clan already think you're screwing each other. The idea of being in love isn't exactly far-fetched. It might go a long way to convincing people about the rajkumar's loyalty to you—and, by extension, to us."

Irritating as it was to admit, Lalit was right. Love was the most logical reason for otherwise outlandish behavior.

"I'm *not* acting giddy around him," she warned.

A soft, warm laugh escaped Navin's lips. "Don't ever challenge a soul magus like that, Roshni."

"Nothing less than magic would work on her anyway," Lalit agreed. "The only creatures Roshan acts giddy around are wounded beyond repair. Or wild horses."

The men laughed. Roshan's lips tugged into a brief smile.

Rumors about her being in love with Navin would help in other ways, too. The prince could sleep in Roshan's room, which would allow her to keep an eye on him—and defend him, if necessary.

As if sensing her thoughts, Lalit reached into his left boot and placed a dagger on her trunk: a freshly sharpened Ambari jambiya in a faded wooden sheath. Roshan took it and tucked it into her belt. She'd trained with jambiyas as a girl, was reasonably comfortable with them. Not as much as her katar, though.

"Vijali Fui will get you a new katar from the black market tomorrow," Lalit said, when Roshan mentioned this. "Anything else? You both hungry?"

"Yes," Roshan said at once. "Prison food leeches the life out of you."

She looked toward Navin, who also nodded. "I could eat," he said.

"I'll also need a new amplifier," she continued. "Maybe Vijali Fui can find me something in firebloom wood?"

Roshan hadn't forgotten the jade bracelets she'd confiscated from Navin—identical to the ones he was wearing now. Yet, convenient as it would have been to see if the prince's old amplifiers worked for her, the risk wasn't worth it—not when her footing with the clan was so precarious. A bejeweled amplifier that cost enough to feed a whole village for a year would only draw the wrong kind of attention.

"All right," said Lalit. "Pure firebloom, right? Nothing else mixed with it."

"Pure firebloom," she confirmed.

Once Lalit left the room, Roshan turned to Navin. "You take the bed, Rajkumar. I'll be here." She pointed to a corner of the room near the torch, a space she'd normally use to read scrolls and books. Rumored lovers or not, there was not a chance of their sleeping next to each other tonight.

He cleared his throat.

"What is it?" she asked, with a tinge of impatience.

"You're not sleeping?" he asked. "Aren't you tired?"

"You know what they say about the wicked, Rajkumar." She watched Chotu float into the room, balancing a tray with two bowls on his head. "There's no sleep for us."

ROSHAN'S FIRST AND OLDEST NIGHTMARE HAD BEEN ABOUT fire. Of smoke burning her lungs and crawling into her eyes. Of screams that weren't her own but emerged from her mouth anyway, rousing everyone around her.

"Hush, bitiya!" Baba had whispered harshly when the nightmares grew too frequent. "Learn to breathe. Slow and easy. That's it."

She'd remembered being horrified, deeply ashamed of having frightened her father and the others back then.

"Never reveal your weaknesses to anyone," Baba had told her afterward. "Enemy or friend."

Now, nine years later, when Roshan dozed off, her head pressed against the rock wall of her room, the dream came again, like a demon shedding its skin. Hollowed eyes, nebulous face. Horned laughter that stretched through her skin, immobilizing her.

Roshan. The scent of smoke and a familiar spice filled the air.

Roshan. Someone screamed. A woman she didn't know.

"Roshan? Roshan, are you all right? Roshan!"

Her eyes flickered open, Navin's worried face slowly coming into focus.

"High hell," he whispered. "Do you always hold back your screams like that? Like you're being choked?"

"Maybe," she whispered. She didn't know. It had been so long since she'd had this nightmare. Her tongue was saturated with the taste of blood.

"Have you ever felt trapped?" she asked Navin after a long pause. "Like you're buried someplace and can't get out?"

"When I lived at the palace," he replied.

He was holding her hand, she realized belatedly. This boy who'd pretended to be her friend and now said he wasn't her enemy, his cool fingers brushing her sticky hair off her face. Roshan didn't pull away, too tired to resist when he coaxed her to her feet and onto her mattress, flat against the bunched-up gunnies that formed her pillow.

"Sleep, Roshni."

It was one of the last things she'd remember from this night: his words, the torchlight outlining his shadowed form, and the soft hum of a lullaby finally, blessedly dropping a dark veil over her eyes.

34

BY THE NEXT MORNING, NEWS ABOUT THEIR ESCAPE HAD SPREAD
across the kingdom. Along with a new katar and a pair of firebloom
rings for Roshan, Vijali Fui had brought them a scroll of the latest *Jwala
Khabri*, which went into depth about the "outrageous break at the central
bandikhana" and the "notorious Shadow Bandit of Ashvamaidan," who
had "bewitched Jwala's most lovable rajkumar" into running away with
her. An artist had also illustrated likenesses of both Roshan and Navin
next to the story—Navin's being the most accurate, of course.

For the Shadow Bandit, they'd shown a girl with a broken nose, wide
gray eyes, light brown hair, and a mole on her chin—the false features
Roshan had magicked over her own as a disguise against the Brights.

I didn't fail you in this, at least, Baba, she thought. Thanks to the
illustration, the Shadow Bandit's true face remained unknown to others
outside the clan.

Relieved, she adjusted the neckline of the dark brown tunic and
vest Vijali Fui had dug out to replace the gray prison rags. Even though
the clothes fit her fine, something about them felt wrong—as if she'd
accidentally fallen asleep and come awake in another skin. Then again,
nothing about the past few days had made any sense, least of all the
actions of the boy who sat across from her. Her face steamed—*from the
chai,* she insisted, slowly sipping the brew from a clay cup.

And the embarrassment of breaking down in front of him last night after something as simple as a bad dream, her traitorous brain added.

"Looks like there's no point in disguising you for today's visit to the truth seeker," she told Navin without looking up from the scroll. "Everyone knows you're with the clan now."

A second later, the *Jwala Khabri* was snatched from her grip, and she found herself looking right into a pair of gold eyes.

"Stop it," Navin murmured. "You haven't looked at me once this morning. We're supposed to be lovers, remember? Smile now, Roshni. Come on." He plucked out the clove she'd tucked into a corner of her lip, popped it into his mouth, and chewed.

She laughed as the taste of the spice hit him, his seductive expression crumpling into one of pure disgust.

"Goddess's flaming hair! How do you eat these daily?" he demanded while she continued to snort, wiping at her eyes.

His grimace softened into a smile. "Are you all right?" he asked when she recovered.

"Why wouldn't I be?" She tried to keep her voice light. "It was only a silly dream. You should've gone back to sleep."

Ignoring the comment, he delicately brushed a thumb over her cheek. "Your jaw is tightening again and people are watching us. Smile. Or better yet, look into my eyes and tell me how much they remind you of pools of buffalo urine."

Curse him for stealing another laugh from her. But it worked. For something that had been so difficult for the past couple of hours, looking into Navin's eyes was surprisingly easy now. Steadying even.

"Are you using soul magic on me?" she asked.

An unnamed emotion flickered across his features. Carefully he tucked a loose lock of hair behind her ear. She suppressed a shiver.

"I am using soul magic to read your emotions and react to them," he said. "But I'm not using my power to influence you or make you act a certain way. If I did, your mind would feel the intrusion, however subtle."

"I . . ." Roshan's voice trailed off before she could complete the sentence. She'd wanted to say, *I didn't feel it before.*

But that wasn't true. She *had* felt his magic. In the delicate nudges that had miraculously dissolved her fears about taking him with her on deliveries last month. The growing pressure against her skull the night she was captured. Right now, though, apart from the grogginess of a poorly spent night, Roshan's mind was clear. Entirely her own.

"I won't do it again," he said, his gaze intent. "Not without your consent."

"How do I know that?" she said, unable to keep the sharpness from her voice.

"You can block your emotions from me." He shrugged, as if it was obvious. "It's the first thing they teach us as soul magi. To build walls around ourselves, to secure our innermost feelings. Right now, I see your emotions haloed in an aura around your head, every color as clear as day."

"I have an aura?" Roshan hadn't read anything about auras when it came to soul magi. Then again, the book of magic she'd used to learn from had several pages missing.

"Yellow, blue, and pink." He tapped the air as if checking off an invisible list. "Fear, likely for the future; worry about something, probably the Shadow Clan; and a desire for someone unspecified—or perhaps embarrassment about last night?"

She barely restrained from pulling away. No wonder he'd been able to control her so easily before. A smirk hovered across his lips. He was probably thinking about the last thing he'd mentioned. Her so-called *desire*. It was an itch Roshan would take care of as soon as she had a private moment to herself. Or maybe just pinch herself really, really hard.

But she was also done being embarrassed.

"What's wrong with desire?" She gave him the smile he'd asked for before, heavy-lidded and sultry, noting the darkening of his eyes, the flare in his nostrils.

"Are you flirting with me?" he asked, leaning forward—instinctively or intentionally, she couldn't tell.

She moved even closer, her mouth brushing his ear: "You wish you were that lucky."

He was grinning when she leaned back, a sparkle to his eyes she hadn't seen before.

"How are your new amplifiers working?" he asked, changing the subject.

"They're all right. Workable."

Roshan had strung both firebloom rings on a leather cord around her neck, had already healed various wounds in the clan with ease. But the rings weren't as powerful as her old amulet, her healing magic flowing like water through a partially blocked drainpipe. She suspected that the firebloom was mixed in with a redwood like sappan, which had no amplifying capabilities—even though the seller had sworn on both the fire goddess and the flying mare to assure Vijali Fui that the wood was as pure as could be.

Which reminded her.

"Your teak ring got confiscated in prison," she said. "But your other jewels and amplifiers are still safe. I can return those to you later." It pained Roshan to make the last offer. But the point of a truce was to start over clean. Fair.

"Keep them." Navin waved a hand. "As a token of my goodwill."

"You're not serious."

"Don't look so suspicious." He sighed. "How about this—I ask you for those jewels when I need them. Fair enough?"

She nodded and he grinned, a yet unnoticed dimple creasing his right cheek. She pinched the inside of her thigh.

About ten clan members joined Roshan, Navin, and Lalit on their trip to Alipore to see the truth seeker, including Hemant and his lover, Fariyal, the duo whispering the whole way to the village. Ignoring them, Roshan and Navin kept up their pretense as a couple: hands linked, gazes smoldering, laughs soft and silvery, whenever a clan member was in hearing distance. It was more exhausting than she'd imagined. Roshan hadn't ever been in love, and she had a strong suspicion that Navin hadn't, either.

Eventually, he said: "Relax, Roshni. You don't need to brighten like a lightorb every time I look at you."

"You could've told me that earlier," she grumbled, making him laugh.

"I would like to see Jaya, if possible," he said a moment later. "Talk to her and see if we can get some information about the subedar. Once I pass your truth seeker's interrogation, of course."

"*Once?*" she asked, biting back amusement. "You seem very confident."

"What can I say?" His smile was unexpectedly sheepish. "The truth can be surprisingly easy to relate."

The humor from the moment diminished as they approached Alipore, Roshan's insides coiling when she knocked on the village head's door. Sarpanch Sohail answered, his eyes almost instantly finding Navin.

"So it's true," he said, staring at the gold eyes above the prince's mask. "You *do* have the rajkumar."

After a nod from Roshan, Navin undid the cloth covering his face, revealing it fully to the sarpanch.

"No one has me." Navin was polite but firm. "I came to Ashvamaidan of my own accord. To help you."

"We'll let the truth seeker decide that," Hemant's voice crackled from behind them.

Without turning around, Roshan addressed him: "Speak out of turn again and I'll break every last one of your rotting teeth. Understood?"

Silence. Which was about as close to an assent as she would get from Hemant.

"We wanted to see Parvara ji, if possible," she told Sarpanch Sohail. "To verify Rajkumar Navin's truths."

Sohail nodded. "Have a seat in the living room. My mate is in the kitchen with our children."

Parvara arrived moments later, a delicate silver nath hooped through one nostril, a translucent dupatta covering the cloud of short, coppery curls framing their head.

"Sardar Roshan," they said, nodding at Roshan.

"Thank you for seeing us, Parvara ji. And for agreeing to help us."

"Do not thank me, child. Alipore is indebted to you and your clan." The beads on Parvara's jama tinkled as they gave Navin a short bow. "Rajkumar. It is a pleasure to have you in our home."

"The pleasure is mine, Parvara ji. And please call me Navin. My title has always been the bane of my existence."

To Roshan's surprise, Parvara's normally stern face broke into a rare smile. "All right, then. Lay your hand on my left one, Navin."

Once Navin did this, Parvara held up their right hand, which was glowing—the one way to confirm a truth seeker's own truths.

Lalit began the questioning: "Did you break Sardar Roshan out of the bandikhana in Prabha?"

"I did," Navin said. "Only the head warden or someone of royal blood could do such a thing."

"Truth," said Parvara. "On both counts."

"Did you come here to get access to any firestones or firestone mines?" Lalit asked.

"I did not," Navin said.

"Truth," Parvara said.

The questioning continued for several minutes. Roshan observed the expressions of her clan above their masks, noting how their skepticism was slowly turning into surprise and then wonder. Even Hemant, whose forehead remained furrowed, didn't protest or raise questions.

At the end of the questioning, this much was certain: Whether or not firestone mines still existed in Ashvamaidan (and Roshan still had doubts they did), Prince Navin didn't want access to any of them or their contents. He was here to do exactly what he'd been saying, which was help the people of Ashvamaidan.

"Are there any mental barriers that you sense in Rajkumar Navin, Parvara ji?" Roshan asked, more for the clan's benefit than her own. "Any possibility that the rajkumar is shielding his emotions?"

"There are no barriers, Sardar Roshan," Parvara replied, their right hand still glowing. "The rajkumar has been most generous in offering his truths to us this morning."

Navin bowed his head. "Meherbani, Parvara ji, but you are the generous one. Considering how much pain this interrogation has caused you."

Roshan thought he was merely being polite—until she noted the tremor going up Parvara's left arm.

Curses.

"Parvara ji, I'm sorry," she said guiltily. "I didn't even think—"

"No apologies are needed, Sardar Roshan. It is not your fault, either, Navin; I am more tired today than usual." Sohail's hands curled around his mate's shoulders. Parvara glanced up at him gratefully. "Besides, I can tolerate a little pain if it helps our village."

"And our valley," the sarpanch added. "Both Parvara and I will bring up the idea of launching a protest against Subedar Yazad at the panchayat meeting next week. However, we cannot make promises. We'd still need approval from the remaining council members. And to convince the villagers."

"Meherbani," Roshan said, holding a hand over her racing heart. It was more than what she'd expected. "Any news about Jaya's missing sister?"

A visible shiver went through Parvara again. The sarpanch bent low and spoke something in their ear. To the clan, he said, "Not yet. We sent out several search parties the first two weeks of her disappearance but found no sign of her."

Roshan nodded. She was looking at Parvara, whose mouth had grown thin. As if they were holding back tears.

"Sarpanch ji," Navin was the one who spoke now. "We were hoping to see Jaya. Get some answers from her about what happened, if possible."

"It won't be possible, Navin ji," Sarpanch Sohail said, and Roshan's heart sank at the hard expression on his face. "Jaya died a few days ago. She was cremated by her mother last night."

35

NAVIN TRUDGED BEHIND LALIT AND HEMANT, THE AFTERNOON sun burning his face under his mask. For some reason, Jaya's wounds had reopened on their own—a rare occurrence if the weapons used to injure her were poisoned and the poison was still lingering in her body, Sarpanch Sohail had explained. The village head and Jaya's mother had taken the girl to the hospital in Surag, but by the time they'd found her a hakim, it was too late. Jaya had bled too much. Even a transfusion wasn't enough to keep her going.

It had happened three days ago.

Three days ago, while Navin was still in Prabha, debating the merits and demerits of breaking Roshan out of prison.

His head pounded. Next to him, Roshan walked in silence. She hadn't spoken since they'd left Alipore, her last words a simple refusal when Navin had wanted to see Jaya's mother to offer condolences. "One daughter is still missing. Another's ashes have barely cooled," she'd pointed out. "We need to give her time to herself."

Grief permeated Roshan's aura now, along with a sort of rigid acceptance. As if deaths like these were inevitable, living in a place like this.

"So what are you going to do now, Sardar?" Hemant's voice floated to Navin's burning ears. "Question that old hag, Sultana? Or do you think she'll mysteriously die, too?"

Someone—probably Fariyal—snorted a laugh.

"Shut it." Navin's words shifted the air, stilling the bodies around them. Hemant was so silent that for a second Navin wondered if he'd performed soul magic without intending to.

Until he found himself facing the glowing red arrow of the other man's atashban.

"You dare tell *me* to shut up?"

"Hemant." Lalit reached out to him. "Hemant Bhai—"

Hemant shoved Lalit, throwing the copper-haired boy back nearly a foot. "Stay out of it! This one's between me and this spare wastrel of a prince."

A part of Navin's mind stirred black with warnings. Telling him to step back. To apologize. But then there was the other part. The one that had laughed when they'd flown away from the prison. That remembered what it was like to feel free.

Unafraid.

Magic poured up his arms, his jade bracelets a cool fire at his wrist. He opened his mouth, ready to unleash it and tell Hemant exactly what to do in vivid and painful detail.

"Don't." A firm hand curled around his shoulders. Roshan's words brushed Navin's ears, as soft as a moth's wings. "You will only do more harm."

Before Navin could respond, she stepped between him and Hemant.

"Hemant Bhai, we are all distraught by Jaya's death," she said. "Please. Let it go. I apologize on Rajkumar Navin's behalf."

For a long moment, Hemant did nothing. Then, slowly, he lowered his atashban and spat. Roshan's face remained expressionless. Her aura, however, seethed, muddier than the rocks surrounding them, as dark as the magic now roiling within Navin himself. Unspent. Restless.

"Let's get moving!" Lalit shouted.

No one spoke on the journey back to the hideout.

"Navin?" he heard Roshan calling behind him. "Navin!"

But Navin didn't stop. Didn't turn around until they were back inside her sleeping area, the red torch flickering against the rocky wall.

"*Don't*," he shot her own command back at her when she tried to touch his arm. "Why did you apologize to that man? Didn't you hear what he said about Sultana Bibi?"

"Navin—"

"And how dare you step in between us?" His hands curled into fists, the rage he kept so tightly under his control now swiftly unraveling. "It was *my* fight. Did you think I couldn't handle him? Or did you think he would've killed me?"

"No," she said coldly. "*You* would have killed him with your magic. And that would've been a disaster neither of us would have recovered from."

Her words hung in the charged air between them.

"Let's say I'd let you have your way and kill or injure Hemant," she went on. "What do you think would've happened next? Do you think his minions would've taken it lying down? Or that a full battle wouldn't have broken out once we got back here? Who do you think others in the clan would've blamed once we returned—a man they've known for years or a prince who has just recently had a change of heart about us being more than petty criminals?"

Stinging as her rebuke was, it made Navin deflate. She was right.

"I get angry with Hemant, too." She dropped onto her pallet in a crouch, her shoulders hunching. "But it's my fault he is the way he is."

He listened as she talked about the fight for the Shadow Clan's leadership a year ago, her attack on Hemant's older brother, Deepak.

"Lalit keeps saying that Deepak would've killed me at some point if I hadn't killed him," Roshan said. "But I often think about what could have happened if I simply tried *talking* to him. Would the clan be as divided as it is today?"

Regret colored her aura a deep teal. Navin repressed the urge to sit by her again the way he had last night. To wrap an arm around her shoulders.

"Lalit's right," he said instead. "It seems to me that the Shadow Clan was already divided, Roshan. If your father had survived the attack, do you think he would have *talked* to this Deepak?"

"Probably not. I know this *here*." She sighed, tapping her head. "But the guilt never goes away. I feel like I failed Baba and the clan somehow. Still feel like I'm failing them."

Why would you think that? Navin bit back his words. Who was he to lecture her about being a failure—when he felt like much the same most times?

"Hemant wasn't wrong," she said after a pause. "Apart from Sultana Bibi, we have no other real witnesses against Subedar Yazad."

"Why is Sultana Bibi such a bad option?" Navin asked. "Has anyone bothered to *listen* to her?"

Roshan frowned, not answering.

"We need to try," he continued. "And if we don't get any answers from her, then maybe we'll find someone else. But we can't give up like that."

"No one's giving up." If he hadn't seen the hint of amusement creeping into her aura, he would've thought she was annoyed. "But I'll admit it is strange to hear *you* talk this way."

"Need me to see the truth seeker again?"

A corner of her mouth turned up. The air between them had grown charged again—but in a different way. One that made Navin far too aware of her indrawn breaths, the dark lashes fluttering against her smooth brown cheeks. In the torchlight, she appeared simultaneously too close and too far. A distance he found himself aching to cover in three quick steps. He knew she would not stop him.

"We could talk to Lalit," he said, clearing his throat. "Maybe he knows other people—other witnesses we could find."

A sharp exhale. "Huh . . . Haan." Roshan stuttered. "I'll ask him."

She kept her gaze averted as she brushed past him, not turning to see if he followed.

Navin ignored the rapid beating of his heart. He'd done right to keep his distance. To not indulge in his lust. It was one thing to pretend an entanglement with Roshan for the clan's benefit. Quite another to get involved for real—especially when the trust between them was so new and fragile.

He stalked out, emerging to a general chattering in the cavern, the smell of boiling rice and fried blue onions. A few feet away, he spotted Roshan with a bowl in her lap, talking with Lalit, her eyes crinkling as the other man playfully pinched her nose.

"Will you have daal-chawal, Rajkumar?" Chotu's bright grin filled Navin's vision, startling him. The boy held up a bowl, eyes and nostrils widening comically as he took in the scents of hot ghee and cumin, the yellow lentils soaking up the grain.

Pushing aside the envy that had begun spiraling up his ribs like a vine of nightblooms, Navin sat next to the boy and held out his hands.

"Meherbani, Chotu," he said. He forced himself to sit straight. To ignore the soft voices behind him and the staccato burst of a rich, female laugh. "I will."

36

THEY WOKE THE NEXT MORNING TO RAINFALL—A RARE TOR-
rential downpour that not only confined the whole clan underground
for the next three days but also turned parts of the parched badlands into
sludgy rivers of mud. The risk of landslides was imminent—no magical
barrier, Roshan reminded Lalit, would prevent them from being buried underground—which meant that someone was always posted at the
entrance, keeping an eye out on the land, making sure it was still clear.

Khush, the only one who could freely leave their hideout without getting drenched, provided updates about the weather, usually to
mock an anxious Navin: "The sky's still pissing away, princeling! *Phurrr,
phurrr, phurrrrrrrrrrrr!*"

But apart from Hemant, who continued making veiled threats about
how quickly her month would elapse, Roshan used this time in confinement to reconnect with the rest of the clan, admitting her faults
openly—"I made a mistake trusting the rajkumar"—and then inserting
a little white lie to explain how Navin had his change of heart—"We
fell in love."

Some, like Khizer, Vijali Fui, and Navaz Didi, who loathed Hemant
as much as Roshan did, were more easily convinced. The others, Roshan
knew, were still watching. Deciding whether she was a worthy leader.
The visit to the truth seeker in Alipore had been beneficial, doing a lot to

alleviate the clan's—and Roshan's own—suspicions about Navin. Most people, in general, were noticeably less hostile to the prince, though many still had doubts about his ideas of removing Governor Yazad's yoke on the land—legal or not.

"Even with soul magic, do you think he can find proof or get a witness to testify before a mahadastur in one of those big-city courts?" Vijali Fui had asked Roshan one afternoon as they sat by the entrance to the hideout, sheets of water hammering the landscape overhead. "And how does he plan to rally the villagers *here*—let alone get support from the whole kingdom?"

"I'm not sure," Roshan admitted. "Navin got that bit of advice from Yuvraj Farhad. He's written to his brother, too. Khush delivered the letter today."

The living specter secretly returned to Roshan's room with Farhad's reply the same night.

I am glad to hear you are well and neither dead nor bewitched. However, right now, I'm doing my best to convince our grandmother against putting a bounty on your head or issuing a warrant for your arrest and imprisonment. Please excuse me if I have time for little else.—F

"Brilliant." Navin crumpled the parchment in his hand. "At this rate, I'm better off hawking that rag of a *Jwala Khabri* and telling them my side of the story."

"You're supposed to be bewitched, remember?" Roshan joked. "People will only think *I* forced you to write the whole thing."

He shook his head, looking glum. Then his face brightened. "This hideout is an old mine, isn't it?"

"It is." She had a feeling she knew where this was going.

"Then if we find firestones here—"

"We still have done nothing to prove Subedar Yazad is after them," she pointed out. "Also, you're not the only one who thought to look for firestones here." A couple of days into the downpour, Roshan had found several clan members hammering at the walls of the mine and chipping away shiny rocks of unusual colors. She pulled one out of her pocket now and held it out for Navin's inspection. "Here's what Chotu found."

"Glass opal." Navin sighed.

"Exactly."

The iridescent black rock crackled with color in the sun and had been fashionable among the aristocracy over fifty years ago. But, lovely as glass opal was to look at, it did nothing to amplify magic.

"I had to put a stop to the hammering and talk to Vijali Fui," Roshan said. "Her grandfather had worked in a firestone mine. He used to say that if firestones are present in a mine, you can feel their magic. They're far too powerful to go unnoticed for months on end."

On the morning of their fourth day of confinement, the sun finally emerged. Chotu was the first one out of the hideout, his skinny form cartwheeling in the air.

"About time," Roshan said out loud, her heart lifting. "I felt ready to bite off an arm."

"Me too," Navin spoke, which was a surprise because he hadn't complained once about the rain these past few days. When Roshan mentioned this, he grinned. "I know you think I'm spoiled, Roshni, but even I must concede to the sky goddess and her annual spate of melancholy every monsoon."

"Is that why it's called the Month of Tears? Because of the sky goddess?"

When Navin nodded, she laughed. "I didn't even realize that! But it's so obvious now that I think of it."

"Some truths are always staring us in the face. You taught me that."

The sun burnished his hair, revealing the black roots under the brown. Once again, she felt the urge to bury her hands in it. To pull him close and suck that soft lower lip into her mouth. He wouldn't have resisted. Roshan was not a soul magus, but she was no stranger to desire—evidenced now by his darkening eyes.

"You're wrong about one thing," she said, reluctantly breaking the spell. "I don't think you're spoiled. Not anymore at least."

The last time, when they'd been alone in her room and not surrounded by people, Navin had been the one to step back. To draw a line between what was real between them and what wasn't. Frustrated as she'd been, Roshan knew she wouldn't cross the line first.

Was that surprise she saw on his face? Disappointment? The expression was gone so quickly Roshan couldn't tell. Navin put a hand to his chest, gracefully bowing. "I'm going to take that as a compliment and not an insult, jaan-e-man."

Roshan laughed, though a pang touched her chest at the endearment. Jaan-e-man. Had she been anyone's beloved?

Apart from her fling with Lalit, Roshan's romances—if they could be called that—were usually brief: limited to hungry kisses or occasional rolls in the hay with strangers behind taverns in Surag or other big cities where she remained invisible in a crowd. She barely remembered those boys or their faces, was certain they'd forgotten her, too. But now, as she watched the couples and trios around her, the secret smiles, the subtle brushes of a hand against a lover's back or hips, she wondered if there could be more.

Jaan-e-man. Roshan buried the endearment deep, next to the ache left behind by Baba's death and the parents she'd never known. She was the Shadow Bandit. She didn't have the luxury to dwell on feelings or on anything else that couldn't be held in the palm of her hand.

"All right!" she called out, silencing the chatter. "Let's get moving. We need to visit Raigarh today, maybe even Mohr. See what the situation is like there."

Treks to the far west of the valley were always longer and more treacherous, the land full of curves and bends and steep hills. The rainfall had made things worse, flooding parts of the river and blocking old, well-worn pathways, forcing the clan to find new routes or carve fresh paths through rock, mud, and silt.

By the time they approached the village of Raigarh, the sun was nearly halfway across the sky. A pair of shvetpanchhi battled over the bloated carcass of a tusked jackal floating in the water nearby, their screeches ringing in the heat. Roshan swallowed hard, noting that the bajra fields had been flooded over. More grain would be lost and more blood tithes would be borne by the villagers—unless they did something about it.

Protesting against the governor and his Brights, however, wasn't an idea the village council was willing to entertain—even with Navin by the clan's side.

"We can't do it." The village head, Sarpanch Daria, was quiet yet firm in her refusal. "Not at the risk of our people."

"The Shadow Clan would protect you." Roshan hoped she sounded reassuring. "I give you my word."

"I know you would, Sardar Roshan." Daria shifted her dark gaze, unable to look Roshan directly in the eye. "I've seen you fight, know that you would have your own turban knocked off to protect ours. But your clan cannot save us from being beaten or being arrested for public disturbance. Not even with a former rajkumar on your side."

Former?

"What do you mean by *former?*" Roshan asked, her voice growing sharp. "Rajkumar Navin is still second in line to the throne."

She glanced at Navin, but he appeared to have gone stiff, reminding her of the time she'd frozen his vocal cords.

"He isn't the rajkumar anymore. But please. Don't take my word for it," Daria said, nodding to one of her councilors. "Here, Sardar Roshan."

Roshan slowly unrolled the scroll, the familiar curving letters of the *Jwala Khabri* floating before her eyes.

"Kiran Mahal has announced," she read out loud, "that hereon, with immediate effect, Navin of Clan Behram, son of the late Yuvrani Athiya and Peri Tir, has been disinherited and stripped of his title. Henceforth, he will no longer be a prince of Jwala."

37

The words from the *Khabri* sank into his brain as if through holes in a sound barrier, a persistent buzz accompanying each one.

For as long as he could remember, Navin had never taken his title seriously, acutely aware of the distinction between the prince and the crown prince, the distance he'd had to maintain between himself and Farhad during every state ceremony. Always four steps behind, as the palace steward had instructed. Never allowed to catch up.

Farhad's letter should've tipped him off to the situation. And it had—if Navin was being honest. He just . . . he hadn't *really* expected to be stripped of his title and disinherited.

A moment later, the scent of cloves and summer air wafted to his side. "Do you want to go back?" Roshan asked quietly. "We can visit Mohr on another day."

His heart said yes. He was tired. So tired of everything. But when he spoke, the words that emerged from his mouth were different: "The weather's been bad and we only have twenty-five days left. I don't want to waste more time."

Hemant's one-month ultimatum did not bother Roshan, who'd shrugged it off whenever Navin mentioned it to her. But the thought hung over Navin's head every day, kept him awake at night while she fell asleep. He may have lost his title and inheritance, but he didn't want Roshan to lose credibility with the Shadow Clan—the only family she'd known.

Navin's family had given her people enough grief as is.

The village of Mohr lay across the river, accessible via a rickety wooden bridge. "It's more of a hamlet now," Roshan explained. "The only non-magus settlement of farmers left in the valley."

"What happened to the others?" Navin asked, forcing himself to concentrate.

"They left. It's hard to grow crops in this land with magic. Without any, it becomes near impossible." Roshan frowned. "I thought it would go easier with Sarpanch Daria—she's always been cooperative in the past."

"The Brights probably threatened her village before the rains began," Lalit said. "It isn't exactly a secret that Navin came here with you after escaping Prabha."

It took a second for Navin to realize that Lalit hadn't called him by his title the way he usually did. There might've been a flash of pity in the other boy's hazel eyes. Navin averted his gaze, unable to confirm the same in his aura. Did the Shadow Clan also think him useless now—like the sarpanch of Raigarh?

"We don't know what has happened in Alipore, either," Lalit was telling Roshan. "If the sarpanch there has been able to convince his panchayat."

"Navaz Didi will find out," Roshan said. "I sent her and Khizer there today to talk to the sarpanch and also to scout the area around the old firestone mine."

Navin reached up to touch the outline of the feather he always kept tucked in an inner pocket of his jama. It was tempting to reach out to Tir, to ask his father to come fly him away from this.

But where would I go?

He turned, found a pair of familiar dark brown eyes watching.

"You don't have to do this." Roshan's aura reflected her truth. "You can go back home to Prabha. Tell Parasmani Bhairavi you made a mistake."

Navin breathed in the hot air. His mouth was exceptionally dry, every blister scar within aching. His feet hurt and his stomach felt as if it were filled with lead. Yet somehow, despite everything, he was still here. Standing.

"In Prabha, people call me the Peri Prince," he said. "But few see me as a person. In Aman, I'm my father's child but still not considered fully peri. Those places aren't my home, Roshni. Haven't been for a long time. There's nowhere to go."

Nowhere but forward, one step after another, until they were inside Mohr, the dusty trees and huts a blur around him. Only the girl walking next to him was clearly visible, her aura a blue cloud around her head, her troubled silence weighing on him.

Breathe, he told himself as they approached the village elders. *Focus.*

"Shubhdin." Roshan joined her hands in the greeting. Everyone else around her did the same.

One of the councilors tottered to his feet, a man who must have seen eighty blue moons in his lifetime. His bushy brows were burnished gold with age, and his heavy white turban nearly covered one eye. The long bamboo staff marking him as village head appeared to be the only thing keeping him upright. Navin noted the lack of an aura around his weathered face and the stiffness of his puckered brown lips. It was like meeting the parasmani again, except this man had no magic in his veins—nothing to repel Navin except sheer determination.

Intrigue bubbled somewhere under the thick fog in Navin's skull. Before they'd arrived at the villages, Roshan had asked him to scan the auras of the councilors to see if he could influence them. Raigarh, of course, had been a disaster. But now as Roshan spoke to the old sarpanch, Navin forced himself to listen and pay attention to the man's body language and gestures. The bracelets at his wrists warmed, his soul magic reaching out . . . hitting a wall of mist and earth, a complex, shifting barrier that let no emotion seep through.

"Roshan Chaya," the sarpanch said, the rumble in his voice reminding Navin of Tir. "We would help you if we could. But we are non-magi. Surely you understand how much you ask of us. Especially since we cannot protect ourselves against the Brights and their cruel spellwork."

"I understand your fears," Roshan said, her voice and aura brimming with compassion. "But we both know that things are not going to change for the better. The villages around you were swallowed by ravines. Many had to move or abandon the valley altogether. If this continues, you might have to do the same."

"If so, what?" the sarpanch demanded. "We will be safe, won't we?"

"Do you truly believe that, Sarpanch ji?" Navin found himself saying, his voice quiet, yet clear. "Or is that your hope?"

Heads turned in his direction, and Navin wondered if he'd made another blunder. But then Roshan nodded, pushing past the haze of annoyance in her aura. *Go on.*

"This is your land, Sarpanch ji." Navin met the village head's flinty gaze. "Yours, not Subedar Yazad's. When Jwala was breathed to life by the fire goddess, Parasmani Behram had vowed to keep its inhabitants safe and also help them thrive under the leadership of old clans like the Aspas, who'd chosen him as their king. What's happening now in Ashvamaidan valley is a violation of that vow, and it must be challenged in a court of law."

The magic in Navin's veins itched to be used. But he held back, watching the auras of the councilors who sat behind the sarpanch. Waiting until the pale blue of suspicion darkened to curiosity.

"I have no right to ask you anything," Navin went on. "I am not a rajkumar anymore, and I have nothing really to speak of—except for my mind and the clothes on my back. I am also afraid of the future." He pressed a hand to his heart, which was pounding under the feather in his chest. "But, despite everything, I am more afraid of doing nothing. Of sitting, hand folded over hand, watching the life around me drain away."

Moments trickled away in silence. No one spoke. But Navin could tell they were listening, bandit and councilor alike. Faces pinched. Breaths held. Waiting for the sarpanch to respond.

The old man cleared his throat. "You say you are no longer a rajkumar," he addressed Navin. "This is unfortunate because I don't doubt your sincerity. But when I became sarpanch, I made my own vows, along with the council behind me, to the people of this village, who now depend on my protection. Do not think us ungrateful," he said, turning to Roshan. "The Shadow Clan helped us when no one would. You still do so. But I am sorry. Right now, at least, the councilors of Mohr and I stand firm in our decision."

Roshan's body was coiled tight, her fists held close to the sides. But when she spoke, her voice was calm.

"I understand," she said. "Shubhdin, Sarpanch ji."

"Shubhdin, Roshan Chaya. Young man." The old councilor looked sad. "Goddess be with you both."

38

"STAY ALERT," ROSHAN WARNED THE CLAN AS THEY LEFT THE village, her hand on her katar.

Ever since Baba was killed in a village nearby, she'd never liked traveling to this part of the valley, her mind flashing images of his severed head floating ahead of her on a pike.

It wasn't until they were well beyond the western pass that Roshan allowed herself to breathe. To evaluate everything that had happened. She'd anticipated failure on some level, of course. But with Navin at her side, she'd also expected to do better. She glanced now at the prince, who appeared lost in thought, having forgotten to put up his mask.

She tucked it into place. Like the caring lover she supposedly was.

"You didn't use soul magic on them." She kept her voice low, hoping it didn't sound as cold as the fury in her chest. "I could tell you wanted to. I felt your magic reaching out."

She'd been surprised to sense it—much like she would a magical barrier, only more delicate. More probing.

"You could? Interesting." The surprise was clear in his gold eyes. "Must be our bond."

Her stomach flipped. "Our bond?"

"Yes, Roshni." She had the feeling he was smirking at her now and instantly regretted masking him. "We began bonding as early as our first meeting, when you spoke my name. An old soul magus trick. But for you to sense my magic is unusual on many levels. It's the sort of thing that comes with a deeper relationship. With trust—on the soul magus's end."

Guilt warmed her cheeks. But Roshan still needed an explanation.

"So why didn't you use your magic?" she asked. "I understand Raigarh was a bust, but you could have influenced the sarpanch of Mohr."

He sighed. "Imagine this. You see someone's house. To enter, you can knock on the door—or break it open. Knocking would work, if someone trusted you. Breaking in would be a last resort—an incredible violation. Now think of the house as a mind. Sheltering someone's emotions."

For long moments, Roshan didn't speak. Then: "Was there no window?"

Gold eyes shuttered slightly, as if baffled. "What?"

"Was there no window to peek into the sarpanch's hou—mind?"

A soft laugh escaped him, and she got the feeling it was real.

"No," he said, focusing on the land ahead of them. "There wasn't. In a way, I wasn't surprised. Jwala may have ended magical segregation earlier than the other kingdoms of Svapnalok, but non-magi, in general, still distrust magi. A certain level of suspicion—even dislike—is needed to create the sort of walls that repel soul magic so thoroughly."

Roshan was grateful he was turned away from her right now and couldn't see the embarrassment—and the desire—that was surely lurking in her aura. Dislike wasn't an emotion she'd felt for Navin in a while now.

"I thought you'd take the easy way out," she admitted.

"In the past, maybe. My old tutor always said that the best soul magi used their power at exactly the right time. Back then, I didn't understand what he meant. Now I do. Using my power on the sarpanch would've worked in the short run. But once we were gone and my magic wore off, we'd have been worse off than before."

Frustration crept up Roshan's spine. His words made sense. But noble as his intentions were, they did little to help their cause.

At the hideout, Navaz Didi and Khizer brought more bad news.

"Sarpanch Sohail and Parvara ji were not able to convince all the councilors to protest," Navaz Didi told Roshan grimly. "It was three against two. They said they'd try again. But they didn't seem very hopeful. Especially with today's . . ." her voice trailed off as she glanced at Navin uncertainly.

"It's all right," Roshan said with a sigh. "We know about the *Khabri*. What about that abandoned firestone mine, Khizer? Did you see anything suspicious?"

"Khush tried to slip in at first," Khizer said. "But there were barriers around it—the sort that keep out living specters. We decided to scout the area and keep watch. For hours, no one came by. But then this one Bright passed through the walls."

"An enchantment," Roshan said, frowning. "So the mine's exterior is probably false."

"That's what we thought, too. Obviously, there's no way of knowing for sure—unless one of us turns into a Bright."

"So if someone from the clan infiltrates the Brights," Navin began, hope creeping into his voice, "we could—"

"We could be caught and skewered," Hemant interrupted. He'd been silent until now. "Sardar Roshan should know. Her dear father tried this in the past, didn't he?"

Roshan's throat tightened. Her hand curled over the hilt of her katar.

"The great Bhim Chaya!" Hemant continued, voice rising. "You would've thought he'd go himself. But did he? No! He sent someone else to infiltrate the Brights. A credulous, loyal village boy who'd seen only seventeen blue moons in his life—a boy whose corpse we ultimately found by the river, violated beyond belief."

Navin said nothing, his face ashen with shock.

Roshan, for her own part, couldn't fight back nor deny the truths Hemant spoke. Her baba had loved her more than anyone else in the world, had fought to the death for the Shadow Clan and the villagers of Ashvamaidan valley. But he hadn't been perfect. Not as a leader. Nor a man.

"You're right, Hemant Bhai," she said. "My baba did wrong by that boy. I cannot change the past, but I can promise this much: No one will have to risk themselves and infiltrate the Brights. If the time comes, I will face Subedar Yazad on my own."

She stalked off before she could register anything more than surprise on Hemant's face. Her vision blurred, and for a while, she wasn't even sure where she was going. She finally paused at the staircase leading to the single entrance and exit of their hideout. Testing the air for the telltale cold of Khush's invisible presence and finding it clear, she sat on the third stair from the top, carefully unraveling her turban and freeing her hair. The sky was awash with orange, gold, and mauve. Somehow, despite everything, sunset in the valley was still the most beautiful time of day.

"You all right?" a voice asked.

She squeezed her eyes shut. A pair of hot tears slid out. "Go away, Lalit."

"It's not Lalit."

A shuffle of feet, a rush of air scented with dust and grass and boy. She didn't open her eyes until she felt the weight of his back hot against her knees.

"Awful day, haan?" Navin said. "Like everything got worse as we went along."

"You could say that." She wiped her face. "It's fine. You can face me."

"Thank goddess." He slowly turned, his broad frame angling awkwardly on the stairs. "Or maybe not."

A giggle escaped her lips. She hadn't done *that* since she was ten.

"Don't laugh at my predicament, Roshni," he scolded. "Not all of us can fit into small spaces with finesse."

"The lower steps are wider," she said on an impulse. "We can both sit there."

She waited until he chose the sixth stair—which still revealed a sliver of sky from above if she looked up—and squeezed in next to him. Her arms warmed, partly from their shared body heat, partly from a reason that had nothing to do with temperature. But she didn't move away. Regardless of what she'd said earlier, Roshan really didn't want to be alone right now.

Even though she suspected he'd ask her what her plans were next. Dreaded the idea of telling him she didn't know.

Instead he said: "Roshni, I need to tell you something. When I'd been captured here, I would often hum songs. It was how I—"

"Did soul magic," she said, the realization sinking in. "Somehow, your singing amplifies it."

His stunned expression nearly made her laugh again. "You knew?"

"I just figured it out. It makes sense when I think about it. How else could you have done the things you did?"

He looked genuinely ashamed. "I'm sorry."

"You were in captivity. If I were you, I'd have done my best to escape as well." This much at least was true.

He raised an eyebrow. "So why did you let Lalit beat me up?"

"I'm not saying I'm perfect."

He laughed. "Good thing you're gorgeous," he said softly. "It's the only way I'd let you get away with something like that."

She'd have thought he was joking again—if not for his eyes, which appeared to glow in the dim light, and his mouth, which parted now, the lower lip slightly wet.

"You don't have to do that," she said. Shame—mostly at her own unruly wanting—made her insides coil.

"Do what?"

"Act like you really want me." Her nails dug into her thighs and she turned her head up again so that she could catch the last red sliver of the sun. "There's no one here to see us. You don't need to pretend."

"What if I'm not pretending?"

Her answer stuck in her throat.

"Roshan." Fingers, calloused from the time he'd spent here with them, lightly traced her cheek. She shivered and turned to face him.

"You didn't want to a few days ago," she insisted. "That time you—"

"Are you afraid?" He cut off her breathless words. "Have you heard of me destroying my lovers with merely a kiss?"

"Who said I wanted to kiss you?"

His laughter slid across her skin, warmed her insides like wine. "Your aura betrays you, Roshni."

Curse the gods.

"*You* don't want to kiss me," she went on stubbornly. "Joke all you want, Navin, but I'm no one's fool."

"No." The mirth left his face, which remained partly shadowed. "You're not. But I may've very well been foolish to think I could stop wanting you."

She could feel his breath on her too-hot cheek.

"Do you want me to go?" he asked. "If so, I will. I won't ever push you."

Say it, her brain commanded. *Tell him to leave.*

"A mere kiss does not destroy," she found herself saying. "I've kissed people before."

"Prove it."

Bad idea, the sensible part of Roshan's brain warned. *You don't need to prove anything.*

Yet.

Here, in the near dark, no one would see them. Here, in this moment, Roshan could pretend she was someone else, kissing someone who wasn't a former prince, but merely a boy whose stubble she itched to feel rubbing against her skin.

A kiss. Just a kiss in the dark.

Navin, as promised, waited for Roshan to prove her point—to cup his cheeks in her palms and gently lean her forehead against his. He made a sound that could have been a resigned sigh. Or a laugh.

Bastard.

She brushed her lips against that smug smile, feathered the seam lightly with her tongue. He released a breath, sharp and hot into her mouth, his hands curving around her hips, his mouth molding carefully to her own.

She did not detonate. Did not even feel the earth shift under her feet. The kiss was oddly delicate, a flickering, barely there flame that made her toes curl deep in her boots.

"Have you destroyed me yet?" she whispered against his mouth.

"I don't know. But you're most certainly destroying me."

She was about to laugh shakily, to say something mocking, when his head angled sideways, fusing their mouths deep, sucking lightly on her tongue. The kiss jolted through her like lightning, turning every nerve and limb to jelly. In response, his fingers delicately feathered her spine, wrenching sound upon tiny sound from her throat. Long moments went by before he broke off, his voice tickling her ear.

"Don't tell me you're moaning over a mere kiss, Roshni."

"A moan does not equate to destruction," she shot back. Or maybe it did.

She'd have wondered if she was the only one affected if not for the press of his body against hers. The feel of him hardening against her hand.

She reluctantly pulled back. "Do you want to stop?"

His face was drawn tight as if in pain. "Do you?"

"No, but—"

His lips captured her errant words, and the last bit of her resolve melted like sugar on her tongue. His mouth moved from her lips to her neck and then farther below, her jama coming undone with ridiculous ease, her breasts pebbling in the cool air, under his hands.

"Is this all right?" he whispered, his mouth hot against her skin. "Tell me, Roshan. I won't go on unless you tell me to."

"Don't. Stop."

He didn't.

Didn't complain when she pressed her own lips to his throat, nearly ripped his jama while opening it. A hiss left his mouth when she pressed her lips to his tattoo, the delicate gold feathers curling around his chest. As her hand curled lower, her brain flashed a warning, reminding her of the herbs she'd have to drink afterward to avoid an early pregnancy.

But it was Navin who suddenly reached out, stilling her hand. "Wait."

She paused, bemused at first as he moved down a step or two, knelt again, understanding, then awe growing as he pushed the hem of her jama up to her waist and undid the drawstring of her trousers, baring her flushed skin to the cold air. He glanced up, eyes hooded. Waiting for permission.

She swallowed hard. She'd heard of people doing this before but had never experienced it herself. She nodded and then gasped as his mouth touched her, scattering her thoughts.

The world expanded.

Shrunk.

Disintegrated to stardust.

When she came down from her high, Navin was wiping his mouth with the edge of his sleeve.

"You liked that." There was no question in that too-smug voice. In that lascivious grin.

"Bastard," she whispered. But the word had no heat to it. She smiled, hand reaching out to touch him, only to find that—

"I . . . might've exploded when you did," he admitted, sounding sheepish. But only a little. He was much too pleased with himself, a part of the starry sky reflecting clear in his eyes along with the ghostly smile of Sunheri's moon.

Roshan's heart throbbed in her chest. An unnamed emotion rose through her like a wave. She did not know what it was—this thing between them—and, if she was being honest, she didn't want to. Not right now, when so much was hanging over their heads. Not when tomorrow could usher in another, higher hell.

All Roshan wanted was to live. In this moment, with this marvelous, ridiculously beautiful boy, who made her feel both like herself and not, who was somehow drawn to her, curves and jagged edges alike, as she was to him. She allowed her fingers to stroke his chest, her nails circling his nipples and then lightly scoring the skin stretched tight over his hard muscles.

"*You* like that," she whispered, unable to resist a smile when he groaned.

A shadow flickered across his face. For a second, her heart stilled and she wondered if he'd seen something in her aura—something that had scared him off. But then he smiled back. His thumbs traced the delicate skin behind her ears, sending another shiver up her spine.

"I love your hair." He breathed in its scent. "So very much."

And when they kissed again, Roshan ceased to think at all.

39

THE NEXT THREE DAYS BROUGHT ONLY MORE BAD NEWS. Firozgar's village elders politely refused to join any protests despite the extra sack of grain Roshan and Vijali Fui brought with them to offer as a gift. Sarpanch Vilayat of Jyoti was more open about his feelings, spitting throatily upon seeing Lalit and Navin and denouncing the latter as a "blood traitor."

"At least he doesn't think I'm bewitched," Navin told Lalit as they walked out of the village, more fatigued than disappointed. Navin hadn't expected success in Ashvamaidan, not right away. But he hadn't imagined failing this badly—not when he knew and had heard firsthand about the atrocities the Brights had committed across the valley. He raised a waterskin to his mouth, took a long swallow.

"Not bewitched?" Lalit asked with a snort. "You mean the sounds I heard from Roshan's sleeping area these past couple of nights weren't of you two playing hide-and-seek?"

Water dribbled down Navin's chin. He met the other boy's knowing eyes. "You have a problem with that?"

He was more curious than offended. By now Navin had overheard various people in the clan having talked about Roshan and Lalit being lovers in the past.

Lalit laughed, a silver cloud of pleasure surrounding his turban. "No," he said. "It was about time something happened."

Navin's face burned. *About time*, as if their becoming lovers was inevitable—though it still felt like a dream to Navin. In the days that had followed the night on the stairs, neither he nor Roshan had been able to stay away from the other. They found excuses to talk, to touch, even when doing something simple like walking across the cavern or eating a meal together. The nights, they spent entwined together, neither mentioning the feeling that hovered in the air afterward, one that rushed simultaneous waves of exhilaration and terror through Navin's veins.

Was it love?

Navin was afraid to use the word, though what he felt for Roshan was more than lust and deeper than friendship. Roshan's aura remained equally muddled, as if she, too, had yet to decide what she really felt about him. It was perhaps why she'd sent Lalit with Navin to Jyoti today instead of going herself—though, right now, Navin was relieved she wasn't there to see him fail.

At the hideout, they walked into clouds of smoke and a shouting match between Hemant and Vijali Fui, the latter's hands glowing red around her dagger.

"Aye!" Lalit marched between them. "What's going on? Where's Roshan?"

"In the black market, getting clothes for Chotu," a voice announced. Khush cackled from somewhere above, clearly enjoying the fight.

"Fariyal cooked up the last sack of our rice and *burned it*." Vijali Fui spat out the last two words, and for the first time, Navin noted the smell of charred rice amid the smoke. "She needs to pay up in coin!"

"You're not getting any coin from Fariyal, old hag!" Hemant snarled, his atashban sparking the air. "If anyone should be replacing our grain, it should be you and our sardar, who *gave away* our food to those cursed villagers! You—" At this point Hemant said something so nasty that the air around Vijali Fui grew dangerously charged. She raised her dagger, ready to strike with a spell, when Navin spoke:

"*Silence.*" His voice reverberated through the cavern. "*No one will fight.*"

Navin did not know why he'd chosen to sing instead of speak the command—or why he'd thought to do it now, right before Vijali (likely deservedly) reduced Hemant to a pile of bones and ash. But, somehow, he knew he'd done right. As if he'd allowed two disparate parts within himself—mother and father, soul magic and song—to finally come together and fuse into a flame that pulsed steadily at his throat.

It was to this that Roshan and Chotu returned: a tableau of slowly thawing faces and angry, twisted bodies, and Navin between them, the inside of his cheek bulging with a new blister.

Roshan dropped the small sack she was carrying onto the ground. "What in high hell is going on? And why does it smell like the cavern's burned down?"

"Fariyal burned our last rice." It was Lalit who spoke, the first of the lot to unfreeze. "Vijali Fui wanted her to pay up to replace it. Hemant feels she shouldn't have to since you gifted some of our extra rations to the villagers."

Red wafted in Roshan's aura. "I gifted the rice with the clan's approval," she said.

"Not mine!" Hemant had unfrozen at last, his voice lower than before, but still angry. "But you people never listen to me, do you? And now we don't have any rice and *Vijali Fui* here wants Fariyal's coin!" He spat again.

"No coin will be taken," Roshan said, shooting a warning glance at a furious Vijali. "We still have a couple of sacks of bajra. That should tide us through till tomorrow night's raid."

A raid? Navin's body grew cold. *So soon?*

The lack of surprise on Lalit's and Vijali's faces gave him pause.

Navin thought over things again. Realistically, it wasn't that soon. He and Roshan had been back in Ashvamaidan for over a week now, and they'd spent much of that time confined to the hideout because of inclement weather. The clan's food supplies had to be running low; in fact, Navin now faintly recalled their portions this week being smaller than normal. It had been the one time he'd barely noticed the lack of food, his mind too full of Roshan and the nights to come.

Roshan, on the other hand, had been thinking of other things. Like food shortages and raids that she'd discussed with others in the clan but not Navin. Not in passing. Not once during the whole three days they'd been together.

You're her lover, Navin. Not her mate.

Yet what really stung was that, despite everything that had happened between them, she still didn't think of him as her ally. Certainly, she didn't trust him enough—not when it came to this.

"Roshan!" he called out as she stalked toward her room. "A word."

She turned around to face him once he ducked into the small space. "What is it?" she asked warily.

Why didn't you tell me about the raid? He stilled the words before they left his lips. Rationally, he knew he had no right to ask her that question. Also, the fact that she'd hidden the information from him wasn't as important as the fact that she was planning to do the raid at all.

"I think it's a bad idea to do a raid," he began. "It will wreak havoc on the Shadow Clan's image."

"Image?" she asked, a tired note entering her voice. "We're bandits, Navin. Looting is what we do."

It sounded so natural when she said it. As if looting *was* what she'd been born to do. But Navin knew better. He'd seen her glow bright with magic to soothe an old woman, assess an aging priest's tumor, seal a bleeding girl's wounds. He now saw her aura, the fear and sorrow feathering the rage—as if she wasn't really that sure of herself.

"Listen," he said. "I understand we need food. But a raid won't help us right now. Our biggest problem is that people see you and the Shadow Clan as criminals and Subedar Yazad and his Brights as victims. No one knows the truth about what's going on. If you continue looting him, no court will recommend legally removing him from governance, let alone giving you and the villagers back your lands."

"Who cares?" Roshan snapped. "No court is here to help us now! Given a choice between starvation and stealing, I'd rather steal and live another day."

Navin's mind raced as he forced himself to pull together the threads of every disastrous thing that had happened this week. Everything led back to his disinheritance and his title—the one thing he'd never really cared for but always taken for granted. An idea, as fresh and tender as new grass, budded in his mind, gaining vigor the more he thought about it.

"What if I write to the *Jwala Khabri?*" he began, and then held up a hand as she started to protest. "No, wait. Listen . . ."

He told Roshan about the first day of Hashtdin, the massive crowds near the royal balcony unfurling banners and chanting his name.

"Maybe I'm not a prince anymore," he said. "Not even a spare one. But does that mean Prabhavasis—or even Jwaliyans—have lost interest in me? The story about my disinheritance had no explanation, correct?"

Roshan frowned, thinking. "I don't think it did."

"Right," he said. It was exactly his grandmother's style: No questions entertained, no explanations offered. But Jwala's inhabitants weren't a five- or even nineteen-year-old Navin, who'd remained easily cowed. "There have to be questions about my sudden removal. Some rumor or conjecture. When I was kidnapped, no one talked about disinheriting me. Even when the news first broke about our escape, people assumed I'd been 'bewitched.' Now, suddenly, without explanation, I'm no longer a rajkumar? What's that saying in the Common Tongue: *There's dirt in the daal?*"

"*There's something black in the daal,*" Roshan corrected. But her amusement soon faded. "That still doesn't solve our most pressing problem for food."

"I may have a solution to that." He held up his wrists, revealing his jade bracelets. "You have another pair of these, do you not?"

"I . . . I'd forgotten about those."

"Some bandit you are. Sell them off. You probably won't get full price for them, but there'll still be plenty of coin to buy food."

"I don't like this."

"You mean you don't trust anything you can't punch or kill." He grinned as she shot him a death glare. "Come on, Roshni. Have a little faith."

"Let me ask Lalit and Vijali Fui what they think," she said, sighing. "I can't make such a big decision without their advice."

The two bandits, to Navin's relief, fully approved of selling the jewels.

"It hurt my heart to burn your expensive clothes," Vijali Fui admitted. "Such fine fabric that was—even when stained with vomit."

Navin and Lalit laughed as Roshan shook her head.

"Ask Khush to bring the jewels here tonight," Vijali advised the Shadow Bandit. "Give them to me tomorrow and I'll make sure I get us the best deal at the black market."

"All right," Roshan said slowly. "So we'll hold off the raid until you return from the market. What about Navin's idea of writing to the *Jwala Khabri*?"

"It's clever," Lalit said. "It's one thing for them to ignore a common villager. But they'd be fools to not print a letter from someone of royal blood—even if he isn't titled anymore."

"What if they do the opposite and depict Navin as the fool?" Roshan asked quietly. "Or worse: What if they don't publish it?"

The words hammered Navin's skull. He knew she was right. Someone at the *Khabri* could very well inform Queen Bhairavi or even Governor Yazad about his letter.

"There's no harm in trying, is there?" Navin asked. "If I fail, well, then I fail. But I'd feel worse if I sat here, doing nothing."

Lalit grinned and clapped his shoulder. "Do it, Rajkumar. We're with you."

"We are," Vijali Fui agreed.

They turned to Roshan, but she said nothing, her aura still tinting her hair blue.

"Roshan?" Navin asked hesitantly. "Are you with us?"

"Yes. Of course. There's parchment and ink in the trunk." There was an edge to her smile—one that Navin couldn't quite figure out. But before he could examine her aura, Roshan pushed past him and the others, leaving them to stare after her awkwardly.

That night, she didn't come to Navin at bedtime. Neither did he find her in the cavern or the stairs by the entrance or the bathroom when he got up to look. The old glass opal mine had many empty passageways, and Navin heard moans and knowing laughter coming from a few. Neither of them sounded like Roshan. He even glanced into Lalit's sleeping area, but the other man was snoring, drool seeping from his mouth.

Instead of being relieved, Navin's stomach tightened even more. In some ways, it might've been easier if Roshan had been with Lalit. At least he'd have known where she was.

At one point, he thought he saw a figure hunched at the end of a long passageway, a glint of red hair under a torch. But before he could step farther, he found himself being pushed backward by a pair of small, invisible, inhumanly strong hands.

Khush, he realized, his torso prickling with cold at the contact. The living specter hooted, predictably teasing Navin about his disheveled appearance.

"Patience, princeling," Khush said. "Your little hakim needs time to herself."

Patience. The word sank in, settling some of Navin's earlier queasiness.

He returned to Roshan's empty room. Instead of lying down on the pallet next to hers, he sifted through her small trunk and found the parchment and ink she'd mentioned.

To the editor of the Jwala Khabri, he addressed the finished letter, folded and tucked carefully into a square. *From Navin, son of Yuvrani Athiya and Peri Tir.*

It was strange not using his title anymore. Yet, somehow, it wasn't as bad as he'd expected. He rose to his feet, ventured again toward the corridor where he knew Roshan was crouched that night.

"Khush?" he called out.

A moment later, he sensed the specter's presence. "Princeling?"

"Would you deliver this for me?" He held out the letter. "It's for—"

"The nasty little news scroll that announced your disinheritance." The letter floated up from Navin's upturned palm and vanished into thin air. "I will deliver it."

A smile tugged at Navin's lips. He was tempted to tell Khush he wasn't a *princeling* anymore. But then he recalled what the specter had called Roshan in turn.

Your *little hakim.*

The thought stilled his words.

"Meherbani," Navin said, bowing in the specter's general direction.

It was silly, he told himself. *To believe a specter so fond of pranks.*

Yet, under his jama and the feather he always kept there, Navin's heart beat a hopeful rhythm. The sort he hadn't felt in a long time.

40

Hope was an emotion Roshan had learned long ago to never entertain—one that would betray her the moment she allowed it to lift her heart. Hope was also exactly the feeling Navin had triggered with his suggestions, a wave of surging lightness that terrified Roshan so much that she'd been unable to face him for the rest of the evening, deciding instead to focus her energies in getting back his jewels from the old hideout.

"Is he gone?" she asked Khush.

"He is, my little hakim. Though he isn't the one you should be punishing right now."

The rebuke in Khush's high voice startled Roshan. His invisibility to everyone except Khizer and his natural fondness for mischief made Roshan sometimes forget that Khush was nearly as old as she was, an eighteen-year-old spirit trapped in the form of the child he'd been when murdered.

"I don't mean to punish him," she said, staring at the jewels peeking out from the bundle before her. She picked up a jade bracelet. The amplifier was cool to the touch.

"I guess I'm afraid of what will happen if I put too much faith in him," she admitted.

Faith was a dangerous commodity in these parts—sold to the

gullible, easily broken. Even Khush did not argue that. Though he did reveal a teasing glimpse of the letter Navin had given him before disappearing from the cave.

Vijali Fui left for the black market before dawn—the jeweler worked only during the first hour there before sneaking away to his shop in Surag. To everyone's surprise, except Roshan's, the old lady returned well before breakfast, her face set in a scowl.

"Bastard jeweler tried to swindle *me*," she groused. "Said I should sell him the whole lot for ten mohurs. *Ten*, when it's probably worth thousands!"

Roshan glanced at Navin for the first time that morning.

"What do you mean?" he asked, face pinched in confusion. "Surely he sees the value—"

"Of course he does!" Vijali Fui said, despair ringing in her voice. "He was driving down the price on purpose. He told me if I wanted to do better, I should go directly to Surag. Every shop there reports to the Aspas. We'd be better off looting them than expecting an honest transaction."

"What if you broke up the jewels?" The suggestion, surprisingly, came from Hemant, who was eyeing the bag in Vijali's hands. "Sold them off piece by piece?"

"A good jeweler would know," Vijali said. "Goddess's hair, even a bad one would! Each gemstone is probably embedded with the royal seal."

No one spoke for long moments.

"It's decided, then," Roshan said, her voice hoarse. "Ready yourselves to raid tonight. We'll be targeting the Bagbol granary."

"Bagbol?" Lalit sounded startled. "I thought we were going to raid another cargo dhow!"

"I've given it some thought and changed my mind. We've raided enough dhows by now for the Brights to add more barriers and protections. The granary is relatively isolated in comparison. Hardly anyone protecting it on most days."

"But the granary is also inside the village!"

"So? It doesn't belong to the village. It belongs to Subedar Yazad. Besides, we raided places inside villages in the past when Baba was still alive."

"And then we stopped because it got too dangerous!" Red mottled Lalit's pale cheeks. "Because innocents could die in any ensuing crossfire!"

"There are no huts in the vicinity of that warehouse," she replied, dismissing his concern. "Though Bagbol is not exactly innocent. Nor an ally of ours."

Not that Baba hadn't tried to turn the village into an ally, taking them gifts of grain and an atrociously expensive firebloom madira, along with having Roshan magically cure their sick and injured. He'd even—to her fury—brushed aside the village council's attempt at getting the Shadow Clan ambushed by local darogas working in league with Governor Yazad.

"You cannot fault the desperate, bitiya," Baba had told her. "They're only trying to survive."

Only now, Baba wasn't here and Roshan was alone, struggling to hold everything frayed and broken—including herself—together.

"I still think—"

"Get the atashgolas ready," Roshan cut through Lalit's argument. "That's an order, Lalit!"

A tick went off under Lalit's beard. She heard him swallow. But he didn't argue.

"We'll gather here right when the fifth torch goes blue," she announced to the others, who were watching them with curious expressions. "Keep your weapons sharp and ready. Is that understood?"

"Haan, Sardar!"

Roshan turned, leaving behind a chorus of whispering in her wake. A moment later, she heard someone calling her name. She ignored it.

"Roshni!" Navin caught her by the arm, his grip firm but not strong enough for her to want to truly fight him. "Wait!"

"*What*, Navin?"

"I know what you just said," he said, his voice far calmer than hers. "But I still want you to reconsider the raid. Or at least wait another day or two until the next edition of the *Jwala Khabri* comes out. We've come so far!"

"I don't have the *time* to wait that long!"

"But, Roshan, the clan—"

"Unlike you, I've had to fight for everything I've gotten so far," she said. Her heart shriveled, hardening like a melon in the heat. "Everything. So don't you tell me to wait for a stupid news scroll's approval. And don't you *dare* tell me what I need to do to protect this clan!"

A wild look came over Navin, his eyes filled with such loathing that for the smallest of moments Roshan felt a genuine inkling of shame.

But then he dropped her arm.

"Be my guest," he said. His gold eyes clouded over with a cruelty she'd forgotten he possessed. "Sardar."

THE RAID STARTED OFF SMOOTHLY, THEIR WAY TO THE GRANARY
unhindered, not a villager in sight. There were no guards, either, nor
Brights posted by the door.

At this point, Roshan should've grown suspicious. She should have
told the clan to wait. To hold back a little.

But her head was pounding from lack of sleep. She'd also heard several stomachs—especially Chotu's—growling on the way there. Navin
was the only one who hadn't left the hideout. *He's probably thinking of
ways to get back to the palace,* she thought bitterly. Roshan had been
tempted to leave him a charm to bypass their barriers in case.

Mud caked their boots and the knees of their trousers, bodies aqui-
ver and teeth chattering from having waded the shallowest part of the
freezing Behrambodh.

An owl hooted above. She glanced up at Chotu, his body nearly
invisible, having taken on the shades of the starry sky.

Someone was coming.

A pair of Brights, then a dozen more, helmets gleaming gold in the
dark.

"Leave!" their leader boomed. "Back away and you will remain
unharmed!"

Next to her, Lalit sucked in a breath. His always steady hands trembled on his atashban, alarming Roshan.

"What's wrong?" she whispered. "Are you all right?"

Lalit didn't reply for a few seconds, still staring at the leader of the Brights. "It's him," he whispered. "Altaf."

"Who?" But Roshan realized who it was even as she asked the question—more so from the pinched skin around Lalit's eyes and between his brows.

Altaf. It was the first time Lalit had revealed the name of the boy he loved.

"You said he was a villager." She forced herself to keep her voice low so that the others wouldn't hear. "Curse the gods. He's a *Bright*, Lalit!"

"I know." Lalit sounded like he was gritting his teeth under his mask. "But he wasn't a Bright when we met. Only talking about joining them. I kept trying to talk him out of it. It's why we split up."

A pang of sympathy went through Roshan. "You still love him."

"I do. But I'd have hated myself for joining ranks with the people who killed my family. *When they don't give us our birthright, we steal it.*" The clan's motto still resonated strongly in Lalit's voice. But it also sounded hollow.

"Sardar?" someone else whispered behind Roshan. "What do we do?"

"Wait for my signal," Roshan told them. She turned to Lalit again. "Are you sure you can do this raid? Tell me now, Lalit. Or walk away."

She couldn't afford any more casualties in the clan. Not now. Especially not on her watch.

Lalit hesitated. Then nodded once.

Fine.

"Arms at the ready," Roshan's whisper carried down the group. As the Brights raised their atashbans, she shouted, "*Now!*"

It should have been easy. There were fourteen Brights to the Shadow

Clan's forty-four, and apart from Altaf, none of the goldplates seemed to know how to shoot an atashban properly, weapons sparking or shots going wide.

But the Shadow Clan's best shooter was hesitant that night. Aiming for arms and knees instead of heads and hearts, while the Brights did exactly the opposite, their wild spells forcing Roshan and a few others to duck for cover, rolling messily out of the way. With a roar, Roshan leaped up and jammed her katar through a Bright's throat. Vijali Fui dispatched another, Khizer a third.

"Shoot him!" someone was shouting. "Shoot him, Lalit!"

Roshan turned, her gaze instantly drawn to two figures dancing around each other. Altaf took aim, his death spell deflected by the glowing orange burn on Lalit's shield.

Curse you, Lalit, shoot him.

She was about to shout the words when a spell hit Lalit in the back, surrounding his body in a wild red glow. The Bright wielding the atashban was already dead—jabbed through the throat by a furious Vijali Fui—by the time Roshan reached Lalit, her throat raw from screaming her best friend's name.

Lalit groaned. Still alive. Next to him knelt Altaf, his helmet gone, his handsome face ashen, his hand dark against Lalit's pale face.

"If you don't get out of here this instant, I will kill you," Roshan told the man. "Do you understand me? Altaf?"

His name startled the Bright more than the venom in her voice. Roshan punched, her katar aimed right at that perfect nose. He blocked the blow, her blade finding his cheek, which now bled like a river. Altaf rose and without another glance at Lalit, ran.

"No!" Roshan held back Hemant, who had raised his atashban to shoot his retreating back. "We do not shoot like cowards. Start loading the gunnies on your backs. We might not have much time before he gets more forces."

"That wouldn't be a problem if you let me shoot him," Hemant retorted. But, for once, he didn't argue. The prospect of food occupied him and the rest, while Roshan focused her energies on Lalit. The atashban wound, she saw with some relief, was localized to the muscles of Lalit's left shoulder, leaving his bones and organs intact.

She allowed her fingers to lightly trace its edges. Waited for her magic to come. The firebloom rings at her throat warmed. With aching slowness, magic crept up her arms, gold specks of it glittering at the tips of her fingers.

Roshan focused on every good memory she had of Lalit: the sparkle in his hazel eyes, his full-throated laugh. Yet, even with the amplifiers now burning between her clavicles, Roshan knew it wasn't enough. Most of the poison was now gone, but Lalit's wound was knitting together too slowly, her amplifiers unable to draw the magic she needed for early healing.

Not that it helped with the migraine. Roshan's head began to pound, hard and fast, her vision blurring from the pain.

No. She couldn't collapse. Not now.

But she did, voices blurring in and out of hearing. When she finally came to, strong arms were heaving her over a pallet. Navaz Didi had carried her back to the hideout as if she were no more than a child again.

Shadows spoke, asking if she was all right. Roshan's head hurt, her eyes wincing at the slightest brush of light.

"Lalit," she whispered. "Is Lalit—"

"Lalit's fine." Navin's low, soothing voice feathered her ears. "The others are tending to him. You saved him, Roshni. And you got us our food."

Something sharp and painful balled in her throat. To her horror, tears burned her eyes. Threatening to flow.

Navin murmured something to the others, chasing them from her room. He helped Roshan sit up and drew her to his broad chest.

"Cry," he commanded. "Cry, stubborn girl."

His magic brushed the inside of her skull. "Let it all out," he hummed.

She did, allowing a dam within to break and flow over the front of his jama.

Lalit. She'd nearly lost Lalit—her best friend in the whole world—because of a few stupid sacks of grain. Because she couldn't bear to admit that Navin, a boy she was terrified to love, might've been right about the raid, might've been right about her banditry all along.

If Navin sensed the truth within her wildly shifting emotions, he didn't mention it. His hand curled gently around her head, his arms steady and unflinching against the maelstrom of pain she'd unleashed. A tiny voice in Roshan's head called her weak. Pathetic for breaking down so thoroughly.

But for once, she didn't care. Nor did she fight for control.

For once, she stayed exactly where she was.

41

"BETTER NOW?" NAVIN ASKED, ONCE ROSHAN STOPPED SHAK-ing. He felt, more than heard, her whisper of assent against his chest.

"You were right," she said, her voice raw. "It was a bad idea to do the raid. I . . . I'm sorry for what I said to you before. You must hate me."

He did hate her—for a while. A couple of hours ago, he'd wondered if he'd made a colossal mistake coming here in the first place. But even Navin couldn't ignore the shame that colored Roshan's aura now, mingled in with guilt and regret.

"I don't hate you," he said, meaning the words. "Besides, I'm the purveyor of bad ideas, Roshni." He paused as she chuckled and then groaned, holding up a hand to her bruised jaw. "Do you want a draft or something? Navaz Didi said she had sleeprose."

"N-no." Her voice, though shaky, was certain. "Sleeprose alters memories. I . . . I don't want to forget what happened tonight."

A pause.

"Are you able to look at me?" He stroked her hair, which was vivid under the torchlight. "Or is your vision still too sensitive?"

Her body shrank slightly before she slowly raised her head. One eye opened to a slit while the other remained squeezed shut. At Navin's snort, she gave him a familiar scowl.

"What are you laughing at, Rajkumar?"

"You," he said without hesitation. "You look hilarious."

Her mouth trembled the second before she laughed. "I know. It's always like this after a migraine, though. The dark remains preferable to light." A pause. "Sometimes I wonder if the fire I was placed beside as a child should have swallowed me whole. Maybe then I wouldn't be here. Screwing everything up."

"*Have* you screwed everything up?" Navin asked. He might've warned her off against raiding, but he could admit she'd done a good job of it. "You said you'd get food for the clan. They brought in sacks of bajra and rice. You went out with over forty people, including a ten-year-old boy. They all returned alive and mostly intact. Are you telling me no one gets injured on a raid?"

Roshan bit her lip. "I've lived in fear my whole life, Navin. Worrying that I'll never match up to Baba, even as I craved to take his place. I worry even now if I put a single toe out of line, things will fall apart."

"You're not your baba, though, are you? Roshan, I used to compare myself with my brother, Farhad, every time. I still do—especially after being disinherited. But I'm beginning to realize that Farhad is a different man. One who has chosen his fetters, though, supposedly, he's the most powerful person after the parasmani herself. I was a little like that, too. But I can't be like that anymore," Navin realized as he spoke the words. "I can't keep my mouth shut or wrap a blindfold around my eyes. And maybe that's not such a bad thing."

"But you don't want to be parasmani of Jwala," Roshan pointed out. "Baba and I wanted the same thing—for the villagers and the clan to get their lands back. I still want it."

"Then maybe you're going about it the wrong way. You keep thinking what Bhim Chaya would do. But what would *Roshan* do?"

She said nothing for long moments, her brow furrowed in thought. "Outside Ashvamaidan, people think we're brigands, which we are. But you said we need the rest of Jwala's support for our freedom."

"Right."

She exhaled sharply. "It's impossible. The others won't agree to stop looting the subedar."

"Did your baba imagine he'd get support from anyone when he started the Shadow Clan? Don't let fear hold you back from changing the narrative, Roshni. Good leaders know when to fight. But they also know when to step back and change tactics. Or so they taught us during those boring lessons they give princelings in case we become parasmanis."

"Princelings? You've been talking to Khush, I see." Her smile faded. "I . . . I need time to think."

Navin nodded. As quickly as he wanted her to make a decision about this, he also understood now that they were, as the old proverb went, teetering on the edge between a well and a ravine. Was this how his grandmother had felt? Was it why she'd eventually made that awful deal with Governor Yazad?

It was discomfiting, but different as they were, Navin couldn't help but see the similarities between Roshan and Queen Bhairavi and the choice they had to make between holding on to power and fighting for freedom.

What if the queen had refused the governors their demands? What if she'd fought harder? Negotiated more? Navin didn't know, nor could he change the past. All he had was now—this moment and this hard-headed, remarkable girl whom he somehow trusted more than he ever had his grandmother.

His hand reached for the feather Tir had gifted him. His father's promise of help was reassuring. But Navin knew now wasn't the time to ask for it.

"Sleep," he told an exhausted Roshan. "It's been a long night."

"Where are you going?" Her hand caught hold of his arm.

Navin hesitated, still smarting from yesterday's rejection. "I thought you wouldn't want me around anymore."

"You thought wrong."

In the dim light, her eyes were so dark they looked nearly black. An emotion, delicate and tentative as smoke, curled around the top of her left ear. Navin's heartbeat quickened. He'd seen it only once, several years ago. Glowing in the auras of a pair of beggars crouched by a sidewalk during a Hashtdin procession in Prabha. It had been the first time he'd seen every shade of the rainbow intertwine without mingling, forming a rope of sorts that circled the two women's veiled heads like the frayed blue-and-gold binding bracelets they wore around their wrinkled brown wrists.

"What's that emotion, Dastur Jamshid?" he'd remembered asking his tutor. "There, around those two women?"

"That? Why that's love, Rajkumar. The rarest, most generous emo-tion of them all. Love knows everything. Sees everything. But wants and cares in spite of it."

Love. The thought sang in his veins, like the first tentative note in a raag, bringing everything around him into sharp focus: the musk of sweat and cloves in the air, the liquid depths of Roshan's eyes reflecting his own.

Love, he thought as Roshan's mouth found his, blood a steady throb in his ears and his heart.

Love, when he let her push him flat on his back and then slide down his chest.

Love, as they lay afterward, limbs entangled, when Navin finally allowed himself to see his own aura, finding confirmation in the swirling, iridescent bands of color that formed a truth he couldn't speak aloud.

THE DAY AFTER THE CLAN'S RETURN FROM BAGBOL, THE BLACK market near Surag was raided by the local darogas. Stalls were forced to shut down, including one that sold cheap copies of expensive books and the latest scrolls of the *Jwala Khabri*.

"Funny," Roshan commented when Khush brought her the news. "The black market has always been there—and the darogas know about it because that's how they get their weekly baksheesh."

Yet even bribes hadn't been enough to prevent the raid—which meant the orders had come from higher up.

"Higher up?" Navin asked. "You mean the Ministry of Peace?"

"Well, not that high up," Roshan said dryly. "The only peacekeeping done over here is by men in gold armor."

Why would Subedar Yazad care about the black market? Navin wondered.

He got his answer three days later—on the twenty-third morning of the Month of Tears, when Khizer and Navaz Didi returned from a delivery with grim looks on their faces.

"What is it?" Roshan asked them, her aura clouded with worry. "Have there been more blood tithes?"

"Raigarh's gone," said Khizer in his soft voice. "Swallowed by the ravines. Most of the houses we looked into are abandoned now. Only Sarpanch Daria had remained. She was waiting for us. She gave us these." He held out two scrolls of the *Jwala Khabri*. "Navin Bhai, I can't read, but she said this might interest you. And that she's sorry for how she acted the last time you and Sardar Roshan went there."

A pang went through Navin. Even though Raigarh and its sarpanch had refused to help them in their fight, no one deserved to lose their home. Also—

"That explains the raid by the darogas," Roshan echoed his thoughts. "The *Khabri* must've published your letter, and the subedar isn't happy about it."

"Still doesn't mean what's in there is good," Navin told her. He braced himself for the contents of the first scroll, the one dated 20 Tears, 40 Bhairavi Kāl. He knew how news scrolls manipulated stories, how they sensationalized rumors, blurring the line between what was true and what wasn't.

To his surprise, the *Khabri* had published his letter in its entirety, the words exactly as he'd drafted them. Next to it, the editor of the *Khabri* had also written a note:

Imagine, dear Jwaliyans, my surprise when a spectral presence dropped this letter into my daal bati last night—"I dropped the damned scroll in his lap, not his food!" Khush screeched as Navin read the editor's letter aloud to the rest of the gathering clan.

Navin, the erstwhile prince of Jwala, or the Peri Prince as he's still popularly known, infamously broke out the Shadow Bandit, Roshan Chaya, from Prabha Central earlier this month. We at the Khabri questioned this strange behavior, wondering if the prince might've been under the influence of dark magic or a strong enchantment spell.

The Peri Prince's disinheritance raised more questions, neither of which Kiran Mahal agreed to provide answers for. Yet here, in this outrageous and enlightening letter, we finally have answers. Are they true? Is Subedar Yazad Aspa of Ashvamaidan as heinous as alleged? Or is this letter merely the ravings of a poor, lost soul? What do you think, readers? Hawk us your answers at the old haveli next to the watering hole in central Prabha.

"Well," Navin said. "That wasn't as bad as I thought it would be. I half expected him to go on a rant about my rabid winged ancestors eating our own when he called me the Peri Prince."

Anger, as cold as ice, flooded through him. But now wasn't the time to address the bigoted commentary he'd come across about his Pashu heritage in the *Khabri* over the years, nor the part his grandmother's own prejudice might've played into how human Jwaliyans saw others of his race.

"Patience," Dastur Jamshid had told him. It had been the first time Navin had heard the word, his tutor carefully rolling up his sleeve to reveal the patch of shimmering green scales embedded into his dark brown skin. "Change will come for those of us who appear more human than Pashu, child. Perhaps you will bring it."

A snort cut through Navin's thoughts.

Lalit was lightly rubbing his bandaged shoulder. "That's a load of horse dung," the bandit commented. "My ma used to tell us stories about the peri and other Pashu, and she always said that the Pashu fought hard for their own, making great sacrifices to save their kin. Here, our parasmani does not care if we live or die. Goddess take her and her royals to the highest of hells. With exceptions," he amended with a quick glance at Navin.

Navin ignored the spasm under his ribs. "I'm not a royal anymore, Lalit."

"Maybe, but not all Jwaliyans think so," Roshan said. She'd already begun scanning the subsequent edition of the *Khabri*. "This paper's from today, and it has published reactions from citizens in each of the four provinces. They're mixed, obviously. Some people do think you're still bewitched or that you've lost it. But others don't seem to think so. Kumari Damini from the eastern province of Tej says, 'Rajkumar Navin is the last person I see having his head turned by enchantment, for he's an enchanter himself. If he thinks the Shadow Bandit of Ashvamaidan is telling the truth, then she probably is.'" Roshan raised an eyebrow at Navin, who suddenly found himself trying his hardest not to avoid her stare. "Former lover?" she asked coolly.

"Former betrothed." Navin coughed. "It was political. Her father's the Minister of Treasure. Our split was . . . not good."

Vijali Fui's cackle broke the tension. "Well, that's a decent endorsement."

Roshan looked at him for another moment, her aura shifting from annoyed to amused. She went back to reading:

"Here's a letter from the province of Atash Koh: 'I am a sipahi from the northern mountains who has followed the story of the Peri Prince with interest. He is a kind man, who protected my kinswomen when they were at risk of losing their jobs as his guards. I also don't understand why people assume he has been bewitched. Rajkumar Navin is a soul magus, which makes him more than capable of withstanding common love potions, jadu tona, and other forms of enchantment. It is hard to believe someone like the Shadow Bandit can capably bewitch the rajkumar from within the confines of Prabha's central bandikhana, especially when she's no soul magus herself.'"

Roshan paused as a few cheers rang out. Navin pushed back the hope wavering in his chest. "That's only two people," he said.

"And here's a third," Roshan countered, her voice growing intense. "This one's from Ashvamaidan and it's anonymous. 'Rajkumar Navin and Roshan Chaya healed a girl in our village, one who'd been badly injured. The Shadow Clan have looked after us when no one else did, when the subedar's blood tithes would have otherwise had us die of starvation. We don't want you here, Yazad Aspa. Yazad Aspa Murdabad.'"

Death to Yazad Aspa. Navin's blood chilled at the letter's ending. These weren't simply words of support. This was a battle cry long withheld, now spoken for all of Jwala to hear.

"Yazad Aspa Murdabad!"

"Yazad Aspa Murdabad!"

The chant began somewhere behind Navin, Chotu's and Khush's voices, soon accompanied by others, growing louder and louder. It felt surreal. As if he were living in a daydream. Navin wasn't sure how he felt about the chant itself. It was common enough. One that people often made in Prabha against ministers or priests, when angered. The difference was that most Prabhavasis weren't armed with daggers and atashbans the way the Shadow Clan and the Brights were. Navin had been fighting so hard to simply get the villagers to rally against the subedar, he hadn't thought about how things could go wrong—or how violent a protest could become.

Navin looked up to find Roshan watching him. She was the only other person in the cavern not chanting the slogan. Eventually, she raised a hand and called for silence.

"Let's save the chanting for an actual protest—if one materializes. We have deliveries to make now. Come on." Waiting until Navin rose to his feet and approached, she asked, in a quieter tone: "Are you all right?"

"I'm fine," he said, forcing a smile. Roshan continued watching him, as if she didn't believe the assertion. To his relief, she didn't push for an answer.

The dread in Navin's belly deepened on accompanying Roshan to Alipore that afternoon, when the council asked to speak to them both. A crowd had gathered around the giant neem under which the village council sat on a raised platform.

"We wish to personally apologize to you," Sarpanch Sohail addressed Navin. He rose up and pressed his palms together in a gesture of humility. "As sarpanch, I wish I had fought harder for the solution you'd proposed. But I, too, had believed your disinheritance would render any protests on our part useless. We were wrong. You were brave to come back here to our province, braver to write to the *Jwala Khabri* about our problems."

"Someone among you was brave, too," Roshan said. "Someone from this village wrote to the *Khabri*, corroborating our story. Was it you, Sarpanch ji? Or your council?"

"It wasn't me." The sarpanch shook his head.

The council murmured similar denials.

A throat cleared from the crowd in the back, where a lone figure had risen. It was Jaya's mother—only Navin could barely recognize her from the last time he'd seen the woman, her face hollowed, the skin around her eyes so dark it appeared bruised.

"I wrote the letter," she said. "For my daughter. For both my daughters and the man who murdered them. Yazad Aspa Murdabad."

The quiet words and the grief in the woman's aura hit Navin harder than any chant could have. Guilt and shame churned his belly. To think he'd worried about a single rally growing violent when people here faced violence daily, having their food, land, even their families snatched away.

"There are Jwaliyans who still see you as their rajkumar," Jaya's mother told Navin now. "And so do I. I will pledge my support to any protest you and the Shadow Clan organize against Subedar Yazad Aspa."

"Rajkumar Navin Zindabad!" someone shouted from the back. "Goddess bless our Peri Prince!"

The chanting for his long life rose around Navin, pulsed through his bones. He made note of every hardened face, from the oldest to the youngest, standing next to their parents, sticks clutched in their small hands, their auras black as thunderclouds. They trusted him. These people, who'd faced so many troubles in their life, trusted *him*.

Navin hadn't realized that his hands had begun to shake until Roshan caught hold of one.

"What is it?" she whispered. "And don't tell me it's nothing, Rajkumar. You've been quiet the whole way here."

"They . . . they believe in me. I've never had anyone believe in me before."

Her gaze softened. "You're hard not to believe in. Or to love."

What? Navin stared at her as the chants still continued behind them. He wanted to ask her to explain herself. To demand she say the words again, despite the iridescent aura rippling around her deep red hair.

But before he could, the sarpanch called for silence.

"On behalf of the village of Alipore, I officially pledge our support for a protest," Sarpanch Sohail said. "But we will need the Shadow Clan's support."

"And you will have it," Roshan said. Navin could feel the certainty of her aura reflected in the pulse at her wrist, steady and warm and purposeful.

"Parvara has been corresponding with other villages, too. Have we heard back from them?" Sohail asked his mate.

Parvara rose to their feet. "We've heard from Firozgar and Mohr, who have agreed to participate," they announced in their clear voice. "Raigarh has been forced to evacuate and find a new place to stay, as you know. But Sarpanch Daria says she will support us if there is a protest."

"Well, Sardar Roshan?" Sarpanch Sohail cleared his throat nervously when a brief silence followed. "What do you think?"

"I think we should gather by the big fire goddess's temple in Surag on the twenty-seventh of Tears, which is four days from now," Roshan said. "That will give Mohr and Raigarh enough time to make the journey on foot. And I think we should do exactly what Na—Rajkumar Navin—advised us to. Let's take back our lands."

"Take back our lands!" Lalit cried.

"Take back our lands!" the village boomed.

Love. The word, spoken with that rasp Navin had grown to crave, echoed through his skull even as the chanting stopped, the sarpanch promising to send word to the other villages about the protest.

It lingered as he finally caught up to Roshan and took hold of her elbow outside the village.

"You can't leave me hanging after what you told me last," he told her, struggling to keep his voice low.

Her eyebrows nearly vanished into her turban. "What *did* I tell you last?"

Any other day Navin would've appreciated the teasing. But right now his nerves were like a rope frayed to its breaking point. Reaching out behind her left ear, he ripped off the mask she always wore.

A couple of gasps rose behind them, but neither Navin nor Roshan looked away from each other. Roshan, for her part, appeared more entranced than astonished, as if she were seeing him for the very first time.

"Call me a princeling or a spoiled brat," he said, his voice hard. "Make fun of me if you want. But don't mess with my head, Roshni. You said I was difficult not to believe. Or to love."

Her mouth curved up in a smile so soft he could hardly believe it was her.

"I meant it," she said quietly, gesturing to the space above her turban—at the cloud of midnight hovering here, glimmering intermittently with flashes of the rainbow. "Satisfied by what you see there, my spoiled princeling?"

He kissed her quick enough to swallow the laugh that followed. Hard enough that they might've toppled over and fallen, if she'd not kissed him back with equal fervor.

Among the whistles and lewd shouts ringing around them, he broke apart from her and whispered, "You're difficult not to love, too."

THEY WALKED BACK, HAND IN HAND, GRINS WIDE AND GOOFY on their faces, Roshan not bothering to pull her mask back on.

Yet, the closer they got to the hideout, Navin saw her aura shift to one that was blue and thoughtful. A moment after they crossed the barrier leading down to the stairs, her hand slowly slipped out of his.

"Lalit," she said. "Vijali Fui. I need to talk to you both. Alone."

A few days ago Navin might've felt hurt at being left so obviously out of the loop. But something had changed between him and Roshan since the night of the clan's last raid, since this afternoon when he'd seen the rainbow hues of her aura.

Trust, Navin realized. He trusted this girl with his whole heart.

"Go on, Sardar," he told Roshan. "I'll find a way to amuse myself."

He spent the rest of the afternoon washing dishes with Navaz Didi in the kitchen and later playing chaupar with Chotu, teaching the boy the best ways to trick his opponents at the game.

Around sunset, when the fourth torch turned blue in the cavern,

Roshan, Lalit, and Vijali finally returned. There were grim looks on their faces.

Navin's heart skipped a beat the second before Roshan dropped the announcement, one that exploded with the force of an atashgola, reverberating through a space that suddenly felt too small:

"I think we should stop looting the subedar."

42

"Outrageous!"

"What in high hell?"

"Have the lot of you been bitten by wild dogs?"

Roshan braced herself against the accusations, the clan's fury mounting the longer she remained silent. Yet, now that the words had left her mouth, she felt strangely relaxed. As if saying the words had stiffened something in her spine, holding her like a rock amid the chaos.

A second later, she unsheathed her katar and threw.

Heads rolled sideways as the dagger flew overhead, its triangular point finding a crevice in the cavern wall. Jamming there.

They turned back to Roshan, utterly silent.

"Now may I explain?" she asked, her voice calm. She nodded her thanks at Vijali Fui, who retrieved the katar. "I know this sounds extreme, but I'm not making this suggestion lightly. In fact, I fought with Navin the first time he suggested it."

She glanced at Navin, whose look of astonishment had settled into one of curiosity.

"We have, for the longest time, been forced to live a life on the margins," she told the clan. "We are thieves, murderers, and criminals. But before that, we farmed the land, fished the river, herded animals, most of which we owned. Well, you did. I was an orphan born to burn in a garbage heap. Bhim Chaya saved me. *You* saved me. You trusted me to be your sardar after Baba died. Please trust me again when I say that we now have a chance to not only save but also free ourselves of the subedar's tyranny.

"Navin's letter to the *Jwala Khabri* has earned us unexpected support from the rest of Jwala—and more important, from three of Ashvamaidan's villages. Now that we have this momentum, we need to add kindling to the fire, as the old saying goes. And we can't do this if we keep looting Subedar Yazad and killing his Brights. No one is saying they don't deserve it," she added, looking right into the mutinous faces of a few older clan members. "But to most people outside Ashvamaidan—the people whose support we desperately need for the palace to start an inquiry against Subedar Yazad—we only look like villains."

A hand shot up. "Yes, Navaz Didi," Roshan said.

"What about food? How will we eat?" she asked. There were several murmurs of assent.

Roshan nodded. "It's a great question. It was exactly why I fought with Navin at first. Initially, we had tried to circumvent this problem by selling some of Navin's old jewels to the black market. Unfortunately, that jeweler was trying to loot *us*." The scattered laughter made Roshan smile, relieved. "But Vijali Fui now says we may have more options. Isn't that so?"

"Yes," the older woman said. "I have a contact at the eastern border of the province who might be able to help us find buyers. Now, with Rajkumar Navin's letter gaining such popularity, we may find more benefactors than before."

"We're planning to head there tomorrow," Roshan said. "I don't know what will happen, honestly. But we have to try something we haven't before. It is our goal, isn't it, to get our lands back? To leave this behind?"

She gestured around the cave, to the worn sleeping pallets rolled up against the walls next to gunnies marked for deliveries. Nearly half the angry faces had softened. For the first time in over a year, Roshan wasn't worried about sounding like Baba or exuding the same confidence.

Even when Hemant spat on the floor and said: "You're a fool if you think a protest is going to change anything or get us back our lands. I don't agree with this!"

"You have every right not to," she told him. "So do the rest of you. This will be up for vote and everyone will have a say. The majority will decide the outcome." She took a deep breath, focusing her attention on the others. "I'm not going to lie to you. I'm scared. I worry that things will go wrong, that more people will get hurt or die before any of this comes to an end. But then I think about the life I'm living now. Day to day, hand to mouth, only fear pushing me onward. I think of choosing between this life and fighting for something better. Maybe the best possible life that I can live. If you were me, what would you choose?"

There was a long pause before a throat cleared. "I'm not a clan member, but I'd choose to fight," Navin said, his voice resonating through the room. He gave Roshan the lazy half smile she'd once thought she hated.

"So would I," Lalit called out.

"And I," Vijali Fui said.

"And I." Navaz Didi.

"I." Khizer.

The sound reverberated through the cave, one voice adding to another. By the time Roshan called for a vote, thirty-five of the forty-four bandits called to put an end or at least a pause to banditry for now.

"Curse the gods! Have you all gone mad?" Hemant demanded.

"If you feel that way, you're free to leave," Roshan said. Exhaustion crept up her bones, but she held firm, not looking away from the other man's furious gaze. "But if you choose to stay part of this clan, you must do what the majority voted on."

For long moments, Hemant said nothing, a vein pulsing under his beard. Then he spat on the floor and stalked farther into the mine, Fariyal and a few others following.

"Roshan, do you really think it's a good idea to give him that option?" Lalit asked as chattering broke out around them. There was a frown on his face. "He could go to the subedar and—"

"Do what?" Roshan asked. "He's magically bound by the contracts everyone signed for Baba, pledging their fealty to the clan. Even if he goes to the Brights, he has nothing to offer."

"I wouldn't say so, Roshni."

She turned to face Navin, who raised his eyebrows. "I didn't have to break your magical contract to find a way around it. It was difficult and I very nearly asphyxiated, but I managed to do it."

There was a brief silence. "I really don't like this," Lalit said at last.

Roshan didn't, either. But they didn't have much of a choice right now—apart from possibly confining or killing Hemant, along with eight other people.

"We'll have Khush and Khizer keep an eye on Hemant when we go out tomorrow," she said finally. "Navin, you'd better come with us. You'll have a better idea of the value of those jewels."

"Also, he can persuade the jewelers to give us a better deal," Lalit said. "Most people fawn over him regardless of the soul magic."

The joke did little to put Roshan at ease. She half expected Hemant to leave, but he was still at the hideout come dinnertime, his cronies throwing occasional scowls Roshan's way.

To the highest hell with them, she decided as she followed Navin back to their sleeping area. For now, at least, Hemant was going nowhere.

THE MORNING OF THE TWENTY-FOURTH DAY OF TEARS DAWNED bright and quiet. They left the hideout shortly before sunrise, hiking to Firozgar, where they borrowed a boat from one of the villagers. Under the careful eye of its owner, Navin and Lalit pushed the boat into the water and then jumped in as Vijali Fui pressed a pair of glowing hands to the bow, making the vessel move on its own accord, without oars.

"How do you do that?" Navin demanded, sounding envious.

"A propulsion spell, Rajkumar." Vijali shot him a gap-toothed grin. "They're easy enough if you have magus blood. All you need to do is learn how to agitate the water."

"Unless you're like me and the water agitates you by not cooperating," Roshan whispered into his ear, and then smiled innocently as he laughed and Vijali looked up, bemused.

Next to Navin, Lalit moved his uninjured arm, murmuring a few words as he cast a web of light around the boat—a shield that faded from view seconds later even though Roshan could feel it buzzing against her skin.

She'd tried healing Lalit once more a couple of days ago and again had trouble channeling her magic properly with her new amplifiers. Eventually, her friend had told her to stop and save her energy. Roshan's glance went to the bag on her lap, one that held Navin's jewels. It was tempting to try out the jade bracelets and see if they worked. She was pretty sure Navin, at least, wouldn't mind.

No, Roshan.

The clan and Ashvamaidan needed coin for food. Roshan wouldn't risk that—even if it came at the price of weakened healing magic.

Vijali Fui's contact lived at the House of Scryers, a monastery bordering Ashvamaidan's eastern edge, a little farther away from the port of Surag. It was dangerous traveling through enemy territory like this, but trekking to the monastery on foot through the ravines would've taken them nearly a whole day. The boat would get them there in a couple of hours, tops—*if* nothing else hindered them on the way.

As the sun rose, the landscape around them changed, hills and canyons flattening to tangerine-colored firebloom orchards rising in the distance. Roshan's heart quickened at the sight of Surag's flat-roofed stone havelis, the imposing white marble Ministry of Treasure they'd broken into last year, red flags with the royal homāi emblem fluttering from its peak.

They sucked in a collective breath on passing a dhow marked with the Brights' distinct brand of shield spells, quickly tugging their blankets over their heads. But no one stopped them. No one turned to look—even from the docks, which now bustled with people boarding bamboo-roofed houseboats, dhows, or small fishing vessels like theirs from either side of the coast.

"Slowly, Vijali Fui," Roshan warned as they fell in line after a pair of boats navigating a bend in the river. "We don't want to draw attention."

But Lalit's shield spells somehow made them less noticeable. Or that's how it felt to Roshan. Soon, they were sailing alone again, the river broadening as they left the city behind.

They reached the House of Scryers without incident, the boat swaying as they dropped anchor and beached at a small dock. The monastery stood a hundred yards away, its marble domes interspersed with stained glass windows. Roshan had never been to this place, but even she could tell that those who lived here weren't lacking for coin.

"I think it's best if all of us don't go in," Vijali Fui said. "Navin, you come with me. You two stay here and keep an eye on the boat. We don't want to lose it to other petty thieves."

Roshan and Lalit nodded, watching as Vijali and Navin walked to the monastery, the sack of jewels in hand, and disappeared somewhere behind the walls.

"I wonder who Vijali Fui's contact is," Roshan mused. "A monk?"

"A monk who happens to be her sister."

Roshan stared at Lalit. "Fire and ashes, you're serious? I didn't know Vijali Fui had a sister! Didn't she lose her family in one of the Brights' raids?"

"She did. But her sister, who could scry the future, had been sent away to live here long ago, when she was a child. Vijali Fui had always written to her sister, and she'd written back. The sister wanted Vijali to leave the clan, had begged her to do so several times over the years and come here."

"Why didn't she?"

"She met Navaz Didi," Lalit said simply. "Also, Vijali Fui has never been one for monastic life. She trusted Sardar Bhim to get back her land. She trusts you, too."

The words, far from uplifting Roshan, weighed heavy on her. By the time the sun reached the sky's center, a pair of figures emerged from the monastery—Vijali and Navin, both grinning widely.

Navin handed Roshan a pair of sacks heavy with—she opened one to see the glint of gold. "You made a good deal?" she asked.

He nodded. "Ten thousand mohurs for the lot. Scryer Devyani—the monk—asked me to use soul magic while dealing with the jeweler. She said outright he was a crook."

Vijali laughed.

Roshan said nothing. The day had been successful—more so than she could have hoped. But a strange feeling crept through her now, compounding as they set sail again.

"Are you all right?" Navin asked, keeping his voice low so that the others wouldn't hear. When she started shaking her head, he raised his eyebrows. "Don't do that, Roshni. I can see your aura, remember?"

Of course he could. She sighed. "I have a bad feeling."

"About what?"

"I'm not sure. Just . . . something feels wrong."

Even though she couldn't pinpoint what it was.

Roshan's instincts had never lied to her about danger, so she remained alert as they cruised through Surag again, even more when they reached Firozgar and hauled the boat back to the village. By the time they reached the Shadow Clan's hideout, the sun had begun to set, glowing behind clouds like lines of molten ore.

The odor tickled Roshan's nostrils seconds after she passed through the barriers, cloying and distinctly familiar in the bitterness she tasted in the air.

Sleeprose.

Bodies were slumped over the cavern, half-eaten plates of food lying nearby. Lalit picked up one of the plates and sniffed at the rice.

"Sedated," he confirmed, nose wrinkling. "The whole lot of them. The dosage appears heavy, too."

Roshan scanned the cave, pausing at Khizer, who was passed out over the stone bench Navin normally sat on, drool seeping from his mouth.

"Hemant," she said. "Where is he? And where's Khush?"

"I can't feel him here," Navin said. "It's too warm."

"I don't see Fariyal, either," Vijali said. "Or the rest of that lot."

So Hemant and his cronies had run away. But why drug the whole clan to do it?

Roshan's insides twisted with dread. She was about to count heads when a wail rang out somewhere behind her.

"Khush!" she shouted. The room's sudden chill announced the specter's presence, along with his cries of utter fury.

"Those *bastards!*" Khush screeched. "That turd-faced, goddess-forsaken swine!"

"Khush, what happened?" she tried to talk over the swearing. "Tell me!"

"Hemant happened!" The specter sounded more distressed than Roshan had heard him. "He and his minions drugged everyone's food and took Chotu! I tried but couldn't stop them!"

"Chotu?" Roshan's heart lurched. "Where did they *go?*"

"To that bastard subedar's warehouse outside Alipore!"

For a moment, every sound grew dim in Roshan's head, narrowing to a single, high-pitched whine.

Chotu. Roshan tried to speak but couldn't. *Subedar Yazad had Chotu.*

"I followed them!" Khush went on, sounding close to tears. "But that cursed warehouse is blocked to me. Then Fariyal came out and handed me this."

A scroll appeared out of thin air, trembling like a branch in the wind.

Lalit watched Roshan and, when realizing she wasn't going to move, took the note and read it aloud:

"The boy will be dead before sunrise unless the sardar of the Shadow Clan offers up herself in exchange."

43

The first time Roshan had seen Chotu, he was in irons: chained to the table of a tavern in Surag, next to a merchant who'd acquired him from the town's flesh market.

"You need to see him to know what he can do!" The merchant was booming, already deep in his cups, gesturing to the boy as if he were a prize mare. Baba had been with Roshan at the time, both cloaked and hooded as they slipped in through the back door. While the tavern owner had haggled with Baba over a crate of bootlegged palm toddy, Roshan had inched closer to the merchant's table. She'd noted the cuts on the young boy's face and arms, the bleeding soles of his feet.

Roshan had not known then about Chotu's magical gifts. All she knew was that she needed to get him out of there as quickly as possible—without anyone noticing. So she'd sneaked a few drops of sleeprose into the merchant's next drink. And the next. While the merchant snored like a baby, the crowd around him drifting away, Roshan had crept up to the boy and whispered, "Tell me where he keeps the key."

It would not have worked if the shackles had been made of magic instead of iron. Breaking those required death magic and a skill that not even Baba had mastered. But luck was on her side that day. No one spoke to or even looked at Roshan as she walked out of the tavern, Chotu's too-thin frame hidden in her overlarge cloak.

"You're free," she told the boy outside. "You can go wherever you want."

Chotu had whispered: "Can I come with you?"

And he'd been with the Shadow Clan ever since.

Now, four years later, Roshan once again feared for Chotu's life in a way she never had—not even during their most dangerous raids.

Somewhere in the distance someone—Lalit, perhaps—talked about waking the others from their induced slumber and putting together a rescue plan to get Chotu out before he died.

"Chotu won't die." When Roshan spoke again, she found herself growing calm. "I'll go."

Vijali Fui's eyes widened with horror. "No, bitiya. There has to be another way. I can go and—"

"There *is* no other way," Roshan cut in. "Also, you're wrong to think I'd ever let you or anyone else go in my stead."

Lalit's mouth trembled. He wanted to argue, Roshan knew. But he also had known her long enough not to. Vijali Fui, on the other hand, refused to exercise any such restraint. "Send in a decoy!" she insisted. "Disguise my face so that I look like you and—"

"If you do that, you'll get caught or die before even getting to Chotu," Navin said gravely. "Roshan is right. It's her the subedar wants. But we still need a plan in place. Waking up everyone else, as Lalit said, is a good idea. Also . . ."

As Navin spoke, Roshan realized he'd used the word *we*.

We *still need a plan in place.* As if he was one of them now.

And maybe it was true, because by the time he'd finished speaking,

Roshan knew that everything could go one of two ways—miraculously right or horribly wrong.

Which was generally how most of the Shadow Clan's schemes worked.

She glanced around at the immobile bodies around her and nodded.

"Let's wake everyone up," she said.

Moments later, several people sputtered, shaking off the cups of water—or, as in Khizer's case, cold milkless chai—that either Navin, Roshan, Vijali, Lalit, or Khush poured over their faces.

"S-sardar," Khizer began stuttering almost at once. "Hem-Hemant—"

"I know," Roshan interjected gently before looking at the rest of the bedraggled clan. "I know what Hemant did."

She read the subedar's note aloud this time, shutting down the protests that broke out.

"This is no more than another raid," she told them. "If we stick to Navin's plan, then everything will work. But you must wait at least an hour before attempting to break into the warehouse—no matter what happens. Do I have your word?" When no one spoke, she repeated herself, voice rising, "*Do I have your word?*"

"You have our word, Sardar." Lalit sounded tired, resigned. The others—including a worried Vijali Fui—chorused something along the same lines.

"Do you think Hemant and the others are at the warehouse, too?" Khizer asked.

"I doubt it," Roshan said. "Hemant and his crew hated this life. He probably took whatever coin the subedar gave him for kidnapping Chotu and absconded."

A small part of Roshan wanted to go hunting for the man. To punish him for what he'd done. But Chotu's face loomed before her, larger than before.

If Chotu comes out of this alive, it will be enough.

Roshan tucked the end of her turban over her mouth and nose. "Khush?" she called out.

"Ready, Sardar," the specter called. It was the first time he hadn't called her his little hakim—and Roshan wondered if it was because he expected her to die at that damned warehouse.

A hand caught hold of her arm.

"Promise me you'll come out of this." Navin's eyes were hard, glittering gems. "Alive."

Her throat tightened. "Navin, I can't—"

"Will you stop being stubborn? For once?" If she could see Navin's aura right now, she'd have probably seen anger in it. But behind that, there was also anguish. And another emotion that Roshan knew would break her if she watched him any longer.

"All right," she said, linking her hands with his. "I promise."

44

ALIPORE WAS ASLEEP. SUNHERI ROSE LIKE A STAINED SICKLE IN the sky, casting a dim orange glow over the roofs of the distant village. The plan was for Roshan to go alone to the warehouse, no other clan members in sight. She left Lalit, Navin, and the others at the village gate and trudged an invisible path in the dark, her feet knowing the way better than her eyes. She paused before an old haveli with crenellations like broken teeth, its latticed windows boarded up with wooden planks from the inside.

A pair of Brights were waiting for her next to a bolted door, the tips of their atashbans glowing red in the dark.

"Weapons," one of them ordered, a man who appeared a couple of years older than Roshan herself. She handed him her katar and the dual-edged jambiya strapped to her calf.

"Search her, Manek." This Bright was older, his weathered face a river-bed of lines.

Roshan didn't object when the young Bright patted her down, finding the silk pouch of cloves in her kamarband and tossing it aside, his hands slowing as he reached her hips, his gaze focused at the juncture between her thighs. Roshan's stomach twisted. Her hands were balling, readying for a fight when he rose to his feet.

"Clear," he said flatly.

Roshan released an inaudible breath. The atashgolas were still nestled against her groin. Safe for the time being.

"Where's Chotu?" she asked the older Bright. "Show him to me."

"He's inside. We'll let him out when the subedar is certain you are the Shadow Bandit and not an impostor."

Roshan grimaced from behind her mask. If she refused to go with them, she'd be giving Chotu the equivalent of a death sentence. Taking her silence as assent, the older Bright tapped the door with his atashban until it began to glow. As Roshan slid through the door, a rush of cold air breezed past, raising the fine hairs on her nape.

"Curse the gods for this weather," said the old Bright.

Roshan's heart thudded. She hadn't known if the trick would work. But somehow, neither Bright seemed to have figured out that the chill belonged to a living specter: Khush, who'd finally managed to circumvent the barrier they'd temporarily lifted.

Soft creaks permeated the brick walls of a passage, growing louder the farther she went into the warehouse. The sounds were oddly nagging in their familiarity, even though, for the life of her, Roshan couldn't place them in this moment. She hesitated, sweat beading a cold, thin trail down her back.

"Move!" The younger Bright's atashban nudged her spine.

She followed the older Bright into a cavernous room laden with sacks of grain. A chandelier burned overhead, hundreds of tiny flames flickering in glass lanterns, casting light over a small figure floating in the air several feet below, shackled and gagged, his green jama spotted with blood. The pit over which Chotu levitated was where the creaking sounds were coming from. Her stomach churned.

Yet it wasn't until she heard the high squeal that Roshan recognized the bone demons for what they were.

"Take off your mask." The voice that spoke was velvet-soft and smooth with authority.

Reluctantly, Roshan lowered her gaze at the group of gleaming gold figures standing before her. "Not until you release Chotu," she said.

"You have no room to bargain, girl."

The speaker was an old man at the center of the group. He leaned against a cane, sandaled feet peeking out from beneath his long black jama, toes curled inward from arthritis. Only the feathered pin on his plain white turban marked his status: an enameled mosaic of the flying mare at the center, surrounded by clusters of bright blue seaglass.

Roshan had seen Governor Yazad Aspa once before from a distance. He'd been giving a speech in Surag, moments before she and the Shadow Clan had broken into the city's Ministry of Treasure. But it was different seeing him face-to-face, to not feel anger exactly but a sense of surreal disbelief on taking in this man with his hunched shoulders and stooped back, the thick green veins that protruded from beneath his wrinkled brown skin. His cold gray eyes assessed her the way one would a wild animal.

"Mask off," he said. "I need to make sure you are who you say."

You cannot be seen. Nor recognized.

Baba had drilled the words into Roshan since she was a small child, and she'd taken them seriously, wearing a mask everywhere, even in allied villages. Outside the clan, few had seen Roshan's face in its true form, without disguises, thanks to the *Khabri*'s false illustration.

But now, she had no choice.

Ignoring every nerve in her arm that protested, Roshan unhooked the knot behind her ear and let her mask fall to the side. The governor's face showed no expression. Indeed, if not for the hand curling tight around his cane, Roshan wouldn't have known that he'd even seen her, let alone registered anything about her features.

"S-subedar," the older Bright next to Roshan said, almost sounding like his throat was being held in a vise. "Subedar Yazad, I can explain . . ."

She had a second to dodge the death spell that was now pouring into the Bright beside her, its fire outlining the skull and bones within.

Governor Yazad lowered his cane, its tip still glowing red, and walked to the lifeless Bright crumpled on the floor.

"Dear Firdaus," he said. "Always so loyal to me. Except in the things that mattered the most."

In the bandikhana, Roshan had learned that a warder's wrath could be earned when she did something wrong—and even when she didn't. Yazad Aspa was much the same, she realized from the faces around him: sweat-lined, looking elsewhere in terror. Even Shera, whom she spotted behind a pair of Brights, swallowed hard, as if holding back questions he longed to ask.

The governor's pale eyes studied Roshan, who was still crouched on the floor, pausing at the wooden rings corded around her neck.

"Tell me, girl." His cane tapped the amplifiers lightly before curving into the hollow between her clavicles. "Are these made of firebloom wood?"

When Roshan didn't answer, the tip burned, making her jerk back. Shackles stung her wrists and ankles, the spell so quick she barely had the time to register it.

"Tell me," the governor repeated, his voice growing softer, "are these made of firebloom wood?"

Again, Roshan didn't answer. Again, he dug the cane in, and this time, the burning intensified, like a hot knife etching her skin, the pain so intense that Roshan was certain she was about to faint. A gasp left her mouth when the governor lowered the cane.

His eyes narrowed as the wound in her neck began healing itself. "Interesting," he murmured. "But clearly not firebloom. If it was pure firebloom wood, you'd have healed instantly."

Behind him, Chotu was still levitating over the pit of bone demons—*with his own magic*, Roshan realized, horrified, when the little boy began to sink and then struggled again to inch upward.

She forced herself to temper her rage as she spoke to the governor. "You asked me to come here. I have. Please let Chotu go."

"Strange how much you sound like your mother right now."

A smile flickered across Governor Yazad's face on registering her surprise. "What would you like, girl? For the boy to go free? Or would you like to hear more about the mother you never knew?"

My mother? A part of Roshan wanted to throw the offer back in his face. To say she didn't care about a woman who'd abandoned her at birth. But something about the governor's expression made her bite back her words.

"There was a girl once," he said, his voice low, reminiscent. "Her body, too, would heal no matter what wounds were inflicted on her. She had your hair, your face. Right down to those acne scars." Roshan tried to pull away when he touched her chin, but the governor held fast, his grip like stone.

"She was sweet, my little Laleh. Beautiful like her mother. Unlike her mother, though, Laleh died while giving birth. It was the first day of Hashtdin, nineteen years ago. A day of celebration. Only this child should have never been born. My Laleh died, gifting the brat not only her rare healing magic but also the protection of her own firebloom amulet."

It wasn't true. It couldn't be.

"You have your father's eyes," the governor noted, almost absently. "Kaifi was quiet, efficient, educated. Poor as dirt. I took pity on him and gave him a job here, in this warehouse. It should have been enough for him, right, little bandit? But Kaifi got greedy. He had to go digging for more. He seduced my daughter and then persuaded her to elope with him when I refused to bless their binding.

"I took care of Kaifi eventually. Slit his throat with my own hands. But Laleh wanted you so desperately. And, fool that I was, I couldn't help but grant my daughter this one wish. When she died, I couldn't keep up the pretenses anymore. I gave you to Firdaus—told him to deal with you." He gestured to the old Bright lying dead on the floor. "Instead, he left you alive for Bhim Chaya and his bandits to find."

Now that he'd spoken the words, she couldn't help but see the similarities between them. The shapes of their eyes and brows. The rounded faces. The Jwaliyan red hair—only his was peppered with gold.

"Don't know who illustrated your portrait in the *Khabri*," the governor muttered. "Then again, it wouldn't be the first time that news scroll got its facts wrong."

A younger version of Yazad Aspa stood nearby. Shera, his complexion ashen with shock. Shera, who'd brutally murdered Baba, who'd tried to kill Roshan herself. Her mother's brother.

"Bring them out," Governor Yazad ordered.

From somewhere in the back, a Bright wheeled in a long wooden casket, whose power seemed to roll out toward Roshan in waves—even at this distance.

Firebloom wood.

Her stomach began churning, grew worse when she saw the person who limped behind the casket between a pair of Brights, his wrists shackled like hers, his bruised face twisting when he saw her.

"S-subedar ji," Hemant sputtered. "S-subedar ji, I p-promised I'd b-bring her. I—"

"Quiet," the governor said, and though his voice was low, Hemant shut up at once.

"See him, girl?" Governor Yazad gestured to Hemant. "The one who betrayed you? He wasn't any better to his companions. When the time came to choose between his life and theirs, he chose himself. Even when his lover screamed for mercy. The promise of gold was much more important to him. Indeed, my mohurs made him a useful informant for a whole year. But I've never been the sort to trust a man who betrays his own clan. Tell me, granddaughter. How would you like him punished?"

Tears slid down Hemant's face. He began blubbering, begging the subedar for mercy.

Angry as she was, Roshan couldn't help but pity him. A part of her—the one that still regretted killing Deepak—understood Hemant's hatred. His need for vengeance. But right now, Hemant wasn't a priority.

"I don't care about him," she told the governor. "You can let him go."

"Is that so?" The governor turned to nod at the Bright nearest to the casket. "It seems then that I must."

The governor snapped his fingers, and it was only then that Roshan realized her mistake. Hemant began screaming as the Brights dragged him near the pit Chotu was levitating over and made him lie flat on the ground.

"Sardar Roshan!" Hemant was screaming. "Sardar, help—"

"No!" Roshan shouted. "I didn't mean . . ."

Her voice died as the governor pressed the tip of his glowing cane to Hemant's rib cage and then began to saw, carving out a hollow through flesh and bone. Something rancid crawled up her throat and burned as she vomited onto the floor. When Roshan's vision cleared, she saw what the governor had wrenched from the dead man's chest. The long curve of a rib bone in one hand, his heart in the other. Still throbbing, as if alive.

Cane tossed aside, the governor hobbled to the casket, which had been opened sometime during this horrific extraction, his whole body glowing green with a magic that Roshan had seen among farmers infusing their power into the soil during the Month of Tears. The glow permeated from every bit of the governor, fissuring the earth under his feet.

"Pasli o rakht, aye zameen," the governor chanted in Old Paras, tossing Hemant's bloody rib into the crevice.

"Dil o atash, aye zameen." The heart burst into flames, its ashes raining over the bone.

He began to kneel, wincing as pain crept up his legs. But when Shera staggered forward by a few steps, his father threw up a bloodied hand, silently commanding him to stay back. Governor Yazad prostrated, glowing even brighter as his turban brushed the ground.

"Let the earth give back what was taken from me." His words rumbled through the earth, making it quake. "Let my daughter be reborn."

Roshan watched, horror mingling with disgust as a body began rising from within the firebloom casket. The corpse's black-red hair was braided in a bun over a high-necked jama, her gray skin like molded wax over a face that appeared skeletal but otherwise perfectly preserved—a near identical match to Roshan's own. The thing that might once have been her mother turned its head, eyelids flickering in the moment before it collapsed back into the casket, the soft *thud* palpable, even though Roshan was several feet away.

Governor Yazad didn't speak. His rage revealed itself in the aftershocks that rattled the earth after his daughter's failed rebirth, forcing everyone in the warehouse to widen their stances or lean against walls to steady themselves.

The quakes. The land draining of magic. The sudden, inexplicable eruption of ravines. Roshan's head spun. *This* was causing them. Governor Yazad drawing on the earth's magic to resurrect his dead daughter, corrupting the valley with his abominable sacrifices.

Roshan's stomach lurched again at the sound of flesh ripping behind her. She forced herself to turn, to watch as Hemant's skeleton rose, bones plucked clean of the bloodied mass that once was his body, entirely intact apart from the rib Governor Yazad had removed. He screamed as his skull glowed and then narrowed, shaping like a bird's.

"Well, granddaughter?" Governor Yazad's voice was soft. He'd risen to his feet sometime during Hemant's transformation into a bone demon and now watched the creature howl. "Would you like me to let Chotu go as well?"

45

When Roshan was little, Vijali Fui got bitten by a river krait, her body slowly succumbing to the snake's venom, her stomach cramping before her muscles began to grow stiff, her lungs slowly losing the ability to process air. Baba had risked life and limb to get her to a hakim in a nearby town, had kept talking to her throughout the perilous journey to keep her conscious. "I thought I was as good as dead," Vijali had told Roshan. "I could barely breathe."

Now, years later, Roshan was equally starved for breath as she watched Chotu levitating desperately in the air, growing more and more exhausted. Only the cool presence of the living specter in the room steadied her somewhat. Reminding her of what she needed to do.

"People call me a criminal," she told the governor. "But it looks to me like we're both branches of a tree sprung from the same rotten root."

Governor Yazad didn't speak. His attention was fully focused on her.

"The only difference is, I don't kill the living to bring back the dead," she continued, forcing herself to glare into those icy eyes. "Nor do I take away the villagers' land from them and drain it of magi—"

A hard smack cut her off midsentence.

The slightest tremor lined the governor's thin mouth. "The *villagers'* land?" he whispered. "Or do you mean the valley that one of my own ancestors had—in a moment of delirious nobility—*gifted* to revolting peasants as a gesture of goodwill? By the time our lands were united as the kingdom of Jwala under Parasmani Behram, nothing could be done to get the valley back. We of the Aspa Clan, blessed by the flying mare herself, were reduced to *governing* what was ours by birth. But it does not matter anymore, does it? Slowly the scales grow balanced. Slowly, I will take back all that is mine."

It wasn't a confession. Not quite. The governor was far too careful to outright admit to unfairly annexing the farmers' lands, even among his own soldiers. To convict him, she'd need more. A whole lot more.

The bone demon's screeches clawed at Roshan's ears, its cries mingling with those of the others in the pit: dozens of small feet scratching the earth, their sounds echoing the way they normally did in the—

Tunnels, Roshan realized, suppressing a shiver.

There was a tunnel under the warehouse—one that probably led all the way to the Maw. Her mind raced, latching onto something the governor had said about her birth father. Something about how Kaifi got greedy. How he went *digging for more*. It was a peculiar choice of words—one that now made her skin prickle.

Had Kaifi discovered a firestone mine? Had Navin been right about that?

Before Roshan could say anything, voices rang out in the warehouse—Shera's the loudest.

"Baba!" he called out. "Baba, the boy!"

Roshan's gaze instinctively danced to where Chotu levitated over the bone demon pit.

Or rather: Where Chotu had *once* levitated over the bone demon pit.

The boy appeared to have vanished into thin air, his body nowhere to be found—not in the empty space above the pit through which the Brights' spells passed without finding a target; certainly, not among the screeching creatures within the pit, growing more restless by the minute.

"Aye!" Shera used his atashban to send a beam of light at the newest bone demon—Hemant—who was howling worse than the rest. "You! Get in there with the others!"

For a second, the bone demon's hollow eyes looked right at Roshan. Did it know?

Did some part of Hemant still live in that thing? Had it sensed Khush turning Chotu invisible and carrying the boy away from the Brights' firing?

If so, Roshan couldn't tell. The bone demon howled one last time, glowing a brilliant white as it dived into the pit.

When she turned around, she noted that the governor was not watching the pit. He was watching her, a curious expression on his face.

"You've done something," he said. "I don't know what it is, but it's clever. Your mother was clever, too. For so many years I've been trying to resurrect her—and failing. But maybe there was a reason for that. Maybe the gods have, at long last, sent me exactly what I needed. A rib of her own rib. A heart of her own heart."

Roshan stared into those murderous gray eyes, thinking of every possible way she could delay him from ripping into her chest, when something Baba used to say floated through her head: *Put jaggery on his elbows and let him lick it off with his tongue.*

She was the jaggery here. The sweet solution to Governor Yazad's problems.

And she had maybe one chance to escape.

One chance to get the governor close enough to kill.

As the subedar's fingers curled around his cane, Roshan spoke:

"I still hear her in my dreams sometimes, you know. My amma. She's talking to me. Then there's only smoke. Fire."

The words made the governor freeze in place. His cane remained on the ground.

Fighting the instinctive urge to suppress the nightmare she'd fought as a child, Roshan forced herself to remember. To recall every little detail.

"She called me her ladli," Roshan whispered. "Didn't she?"

Her ladli. Her dearest one.

A tremor went up the governor's arm. No one spoke. Not the Brights. Not even Shera, who was listening to Roshan as if captivated.

"I felt her hand in my hair." Roshan's throat tightened as she recalled her old nightmare about the fire. "The air around us smelled of . . . *cloves.*" The word burned the back of her throat.

"She never could get enough of them," Governor Yazad said quietly. "Always had one tucked in the corner of—"

"—her lip?" Roshan finished. "I do that, too. You don't believe me?" she asked when he didn't respond. "Come closer and look. See the cloves in the pouch I always carry in my kamarband."

She expected the young Bright who'd searched her—Manek, she recalled the name—to refute the statement. To warn the governor that there was no longer a pouch in Roshan's wide belt. But the Bright remained quiet for some reason. Or maybe he hadn't heard her properly.

Her heart beat faster as the governor hobbled toward her. As much as she itched to move, she forced herself to wait until he got closer. Until she caught a whiff of his scent. Fireblooms, smoke, and blood.

"When you don't give us our birthright, we steal it," she said, so soft that only he could hear. "Isn't that so, grandfather?"

And then, before Governor Yazad could respond, Roshan plunged her shackled hands into her trousers for an atashgola and broke the safety knob with her teeth.

46

Where were *they?*

Navin tried to remain calm as minutes and then an hour trickled by. He was waiting with the Shadow Clan about a hundred yards away from the warehouse, behind an outcropping of rocks.

"Lalit?" Navin whispered. "Should we try to break in now?"

"Not yet." Lalit's eyes were narrowed above his mask. "I don't want to start bombing the place and accidentally hit one of our own. You're sure your father heard the song, right?"

"I'm sure," Navin said. *I think.*

He reached out to touch the peri feather inside his jama, pulled it out again. He'd sung to it the moment Roshan had disappeared into the warehouse, ignoring the partly surprised, partly captivated audience of bandits, and felt it grow warm in his hands. The last time that had happened, his father had heard his voice—and had appeared shortly afterward.

Patience, Navin told himself. If Peri Tir hadn't wanted to help him, he wouldn't have given Navin the feather at all. Besides, Ashvamaidan valley was much farther away from the Pashu kingdom than from Jwala's capital, which meant it might take his father longer to get here.

Several moments later, someone next to him gasped. "Look! There!"

Navin glanced upward, spotting two winged peri looming against the gold of the moon. Next to Tir's familiar silhouette flew another, slightly smaller, peri.

They swooped low, their wings bringing in drafts of cold air with them. His father alighted first, his talons scraping the rocky ground. An adolescent male of around thirteen years landed lightly next to him, the square shape of his jaw identical to Tir's.

Navin stared. He hadn't seen his half brother for a decade and, in that time, Adi had already grown a little over six feet, towering over most of the humans. The young peri adjusted the quiver slung over his shoulders, his gold eyes scanning the Shadow Clan, brightening when he found Navin.

"Navin Bhaiyya," Adi announced, his face breaking into a wide grin. A faint, silvery aura glowed around his curly black hair—happiness Navin couldn't fathom. "We came as soon as you called."

"What Ardeshir means is that he insisted on coming with me," Peri Tir corrected. His face, as always, was devoid of expression, his aura blank. But Navin had begun learning to read the silences that followed his father's statements. *Was this all right?*

"I'm glad you came, Pitaji. You too, Adi," Navin said truthfully. And then, before anyone else could speak, he turned to his brother, craning his neck slightly to look him in the eye. "I'm really sorry for what I did when we were children. I know I have no right to ask you for forgiveness, but . . ."

Navin's voice died when, without warning, Adi nocked an arrow in his bow and pointed it at him.

For long moments, no one spoke.

Then Adi twittered a laugh before lowering his weapon. "There,

Navin Bhaiyya. You tried to kill me when you were nine. I tried to kill you a moment earlier. We're even now."

A flurry of nervous laughter followed. Heart still throbbing, Navin laughed as well. "Goddess's hair," he said. "I guess I deserved that."

Adi's grin widened. His mouth parted as if he was about to respond when a blast echoed in the distance, the sound reverberating to a pitch that hurt Navin's ears. The warehouse's barrier flared into visibility—a fiery orange dome that crackled with energy, obscuring the warehouse.

"Roshan used her atashgola," Lalit said. Worry flickered through his aura. "It's time to break in."

Navin found himself growing numb. This had been their plan, for the most part. To sneak Khush in with Roshan. To make Chotu invisible if foul play was afoot and fly him to a safe spot before Roshan tried firebombing the place, weakening it from within. But the warehouse's barrier appeared strong. Navin recalled the look on Roshan's face, the utter resignation in her aura even when she'd promised him she'd come out alive.

She would. She had to.

"We'll need you both to shoot at the warehouse's barrier," Lalit told Tir and Adi. "If we attack it together at once with atashgolas and death magic, we may have a chance at breaking it."

Peri Tir made a clicking sound in his throat—one Navin knew meant he disagreed.

"Bad idea," Tir said. "Even simple barriers are designed to rebound most spells and firebombs, and this barrier is much stronger. To breach it, you need to target its weak points. The Pashu call them makhūshi surākh in the Old Tongue, which roughly translates to 'magical gaps.'

We look for these gaps and try to widen them. Some barriers are stronger than others, of course. But none are indestructible. A peri's voice can, for instance, break any sound barrier."

"So that explains it," Navin told himself, thinking about the barrier he'd broken in the Maw.

"Explains what?" his brother asked.

"Long story." Navin forced a grin. "Maybe one day I'll tell you. If we get out of this alive."

"Ardeshir and I can try to find the gaps first," Tir told Lalit. "Once it's safe, I'll raise an arrow in the air and you and your clan can charge forth. Isn't that right, son?"

"Haan, Pitaji!" Adi said.

The young peri looked confident. Fearless in a way that spurred amusement and envy into the aura of several clan members.

Navin, on the other hand, only felt a creeping anxiety that grew as both peri flew to the glowing orange dome and were quickly forced to dodge what looked like lightning streaking outward from it.

"Who's shooting at them?" someone asked. "Is it the Brights?"

"No, it's the cursed barrier itself," Lalit said, both awed and frustrated. "I've never seen anything like it!"

Neither had Navin. He lunged forward when fire from the barrier caught one of Adi's wings, panic flaring, but a pair of hard hands held him back.

"Don't!" Lalit shouted in his ear. "Navin, *don't!*"

"That's my *brother* up there! I'm not going to stand here and watch!"

"There's no need for you to do anything. He's fine. He's still flying. Look!"

Navin looked and saw that . . . Lalit was right. Somehow, Adi had managed to put out the flames on his own. And, though a little unsteady, he was still airborne.

"If you go racing to the warehouse now, one of two things will happen: The barrier'll shoot you or one of the Brights keeping lookout will," Lalit said. "You'll be dead before you know it. Have patience, Rajkumar."

Patience. Navin had never hated any word more. But he knew that Lalit was right. Heart in throat, he watched Tir shouting from a few feet above the top of the barrier's dome, gesturing to Adi to join him.

As one, the peri took aim, their arrows converging on the barrier at a single point.

For a long moment, nothing seemed to happen.

Then, like glass fracturing from impact, cracks webbed the orange dome, which began to dissipate, releasing a noxious-looking green smoke.

Tir faced the clan and raised an arrow high in the air.

It was time.

"Arms at the ready!" Lalit shouted. "Charge!"

But, unlike the others, Navin didn't move.

He was watching the figure behind Tir, noting the odd spasms passing through Adi's injured wing. He thought he screamed something: maybe for his father to turn, maybe his brother's name. He couldn't tell.

Later, when he recalled this moment, all he would remember was Tir spinning around a second too late, Adi's wings collapsing, his body tumbling through the air and disappearing into the smoke.

47

As anticipated, the atashgola didn't destroy the warehouse's barrier. It did, however, make Governor Yazad and every Bright within a two-foot radius of Roshan back off as she spun around, swinging it hard at the passageway leading to the entrance. The ensuing explosion spewed chunks of rock and wood everywhere and made a sound that lanced her eardrums even though she dragged her shackled hands up to her chin and plugged them with her fingers as quickly as she could. Amid the smoke that filled the room, stinging the back of her throat and her watery eyes, she spotted bodies on the floor—a pair of Brights who'd been caught in the explosion and hadn't made it.

"Secure the doors, fools!" the governor roared. "Shera, where is the witch? Shera!"

"I can't see her, Baba!" Shera shouted back. "There's too much smoke!"

There *was* too much smoke. It gave Roshan enough cover to crawl behind a pile of gunnysacks—and crash straight into another obstacle: the younger Bright who'd searched her outside the warehouse, his beady brown eyes and a hooked nose floating above an atashban pointed right at her.

"Don't move," Manek warned. "Unless you want me to raise an alarm about the *other* atashgola still hidden in your trousers."

Another quake thundered the building. The chandelier flickered, swaying dangerously overhead.

"Breach!" someone shouted as a siren wailed through the warehouse. "The barrier has been breached!"

Roshan barely heard the words. She eyed Manek and his glowing red weapon. "What do *you* want?" she asked him. "My liver? Or half a lung?"

His mouth twitched. "Neither."

"Then why keep my secret about the atashgolas? Are you even a Bright?"

No Bright—or at least no loyal Bright—would've let Roshan sneak in illicit firebombs nor gone a single minute without trying to capture her or raise an alarm.

In response, Manek rolled up one of his gold leather sleeves, exposing the swirling flames of a faded black tattoo on his forearm.

Roshan's heart thudded in her chest. She'd heard of these tattoos, though she'd never seen one up close. They were used to communicate with others of their kind over long distances, inked into the skins of Jwaliyan cadets when they graduated to join ranks with the queen's most elite soldiers.

"Lieutenant Manek Atashin," the sipahi whispered. As he spoke, he pressed a finger to the tattoo and the flames began to glow, crackling under his warm brown skin like embers.

"What are you doing here?" Roshan whispered. "Did Parasmani Bhairavi send you?"

"I—"

An atashgola exploded, so close that it blocked all sound. Coughing against the smoke, Roshan rolled sideways—and found herself staring into the glowing red tip of Shera's atashban.

"Up," the tall man whispered, sweat and blood beading his pallid face. "Now, witch."

Roshan's fists curled inward. She had no amplifiers on her, but she wasn't as weak as she had been in prison. She could try and tackle Shera. See if she could incapacitate him without magic. But then she spotted Manek standing behind the governor's son, shaking his head ever so slightly.

"Hands above your head!" Shera ordered. "And move!"

Roshan didn't know what game the sipahi was playing. But, so far, he hadn't done anything to actively harm her. She did as Shera commanded, slowly raising her arms.

The smell grew worse as they moved farther, smoke from the atashgolas mingling with acrid green fumes that seemed to come from somewhere above. Roshan's boots clanged against something on the ground—the gilded armor of a Bright corpse, the copper stench of blood rising from it. There were more corpses the farther they went along, Brights seemingly affected worse by the Shadow Clan's bombing.

But the clan had taken hits, too. The sight of Navaz Didi's bloodied form and glassy eyes nearly brought Roshan to her knees. She winced as Shera's atashban grew hot against her back.

"No time for mourning, witch," Shera said. "Aye! Shadow Scum! Look what I have here!"

He forced Roshan forward until she stumbled into a space clear of smoke.

"Drop your weapons or I kill the witch!" Shera warned. "I'm giving you until the count of three. One. Two—"

"Wait! Wait!" Lalit hollered. "We're doing it. See?"

Figures began to bend, the clan laying their weapons on the ground. As Lalit rose, a Bright captured him from behind and shackled his hands.

A few feet away, Governor Yazad's black-robed figure hunched over, his cane glowing green as the earth collapsed around Laleh's casket, swallowing it whole.

"Shera!" he snarled. "Hurry!"

Over the governor's turban, amid the fumes, Roshan spotted something else.

The flicker of a gray beak. The flare of a gold wing. The black gleam of an eye under a flaming feathered crown.

Roshan didn't know if she was dreaming. If the apparition truly was the homāi or merely shapes formed by smoke and a wayward spell.

Was it fate? Or folly? she thought—right before a pair of hard hands pushed her in the back and sent her headfirst into a hole in the ground, her world turning into a pit of bone demons screaming in the dark.

48

As a child, when Navin had drawn his brother to a river full of hungry makara, he'd not considered how things would be afterward. How it would really feel to have Adi gone.

Now, years later, Navin was running. Faster and faster, a stitch arcing up his side as the clan raced to the warehouse, aiming a flurry of spells and atashgolas at the entrance.

The last thing Navin expected was to be hit by an invisible force— one that knocked him flat on his back.

"Where are you off to, princeling?" a voice hissed in his ear. "Plan on dying with the rest of them?"

"*Khush?*" Navin sat up, clutching his spinning head. "What are you doing out here? Where's Chotu?"

"Here, Navin Bhaiyya," a hoarse voice said.

As if appearing out of thin air, Chotu's small, hunched body revealed itself behind a large rock, his brown skin ashen, teeth chattering from being in Khush's presence for so long. Relief rushing through his veins, Navin took off the blanket tied around his shoulders and wrapped the shivering boy with it.

Their mission had succeeded. Well, at least a part of it.

Roshan was still stuck inside with the Brights. And Adi—

Navin looked up at the smoking rooftop and tried to rise to his feet again—only to be thrown back on his arse by a pair of cold, preternaturally strong hands. "Goddess's flaming hair, Khush! I have to get to my brother!"

"Why run to him when he flies to you, silly prince?"

Navin craned his neck up. The specter was right. A pair of large winged shadows loomed overhead. Tir and Adi were flying to them—together. Despite the jerky movement of his injured wing, Adi landed well enough, right next to Tir.

"He's fine," Tir announced before Navin could ask, his voice as soothing as a sunbeam. "It was only the smoke pouring out from the barrier that got to him."

"Sorry," Adi said, giving Navin an embarrassed smile. "Looks like I worried you without reason."

"I'm your brother. If I don't worry about you, there's a problem."

Tir's and Adi's smiles were identical in their surprise and pleasure.

"What about Roshan?" his father asked. "Is she—?"

Another atashgola exploded within the warehouse, cutting him off. A figure catapulted out of the place and raced toward them.

"Sardar Roshan . . ." Khizer barely managed to get the words out. "Shera . . . Subedar . . . they . . ."

"Breathe, Khizer," Navin commanded, ignoring the sting of pain under his lower lip, a blister forming right in the hollow beneath his gums. "Tell us where they took her."

Khizer's aura calmed under Navin's soul magic, his eyes taking on a familiar, glassy sheen. "The bone demon pit," he said, his voice hoarse but calm. "There's one inside the warehouse. Shera shoved Roshan in and he and the subedar followed. The earth closed itself over them and a layer of rocks formed over that."

Something inside Navin went numb. He pinched himself to remain in the present. "What happened to the rest of the clan?"

"Most were captured by the Brights. I was lucky. I was closer to the door, throwing atashgolas, so I slipped away."

Roshan, Navin thought. He needed to get to her. But—"We need a plan," he said.

"You tell us, Rajkumar," Khizer replied. "You're the best planner among us."

"What? I'm not!" Navin protested.

"You are! You planned this raid and Chotu's rescue. You brought us this far."

Navin expected someone to rebut Khizer's statement. To echo the thought now in Navin's head—that only luck had brought them so far.

But no one did. Not even Khush, who was known to mock most suggestions, no matter how serious they were. Navin sucked in a deep breath, overwhelmed with an emotion that felt too big, too deep to hold in his ribs.

Think, Navin.

"Pitaji." He turned to Tir. "I know I don't have the right to ask you to fight in a human war, but—"

"I wouldn't be much of a father if I *didn't* help you right now," Tir cut in. "Tell me what you need. I am at your disposal."

"Me too!"

"Thanks, Pitaji. Adi," Navin said. "I thought it would be best if we all split up. You and Adi can fight with magic—and you're also armed. Maybe the two of you could attack the Brights in the warehouse and help free the clan? Is there a way?"

"There is," Tir said after a pause. He turned to stare at the empty space above Chotu. "But we'll need your help, Khush ji."

"You can see me?" Khush sounded more curious than startled about this.

"Pashu can see living specters. Well, most of us can," Tir amended with a glance at Navin, who was shaking his head. "Adi may need to mask up, but I'm sure he and I can find a way into the warehouse through the roof. For my plan to work, I need to ensure that the Shadow Clan have their ears fully covered. Khush can whisper to them—warn them beforehand. We will sing to the Brights, and it will not be pleasant."

Meaning their eardrums would split open and ooze blood.

Pushing away the grisly image, Navin turned to Khizer. "I think you and Chotu should go back to the hideout. This place won't be safe much longer."

As he spoke, Brights began trickling from the warehouse, shouting instructions to one another.

"What about you, Navin Bhaiyya?" Adi asked. "How will you get to Roshan?"

Navin wasn't sure. Waiting for Tir and Adi to bring the warehouse under control would waste too much time. Roshan would already be dead by then.

He thought hard. "If they took her into the bone demon pit, there has to be a tunnel underground."

But how to get to it? The only other tunnel Navin knew of was the Maw—and that was much too far from Alipore.

Goddess of Fire and Light. Help me find a way.

The prayer had been instinctual, almost a habit. Navin didn't expect an answer. Nor initially understood the meaning of the soundless sparks erupting before his eyes, swirling like fireworks during Hashtdin.

"Navin Bhaiyya?" Adi prodded. "What is it? Why are you so quiet?"

"Don't you see them?" Navin gestured to the sparks, which were now dancing and shifting. Growing, it seemed, into something even bigger.

"See what?" Khizer asked, sounding confused.

"Those sparks!" Yet, even as he spoke, Navin sensed that Khizer couldn't see them. No one else could.

"Do the sparks have feathers and a crown?" Tir asked, his voice quiet.

"Both," Navin whispered. Flame-feathered and onyx-eyed, the homāi hovered in place, an act that could have been mistaken for patience—if not for the restlessness with which she tossed her head.

The time for patience was over.

"I'll follow the homāi," Navin said. As he spoke the words, blood rushed through his limbs. Warm and hopeful. "She'll show me what I need to do."

Ignoring Khizer's and Adi's shouts, Navin chased the bird, who now streaked sideways, flying toward the ravines. There, between a cluster of rocks, opened a passage big enough for one person.

What lay inside the tunnel? More bone demons?

Before Navin could ponder that, an explosion rattled his ears. The Brights were shooting dozens of flaming arrows from their atashbans up at the flying peri and below at a fleeing Khizer and Chotu. Somehow, though, a blink before hitting wing or flesh, the arrows curved slightly, as if turned by the air itself. By the time the Brights thought to chase after the two humans, the latter had already disappeared within the ravines past Alipore village.

None of the soldiers looked Navin's way; it was as if following the homāi had made him invisible as well.

Or so he thought until an arrow whizzed past his ear, piercing a hole in the rocks.

Move. The homāi's magic tugged on him. *Now.*

He had no choice. Navin dived into the passage seconds before another spell hit and the rocks by the entrance collapsed, trapping him inside.

49

THE PIT STANK OF BLOOD, OLD WOOD, AND ROTTING MEAT, THE bone demons' squeals echoing in Roshan's ears. For some reason, they did not attack her. It was as if something—or someone—was keeping them at bay. Voices floated overhead as she lay on the ground, her head throbbing from having hit something, a hand lightly smacking her cheeks.

"What happened, Baba?" Shera sounded agitated. "Is she dead?"

"Only knocked out." Governor Yazad's cold voice made her skin crawl. "Never mind. Carry her, will you?"

Carry me where? Roshan wondered.

She didn't move as a pair of hands—likely Shera's—tapped her ankles, shackling them, before he caught hold of her by the waist and tossed her over his shoulder.

The bone demons' screams grew louder, angrier. Roshan tried not to twitch as something swiped at her hair, pulling out a few locks.

"Patience, children," the subedar crooned. "You will have her soon enough."

Her cheek flat against Shera's back, Roshan risked peering through a slit in one eye, trying to make sense of where they were. Darkness all around. Rocks and old bones jutting from the walls.

A glow up ahead—a lightorb perhaps, leading down a tunnel as she'd suspected. She nearly jerked when a howling bone demon burst from the wall, its body glowing amber.

"Here's the new one, Baba," Shera said, his voice flat. "It's still glowing with unused energy."

"Perhaps then, it can take us there," the governor said. "Go on, Hemant. Take us to the place you wanted to see most when you were a man."

Hemant—or the thing that was once Hemant—skirted sideways, ramming its skull against the tunnel wall. The amber light shrouding its skeleton veined every crevice in the rocks before crumbling, forming an archway wide enough to let a grown human through.

"A new way?" Governor Yazad seemed intrigued. "Will this be a shorter path?"

Roshan felt Shera's pulse kick up a notch. "Baba, do we really need to explore this *now?*" he demanded.

The governor didn't seem to be listening. The lightorb flickered as he hobbled in after Hemant, who made a sound reminiscent of his voice when he was still alive. Shera muttered something Roshan couldn't hear. But eventually, he followed them, too, his arm clutching Roshan's knees in a grip nearly as painful as her shackles.

Fiery trails molded the walls and ceiling around them like rivers of molten iron, the tunnel curving and shaping itself to suit Hemant's whims. Heat crept up Roshan's back and skull. It was like being inside the warehouse again—as if the tunnel were full of smoke, even though she could see no sign of it. Scratching and squeals echoed in the walls, the sound cutting off abruptly as Shera followed the governor through a barrier that scratched at Roshan's bare skin.

She barely noticed. Her eyes opened wide as she took in the walls, alight with color and embedded with gleaming shards of rock: from the palest yellow to the clearest glass, from rich, velvety greens to deep ambers and the reds of congealed blood. A well-used pick and shovel lay in one corner, next to a barrow heaped with glittering dust and gems.

Firestones.

A mine full of them.

Roshan's back struck the ground, the impact so sudden that everything around her began spinning. The shackles on her wrists and ankles burned, and there was no way for her to hold in a gasp.

"Looks like she's awake," the governor said, his face shadowed by a lightorb overhead. "Come now, Shera. Let's begin."

"Baba, are you sure you want to do this again tonight?" The hesitation in Shera's tone surprised her. "Your leg—"

"There's nothing wrong with my leg! Now do something useful for once and draw up Laleh's casket!"

Shadows partly shrouded Shera's face, nothing visible except the pale tint of his pursed mouth. He turned and knelt, pulling on a lever. The ground parted and the firebloom casket rose from within, caked with dirt and maggots, as if it, too, had traveled with them all the way here.

Roshan's throat tightened. She cursed herself for listening to Lieutenant Manek—whoever he was—and not killing Shera when she had the chance. Now she was fully shackled and stuck underground in this gods-forsaken mine while Hemant scampered restlessly from one corner to another.

"Laleh." Governor Yazad's voice was soft as he brushed the dirt from the casket. "Bitiya. Soon we will be together. Our family will be whole again."

Roshan's gaze slithered to Shera, noting the way he stiffened at his father's words.

"What about your son?" she asked, her voice raw but still clear. "Do you care he exists at all? Or have you forgotten the living in favor of the dead?"

Pain lanced through Roshan's shackles as Hemant lunged, his sharp teeth latching onto her left thumb. The pain made her eyes water, turning everything a blur. What felt like hours later, a sharp buzz in her wrists and ankles jolted her back into consciousness. Her throat ached from screaming.

The governor must've called him off at some point, because Hemant was whining as if being denied a treat. He bounced in place, his sharp teeth streaked with Roshan's blood.

A sliver of bone peered through the mess of blood and flesh on her gnawed thumb. Her hand warmed, her magic reacting almost instantaneously to heal the wound. But the throbbing in her thumb did not ease. Neither did the flesh and skin begin knitting back together as quickly as they normally would.

"Stupid girl," the governor said coldly. "Don't talk about things you don't understand."

Roshan gritted her teeth against the pain and exhaustion creeping up her body.

It was tempting to stay quiet. To accept the inevitability of what surely must be a slow, agonizing death. But then she looked again at her bloodied thumb and nearly threw up in her mouth. Governor Yazad had already stolen their lands and her baba. She wouldn't give him the satisfaction of stealing her mind as well.

The gleam of firestones in a nearby barrow caught her eye, an idea beginning to form in her head.

"You're wrong," she said. It was an effort to say the words. To speak clearly when she wanted to wail. "When you say that I don't understand what you're going through."

As she spoke, she shifted her hips, inching toward the barrow. Her shackles jolted again, but the pain was nothing compared with her left thumb.

The governor stiffened but did not turn to look at Roshan. Shera didn't seem to be listening to her at all. Something about tonight had drained him of his usual bloodlust.

"I understand what you're going through," Roshan went on. "I, too, was someone's bitiya once. If I could, I would do everything in my power to steal his life back."

A brief silence. Next to her, Hemant growled, as if itching to bite her again.

The governor didn't move.

Roshan could feel Shera turning to look at her. But instead of eyeing him, she forced herself to turn to the bone demon, addressing it the way she couldn't bear to address Hemant when he was still alive.

"I was angry. So angry when Deepak Bhai betrayed Baba. But I didn't try to stop myself. To pause and think of the devastation I would cause others when I killed him. I was only thinking of myself." As she spoke the words, she realized they were true. "Given a choice, I would've brought Baba back to life again. When I couldn't, I decided I would take his clan instead. Ultimately, I wasn't able to hold it together. You were right, Hemant. I was—am—a failure as a sardar."

Hemant's growl softened to a whine.

She turned to Governor Yazad, who was watching her with narrowed eyes.

"You're thinking about your daughter now," Roshan said. "And I don't blame you. But you forget that she's my mother, too. If you succeed in resurrecting her, do you think she'll forgive you for killing her only child?"

"Enough," the governor whispered. "Shera. Grab her."

Time to move.

Relying on a strength she didn't know she still possessed, Roshan dived for the barrow, her hands closing around the rough-hewn edges of a large red firestone, so hard it felt as if she'd pierced skin.

It was a risk. A major risk that could backfire worse than she'd anticipated.

However, for once, fate was on her side. Magic flushed her skin, her whole body feeling like it had been thrust into heat after being frozen for hours. Life magic, glowing gold on her eyelashes, her cheeks, on every tip of her finger.

Her thumb snapped painfully back into place, flesh and skin knitting together a second before the bone demon landed on her back, its claws digging into her shoulders.

Crack.

Hemant's skull shattered to bits under the impact of the firestone in Roshan's grip, fragments of bone clattering to the ground. Without really understanding why, she brought the stone down on the shackles with a scream, her body still glowing with life magic.

Boom: The sound rattled her teeth as her legs burst free and then pierced her ears once more as she focused the firestone on the shackles binding her wrists.

The world began to blur around the edges. Roshan's head throbbed, partly stunned, partly dizzy from having used magic this way. Life magic to break shackles—she hadn't even known such a thing was possible. But there was no time to ponder. No time for anything except the intense, blinding pain that seemed ready to rip her skull apart. Along with the migraine, a voice echoed in Roshan's head. Low and sonorous at first, it grew louder like the crush of a waterfall, the flap of tens of thousands of butterfly wings.

Was this what death felt like? Roshan wondered as darkness descended. Had she broken her shackles only to have her own magic kill her?

In the midst of the black river she was floating on, a light sparked. Scattered like stars.

The homāi's black eyes were soft, warm even, as she spoke in the voice Roshan had once thought a figment of her imagination:

"It is not your time yet, ladli. This place is not for you."

Amma? Roshan was unable to say the word out loud. Was that really her mother?

"My baba has grieved so long. Hurt so many people for my sake. But his jewel cannot return to him," her mother's voice grew more urgent. "Tell him that, ladli. Tell him to let me go."

Roshan wanted to weep. To reach out and touch her mother just this once.

But before she could, the homāi burst into flames and Roshan found herself flying out of the river—back into the light of the living world.

50

SOUND.

A complete and utter lack of it, along with a darkness so absolute that if not for the homāi hovering ahead of him like a beacon, Navin would've thought he'd gone blind as well as deaf. He pressed a pair of fingers to his throat, preparing to sing and break the barrier when the light ahead of him flared sharply, making his eyes water.

Don't. The warning was clear even though the homāi had not spoken a word. *Not yet.*

She flew farther, illuminating a long tunnel branching off several ways. If he'd blinked, he would've completely missed the path she'd taken. Several times, his arms and legs scraped rocks, and once a bone jutting from the walls of the narrow space.

Curse you if you die on me, Roshni.

As if in response, he felt something brush softly against his cheeks. A sigh that tickled the inside of his ears.

"Sing, hatchling." His father's voice poured from the homāi's beak, the only audible thing in the silence.

Navin sang. Of moonlight glinting on a dhow floating across a river. Of lies and truths, hope and heartbreak. Of the sun streaking a sky outside a dark cave. A rainbow tinting the aura of a girl with black-red hair.

The sound barrier broke. Along with it, so did the darkness, a hole crumbling through one of the walls, the force of the explosion turning Navin nearly dizzy as he stumbled into a . . . was it a room? No. It was a cave.

Glittering with firestones and swelling with chaos.

The homāi was gone.

"Roshan!" Navin shouted, ducking Governor Yazad's death spell and trying to reach the motionless girl.

Here, he was blocked by a glowing red atashban and Shera at its other end.

"Drop your weapon. You are not to shoot nor kill anyone," Navin commanded, magic resonant in his voice, which echoed through the cave. "*Now, Shera.*"

Shera's arms moved jerkily, as if fighting the order. His aura was red. But by the time Navin realized his mistake and opened his mouth to rectify it, Shera had already thrown his weapon aside.

The soul magic in his earlier command would prevent Shera from killing him. It would not, however, stop the man from beating him to a pulp. Shera pummeled Navin's face, breaking his nose and slicing his lip with a few well-placed punches. A blister burst in Navin's mouth. His hands searched the ground, found a rock with jagged edges. Shera deflected the blow easily, his grip on Navin's wrist so painful that it was an effort not to cry out in pain.

"Drop," Navin forced the word out, magic singeing his lips. "My. Hand."

Shera did, after a struggle, his curse lost in another new sound.

Footsteps hammered the tunnel, followed by voices rising in the air.

"La-Lalit!" Navin shouted, recognizing one of them. Before he could say more, Shera punched Navin again, so hard that he saw stars.

But his ears were still functioning perfectly. And they heard Governor Yazad's voice crawling through the cave along with the bone-chilling magic of a verse in old Paras. A command Navin couldn't decipher except for one word.

Ahriman.

Demon.

From all around them, as if they'd always been hidden in nooks and crannies, shadows emerged, solidified into bone demons larger than any Navin had seen before, their hollow eyes glowing scarlet instead of green, their ruddy jowls stained with old blood. They swarmed into the tunnel, which burst into screams and webs of red and green light.

As Navin struggled to his feet, another punch rattled his jaw. Shera raised an arm, about to hit him again, when a figure dived between them, her familiar shout sending a rush of adrenaline through Navin.

As Roshan and Shera grappled on the floor, Navin grabbed a dusty shovel lying nearby. He raised his arms, about to slam Shera in the back, when something sharp curled around his feet and ankles, rapidly snaking up his legs. Navin's nerves screamed in agony as the thorny shrub punctured his skin, forcing him to his knees.

"Foolish prince," Governor Yazad said, sounding almost disappointed. "I suppose you are truly bewitched by her. But tonight, I will end it. Tonight, the world will be righted again."

Navin tried to speak. To move. But his limbs were frozen. His mouth could do no more than twitch. He could only watch as Shera wrenched the firestone from Roshan's grip and began dragging her by her hair to an open casket.

Were they planning to bury her alive?

"I saw her!" Roshan screamed. "Laleh! She talked about you, Subedar. She said that your jewel cannot return to you. You need to leave her in peace!"

The subedar's daughter, Laleh? But wasn't she . . . ?

Navin stared at the casket, years of conversations with Shera about the governor's grief and his inability to forget his daughter gaining new and terrible meaning.

The governor's face had twisted at Roshan's plea. Turned into something ugly. Unrecognizable. His aura, which until now had remained invisible to Navin, flared to life. A grief as deep and green as an ocean. One that had turned to venom.

Navin knew then it wouldn't matter what Roshan said or did. The governor would kill her before the night was out.

Navin closed his eyes, feeling the cool weight of the jade bracelets at his wrists, picturing the magic that now hummed in the skin underneath climbing up his arms. Warming his throat, unraveling his frozen tongue.

"Save yourself." As Navin spoke, his voice filled every empty space in the cave. "Save yourself, Roshan."

Through a fog, he watched her hands reach up and twist hard, loosening Shera's grip in her hair. As she, somehow, miraculously slammed the bigger man to the floor, Governor Yazad raised his cane, his limbs trembling.

No. Navin wanted to say. *You will not hit Roshan.*

The words that left his mouth were entirely different, spoken in a voice that sounded at once like a hundred peri singing, like the crackle of a thousand fires:

"*Let her go.*"

As pain knifed Navin's throat, blood filling his mouth, the governor's bad knee gave way, his spell arcing in the opposite direction like a scythe, setting Laleh's open casket aflame.

"Baba! Baba, no!" Navin could barely hear Shera's shouts over the explosion that shattered the casket, the governor's anguished wails. "Baba, she's gone! Gone, you hear me?"

More bodies burst into the mine: Shadow Clan members, including a bruised and bloodied Lalit and Vijali Fui, followed by a young Bright in gold armor, his forearm held high, a royal messenger tattoo glowing on his skin.

"Drop your weapon, Shera Aspa!" the sipahi ordered. "By order of the crown prince of Jwala, you and Subedar Yazad are under arrest for various criminal activities, including, most recently, the murder and desecration of the bandit Hemant . . ."

Sound faded from Navin's ears as more sipahis poured through the tunnel, filling the mine with their round, homāi-emblazoned shields, marble-tipped atashbans pointing at the governor and his son.

The last thing Navin saw was Roshan's face, light limning her form—from dark red lashes to dirt-tipped fingers—her lips saying a word that might have been his name.

With the blessings of our Goddess of Fire and Light, we bring you

THE
JWALA KHABRI

THE ORIGINAL
Voice of the Kingdom

Day 1 Flowers, 40 Bhairavi Kāl

JWALA'S PERI PRINCE RETURNS

The erstwhile prince of Jwala, Navin of Clan Behram, arrived in Prabha early this morning by boat, under heavy guard, amid fervent cheering and binding proposals by delirious citizens, some of whom have declared themselves devotees of the Peri Prince.

Two other armed barges docked at Prabha later in the day, the first containing Ashvamaidan's disgraced provincial governor, Yazad Aspa, alongside his son and lieutenant governor, Shera Aspa, arrested seven days earlier by royal sipahi forces outside Alipore village, twenty-five miles west of Surag. Several charges have been laid against the Aspas, including murder and the creation of bone demons, all of which have been severely contended by the governor's dasturs, who insist they will fight the allegations in court.

The other barge contained the notorious Shadow Bandit, alias Roshan Chaya, the Peri Prince's alleged lover, who was arrested by the sipahis along with several other members of the Shadow Clan. However, the Shadow Bandit seems equally if not more popular than the Peri Prince, her arrival spurring a protest of hundreds of Jwaliyan citizens—including masked and turbaned university students who congregated outside the palace gates and balcony, chanting slogans of freedom and justice for Ashvamaidan's farmers. While the *Khabri* did not receive an official response from Kiran Mahal to any of our hawks, an anonymous insider tells us that "the protests have caused agitation among many a courtier and even royals—including our exalted parasmani."

Our sources have further suggested the existence of an active firestone mine near Alipore. Firestone, a powerful mineral with magic-amplifying qualities, was believed to have gone extinct half a century earlier. Lieutenant Manek Atashin, the officer in charge of investigating the Ashvamaidan saga, as we now know it, declined to answer our questions about the mine, only calling the mission "a success beyond imagining."

51

NEWS FLEW IN ON A PALACE HAWK'S WINGS, THE BIRD DROPPING the note on the pavement in front of Navin while he strolled through the gardens at Kiran Mahal, burly sipahis surrounding him on four sides. He paused, waiting impatiently, as one of the men picked up the scroll and scanned the name on it. Snatching it once it passed inspection, Navin broke the familiar seal and unrolled the parchment. Insects buzzed around him as he read the few lines that were written there. Once. Twice. Again to make sure he wasn't dreaming.

"I'd like to see the parasmani," he told the guard who'd handed him the note.

Navin had to remind himself to speak low, to avoid exerting his voice more than needed. The poison from Governor Yazad's plant had damaged his vocal cords, making speech painful. The palace hakim, who'd examined him on arrival, said that Navin was lucky to have a voice at all.

"Whoever healed you drew out most of the venom at the right time," the hakim had commented without mentioning Roshan by name. "Thankfully, your magic is functioning as normal and you should still be able to see auras. But I advise giving your vocal cords as much rest as possible. No soul magic commands or singing for at least a year."

A whole year. Three hundred and sixty days of recovery and a twice-daily potion of raw shvetpanchhi egg mixed in with diluted blood bat venom. Navin would've been tempted to flout the instruction if his throat didn't hurt so much. The irony was that the one time he *did* decide to follow orders, no one seemed to believe him.

The sipahi he'd spoken to right now, for instance, and his guards kept their ears stuffed with cotton so that Navin couldn't use magic on them. The trouble was, neither of his guards could read lips. It was only when Navin mimed walking and a crown on his head that the guard seemed to get the gist of the message.

"You wish to go to the parasmani. Ji, Rajkumar." The sipahi bowed.

Navin wasn't fooled by the false servility nor the placating use of his former title. He was a prisoner here as far as the sipahis were concerned—a threat they'd surrounded with no less than three magical confinement barriers the moment he'd stepped off the barge that had brought him to Prabha two days earlier.

At this rate, it might be better if they dropped all pretenses and put Navin in regular old stinging shackles or took him to the central bandikhana along with everyone else: Governor Yazad, Shera, the Brights, Roshan, and the other members of the Shadow Clan.

Roshan. Navin still hadn't been able to find out much about what had happened to her since the sipahis' raid of Alipore's mine—despite religiously combing through the latest scrolls of the *Jwala Khabri*. After Navin's use of soul magic and subsequent collapse in the firestone mine, the sipahis had only waited long enough for Roshan to complete healing him before they'd separated the two. Then they'd taken Navin to a heavily guarded inn somewhere in Surag. Not that it had mattered. Navin had been spitting out blood most of the time, his upper lip and the inside of his mouth scarred from blisters, his throat so raw that he'd not wanted to eat or drink, let alone break the sound barriers guards surrounded him with day and night.

He hadn't heard from the peri side of his family, either, Tir's feather having been broken during the scuffle in the mine. Inquiring with the sipahis or demanding answers from the parasmani yielded—as expected—no results. For the last couple of nights, Navin waited for hours on the balcony of his room, where he was imprisoned, hoping to catch a glimpse of a winged form or two. But there had been nothing except for a lonely crescent moon, surrounded by ragged gray clouds.

They're all right, Navin assured himself now for possibly the hundredth time. *They have to be.*

He followed the guards through the Royal Wing and into the study, where all of them waited before the desk in silence. A moment later, the figure behind it looked up at the sipahis and said: "Leave us."

"Parasmani ji," they demurred, bowing deeply.

Navin barely noticed them leave. He was staring at Farhad—no longer Jwala's crown prince, but its king—dressed in a cobalt jama of the finest silk, a sarpech of yellow conch pearls and ostrich feathers pinned to the side of a blue-and-red turban wrapped in the multilayered, ceremonial style Navin had seen their grandmother wear during state dinners.

Queen Bhairavi was nowhere in sight.

Farhad waited for the door to close before turning to Navin. "Sit, brother. You look well. Much better than when you first arrived."

You mean I'm not dead yet, Navin would've joked if they were on better terms. But right now, Navin wasn't certain of his position in the palace. Or with Farhad.

"I read your note," he said instead, taking a seat in a plush, high-backed chair. He held up the scroll Farhad had sent him—an official declaration of abdication signed by Queen Bhairavi, appointing Crown Prince Farhad as her immediate successor, along with the signatures of every minister at court appearing as witnesses. "Care to explain what exactly is going on? And how long you've been planning this coup?"

Farhad's mouth flattened. His aura was blank. "The coup wasn't really a choice on my part," he said. "After you broke the Shadow Bandit out of prison, I panicked. Our grandmother wanted to disinherit you. She . . . she said some really . . . terrible things about you and your father. I was so angry with her. But I also knew I couldn't reveal it to her directly." Farhad released a breath. "So I let her do what she wanted—all the while secretly making inquiries within the royal forces. I found a young, honest lieutenant who was eager to make a name for himself in the sipahis. I took him in my confidence, gave him a small troop of forces, and told him to go to Ashvamaidan to infiltrate the Brights."

Though Navin had suspected Farhad's involvement in this matter, it was still surprising to hear out loud. His brother loved Navin, but Farhad had—until now—never broken a single protocol, let alone *considered* defying their grandmother to send out secret forces.

Why now? Navin wondered. *What had changed?*

"Lieutenant Atashin was excellent," the new king went on. "He managed to infiltrate the Brights without detection. But he was having a hard time collecting evidence. To do that, he had to get into Subedar Yazad's inner circle. To quietly witness the Brights butcher someone for the subedar to make a bone demon.

"It was pretty awful. He nearly abandoned the mission because of it. But I persuaded him to stay longer. Then the *Jwala Khabri* published your letter, which began raising questions here in Prabha. Uncomfortable questions that the parasmani kept refusing to answer until she could no longer avoid them.

"After Atashin's discovery of the firestone mine in Alipore and his arrests, I knew I had to act quickly, to do something to save our family and the throne. So I had a chat with the parasmani. Told her that she needed to abdicate and go into hiding at one of our southern estates. Her only other option was to face corruption charges, which were bound to come forth from the Aspas. And they have—this morning." Farhad wearily held up a scroll marked with the seal of a court dastur. "Our ministers and dasturs assure me that my position as the new parasmani will be safe as I had nothing to do with our grandmother's deal with Yazad Aspa. But I'm still not looking forward to that trial, let me tell you."

Navin's mouth opened. Closed. Unable to articulate the emotions roiling through him right now—surprise, gratitude, sorrow, joy, and confusion—all for the man who now sat before him.

"Meherbani," he said at last. "For your help. But I still don't understand why I'm here."

"What do you mean?"

"Under Jwaliyan law, I am considered a criminal for breaking Roshan out of prison. I should be at the bandikhana. Not here."

Farhad laughed. "Navin. You're a prince."

"I thought I was disinherited and stripped of my titles."

"I'll reinstate everything." Farhad waved a hand.

"What if I don't want to be a prince anymore?"

The silence that shrouded them both was so thick that Navin could barely hear more than their collective breaths.

"Why," Farhad began slowly, "in the highest of hells would you say that?"

His brother's aura burst forth, the anger in it surprising Navin. Along with the pain, which evoked an answering pang in his chest.

"Don't be upset," Navin said, keeping his tone gentle. "You are my brother by blood and nothing will break that bond. But I don't belong here the way you do. Here, I am a misfit—someone who wanders around aimlessly, always chafing in my own skin."

"It won't be the same as before!" Farhad countered, his voice growing urgent. "When I reinstate your title, I will give you more powers. We'll work together to make new laws, to bring forth necessary changes in our kingdom."

Navin hesitated. It sounded tempting when put that way. But then · · ·

"I could do that outside the palace, too," he said at last. "In fact, I'm pretty sure I did more for Jwala when I wasn't a prince than in the nearly twenty years that I lived here."

A pause.

"It's not just that, though, is it?" Farhad's voice was hard. "It's that girl."

"Roshan Chaya," Navin spoke her name softly, though n emphatically, "is the only reason I am sitting here today, talking t

Farhad's face remained neutral, but his aura revealed glints ance. "She was in pretty bad shape after healing you."

It was the first time Navin had heard anything about Ros that sent his heart instantly racing.

"What do you mean?" Navin tried not to sound a happened to her?"

For long moments, Farhad said nothing. Slowly, the red clouds in his aura deepened to brown. Acceptance, perhaps. Or resignation. "She's all right," Farhad said. "I went to see her and the rest of her Shadow Clan at the prison yesterday. The hakim over there has stabilized her well enough. You can sit back down."

Heat creeping up his face, Navin did. He hadn't even realized that he'd risen from his chair.

"The warden said she's been asking about you daily," Farhad continued. "She wants to know how you are." A pause. "I could approve of communication between you two—letters only," he clarified as hope leaped in Navin's chest, "while this trial goes on. And afterward, if necessary."

"Meaning, if we both get sentenced."

"I can't stop that. That lies in the hands of the Ministry of Justice. It was difficult enough convincing the court and Minister of Justice to have you put under house arrest at the palace."

Navin frowned but didn't argue this. Farhad might be king of Jwala, but it didn't mean he would circumvent the law. That's what their grandmother had done—and look where it had taken her. He glanced up at a small portrait on the wall, one of Queen Bhairavi during her coronation ceremony.

"What did the parasmani say when you told her to leave?" The question slipped out of his mouth. "Did she blame me for everything, as usual?"

Farhad's aura turned the color of a stormy ocean. His brown eyes were soft. "The parasmani did what she deemed best for her family and the throne. She did love you, in her way. But her love couldn't overcome her grief over our mother's death, the prejudice and immense anger

she'd felt for your father. You are not at fault here, understand? Our grandmother's actions are on her, not you."

"I guess." Navin licked his dry lips. "What about my father?" he asked, changing the subject. "He and my brother Adi were in Ashvamaidan, too, during the sipahis' raid."

"They're all right." Farhad sifted through a pile of scrolls neatly arranged on a tray by his side and drew one out. "This came for you a couple of days ago from Aman. I'm sorry we didn't bring it to you before. I didn't take over the parasmani's study until this morning."

Some of Navin's anxiety eased upon seeing his name inscribed over the seal in Peri Tir's careful handwriting. His fingers rolled over the rough parchment, its edges as soft as a feather.

"Meherbani." For the second time in his brother's presence, he revealed his own aura to Farhad, the truth curling like smoke in his peripheral vision. "You've done more than I expected. Parasmani ji."

"Please. No titles when we're alone." Farhad gave him a faint smile. "I didn't do much, really. Didn't do half of what an older brother should have to protect you."

"You could've done worse," Navin said, thinking of himself and Adi. "I used my soul magic to lead my young peri brother to a makara pond when I was nine."

Farhad's snort turned into a cough. "Goddess's hair! Maybe I should have you thrown into the bandikhana after all."

"It's an opportunity of a lifetime." Navin shrugged and grinned. "The one chance you'll have to get every threat to your throne out of the way."

To his surprise, sorrow coiled in his brother's aura. "I never thought of you that way. You know that, right?"

If his own aura had been invisible, Navin would have lied and evaded another uncomfortable conversation. But he'd run from the truth long enough.

"I didn't," he said honestly. "I always thought I was the one hurdle that you and our grandmother wanted out of your way. It's not a feeling that's going to go away soon."

The new king of Jwala winced. Then laughed wryly. "You even talk like her now. The Shadow Bandit. When I asked her what she thought of me, she didn't hold back her thoughts. I'm not sure if I liked it."

"I didn't. Not at first." Navin's lips stretched outward and up: his first genuine smile that morning. "But I wouldn't have her any other way."

THE ASHVAMAIDAN TRIALS TOOK PLACE A WEEK LATER IN THE throne room downstairs. Twice as many sipahis lined the halls on the day of Navin's hearing, long spears alternating with marble-tipped atashbans. Despite the crowd in the darbar, the air smelled fresh, like lilies and clean river water, old magic humming in the tall marble pillars edging the perimeter of the throne room. Lapis lazuli and gold foiled the walls, shimmering subtly like the Behrambodh at twilight.

Courtiers were arrayed on both sides, seated cross-legged on cushions. Behind them were various familiar faces: the village heads of Jyoti, Alipore, Mohr, and Raigarh. Dinamai was there, too, along with a trembling Sultana Bibi, and Jaya's worn but stoic mother.

The mahadasturs presiding over the cases towered over the assembly on a central platform, scrolls littering their tables, dressed so alike in their floor-length blue-and-orange jamas that from a distance they were indistinguishable from one another. Above the judges sat Farhad on an elevated lapis-and-marble throne, dressed in a pale blue jama, a yellow-and-blue turban on his head. He glanced briefly at Navin when he stepped in but otherwise made no acknowledgment of his presence.

Governor Yazad and Shera were already in the darbar. Even shackled, the governor appeared immaculate in his black jama, his face so worn it looked like a saint was being put on trial. Navin caught Shera's eye for a second, but his former friend looked away, as if he couldn't bear to meet Navin's gaze.

Yet guilt, or otherwise, had little to do with the outcome of a trial.

Within minutes, the Aspas' court dastur began pointing out the lack of judicial proof surrounding the murder allegations of Ashvamaidan's villagers. Sarpanch Vilayat from Jyoti even gave a testimony in favor of the governor—which resulted in jeers from the listening villagers and the mahadasturs issuing a warning for silence.

Only Lieutenant Manek's testimony about Hemant's murder seemed to make a difference, the mahadasturs carefully listening to the sipahi as he recounted his secret mission. Gasps rose from the audience as Manek went into the details of making a bone demon and the reason behind it.

A stray draft brushed the back of Navin's jama. More witnesses must have entered the throne room. He sensed—*knew*, somehow— that it was her before he even turned to confirm this, spotting her next to a nearby pillar, her wrists shackled, her hair like blood and fire under the lightorbs.

Roshan's face was tired, but otherwise she appeared well. She glared at the governor and his son, wisps of ochre, blue, teal, and red haloing her hair. Fear, worry, sorrow, and anger—all tugging at one another as if she was unable to make up her mind about the two men. Her relatives by blood.

Her aura shifted as her gaze snagged Navin's, silver streaking through the cloud of muddled color. It was the first time they'd seen each other since Lieutenant Manek and his sipahis had arrested them in Ashvamaidan. Seven days had passed since Navin had begun writing to her in prison and she'd begun writing back.

A small smile appeared on her face. Navin grinned back and winked, trying to put her at ease. From her last letter, he knew she was nervous about the outcome of these trials. That she didn't trust them at all.

Navin had teased her, calling her a pessimist. But as the trial went on, his heart began to sink. Each dastur played the other as if they were gambling at chaupar, tossing around acts and laws like dice, in a language that, despite being Paras, flew right over Navin's head.

The saga continued for several days as the dasturs called Navin to the stand, then Roshan and Lalit, then the villagers, and then, finally, Governor Yazad and Shera. Some testimonies—such as those of Sultana Bibi and Jaya's mother—were deemed "inadmissible," though the maha-dasturs seemed sympathetic to their cause.

In the meantime, daily protests took place outside the palace, a part of the crowd on the side of Ashvamaidan's farmers and the Shadow Clan, and another part, mostly made up of wealthy aristocrats, clearly on the governor's side.

On the twentieth day of Flowers, instead of being escorted to the darbar, Navin was taken to a small room next to it. There, he found Roshan and Lalit seated before Ashvamaidan's appointed court dastur.

"Good," the dastur said. "You're here, Rajkumar."

"What's going on?" Navin asked. "Why aren't we in the darbar?"

"The opposing side approached me last night. They have offered Roshan Chaya and her clan what is called a sauda," the dastur explained. "Similar to a barter or trade in the Common Tongue. Each member of the Shadow Clan will get only a year in prison for their crimes. I have spoken with Parasmani Farhad, and he has agreed to issue a partial pardon considering the role the Shadow Clan played in revealing corruption in Ashvamaidan and also leading the sipahis to Alipore's firestone mine, which will now be a valuable crown resource.

"In exchange, we are to drop the remainder of our charges against Subedar Aspa and his son, reducing their sentence to five years. Roshan and Lalit asked for you to be brought here. They wanted your opinion before making a decision."

Navin frowned, studying the dastur's aura. But there was no sign of deception there. The man was speaking truthfully.

"May I speak to Roshan and Lalit alone?" he said at last.

"Of course. I'll wait outside with the guards."

Once the dastur exited the room, Navin turned to the two seated figures. "I think it's a good deal, Roshan. You should take it."

"You can't be serious!" Lalit burst out.

"He is. He never calls me by my proper name otherwise," Roshan said. A wrinkle marked the space between her brows. Her aura, for once, was calm, giving Navin no real hint to her feelings. "Why do you think we should take it?" she asked him.

"When the opposition offers a sauda, it means they worry that the case could go on for years," Navin explained. "It also means the judgment could go either way—and they want to cut their losses."

"You mean, we could win," Lalit countered. "Why not take the chance?"

"Because we could lose," Roshan said quietly, not taking her eyes off Navin. "Right?"

Navin nodded. "Your dastur isn't deceiving you, from what I can tell. Besides, if the subedar and Shera go to prison, it also means they won't be governing Ashvamaidan anymore. Isn't that what you wanted?"

Neither Roshan nor Lalit spoke.

"If you don't take this deal, the next sauda could increase a year in prison to five. Even twenty," Navin pointed out.

"I don't care about going to prison," Roshan said. "I only want justice."

"Justice doesn't happen on our terms." Navin thought of his own grandmother, who'd disappeared before he could speak to her, leaving behind an ache that he suspected would never go away. "There's always a catch."

Roshan nodded. Blue curled through the brown of her aura. A lingering worry she'd somehow managed to hide from Navin earlier.

"You've been practicing," he said, smiling suddenly. "Shielding your emotions."

"Only a little." She smiled back briefly. "I'll need to discuss with Lalit and our dastur again before making a decision."

Four hours later, the council of mahadasturs announced their verdict: five years in prison for the former governor of Ashvamaidan and

Shera, now stripped of their titles and land; a year in prison for each member of the Shadow Clan; and finally, six months' imprisonment for Navin at the palace, a decision that didn't really come as a surprise.

What did surprise Navin was Farhad rising to his feet at the end of the hearing, resulting in every other person also getting up in the throne room.

"Sit," the king of Jwala said, waving a hand. "I have been listening to these proceedings with great care. And I understand that the judgment passed here will not satisfy everyone."

A few eyebrows rose among the mahadasturs and the courtiers at this outspoken comment. But Farhad had the villagers' attention now, Navin noted.

"My family has been blessed to rule over this land birthed by the goddess of fire, tilled to fertility by the great flying mare," Farhad said. "And I will do my best to honor the responsibilities I've been given. Starting with decreeing that two-thirds of the proceeds from the Alipore firestone mine, and any other firestone mines discovered in Ashvamaidan henceforth, will go toward rebuilding the province."

Gasps, followed by exclamations of shock from the courtiers and excitement from the villagers.

"There will also be a new governor for the province, chosen by the council of village elders from among themselves," Farhad continued. "I imagine there is no better person to administer you than one of your own."

"Parasmani Farhad Zindabad!" a voice cried out from among the crowd. "Long live our king!"

"Long live our king!"

"Long live our king!"

The chanting went on, soon added to by others in the throne room—eventually spilling over onto the streets outside, where protesters awaited the verdict.

Navin peered over the shoulders of the guards escorting him out of the throne room.

He thought he caught a glimpse of dark red hair for a moment, but it was only a courtier. Just when he was about to give up on finding her, a voice called out his name.

Roshan was waiting with her own sipahis next to a tapestry. One of these happened to be Lieutenant Manek. The sipahi nodded at Navin's guards, who parted, allowing Navin to walk up to Roshan, then pause a few feet away, hesitating. Unsure of what he was supposed to do now.

"What next, Rajkumar?" she asked, smiling. But there was doubt there, too. An uncertainty of the future. Of *them*.

"I've discovered that I'm a patient man," Navin said. "I can wait a year or so. If you want me to, that is."

For long moments, Roshan didn't speak and Navin wondered—worried—if she would sever this delicate, shimmering thread between them. Then a wisp of silver curled over her head: a hope that matched his own.

"I do," she said with a smile.

AN UNFINISHED SONG

SONG

Prabha Central Prison

DAY 20 of the Month of Flowers,
YEAR 2 of King Farhad's reign

52

King Farhad's official coronation ceremony took place the week they released the Shadow Clan from prison—"a most auspicious day," per the astrologer for the *Jwala Khabri*—a day Roshan had half expected to never arrive despite the changes that had already been made in the province of Ashvamaidan, and despite Navin's weekly letters throughout the year, assuring her that all would be well.

Have a little faith, Roshni, he'd written. *If your paranoia was true, no one would have released me. I can assure you that I'm still considered more of a threat to the throne than you are—despite not having a title anymore.*

Faith is the hairy boil on human logic, she'd written back in a moment of sheer obstinacy.

Though—logically—there was no reason Roshan's sentence would be extended to more than a year. She'd remained on her best behavior in prison. In the last six months of her sentence, the prison hakim had also allowed Roshan, under strict supervision, to borrow a stick of firebloom wood and assist him in healing sick inmates.

Such blasphemy! Navin had replied. *It's good that I already love you.*

She'd smiled at the first line, stilled at the second. She'd read it back. Over and over, until the parchment grew worn from her unrolling.

Love. Roshan couldn't tell now if the love Navin wrote about was real or the casual kind of love—an expression wealthy Jwaliyans tended to use about everything from music and the weather to their pet songbirds.

There was, of course, a way to know.

Ask him to come to Ashvamaidan with you.

The thought had struck Roshan more than once over the past few months. She'd considered putting it in one of her letters, too.

But what if he said no? Or worse, what if he stopped writing to her altogether? Roshan didn't know if she could bear having Navin completely out of her life. Was it so terrible to have him as a friend than as no one at all?

"Ready?" a voice asked once Roshan emerged from the change room, dressed again in her old clothes, which were stiff and musty from disuse.

Vijali Fui had grown thinner in prison, her smile no longer the same since Navaz Didi had died. But today she was grinning wide—even dressed in her old jama, which held splatters of dried blood.

"We're free today, bitiya. Free!"

Roshan grinned back. "I'll admit I got a little worried when I found out Lalit and the others were being released yesterday," she said.

Lalit and the remaining members of the Shadow Clan (except for Khizer and Chotu, who'd escaped the sipahis' arrests) had been split from Roshan and Vijali after their sentencing and transferred to another prison somewhere in the north of Jwala.

It's as cold as an ice god's balls here, Lalit had written to them. *But we're all right. Treated well enough. Khush, Khizer, and Chotu are in the kingdom of Samudra now. Chotu enjoys living by the sea.*

Roshan wasn't sure how Lalit had received news about their other friends—though she didn't ask, in case it got Lalit into trouble. She guessed that the northern prison wasn't as heavily guarded against living specters as Prabha's central bandikhana.

Sunlight pricked her eyes as she and Vijali were escorted by a pair of sipahis into the prison yard and toward its tall gates, atashbans glinting at the tops of each lapis-domed watchtower. Magical barriers squeezed Roshan's ribs so hard that she thought they'd crush bone.

"Hurry!" the sipahis ordered. "Keep walking or you'll get injured!"

Roshan did, breath rushing out of her in a *whoosh* as they stumbled out onto the street.

A moment later, she turned, staring at the place that had been home for the past 360 days.

Funny, she thought, *how you could get used to anything in this world.*

A shadow flew overhead. Roshan's pulse quickened, wondering if she'd seen the hint of a gold wing.

"What happened, bitiya?" Vijali Fui asked. "What's there?"

"Nothing," Roshan whispered on spying the bird. A bulbul singing on the branch of a firebloom tree.

She hadn't seen the homāi again since her vision in the firestone mine a year ago. For months, she'd tried to make sense of it—to understand if what she'd seen was real or the product of delirium. The prison hakim, who was Zaalian by faith, told Roshan that even magic acted in inexplicable ways sometimes.

"Ultimately, there is a power—a goodness, I like to think—that restores balance in the world," he'd said. "We Zaalians call it magic. The others call it the gods or the great animal spirits. We must believe in that goodness, even if we don't believe in anything else."

Goodness—or the thought of it—was probably a reasonable thing to attribute to one's parents. Once, in prison, she received a letter from Sultana Bibi, as transcribed by a village elder. In the letter, Sultana Bibi had described Roshan's birth father at length. Roshan learned that Kaifi had been quiet, clever, and occasionally hot-tempered, that he had a tiny birthmark below the left underarm, the way Roshan did.

He loved that girl, the letter said, referring to Roshan's mother. *People say it was about the firestones, but I know my Kaifi. It was never about coin. It was always about her.*

Perhaps it was. Roshan would never know for sure. But over time, she'd learned not to question everything—especially when it came to matters of the dead. News had arrived from time to time about the man called Yazad Aspa, about how he and his son were appealing for a shorter sentence from within another part of the prison.

They would, if the *Jwala Khabri* was to be believed, probably be granted that reduction. The right number of coins in the right hands could go far when it came to undoing justice.

"It's true," Vijali Fui had said when Roshan told her this. "But none of us have clean hands, bitiya. Let go of your anger. It will be better in the long run."

Roshan hadn't known if she could. But now, as she walked out of the prison gates and into the sun, she felt oddly light. Like a stray leaf in the wind.

Her gaze caught and snagged at the figure waiting for her in the shadows. Garbed in a pale green jama and matching trousers, with decidedly less jewelry than she'd seen him wearing the first time. If not for the sipahis trailing him, Navin might have been unremarkable, passing for a modestly wealthy Prabhavasi merchant.

"Look what we have here," Vijali Fui murmured, nudging Roshan. "Go on. I'll see you at the inn later."

Roshan's heart, dulled by the monotony of imprisonment, suddenly came alive, beating a familiar rhythm.

"You're nearly an hour late," Navin announced as she approached him. His voice was soft, raspier than before. Strands of silver peeked through his black hair, not a streak of henna in sight. He was broader, slightly taller than she'd remembered. Only those peri eyes remained the same. Gold, gleaming, endlessly beautiful.

"I didn't realize you were keeping tabs on me," she responded.

"It's been a year, Roshni. Lovely as your handwriting is, I was tired of not being able to see your face." Roshan's yearlong sentence had not allowed her any visitors at prison. Even if they were former princes.

"Charming. I didn't realize how much I missed your flattery."

She wasn't lying. She knew Navin could see it, too, by the sparkling eyes that took in her aura, which must be silver right now, perhaps tinged with a little green. She'd been surprised initially when he told her about auras and the different colors of human emotions. Red for anger, blue for worry, yellow for fear, green for sorrow, silver for joy, black for truth. The one time Roshan had drawn up the courage to ask Navin about the color of love, he'd simply replied: *indradhanush*. Like the iridescent Brimmish metal, love was an emotion that held every color under the sun.

"How are your father and brother doing?" she asked now.

After serving his sentence out at the palace, Navin had left Jwala and spent the past few months in Aman to get to know his peri family a little better.

"They're doing great," he replied, grinning. "Adi's flying like a champ again. My father was helping me strengthen my voice. It's a little slow going. Apparently, the soul magic I did in the mine left a nasty scar in my throat. I *can* do soul magic now and then, but it's exhausting. Singing is worse: I can't even go over an octave now."

If this was true, Roshan wouldn't have known. He hummed a tune she didn't recognize, one that made her flush with pleasure. The music—or maybe his floral attar—drew a pair of bees, who buzzed around them, their striped yellow bodies shimmering in the heat.

"Goddess! They're always following me around." He gently shooed one away before it settled in Roshan's hair. The back of his fingers lightly brushed her cheek.

"I can see why," she said.

Why was she so breathless all of a sudden?

A year had gone by, but it felt like only yesterday that they were both inside an underground cave, his heart beating against her cheek.

His gaze fell to her lips and then back up. Roshan pinched herself. Stop dreaming, she scolded herself.

"Where will you go now?" she asked him. "Back to the palace?"

Navin shrugged. "I've been living with my old tutor, Dastur Jamshid, for the past month or so. It's easier. Farhad—the parasmani, I mean—keeps offering me my title back. I keep telling him no. He thinks he'll wear me down eventually. He still doesn't understand that it's not what I really want."

What do you want, then?

The words stuck in her throat. She couldn't ask him that. She had no right. The idea she'd had about asking him to accompany her to Ashvamaidan seemed nonsensical now. The foolish dream of a girl who still wanted to hold both moons in one hand.

"Your aura's a real mess right now," he commented.

She scowled. "Stop doing that."

He grinned. "I'm not *doing* anything. But I *can* keep pestering you until you tell me what's on your mind."

He could. And he would. Fine, then.

"I'm going back to Ashvamaidan." The words came out of her in a rush. "Sarpanch—*Subedar* Sohail asked me to return to the valley, to help rebuild. They need more healers, he said. And others, besides. If you want to come along . . . I mean, you don't have to. Clearly you have family in Aman, family in Prabha, you're used to a much better life than anything we can offer . . ."

Her voice trailed off as he held up a finger, requesting permission to speak.

"Subedar Sohail wrote to me, too. He said it would help having a former prince on his council," Navin said, smiling slightly. "I suspect my brother—the king, that is, not the peri—has something to do with this offer. But I said yes. I didn't let them know I would've come even if he offered me a job cleaning gusalkhanas."

A wisp of color emerged from the back of Navin's head, shimmering like a rainbow in the sunlight. Roshan pinched herself again, wondering if it was another vision.

"Dastur Jamshid has some interesting books on soul magic," Navin said, watching her closely. "One of them said that if a soul magus's bond with another person was strong enough, that person could see flickers of the soul magus's aura."

"Oh," she said.

His brow furrowed at her nonchalant tone. But something about her aura must have tipped him off. Or maybe it simply was the way the corners of her eyes crinkled, more from joy than from the sun.

A slow, lazy grin overtook his face. "You'll pay for that, Roshni."

Her face heated in anticipation as she saw whispers of an answering pink flush in his aura. "I'll hold you to that promise, Rajkumar."

GLOSSARY

Note: You will find many of the terms below common to our world and the former empire of Svapnalok (consisting of the kingdoms of Ambar, Prithvi, Jwala, and Samudra). However, there are a few words that differ slightly in meaning and/or are used specifically in the context of Svapnalok. These have been marked with an asterisk (*) wherever possible.

aiyaash: Debauched

alvida: Goodbye

*atashban: A powerful magical weapon resembling a crossbow; invented by King Lohar in the kingdom of Ambar

bajra: Pearl millet

ber: A sweet and tart tropical fruit, also known as the red date or Chinese jujube in our world

bhai / bhaiyya: Brother; can also be used as a respectful way to address a stranger

*bidaal: A *Pashu* who is part cat, part human

champa: Frangipani

chawal: Rice

daal: Cooked lentils, usually yellow in color

daroga: A police officer

*dastur: A scholar in the kingdom of Jwala

dhow: A lateen-rigged sailing boat with one or two masts

didi: Elder sister

*ervad: A priest at the fire goddess's temple

gusalkhana: bathroom

haan: Yes

*hakim: A magical healer who works in an official capacity at a hospital or at the palace in Jwala

haveli: A mansion

*homāi: An ancient animal spirit, often taking the form of a firebird; worshipped by the *Pashu*; seen as a harbinger of fate by humans in the kingdom of Jwala

howdah: A seat carried on the back of an elephant, sometimes with a canopy

*indradhanush: A rainbow-hued metal; native to the Brimlands

jambiya: A short, double-edged dagger

ji: An honorific, usually placed after a person's name; can also be used as respectful acknowledgment, in the place of "yes"

katar: A punch-dagger with a triangular blade

kumari: A title used for an unmarried young woman (also Miss in our world)

*mahadastur: A title for high scholars in Jwala, who preside over court cases

*makara: A *Pashu* who is part crocodile, part human

malido: Sweet pudding made of wheat flour, semolina, fruit, and nuts; served in Zoroastrian religious ceremonies in our world

*meherbani: Thank you

murga: Literally means cockerel; also refers to a punishment given out by teachers to naughty schoolchildren, where the child is made to squat outside the classroom and hold their ears

naah: No

*Paras: The official language of the kingdom of Jwala

*parasmani: Official title of the Jwaliyan monarch

*Pashu: A race of part-human, part-animal beings; native to the kingdom of Aman

*peri: A gold-skinned *Pashu* who is part human, part bird

poha: Flattened rice; normally a breakfast dish

raag: A melodic framework used for improvisation and composition of Indian classical music

rajkumar: Prince

*sardar: Title for the leader of the Shadow Clan

*shubhdin: Good day

*shubh prabhat: Good morning (also *suprabhat*)

*shvetpanchhi: A large, carnivorous bird with white and black feathers; native to Svapnalok

sitar: A plucked string instrument used in Indian classical music; can be used for solo performances without a vocalist

sorghum: Ancient cereal grain, usually white or yellow in color

*suprabhat: Good morning

*subah: Province

*subedar: A governor of a province in Jwala

tanpura: A plucked string instrument used in Indian classical music, normally used as background music to support a vocalist or musician

tharra: Home-brewed alcohol

wah: An exclamation of high praise

yaara: friend

yuvraj: Male heir apparent

yuvrani: Female heir apparent

AUTHOR'S NOTE

According to the Zoroastrian faith, good and evil, truth and lies, light and shadow are symbolized by twin spirits: Spenta Mainyu (also called Ahura Mazda) and Angra Mainyu (also called Ahriman). While modern Zoroastrians like myself worship Ahura Mazda as the Supreme God, we also believe in the concept of free will and that the twin spirits symbolize the choices we face in our daily lives.

In hindsight, it may seem obvious that a kingdom named after flames (or *jwala*) would have a fantasy religion inspired by a real-life faith where fire is considered sacred. (Contrary to popular misconception, Zoroastrians do *not* worship fire.) Yet, when I started writing this novel in early 2020, I did not know I'd be drawing inspiration for its themes from so many elements of Zoroastrianism.

At the time, all I wanted to do was write a historical fantasy about gangs in India. My research led me to the badlands of the Chambal Valley in central India, a beautiful, rugged landscape made infamous for its banditry. Records have been found dating back to the sixteenth and seventeenth centuries about bandits in the region, who robbed unsuspecting travelers and strangled their victims.

Many of the primary sources I came across for this time period were authored by the British—specifically an East India Company official named William Henry Sleeman. While social banditry was not always a motive in choosing a life of crime, Sleeman's interpretations about

Indian bandits were often misguided and inaccurate, promoting a narrative that was both racist and xenophobic.

Where colonial history failed to provide me with sufficient answers, contemporary sources came to my aid in the form of India's most famous female bandit, Phoolan Devi. Born into a world rife with caste division, Phoolan was kidnapped by bandits as a young girl and later went on to become a bandit herself. At the time of her surrender to the authorities in 1983, she was wanted on multiple counts of robbery, kidnapping, and murder. However, Phoolan was greatly admired by the masses and, after serving out her prison term, was elected as a member of the Indian parliament. Phoolan's popularity intrigued me. These bandits were not heroes, but they weren't always perceived as villains, either. Indeed, bandits like Paan Singh Tomar (a former soldier and athlete who represented India at the Asian Games) even called themselves *baghi*—rebels fighting injustice.

Of Light and Shadow was, in part, an exercise at decolonizing my imagination and, in another part, letting my imagination run wild. Apart from Phoolan Devi and Paan Singh Tomar, I also drew inspiration from heroic outlaws like Robin Hood and iconic movie villains like the bandit Gabbar Singh from the Bollywood classic *Sholay*. I further added my own spin on the narrative with magic (of course!) and a cast of characters who ultimately showed me that Ahura Mazda and Ahriman exist in us all.

ACKNOWLEDGMENTS

Meherbani:

The Canada Council for the Arts and the Ontario Arts Council for funding this project.

My amazing editorial and publicity teams at FSG Young Readers and Penguin Teen Canada: Janine O'Malley, Melissa Warten, Lynne Missen, Peter Phillips, Hannah Miller, Tracy Koontz, Allyson Floridia, Lindsay Wagner, Hayley Lown, Asia Harden, Kelsey Marrujo, Gaby Salpeter, and Sam Devotta.

My agent, Eleanor Jackson, for encouraging me to work on my idea for a fantasy novel about a teenage bandit queen.

My generous and insightful early readers: Megan Bannen, Erika David, Shveta Thakrar, Eloise Andry, Anushi Mehta, Alysia Maxwell, Mahtab Narsimhan, Sherry Isaac, and Kristen Ciccarelli.

The ultratalented art and design team of this book: art director Samira Iravani, cover artist Johnny Tarajosu, and cartographer Jared Blando. I'm so thrilled I got to work with you!

My parents for your unconditional love and support and my grandmother for showing up when I least expected you to—much like your namesake in this novel.

And you, reader, for picking up this book. I hope you've enjoyed it.

ABOUT THE AUTHOR

TANAZ BHATHENA is an award-winning Zoroastrian author of contemporary and fantasy fiction. Her books include *Hunted by the Sky*, which won the White Pine Award and the Bapsi Sidhwa Literary Prize, and *The Beauty of the Moment*, which won the Nautilus Gold Award for Young Adult Fiction. Her acclaimed debut, *A Girl Like That*, was named a Best Book of the Year by numerous outlets, including the *Globe and Mail*, *Seventeen*, and the *Times of India*. Born in India and raised in Saudi Arabia and Canada, Tanaz lives in Mississauga, Ontario, with her family. Visit her at **tanazbhathena.com**.